# *No Silver Spoon*

Dympna stared. She could feel her eyes getting rounder and rounder as her colour rose higher and her heart sank lower. Surely her mother could not be serious?

To protect Nicholas from helping his family, doing his duty by paying off a loan, she herself must go away from the village, from Connemara from Ireland itself to live as a servant in a strange land? Why, she would not even be working for wages, because she would have been bought, like an ass or a cow.

Did her mother truly mean to let her slave her life away in a house in Liverpool instead of working on the fishing boat, digging in the vegetable patch, helping Micheál or Beatrice herself in all their tasks here at home?

Katie Flynn has lived for many years in the Northwest. A compulsive writer, she started with short stories and articles and many of her early stories were broadcast on Radio Mersey. She decided to write a series set in Liverpool after hearing the reminiscences of family members about life in the early part of the century. *No Silver Spoon* is her eighth Liverpool novel.

# KATIE FLYNN

# *No Silver Spoon*

arrow books

Published in the United Kingdom in 1999 by
Arrow Books

5 7 9 10 8 6 4

Copyright © Katie Flynn, 1999

First published in the United Kingdom in 1999 by William Heinemann

Arrow Books
The Random House Group Limited
20 Vauxhall Bridge Road, London SW1V 2SA

Random House Australia (Pty) Limited
20 Alfred Street, Milsons Point, Sydney,
New South Wales 2061, Australia

Random House New Zealand Limited
18 Poland Road, Glenfield
Auckland 10, New Zealand

Random House (Pty) Limited
Endulini, 5a Jubilee Road, Parktown 2193, South Africa

The Random House Group Limited Reg. No. 954009

randomhouse.co.uk

A CIP catalogue record for this book
is available from the British Library

Papers used by Random House are natural, recyclable
products made from wood grown in sustainable
forests. The manufacturing processes conform to
the environmental regulations of the country of origin

ISBN 0 09 927995 9

Printed and bound in Great Britain by
Cox & Wyman Ltd, Reading, Berkshire

*For my friend Thelma Teader, who reads my books,
lends me her granddaughters, and is everything
a friend should be – except near enough!*

I should like to thank Maureen Corbett of Streamstown Bay for taking the time and trouble to find me a suitable spot for the Connemara side of my story, and various booksellers and local people in nearby Clifden, for helping me to find out about their beautiful town.

# Chapter One

Dympna Byrne was half-way down the cliff, with her collecting bag completely empty of the eggs she coveted, when she heard her brother Egan calling her. For a moment she wondered whether to stay quiet, because if she shouted back she would disturb the nesting birds who were, as yet, ignorant of her presence. But Egan's voice was rising to a plaintive wail . . . perhaps it might be as well to climb very carefully back up again, tell him she was busy, so she was, and find out just why he was bawling for her.

Dympna sighed and began, with great care, to retrace her steps. Without even thinking about it she could recall every move she had made to get this far down, and simply repeated them now, in reverse. First she found handholds, her fingers gripping tiny rocky outcrops so small that few would have realised they were there, then her bare toes explored what seemed like smooth rock face and wedged themselves into every tiny crevice. She was a good and fearless climber, but she went slowly and with deliberation because these cliffs were difficult to climb, which was why the sea-birds nested there in such great numbers – and why she had chosen it as a suitable spot to fill her collecting bag. After a few minutes she rested, looking down from her lofty perch on to the sea below her. How beautiful it all was! The little islands offshore were showing their spring green, the colour intensified by the whiteness of their narrow beaches, and the late afternoon sun shone from a pale-blue, cloudless sky, its rays penetrating the translucent sea water, gilding the sinuous body of an old daddy seal, which was investigating the kelp beds near the foot of the cliffs. So clear was the water that she could see not only the seal but also a shoal of tiny fish, and the greens and purples of the kelp. Seagulls and guillemots bobbed on the little wavelets and puffins, swift as swallows, flew to and from their burrows lower down the cliffs, the incomers with the silvery flash of sand eels in their beaks, the outgoers flying with speed and purpose, for though few of the eggs had hatched as yet, the sitting birds needed food as much, now, as the nestlings would, later on.

'Dympna-aa! I know you're somewhere, so I do! Aw, c'mon, alanna, else Mammy will have me hide, so she will.'

Egan's voice was plaintive and with a sigh Dympna withdrew her gaze from the blue-green depths beneath her perch and sought her next handhold. She was fond of Egan and did not want to get him into trouble – not that it was likely. Their mammy indulged Egan, her youngest child, and was completely soft with Nicholas, Dympna's older brother. It is only with meself that she sometimes seems unfair and harsh, Dympna thought, edging into a sort of chimney in the rock and wedging her shoulders against one side and her knees against the other. I wonder, is it because I'm a girl? Only Mammy was a girl herself once, so she was, so she ought to have more sympathy with me, and more fondness, too, since I'm her only daughter. But it did not seem to happen that way. If there was housework to do, Mammy called for Dympna. If Mammy wanted messages run or potatoes dug or milk fetched from the farm a mile away, Dympna was summoned. If someone had done something they should not, Mammy blamed Dympna. Either it was her fault outright, or if it was clearly Egan's fault, she should have stopped him doing it, for wasn't she the elder now, and hadn't she been told to take responsibility for Egan from the moment he could toddle?

Dympna began to go up the cliff chimney like a caterpillar, humping herself along on shoulders and knees, glad she wasn't wearing anything special, but only the ragged grey flannel shirt she wore for rough work, tucked into an old pair of Nick's trousers. Mammy didn't know about the trousers, mind. Dympna had begged them off Nick, when he'd got a new pair, and you had to admit that Nick was good-natured enough, so long as it didn't directly affect him. 'Sure, take 'em, Dymp,' he had said largely. 'I'll not be wantin' such ragged old t'ings when I'm at the grammar school wit' all me pals.'

So Dympna had hidden the ragged trousers in the hay loft above the donkey's old stone byre, and used them when she was doing something which might spoil anything half-way decent, as now. And very useful they had been – nearly as useful as the old collecting bag, made out of rope and strong canvas, which her daddy had given her for egging trips, and wasn't he fond of an omelette now, and didn't he tell her she was a broth of a girl and better by far than a feller when she turned up with her collecting bag bulging, and half the boys in the village moaning that it was a poor season and they would be thankful for a dozen eggs?

Dympna reached the top of the chimney and began to crawl along an upward-sloping ledge; she glanced up and grinned as Egan's round-eyed face looked down at her. He wasn't a bad kid and now, she knew, he would be holding his breath and saying prayers for her, because he had no head for heights and could not understand her complete lack of fear when it came looking over the cliffs, let alone climbing down them.

'Hey, Egan! Shan't be a minute now, but can you not tell me what the mammy's after wanting me for? It takes a while to get amongst the nests, you know, and I'd not had a chance to take any eggs when I heard you bawling for me.'

'She wants some taters dug,' Egan said. 'Oh, be careful, Dymp! Don't hurry now, take your time. What were you after eggs for, anyhow? It's a late Easter this year.'

'Mammy's birthday,' Dympna said shortly. She felt cross with Egan. Couldn't he have saved her the trouble and dug a few potatoes for their mammy? And how had he found out where she was, anyway? No one could have told on her because she had not confided to anyone else where she was bound. And now if Egan insisted she would have to go all the way home and up to Daddy's field just to dig out a few spuds that one of the others could have done with their hands tied behind them, just about.

'Oh, Egan, why couldn't you dig 'em? And how did you know where I was, anyway? I didn't say anything to anyone, because of it being Mammy's birthday in a couple o' days. I didn't want 'em to know and go telling, see? I wanted to give her the eggs as a surprise.' As she spoke she was climbing, and before Egan had answered she was hauling herself up and onto the short, sweet grass on top of the cliff. 'Now, how did you know where I was? I want to know, wee feller.'

Egan sat down beside her and together they surveyed the sea, the birds and a small boat, way out. 'I didn't know, Dymp,' he said at last, turning his clear brown eyes upon her. 'I tried everywhere else first, then I just guessed, I suppose. Why didn't you ask me to come along wit' you? I know I'm no good on the cliffs, but I could have kept an eye on you, in case.'

Dympna laughed, glancing sideways at him. He was a nice brother, she thought. He had straight brown hair, which fell across his brow in a soft fringe, skin browned by wind and weather, a curving mouth with rather large, very white teeth and round brown eyes, which made him look both simple and innocent. His eyes were very similar, Dympna told herself now, to her father's. Micheál had just that look of simplicity and innocence, though she was very sure that her daddy was neither. But he was gentle, kind and always believed the best of people; perhaps that was what father and son had in common, for Egan tried over and over to defend her from the mammy's criticism, as he would pick up the kitten when it played havoc with Mammy's coarse grey knitting wool and run with it to some place of safety. But although she was fond of Egan she did not intend to let him off for pursuing her here.

So she heaved a sigh and looked sternly at him. 'I'd rather you'd have dug the taters, young feller-me-lad, and left me to me egg collecting. Why didn't you, Egan? Mammy wouldn't have minded, would she?'

'I don't know, but the t'ing is, there was a real bad row going on at home and I t'ink she wanted me out of the way, because they don't often quarrel, our mammy and daddy, do they, Dymp? Today Daddy

5

was backed into a corner, but he was fairly roaring and that's not like the daddy, is it, so? And Mammy was crying and saying he'd got no cause to behave like that just because Dermot wants to better himself and who was he to . . . well, anyway, Mammy told me to fetch you home.'

'You said she wanted me to dig spuds,' Dympna said indignantly. 'Make up your mind, Egan! And if she wants you out of the way, which I can understand if they're having a good quarrel, why should I go back where I'm not wanted, answer me that? The spuds was an excuse, Egan, so we might as well stay here as not, whiles I fetch up the eggs.' She turned her gaze back to her brother's small brown face with its cowlick of soft hair hanging over his eyes. 'Now don't you t'ink we'd be as well off bringing back some eggs for Mammy's birthday as going up to the field to dig spuds, which she probably doesn't even want?'

'Well, 'tis true that Mammy said she needed spuds, but I'm pretty sure she just wanted me out of the kitchen. Only I don't like to see folk shouting, Dymp, specially Mammy and Daddy, so I reckon I'd rather we were at home . . . in case we could stop 'em shouting.'

'I can't stop 'em, and nor can you, so why don't we spend ten or fifteen more minutes here while I go down after some eggs?' Dympna said coaxingly. 'It's for Mammy's birthday, Egan, so I'm not being selfish.'

'I'll come back wit' you when the quarrel's over,' Egan said. 'Sure an' it's a good walk up here, so it is, but worth it, for to get eggs. Come on, darlin' Dymp.'

Dympna considered telling her brother to go back without her, for the April days were still not long enough for evening egg collecting, but when she

6

looked at his anxious little face she sighed, laughed and set off beside him across the short cliff-top grass. 'They'll not thank us for interfering,' she said warningly, however. 'All mammies and daddies fall out sometime, acushla, even ours. Why, think of the Tomases, and the O'Reagans and the Sullivans – they're shouting and fighting half their lives, so they are. So we'll pop our heads round the kitchen door, and very likely it will all have blown over and Mammy'll wonder what we're doin', asking how many spuds she wants dug.'

'Oh, t'anks, Dymp,' her small brother said gratefully, falling into step beside her. 'I'm sorry I was after disturbing your egging, but I'll come back wit' you, honest to God, when you've seen Mammy and dug the taters, if that's what she wants.'

It was a good walk back to the village, but both children were used to walking – not that they walked for long, for as soon as they had crossed the grass of the cliffs and turned onto the deep little lane which would lead back, eventually, to the village, they broke into a comfortable jog-trot which, Dympna knew, would soon have them home. They talked as they went, but kept off the subject of the quarrel and their parents, turning instead to school and their teachers and fellow pupils, for all the children were still at the village school, though Nicholas was being coached for his school certificate by Mr O'Neill and spent a good deal of time sitting in the teacher's study, being tutored, or at home doing the work he had been set. Mr O'Neill had told the Byrnes that Nicholas was very clever and was worth coaching, since when he was old enough he would be fit to take the entrance examination for the university in Dublin.

There were only two teachers at the village school, Mr O'Neill, who was headmaster and taught the older children, and Miss Annie Ennis, who was a pupil teacher and taught the little ones. At thirteen and eleven years old respectively, Dympna and Egan were both in the top class and at the mercy of Mr O'Neill's ruler – which could land with enough force to cause bruising, if not blood – and his temper, which was unreliable. But he had the reputation of being a good teacher, for did not the first four or five in the top class usually get the choice of going on to further education in the town? Many parents – most, indeed – could not afford to send their children to the higher school, even if they won scholarships, because the boys were needed on the fishing boats and the girls at home or as earners, but Mr O'Neill's teaching would, their parents told their smarting children, stand them in good stead one day. Because Mr O'Neill was rising sixty he had taught most of the parents as well as the kids, and they respected him and made certain that their children did too.

So what with gossiping about Mr O'Neill's latest effort – he had the top class all trying to write true stories about their lives which, he said, he would one day put into a real book – and bewailing the fact that school was still considered necessary even if you were bound to end up on a fishing boat or as a housemaid, the time flew past and soon they turned into the narrow lane onto the common land around which the fishermen's cottages stood. The ground sloped away here to join the tiny stone quay and the rock-strewn little beach, and then it began to climb to where the cottages were placed, each one in its patch of garden with its own apple trees, washing line and peat pile surrounding it. The Byrnes' cottage was,

8

Dympna thought, the most conveniently situated, for it was on the cliff about a dozen feet above the shore, with a tangle of furze and hazel trees sheltering it from the beach on one side and the apple trees hiding it from too close a scrutiny from passers-by on the other. And it was the closest of all the cottages to the freshwater spring which came bubbling out of the ground between limestone rocks and hazel copse, to fall first into a round tin bath before chuckling its way over the edge on its intended path down to the sea. The spring, Dympna knew, was the reason that the cottages had been built here in the first place, probably why the stone quay had been built, too, though it had been there many years, she supposed.

A dozen yards from their cottage, Dympna stopped short and gazed. It looked peaceful enough with its goldy-brown thatch gilded by the long rays of the evening sun. Smoke curled up from the chimney and Dympna could smell the cooking smells and knew that it was fish baking on the griddle and potatoes simmering in the big black pot suspended over the turf fire, which was seldom allowed to go out.

'Can't hear anything, Egan,' she said after a moment's rather anxious silence. 'I t'ought you said they were yelling at each other?'

'Well, they were,' Egan assured her. 'Mammy was sort of talking-crying, and Daddy was bellowing – honest, Dymp. But they've stopped now, t'ank the good Lord.'

Dympna smiled. Egan hated arguments no matter how trivial and could burst into tears at the threat of a fight, though to be fair to the boy when he had to fight he fought with the best – punching, kicking and biting – when called upon to defend himself or his friends.

'Well, we'd best go in, anyway, find out how many taters Mammy wants,' Dympna said reluctantly. 'And don't forget, Egan, that you promised to come back wit' me to the egg collecting. Come on in now.'

They approached the cottage cautiously, as though someone inside was listening out for them, but as soon as they were within a few feet of the ancient wooden door, thickly painted with tar against the weather, they could hear the rumble of voices. Egan speeded up and the two of them burst impetuously into the large living kitchen where the Byrnes' spent most of their lives when indoors.

It was a low, dark room, for the windows were set back in the thick walls and the thatch overhung them, but at the moment it was brightened by the sunlight streaming in through the low little back window and as Dympna had guessed fish were cooking over a griddle and the potatoes smoked gently from their big black pot. Dympna saw that the table was not laid for the meal, however, and indeed, her father and mother faced each other across it whilst Nicky stood by, watching, his eyes going from face to face as the two adults spoke. He looked . . . odd, Dympna thought, almost calculating, as though he were weighing up who would win and would then choose which side to take. Dympna and Egan, breathless from their run, stood in the doorway, watching the scene within as though it had been a stage and they the audience.

'I'm tellin' you, Bea, I cannot manage wit'out the boy. It's no use you sayin' that Dermot must be persuaded to stay, he will not do it and I will not ask it of him. Why, 'tis only because he's the third son that he's come to work for me, because his daddy's not got room for him in the *Dancing Dolly*, wit' the other two boys aboard. But now he's goin' to marry young Eileen McCarthy, he'll be better off workin' from her village, an' why should he not do so, when they've been as good as engaged these past five years? And we've been married long enough for you to understand full well what I'm tellin' you. No man can fish alone in a boat, cast out the net and pull it in again, laden wit' fish. The *Fair Aleen*'s heavy for two, she's impossible for a feller alone. When we've the sail up she'll go like the wind and I'd mebbe manage, but when it's calm and it's labourin' I am at the oars, then I need someone at the tiller, someone to jump out to tie up the painter. I've been as proud as you that Nicky's clever, has a great future, but *I can't manage alone!* It's been grand havin' Dermot, despite havin' to pay him a fair share of the catch, but he's goin' to Roundstone to work wit' a much bigger boat than mine, so's he and the girl can marry sooner, and sure and I'd not be stoppin' him even if I could, which I can't. So . . .'

'Nicholas is going to stay on at school,' Beatrice said in a low, dull voice. 'There's the money, Micheál. It's been put away safe for when he's at the university, or maybe when he comes out and needs a start to his career, but if necessary we could use it to get ourselves a different boat, the sort the other men use, a rowing boat. They can manage alone at a pinch, you know they can.'

'No, Bea. The *Aleen* was me father's boat and his father's before him, and I'd no more dream of gettin' rid of her than fly to the moon. Why, no one else in the village gets as much fish as we do, because they can't go so far out, nor so deep. In deed, I'm not askin' you, it's tellin' you I am. The boy's a bright boy, no one knows that better than meself, but it's not as though

I'm asking' him to give up his schoolin' for ever, for indeed I am not. Egan's goin' on twelve, he'll be able to leave school in less than two years. All I'm askin' is for Nicholas to put off his schoolin' for a couple of years . . . it could be less than that, if Dermot's young brother comes in wit' me. He's only got a year more at school and he'll be at the fishin', for he's got sawdust between the ears, has Aidan. So what d'you say to that? And don't be shoutin' me down again, woman, or so help me . . .'

'You can't ask it of him, Micheál,' Beatrice said. She was actually wringing her hands, Dympna saw with considerable surprise. It was an action she had frequently read about but never thought to see in real life. 'The poor boy's worked like a navvy so's he can get his certificates and go to university; he can't just leave for a couple of years and then walk back in. Why, he'd be a laughing stock, still studying with Mr O'Neill when everyone else had left school. Oh Micheál, I've never suggested using the money before, but now, if it'll buy Nicholas his rights . . .'

'I say no, no, *no*!' Micheál roared suddenly, banging his fist down on the long kitchen table. 'You can't use that money to buy a young feller to help me wit' the boat. Woman, why don't you listen when I speak? I've not spoke to Aidan's daddy yet but I'll do so tomorrow, so I will, and if he says Aidan can come wit' me when he leaves school then it's only a year Nick will have to miss out on and a clever feller like him . . .'

Dympna had been watching and listening in silence, taking in what was being said. Now she glanced over at Nicholas, standing there, his narrow, clever face blank as an empty page, only his eyes flickering from face to face. Why did he not speak? Why did he not remind their father how useless he was in a boat? How on the few occasions he had gone to sea with Micheál he had managed to get a hook buried in his finger; had been smitten across the head by the boom when the boat gybed sharply and had been knocked, unconscious, into the waves; had refused to haul on the net because he'd torn his fingernail and was appalled by the sudden loss of blood; had lost them a whole hour on a day the mackerel were running by forgetting the bag of bait and forcing Micheál to return to the harbour to fetch it? But it seemed that Nicholas was not going to say a word in his own defence; he was waiting for his mammy to win the war, as she had won so many others for him in the past.

But not, it seemed, this time. Micheál was turning away, was taking the cauldron of potatoes off the fire and across to the door so that he could strain them outside. He was saying, in a suddenly calm and ordinary voice: 'Then that's settled; I'll speak to Aidan's daddy in the mornin', so I will, and see what can be arranged, and in the meantime, Nick will work on the boat wit' me and explain at school that it's just a temporary t'ing.'

'I'll use the money . . .' Beatrice began, then stopped and looked, for a moment, so totally defeated, so miserably unhappy, that Dympna's heart bled for her. Poor Mammy, so used to getting her own way and finding on this one most importance occasion that Micheál was not to be swayed. And poor Nick, too, because he'd make a terrible fisherman, so he would . . . and perhaps most of all poor Daddy, landed with his most incompetent child as a shipmate and having to put up with his wife's agony of despair over a decision that he must have hated almost as much as she.

'Daddy.' It was her own voice, small and flat; she was surprised to hear it, almost unaware of what she was about to say. 'Daddy, why not me?'

Her father turned from the back door, the huge pot of drained potatoes in his hands. He looked across at her and smiled his slow, gentle smile. 'Why not you, alanna? I don't know what you mean.'

'Why can't I take Dermot's place, Daddy? I can leave school when this term ends, because I'll be fourteen before the next one starts. Oh, I know I wasn't going to leave, but I don't mind – I'd like it very much. And I'm useful in a boat, Daddy, you know I am. And it 'ud mean Nicky could go ahead wit' the big school and the university and all. Why not, Daddy?'

Micheál stared. Dympna knew that it took time to get new ideas into her daddy's head so she said nothing further, just waited, but behind her she heard her mother's sharp intake of breath. It pleased her that this idea should cause her mother to gasp, because it just showed that Mammy had never even thought of her only daughter going off with the fishing fleet. But why should she not? She was as strong as a boy her age, a good deal stronger than Nicholas, with his beautifully kept hands and his dreamy ways, and his formidable intelligence which, nevertheless, let him down constantly over practicalities.

'Dympna, have you run mad? It's quite impossible. What on earth would folk say? No girl has ever sailed with the fishing fleet, it's . . . it's probably bad luck, or something of that nature. No, don't ask your daddy to take a decision like that.'

Dympna stared with undisguised surprise at her mother. Nothing could have been more calculated to put Micheál's back up, for although he was quite as superstitious as every other fisherman on the west coast he always denied it flatly, said that a man who believed in God could not also believe in fairies and ghosts and fabulous beasts. And what was more, she had been to sea many times with the fleet during the long summer holidays and no one had ever questioned her right to be there. Of course, actually working on the boat might be different . . . but time alone would tell, and for now, it would be enough for Daddy to agree that her suggestion was a reasonable one.

But Micheál had turned back towards his wife. 'Shush, woman, while I t'ink this one out, for it will take a deal o' mullin' over, so it will.' He turned to Dympna. 'Dermot won't let me down by leavin' at once, he's made that plain. If I was to ask him to stay until term ends . . . and I'll sound the family out about Aidan at the same time . . . That way we needn't make hasty decisions we might regret . . . why don't you serve the fish round, Bea, an' I'll tip the taters into the big bowl.'

Beatrice bustled over to the fire and began transferring the fish from the griddle to a cracked and crazed oval dish, which looked as though it was about to shatter into a thousand pieces every time you put food on it, only Dympna knew that it had looked like that for as long as she could remember and had never so much as creaked under the strain. The atmosphere in the room, which had been so tense that you could feel the power of it buzzing through your own veins, suddenly calmed, became ordinary, normal. Egan went to the dresser drawer and brought out the tin knives and forks, and the tin plates. He put the big piece of salt onto a side plate and then went out of the kitchen and across to the well, where he cut a piece of butter which he brought back into the room on a dock leaf. Dympna, realising that her small brother was doing the sensible thing in pretending that nothing had happened, fetched the big jar of pickled onions from the cupboard and set that on the table too, then pulled the chairs round.

As though this had been a signal, Beatrice came over to the table with the fish and began to hand it round – three big fish for their father, two for Nicholas, and one each for herself, Egan and Dympna.

'Start,' she said to them. 'Never let good food go cold on the plate, I'll just mash the tea.'

Micheál came and took his place at the head of the table and Nicholas, Egan and Dympna followed him. Micheál speared half a dozen of the big, floury potatoes, then passed the crock along to Nicholas, who took two. Dympna, sitting between her brothers, helped herself and when her father had finished with the salt, reached for it, cut off a small corner and crumbled it over her meal. Beside her, Egan heaped his plate; he had a healthy appetite and filled the chinks his share of the fish left with potatoes at this time of year, though in the summer and autumn, when blackberries, nuts and wild apples were to be had, his appetite for potatoes waned a little.

Beatrice came last to the table, carrying the big tin teapot. Sometimes there was milk from their goat, sometimes not, but the tea was so good, Dympna thought, that even without milk it was a fine drink, so it was. Now, her mother filled five battered cups and handed them round, then sat down before her own plate and began to eat. No one spoke until the plates were almost empty, then Egan said conversationally:

'Can me and Dymp go out after we've done the washing up, Mammy? Or is there work for us?'

Beatrice glanced across the low-ceilinged room. Outside, the sky was darkening, the short April evening turning to dusk as the sun sank beneath the western horizon. 'Not tonight, Egan' she said, her voice calm, untroubled. 'It'll be too dark by the time you've finished clearing away. But you can go off first thing tomorrow, as soon as you've done your messages.'

No one would have thought, Dympna told herself, that only minutes earlier a fight had been going on, with raised voices and turbulent emotions. If an Ennis, or an O'Reagan, or a Sullivan had walked into the kitchen now, he or she would never guess that the Byrnes had been quarrelling. Now they were just a family at their supper, friendly and relaxed after the day's work, whereas as Dympna well knew, when the other families fought there would be kids flying out of the door to escape a fatherly clout round the ear or a motherly slap across bare legs, and an atmosphere of uneasiness and tension would prevail, sometimes for hours, sometimes days. But the Byrnes were different, everyone knew that. Micheál was so calm and good-tempered and Beatrice was not only English, but well-born into the bargain. So since all Irish people knew that the English were a chilly sort of race, not much given to either hot-blooded rages or enthusiastic outbursts, they had simply accepted the quiet good manners in the Byrne household as the outcome of a mixed marriage.

'Right, Mammy, then we'll do our messages and set off first t'ing. That'll be just fine, so it will,' Egan said cordially. He nudged Dympna with a sharp elbow and added, 'Pass the spuds, Dymp.' Dympna put

17

down her knife and fork, but before she could move Nicholas reached out a long arm for the crock and helped himself, prior to handing the dish on to his small brother. Nicholas, who mooned about most of the school holidays, seldom took a second helping and Dympna thought, with an inward smile, that her mammy would encourage more quarrels if she realised it was one way to increase her eldest's appetite, for Beatrice worried over Nicholas's slim build and small helpings.

'More tea, Micheál? Nick?' Beatrice said. Micheál said that would be just grand and held out his cup, but Nicholas merely shook his head. If Egan or meself behaved like that Mammy would have a dicky-fit over us, Dympna thought, waiting her turn for another cup of the strong black tea. Still, there you are; every mammy has to have a favourite, Finola O'Reagan says so, and it's usually a son, so I suppose I shouldn't grumble. After all, Daddy likes me best, though he's not the sort of feller to say so out loud. Well, he likes me and Egan best, she added conscientiously, for her father never showed favouritism between his two younger children. Come to that, he tried very hard to love Nicholas as much as he loved the two of them, but you could tell from his wrinkled brow when Nicholas decided to converse with him on some subject or other that it was uphill work.

'Whose turn is it to wash up?' Micheál enquired presently, when Dympna was clearing the table and Beatrice was pouring boiling water from the steaming kettle into the small enamel bowl set in a rough wooden stand, which Micheál had made himself, ready to wash the crocks. 'I've some netting to do. It's only patching, but whoever isn't washing up can run down to the quay and bring up the big net.'

'I'll go,' Egan squeaked, but Micheál shook his head. 'It's too heavy for one,' he said. 'Nicholas, go wit' him an' give him a hand.'

On another occasion, Dympna guessed, Nicholas would have found some get-out, but with the recent quarrel ringing in his ears her elder brother was sensible for once. 'All right, Daddy,' he said at once. 'Come on, Egan.'

The two disappeared and Dympna set to work to wash the crocks.

All evening Dympna sat by the fire, doggedly helping Micheál to mend the net and wondering what the outcome of her suggestion would be, but knowing that she would be told in due time. Until then, she would only spoil her own chances by what Micheál would probably term 'nagging', though the good Lord knew it was costing her dear to hold her tongue. It was most annoying, probably, not being able to be sure of her mother's backing. Beatrice wanted Nick to stay on at school, and the only career she considered suitable for girls was housework and marriage, but that did not mean she would not agree to Dympna working on the *Fair Aleen*. So far as education was concerned, Beatrice did not think it was important for girls to be educated. She had several times assured her daughter that a clever girl would not get as far as one who brushed her hair a hundred times when she got up in the morning, polished her teeth daily and cleaned her nails with a sharpened matchstick whenever she had a spare moment. 'But brushin' me hair and cleanin' me teeth won't turn me into a beauty,' Dympna had objected once, only to be told sharply that beauty was only skin deep and cleanliness was next to godliness.

19

So heaven knows which way she'll jump when push comes to shove, Dympna told herself despondently as she sat and knotted the tarry string in the firelight. She'll back me if it's the only way to get Nick off the hook though, I'm fairly sure of that.

Presently, when the fire had burned low and the net was mended, Dympna got to her feet and said that she'd like a breath of fresh air before she turned in for the night. Micheál, staring into the glowing embers of peat, said she might go as far as the quay, which meant he would go with her and help her to carry the net, but Dympna stood up, draped the net around her shoulders and said she would be just fine and he was not to bother, and Micheál grinned at her and said, 'Good as any boy!' which made them both laugh, then turned to pick up his pipe.

Nicholas had left the house some while before and Egan was in bed, so Dympna had no company down the sloping, stony track to the little harbour, but she did not mind that. Instead, she looked around her, enjoying the night, the stars in the velvet blackness overhead, the salty wind off the sea, which lifted the soft black hair off her forehead as she descended the track. She had thought about going round to the Ennises' cottage, which was barely twenty yards from their own home, but had decided against it. Finola was her best friend, but she did not want to tell her of the plan she had proposed. If her parents agreed and she went to sea in the *Fair Aleen* then Finola would be deeply upset, for the girls had always done everything together and Dympna knew that when Finola went into service, as she was bound to do, she had hoped that they might go together. After all, there were big houses in the nearby town of Clifden whose owners could afford to employ a couple of kitchen maids . . . why should they not be employed together?

Dympna, however, had always very much disliked the thought of going into service. It seemed horrible, to her, to be shut away from the beach, the sea, the freedom of the wind in her face. She had seen the girls who worked at the big houses coming home for a day off, with their feet pinched by smart shoes and the seal of servitude in their meek expressions. But she knew there was little choice for her in an area where jobs were few and eagerly sought after. In her dreams, however, she saw her future in a very different light. She might not be as clever as Nicholas, but she was by no means stupid and Mr O'Neill had hinted once or twice that she might, if she put her mind to it, win a scholarship as her elder brother had done and this, he told her, might lead to a job as a teacher. Dympna was not sure that she would like to teach unruly children who did not want to learn, nor was she certain that she would enjoy the hard work that would inevitably result if she decided to better herself by this course, but she reminded herself resolutely of the holidays and imagined a neat little house with a big garden and herself the mistress of it, and pushed aside the less delightful side of a teaching career.

However wild Dympna's dreams, though, at heart she was a practical girl and knew that such a career was simply not possible for someone in her position. It would not do to set her sights too high, it would only lead to disappointment. Her parents would need her at work even more because Nicholas would not be earning for many a long day. But now that she had suggested taking Dermot's place in the boat, she realised she would very much prefer to spend the next few years in the open air, with Micheál and the *Fair Aleen*, knowing that she was helping him in his constant fight to keep clothes on their backs and food on their plates. If only her mother would agree, she was sure that this particular dream could easily become fact, for Micheál was proud of his daughter's usefulness in a boat and would probably jump at the chance of having her aboard instead of Nicholas, who fainted at the sight of blood and turned green when the sea became even a little rough.

Dympna reached the harbour and dragged the net, which was beginning to feel as heavy across her shoulders as though it were already full of fish, over to the *Fair Aleen*. She dropped it unceremoniously on the bottom of the sturdy craft, then strolled down the slipway and onto the strip of sand, which was only visible at high tide. Beneath her bare feet the sand felt cold, so she crossed it hurriedly and stepped into the little waves, which hissed softly against the shore. The harbour was not actually on the coast itself but was in a sea lough, well sheltered by the arm of land reaching out into the Atlantic and also by the islands that clustered around this most beautiful part of the coast. But the water was cold and fizzing with small bubbles, and Dympna had to force herself into it, though once the first shock was over it was very pleasant to tired feet. She walked out a little way until the hem of her skirt was in danger of getting wet, then stood still, staring out towards the sea and watching the far-off crests of the real waves, for by the time a wave had come racing up the sea lough, its force was very much diminished. What a lovely night it was, though, with a million stars sparkling overhead in the dark velvet sky and the faint odours of seaweed and salt water mingling with the scent of the gorse blossom up on the cliff top. And what fun it would be to work with Daddy at bringing in the fish. She would far rather be a fisherman – or a fishergirl, she supposed – than either a servant or a teacher.

But it was no time to be standing dreaming down on the beach. For all she knew, when she got back to the cottage Mammy might have made up her mind. Why, Beatrice and Micheál could even now be waiting to tell her that it was all agreed, that she might start work with her daddy as soon as the next term was over.

Dympna cast one last look at the dark sea, the distant crests of the waves and the boats drawn up above the high-water mark. There were four boats there now – the three sturdy, black-tarred Connemara rowing boats with their high, pointed prows owned by the other fishing families nearby and the Byrnes' far more elegant Galway pucan, with its rakish mast and brick-coloured sail. In the *Aleen* I'll sail far out beyond Inisboffin and the other islands, Dympna told herself as she turned away from the harbour and began to climb the steep little lane which led to her home. If only Daddy will agree to my working with him.

Beatrice sat by the last embers of the fire, knitting. Opposite her, Micheál was making clothes pegs with his gutting knife and a good piece of planking cast ashore on the long, rocky beach that edged the lough. Because the cottage was close to the shore the winds could be fierce and clothes pegs – and sometimes the clothes, too – were often casualties of a wild day, and Beatrice, watching him, reflected that she could not remember a time when the two of them had sat of an evening with empty hands. To work as they enjoyed the fire's warmth after a long day came as naturally to them both as breathing, she supposed.

They had not discussed Dermot leaving the village and the possibility of Dympna taking his place in the boat whilst she was out of the way. Micheál did not do anything, he did not even discuss doing something, without considerable thought. What was more, Beatrice had been married to Micheál now for sixteen years and knew him well enough to realise that whilst she might take most of the decisions necessary in their lives, where the *Fair Aleen* was concerned, Micheál's word was law. That this was only right, for fishing was a dangerous and chancy way to earn a living, and a mistake could prove not merely expensive – a sail ruined in a gale was a major disaster – but also fatal. Of the elderly widows living with their children in and around their small community, almost all of them had lost their men at sea.

So because this decision involved the boat, Beatrice knew that she must wait for Micheál to make up his mind, and she also knew that trying to hurry him simply would not work. In fact, it could easily have the opposite effect – he might slow down because his train of thought had been disturbed or interrupted.

So Beatrice knitted patiently on and went over and over in her mind the arguments she would use when Micheál finally decided to open his mouth. They had to be quite subtle, because if she said flatly that a fishing boat was no place for a girl it could have two quite different effects. It might cause her husband to say that she was right and, since the boat was not place for Dympna, Nicholas must do his duty as the eldest son of the family. Or it might have the desired result: that Micheál would insist on Dympna sailing with him.

So Beatrice continued to knit, the coarse grey wool pulling off the ball as she worked, and asked herself, not for the first time, why she felt she had to be so hard on Dympna. But the answers were muddled and confused, as Beatrice's own feelings were muddled and confused. She knew that she resented Dympna, whose birth had seemed to set the seal on her marriage, but she also knew that this was scarcely her daughter's fault.

After Nicholas had been born she had been absolutely worn out, for it was a difficult birth and she was still emotionally scarred from the battle royal that had resulted when her parents had realised she was pregnant. As a consequence of her own misguided behaviour, therefore, the girl who had been waited on hand and foot since the day she was born had suddenly found herself in an earth-floored four-roomed cottage, with scarcely any money, a man she felt she hardly knew in her bed and a child that wailed all day and half the night.

For the first year she had been so ill, so confused, that it was all she could do to get through each long, wearying day, but gradually she had realised that in Nicholas lay her salvation. From the moment of his birth the baby had shared their bed because that was the way of things in this land that was so foreign to her; and because the pain of childbirth and her subsequent illness had made her delicate, she had used the child as an excuse to keep her husband at arm's length. At first she and Micheál had shared his mother's cottage with his two younger brothers – his father had died at sea when Micheál was six – and her mother-in-law, a squat little figure in black with a face like a currant bun and a heart of gold, took Beatrice under her wing and taught her all she needed to know. To begin with, Beatrice had not appreciated that she must learn or fall by the wayside, but by the time she had been married three years she knew how to husband their small resources, how to knit and sew, make and mend, cook and pickle, gut fish and plant cabbage and potatoes in their scrubby upland field. The older Mrs Byrne had taught her, too, to love her baby son and to respect her husband, who was kind and gentle towards her though she must often have puzzled him deeply.

But when Nicholas was three, Micheál's uncle Fergal had offered his nephew the cottage by the quay, which he wanted to leave in order to live with his daughter in Cashel.

'You could bring the pucan down here wit' you, Micheál,' his uncle had urged. 'It's a nice little cottage, so it is, an' you'd find the fishin' easier, wit' the Connemara boats bein' slower an' heavier than the *Aleen*. And you're crowded now, wit' the babby an' wit' your brother Sean courtin'.'

So they had left the little house by the harbour in Galway and come to the cottage, and because of Micheál's deep sense of being away from his mother and her own painful realisation of how she would miss the older woman, she had finally let Micheál become her husband in the true sense of the word. She could not bear his pain, but in bed in the cottage on that first night she had held out her arms to him as simply as though he had been Nicky and had comforted him – comforted him so well that nine months later, their second child had been born and had been christened Dympna after Micheál's grandmother.

From the moment of Dympna's birth she had

blamed the small, dark-haired girl-baby lying in the home-made cradle for binding Beatrice and Micheál Byrne with bands of steel; for making them in truth man and wife. Micheál took it for granted, after Dympna's birth, that Beatrice was now his wife by choice as well as circumstance, and to her initial self-disgust she found herself welcoming his caresses, his tenderness. Shamingly, she even enjoyed the love-making which happened more and more often, now that the loss of his mother and their new independence had lowered the barrier Beatrice had erected between them.

So it was for all these reasons that she could not love Dympna the way a mother ought, as well as for the fact that she feared the girl would behave as she, Beatrice had done, and bring shame to the small family in the cottage by the shore. The respect and mild affection she felt for Micheál she could have borne, but the pleasure she took in his touch, his mouth on hers, was a weakness and a wickedness that would never have come about had it not been for Dympna. So she could not love her little daughter and sometimes she found herself almost counting the years until she could send Dympna off into the wide world and settle down once more to adoring Nicholas and later, to loving her youngest son. For Egan had been born two years after Dympna and was a fat and placid baby who took suck and played with his toes, and seemed to make no demands on anyone. So Beatrice felt confusedly that had it not been for Dympna she could have settled down to doing her housework and taking the donkey and cart in Clifden to sell her fish whilst being simply a dutiful wife to Micheál. He should expect no more, she told herself whenever the thought crossed her mind. After all, he knew very well she had not been in love with him when they married; indeed, she had hardly known him. Her parents had cast her off and Micheál had picked her up; gratitude and hard work should have been the price she paid to him, and therefore gratitude was the only emotion to which she would admit.

But now, sitting by the fire and knitting a jersey for Egan, who was hard on his clothes, Beatrice remembered another lesson her mother-in-law had taught her. 'Patience is a virtue, alanna,' the mammy often said when Beatrice raged against the hours spent simply cooking and cleaning, and waiting for something to happen. ''Tis no good t'ing to be always rushin' about and changin' your mind. A fisherman's wife spends more time waitin' for her man than most, so there's another lesson you must learn. Patience.'

Well, she had learned it, and learned it well. Right now she was longing with every fibre of her being to demand that Micheál tell her what he had decided so that she could pass the news – good or bad – on to Nicholas, but she knew that to do so would, in the end, work against her. Let him sleep on it, she commanded herself, as the fire settled and Micheál finished the last peg and tossed it into a reed basket by his side. Don't ever let him see you're afire with the desire to know what he's going to do.

'Time for bed,' Micheál said. He swept his whittlings into a tidy heap in the hearth and then lounged to his feet, holding out his hands to her. 'Come on, uppadaisy!'

She laughed, because it was an expression her old nurse had used in that other, distant, life, and put her hands in his so that he might pull her to her feet. His palms were hard and callused, yet so carefully did he grasp her fingers that he could have been a fine, idle gentleman who had never done anything more strenuous than lace his boots.

'All right,' she said, on her feet now and reaching up to push her knitting onto the broad plank mantel above the fireplace. 'You go on; I'll just tidy round here.'

She said it every night, and every night his response was the same. 'Sure and isn't it the tidiest room I ever did see, indeed?' he asked. 'And aren't you the best little housekeeper in the world, an' meself the luckiest feller? You come to bed, me darlin' girl, and get a good rest before tacklin' what tomorrer may bring.'

Beatrice looked around her; the floor was swept, the table cleared, the curtains, made of cheap cotton but bright and clean, were pulled across the windows. Even the fire had died down without making a great deal of ash, for the wind had calmed with the coming of darkness.

'Oh . . . had I better check on the donkey and the hens?' she asked next, as she always did, and Micheál smiled fondly at her, shaking his head, then reached his coat down from the peg on the back of the door.

'I'll give an eye to 'em,' he said. 'Now hurry, for I'll not be above five minutes.'

Beatrice lit a candle by the fire's dying embers and went through into their bedroom where she undressed quickly but not hurriedly, for though it was a cold night the warmth from the fire which backed onto this room had taken the edge off the chill. She brushed out her long auburn hair, then plaited it and fastened the end with a piece of narrow blue ribbon. Micheál had bought her a quantity of the ribbon just before Dympna had been born and she always used it at night, and knew it pleased him that she did. Hair plaited, she splashed her face with cold water, rubbed it dry on her flannel and slid a white cotton nightdress over her head. That made her remember how astonished the mammy had been that a young girl should have a special garment for going to bed in, as she climbed between the blankets. She, who had once know the caress of lavender-scented sheets and pillowcases, had long ago given in to the realisation that blankets alone were a good deal warmer, and much cheaper, too, when you knitted your own, than the best of linen sheets.

Presently, Micheál joined her. Ever since seeing her horrified embarrassment on their wedding night when he had expected her to undress before him, he always contrived to be out of the room when she made ready for bed, and although she never felt such embarrassment now, she was still grateful to him for his thoughtfulness.

Now, he undressed with his usual calm delibera-tion, whilst telling her in his deep, slow voice that the hens were all roosting in the hayloft where no fox could get them and the donkey slumbered in the byre.

'And the kids are asleep, too,' Beatrice said thank-fully. She had popped her head round the door of the boys' small room and into the curtained-off space where Dympna's bed was kept, before entering her own room. 'Now we can settle down with a quiet mind.'

Micheál, who never seemed to worry about any-thing, Beatrice thought enviously, merely grunted and put a heavy arm round her waist, pulling her close. Like two spoons, Beatrice thought. Now I must push all my worries out of my head or I'll never go to sleep.

But she was still speculating on what the outcome

of Dermot's leaving would be when, presently, she slept.

It did not occur to Micheál to wonder whether his wife was anxious or not about his decision, because he assumed – wrongly, as it happened – that she would guess his intention. She was a clever woman, worth ten men such as he, so he was sure that her intuition as well as her brain would have realised at once which way the wind blew. Although he had given little evidence of it, the truth was that the thought of Nicholas on the *Fair Aleen* had been more of a worry than a blessing to him. The boy was clever everyone told him, so it must be true, but deep in his own heart Micheál considered his eldest son to be downright simple. A useless ninny who could neither tie a knot that would not undo seconds later nor bring a net inboard without spilling half the catch.

It was not as though Nicholas was even helpful about the place, his thoughts continued as he settled for sleep, one arm around his woman's supple waist. He could just about lay the table for a meal, but when he dug potatoes the fork went through the biggest spud, like as not, and anyway he had no strength in him – he would drive the fork into the soil no further than half-way down the tines, so he raised only half of the potatoes and the rest of the crop would be lost. And fancy impaling his finger on a hook and fainting when it was tugged out by his little sister! Still, no one could help what they were, Micheál decided fair-mindedly. Mr O'Neill said he was the brainiest boy ever to pass through his hands, so he was, and that, Micheál told himself guiltily, was a matter for pride. Particularly if you didn't have to take the boy to sea with you.

Beneath his arm, Beatrice settled into the familiar position she always adopted just before she slept. A hand beneath the pillow, fingers spread, the other arm curling up so that the fingers grasped the end of her long plait of hair. It was a glorious colour still, though she was past thirty now, but to Micheál she was still the beautiful young girl who had come down to Salthill with a family of cousins, for a holiday. Sometimes with them and sometimes alone, she had sunbathed on the flat rocks or gone further along to watch the fishermen as they brought in their boats. Several times she put on a bathing costume, which had all the fellers staring, and splashed sturdily out into the cold Atlantic, there to frolic like a seal or a mermaid in the waves until she scampered ashore and wrapped herself in a huge, striped beach towel, with that long, reddish-gold hair darkened with water and the white skin of her rosy with rubbing.

He had loved her then, of course, but hopelessly. He had never thought to make her his wife because such a girl was way beyond him. But sometimes of an evening she would come and perch on the prow of the *Fair Aleen* and talk, and though at first he had blushed and stammered, soon he grew easier. He had told her about his life; about his mother, working hard to keep him and his younger brothers fed and decently clothed, struggling to bring them up alone ever since his father had been killed in a storm at sea when returning to harbour and rounding Black Head. How Micheál, then a child of six, had been a terrible charge on his mammy until he was twelve, when he had worked with an old friend of his daddy's who had lost his own boat and so was glad to take out the *Fair Aleen*, even with a crew of such tender years. Things were easier now, though, he had assured her, eyeing her pretty clothes, the way her hair gleamed in the light of the setting sun. No one, he thought, had ever been lovelier, nor more unattainable. Yet before the summer was over the two of them had married and in sixteen years he had never regretted their union. Even after Nicholas's birth, when she had pushed him away from her . . . but that was long ago.

He was a lucky man, he reflected now, as the bed grew warm about him and the scent of his wife's hair filled his nostrils. He had a beautiful, clever wife, two handsome sons and a daughter who was bright and loving, and a good companion, which was more than a good many men could say of their daughters. He thought about Dympna and smiled to himself. She did not resemble her mother in the slightest, for she was not a pretty child, though he told himself that thirteen was a difficult age. Dympna was dark-haired, with a small, triangular face, which reminded Micheál of a kitten's, and large, slightly tilted dark eyes. Her nose was an indeterminate blob of putty, her mouth set in far too firm a line, her chin jutted. What was more, her skinny figure resembled a boy's far more than girl's. And despite her dark hair, she freckled in summer until her face was quite brown. But she was a grand help on board the *Fair Aleen*, so she was. Quick, strong, her eyesight so good that she spotted a shoal of fish beneath the waves whilst her father was still staring at the disturbed water, she could haul on the net almost as strongly as Dermot, and certainly her enthusiasm far exceeded that young man's, for her idea of a high treat had always been a trip in the boat, with her father, whereas to Dermot it had been just a means of making a living.

So he would take her out with him next day and see how she did. He told himself severely that he must not make up his mind definitely until he had watched how she behaved when she was not just a helper but his crew. Not that he had the slightest doubt; she would throw herself into the fishing with the same whole-heartedness which she used towards everything she enjoyed. Dermot was in his full strength and had worked well, but for the last six months or so his mind had not been on the job. He had been thinking of his young woman, and who could blame him? So he would take Dympna out next day and give Bea his decision as soon as they got home. She would tell Nicholas. He loved the boy, of course, but sometimes if seemed to Micheál that Bea cared more for her eldest child than she did for either of the other two and that hurt him. He loved all three of them, so why could not his wife do so? Oh, Nicholas was a dreamer and not a useful or practical person, but that did not stop Micheál from appreciating his son's cleverness, his tall, slim figure and the hands of him, so slender and white, yet strong enough when he chose to use them in a way he enjoyed. Nicholas played cricket for the school team and Micheál really admired the way he could bowl, crack a ball to the boundary and leap at a catch. What was more, he had won his scholarship without making any particular effort and, Mr O'Neill had told Micheál, he had come top out of all the entrants.

'You should be proud, Micheál,' Mr O'Neill had said, when Micheál and Beatrice had attended a parents' evening at the school. 'When I think how hard I tried to beat mathematics and some imagination into your thick skull I marvel at your son, so I do. He has a mind like a rapier . . . and the girl does well too, for her age and sex. You'll be proud of both of them one day, I'll warrant. And Egan will probably do well once he becomes interested in his books.'

Mr O'Neill had not hesitated to make personal remarks about Micheál because he had taught him from the time he was seven until he left school, but he was almost ill at ease with Beatrice. 'I daresay it is from yourself that Nicky inherited his brains,' he said rather shyly to her after he had teased Micheál. 'But seeing as I never had the teaching of you, I can't be sure now, can I?'

Beatrice liked Mr O'Neill; she had told Micheál so on many occasions, so she smiled very sweetly and said that she did not know where Nicholas's mathematical brain came from, since she herself had never shone at that subject. Did she like the teacher just because he praised her beloved son, Micheál wondered now, lying content in his bed with his wife warm beneath his arm, or because she saw through the fierce act he put on with the kids to the kindly and concerned man beneath? And what would Mr O'Neill say when he heard that Dympna, for whom he had high hopes, would be leaving school to work aboard her father's old boat? Micheál might not have much imagination, but he found he could imagine all too well the look on the older man's face. He sighed, then shrugged. Mr O'Neill would be just as angry with him if he dragged Nicholas away from his studies – more, probably. It was no use trying to please everyone. As so often happened, he must simply do his best for them all and hope that he let no one down.

'Are you all right, Dymp? Oh, 'tis a long way down you are – go careful now . . . surely you've got enough in your bag . . . oh Dymp, do come back!'

Egan lay on his stomach on the cliff edge, peering over and calling down anxiously whilst Dympna, with her collecting bag far from bulging, shook a reproving head at him and continued to climb down the cliff.

Yesterday had been a fine day, with sunshine, but it had not been a particularly happy one. There had been all the fuss over Dermot leaving, and Mammy and Daddy shouting at each other, and then there had been her offer to take Dermot's place on the boat, and Mammy saying it was all wrong and Daddy saying he must think . . . She had gone to bed not knowing what was going to happen.

But this morning, when she had gone through into the kitchen, she somehow knew that everything would be all right. Micheál's face had been calm, and Beatrice had stood before the table cutting hefty slices off the loaf and spreading them with a big lump of pork dripping, sprinkling them with salt before handing them to each person as he or she arrived, to eat with the cup of hot tea already standing on the kitchen table. There was not much talking; there never was, in the morning. Nicholas ate abstractedly and drank several cups of tea, then got up without a word and went out of the back door. Beatrice shouted after him: 'Will you be coming in for a noonday meal?' and Nicholas half turned and said absently, 'Sure, Mammy,' before disappearing into the light drizzle which was falling.

'Where's Nick going?' Egan had said, but not as though he really wanted to know. 'Are there any messages for us, Mammy?'

'Dig some potatoes and fetch me a jug of milk from the farm, the goat's gone dry on us,' Beatrice had said.

She was still staring at the back door, which Nick had pulled to behind him. She'd turned to her husband, stolidly munching bread and pork dripping. 'Have you talked to him, Micheál? Only I'd not want him to go saying anything to Mr O'Neill, if . . . if . . .'

'I told him he could go one wit' his studies,' Micheál had said through a mouthful. 'I'll go over to visit Aidan and his mammy tomorrow before I take the boat out. Indeed, with that drizzle fallin' and no wind to mention, it's not likely to be a good day for the fishin', so mebbe I'll have a day workin' the field.' He had turned to his daughter. 'Will you get me some seaweed later, alanna? You can mound it up in the corner where the dung's been piled up, for I'll start diggin' in the rotted stuff today.'

'Sure I will, Daddy,' Dympna had said readily. 'But me and Egan want to be off for the morning . . . you know, I told you yesterday what we'd in mind to do.'

Micheál had frowned over this for a moment, then glanced at Beatrice and back to Dympna, slowly nodding his head, a smile beginning. 'Oh aye, I remember. Well, come back for the noonday meal and you can get me the seaweed after that. Have a care, mind.'

'We will,' both children had replied at once, then laughed. Dympna turned to her mother. 'If Egan gets the spuds, Mammy, what'll I do?'

'Clean through,' Beatrice had said curtly. 'There's no fish to sell but I mean to go up to the Sullivans to see whether Mrs Sullivan has anything for me. She's keeping poultry in a big way now and there's often work which I can help with.'

Dympna had sighed. Cleaning through was no light task and would take her most of the morning, which would mean no egg-collecting on the cliffs unless she could think of a good reason to escape the task.

She'd glanced at Egan, who winked at her. 'I'll give Dymp a hand an' then we can both dig the spuds,' he said in a fair-minded sort of way. 'That's all right, is it, Mammy?'

'Sure,' Beatrice had answered, but Dympna very much doubted whether her mother had heard the words. 'Micheál . . . can I have a word now?'

'Off wit' you,' Micheál had said to the children. 'Start wit' the praties, get them out o' the way, an' sure the cleanin' will be done in no time.' He turned back to his wife. 'Come through alanna, whiles I put on me new jersey, for I can't go callin' on Aidan and his mammy in this ould t'ing.'

As soon as their parents disappeared Egan and Dympna had hurtled out of the door, both with half-finished slices of bread and dripping in their hands. 'Get the basket,' Egan said as they roared into the corner shed. 'I'll fetch the fork.'

Five minutes later, armed with the shallow reed basket and the fork, the two of them were running up the side of the hill which climbed behind their cottage. It was rough ground, this, with a deal of gorse, great, grey-nosed rocks and a few spindly saplings, mostly of hazel, but then they were hurrying down the further side, until they reached the place between the hills where the Byrnes' potato patch was situated. Up here it seemed colder and wetter than before, but Dympna dropped the basket, grabbed the fork and headed for the potato clamp. 'I'll uncover 'em, you pick the best ones out,' she said breathlessly. 'Well, I dare say they'll mostly be shooting by now, but we can knock the shoots off and they're none the worse for that. At least there were no bad ones when I last looked.'

'It's been a mild winter,' Egan said. He had watched as his sister removed the outer layer of earth and forked delicately through the straw, to uncover the earthy brown potatoes which lay beneath. Then he began to pick out the biggest, rubbing the shoots off before placing them tenderly in the reed basket. 'They're good spuds, aren't they, Dymp?'

'Aye, very good,' his sister said. 'When we've got enough we'll go and cut a cabbage or two, if there are any worth cutting. Might as well, since there may be no fish tonight.'

The main meal of the day was always supper, and supper was usually fish, but if Micheál did not go out in the boat they would be forced to make do with bubble and squeak, as Beatrice called potatoes and cabbage mashed together and fried in pork fat in the big old frying pan. They ate their own vegetables for as long as they could, but when these were finished they could always buy from the Sullivans, who owned a decent farm three miles further up the lough and were good friends to all the Byrnes. 'Should we pick some of the smaller spuds for the pig?'

'Mammy didn't say . . . but there's no sense in leavin' them here to rot,' Egan agreed. 'Then there's the hens . . . though there'll be scrapings for them, I expect.' He'd picked out half a dozen or so good handfuls of the smallest potatoes and laid them to one end of the basket, then headed up the field to where the cabbages still grew, though there was more empty space than cultivated at this time of the year. 'Hey, they're not too good, are they, Dymp? Shall we cut four, and one of the small, weedy ones for the pig?'

'It won't hurt,' Dympna had decided. She had no

desire to return to the cottage just to be sent back for foodstuff for the animals. 'We'll tell Mammy she should bring Rosa up here in a week or two; the thistles are beginning to shoot.'

Rosa was their donkey, a big-eyed, loud-voiced slip of a creature who had a prodigious appetite for anything even slightly edible, and a good few things that were nothing of the sort. Many a time Dympna had cursed the animal's quickness when her woolly scarf was whipped off and half eaten before she realised, whilst her brothers laughed helplessly at her rage.

Presently, the children had set out to return to the cottage with their prizes. They met Micheál on his way up to the field and exchanged a few words, and Micheál told them that Beatrice had gone over to Mrs O'Reagan to see if she had any salt to spare, for she would not be shopping until the following day. Relieved, for if their mother was out she would be in no position to find them more work, the two of them had hurried back to the cottage, where Egan had tipped some water into a bowl and begun to scrub the potatoes, whilst Dympna held the cabbages near the light coming in from the window and scrutinised each tough green leaf for caterpillars or beetles or slugs. 'Not that they'll live in boiling water,' she had said, fastidiously flicking off any livestock. 'Only you know what Mammy's like if she finds a stewed caterpillar. Give 'em a quick dunk, Egan, while I go and tidy through.'

She was lucky, for Beatrice had made the beds and put away clean clothing, so all she had to do was fold back her wooden bed and brush the hard-packed earth of the floor, which wasn't too difficult. By the time she got back to the kitchen Egan had finished cleaning the potatoes and was throwing the dirty water out through the back door and advising her to get her gear, before Mammy came back and thought of something else they might do.

'Sure I will,' Dympna had said, and fetched out her collecting bag and a hunk of stale bread which was being saved for the pig. She had long ago discovered that if she was attacked by indignant gulls or guillemots she could throw bread at the birds, which at once scared them away from her and gave them something else to think about. 'Come on, then, Egan, the quicker the better!'

There was no sign of Beatrice, so the two of them had grabbed another slice of bread each and bolted towards the distance cliffs.

And now here they were, Egan on watch and Dympna almost among the rough clumps of dried heather and bits of seaweed and driftwood, which constituted nests for the birds that thronged the cliffs. She was going carefully, because the drizzling rain had made the ledges slippery, but visibility was poor; a good number of the birds were out fishing and the rest, being only able to see for a few feet, were unaware of her presence, or at least had not started to make a fuss.

She glanced towards where Egan's face hung, staring down anxiously, and realised she could scarcely make out his features at all. This was becoming a sea mist, so she had better get a move on or there would be no exciting parcel for Beatrice tomorrow morning, when she came into the kitchen at breakfast time.

An hour later, she and Egan were couched in a bed of dead and uncurling bracken, ignoring the drizzling rain whilst they gloated over her haul.

41

'You must have got twenty or thirty,' Egan said, big-eyed. 'Janey, but I was scared, Dymp, when that great gull flew at you! I t'ought you was a goner, so I did.'

'You'll be a goner if you talk brogue within slapping distance of Mammy's good right hand,' Dympna said, chuckling. Though both of them used the local dialect in the village and at school, they never allowed their mother to hear them. She thought it unnecessary, said clear speech was a great asset and tacitly never seemed to notice that Daddy spoke with a brogue all the time. Dympna, when very small, had once mentioned this strange fact to Micheál, who had chuckled, given her a hug and said: 'Your Mammy's an Englishwoman, alanna, so she talks as they talk. And since you're the child of the pair of us, you use both languages, so to speak. You've the best of both worlds, see?'

'Oh sure, I can see the mammy hidin' behind that gorse bush,' Egan said now. He peered into the collecting bag. 'There's a grand mix of eggs in there, Mammy's goin' to have the best birthday present ever!'

'I never took more than one or two from the same nest and birds can't count, Mr O'Neill said so,' Dympna said. The village kids robbed songbirds' nests and blew the tiny, delicately shaded eggs to make ornaments for their mammies' mantels and Mr O'Neill disapproved of the practice. 'How many will we give Mammy, would you say, Egan? She'll not want to eat this lot.'

'Give her a dozen, then she can make a big old cake,' Egan answered, licking his lips. 'Do you remember Mammy tellin' us about her parties when she was a kid, like us? She always had a birthday cake, wit' pink icing and candles on. I wish we could make her a cake, Dymp, only we don't rightly know how.'

'No, because she never makes cakes either, it's mainly pastry an' bread when we see her working,' Dympna said. 'Right, she shall have twelve and the rest we'll sell. Then we can buy her a proper shop present. Come on, let's get moving or we'll not have time to go down to Mrs Bailey's before we get our dinners, and once we're indoors . . .'

'. . . the mammy'll find us some work to do,' Egan grinned. 'Come on, then, Dymp; race you to the first stile on the cliff path.'

By evening, the birthday had been arranged. Dympna's large sea-birds' eggs had fetched a fair price, for they were the first of the season, and with the money she and Egan thought long and hard, and then bought their mammy a box of writing paper and matching envelopes, for she had sisters living in England and wrote to them sometimes. Then, with the very last of the money, they had bought a length of ribbon for her hair. The dozen eggs were put carefully into an old biscuit tin that Mrs Bailey had given them, and then wrapped in blue tissue paper, which Mrs Bailey had said had come wrapped around some china, long ago.

'I've had it put away for years, waitin' for the right moment to use it,' she told them, smoothing the tissue beneath her hand. 'Those lovely eggs deserve a pretty wrappin', so they do.'

'Mammy'll be that pleased,' Egan said triumphantly, as he and his sister stowed their gifts away in the little corner cupboard in the boys' bedroom. 'I wonder what Nick's bought for her, Dymp? And Daddy, too?'

They knew it would be something really good from Micheál, for he had impressed upon them the importance of giving one's mammy the very best one could afford. 'Mammies go wit'out a great deal when the childer come along,' he had told them. 'So her birthday is a day to say "thank you" and to show her she's special. See?'

Dympna and Egan did see, and usually went together over a present, but this time Dympna thought triumphantly, they had really done the mammy proud. And all it had needed was a little thought, for she had bought Mammy a few eggs on other birthdays but had never done such serious – and successful – collecting. 'We'll remember this for another year,' she told Egan as they went back to the kitchen where Mammy would presently appear and begin to get the dinner together. 'Of course, you've got to be the first down the cliffs if you want a good price, but who cares for that? I love egging, so I do.'

And the rest of the day they smiled whenever they caught one another's eye, and hugged their secret to themselves, joyously anticipating the morrow.

When Dympna woke on Beatrice's birthday morning it was to pale sunshine and the sound of bird-song. She lay for a moment, gathering her thoughts, then slithered abruptly out of bed and onto the cold earth floor. It was The Day, and she and Egan had agreed to get breakfast ready and take Mammy a cup of tea to start the day off right. She had no idea what time it was, but threw her clothes on and padded along to the kitchen, where Egan was already lugging the filled kettle over to the fire, which crackled bravely.

'Don't put it on yet, Egan,' Dympna hissed, taking it from him, though not without difficulty. 'Janey,

44

you eejit, you've filled it so full 'tis all I can do to shift it.'

'Well, you should have got up as soon as I shook you.' Egan's lower lip jutted. 'I had to manage for myself, you not bein' around to help. Anyway, you can always empty some out.'

'Well, I will,' Dympna said, carrying the heavy kettle over to the bucket and pouring half the contents back from whence they had come. 'Are you goin' to toast a slice of bread, so's Mammy can have toast in bed as well as tea?'

But this Egan refused to do, on the grounds that he wanted Mammy up as soon as possible, to open her presents. So presently, when the kettle boiled, the two children took two tin mugs of tea through to their parents, since Dympna knew that Mammy would get no pleasure from the tea if she were the only one drinking it.

'Happy birthday, Mammy,' they chorused as soon as Beatrice's eyes opened. 'Many happy returns and many more of 'em.'

'Thank you both; my, what a surprise.' Beatrice took the mug from her son and began to sip at it. 'My goodness, it's hot!'

'Tea's meant to be hot,' Egan said, hopping with excitement. 'Mind you get up as soon as you've finished drinkin', Mammy, because Dympna and me's gettin' the breakfast, so we are.'

'That'll be a treat,' Beatrice said, continuing to sip her tea while Micheál, grinning, sat up in bed with both hands curled about his own mug. 'And what's for breakfast, may I ask? I'm mortal fond of having a breakfast cooked for me, whether it's a coddled egg in a silver dish or a plain old piece of bread and dripping.'

'Oh, it's not plain old bread,' Egan said, hopping a bit. 'It's better than that, Mammy. You'll be surprised . . .'

'No she won't be, not if you tell,' Dympna warned, catching hold of his sleeve. 'Let's get on with it, Egan, else everyone'll be late for everything.'

Back in the kitchen, Egan laid the table whilst Dympna broke two gulls' eggs into a bowl, added flour and milk, and whipped the mixture up to make pancakes. By the time Beatrice, Micheál and Nicholas came into the kitchen the table was laid, the food steamed on the plates and the presents, wrapped with varying degrees of care, were piled in front of Beatrice's plate. Nicholas had done his up in a piece of newsprint which, he told them, he had painted himself. It was the prettiest parcel and the one which, to Dympna's secret disappointment, their mother opened first.

'What can this be?' she said, unwrapping. 'Oh, Nicky!' She held up a china cat with a long neck and very small, pointed ears. 'Oh, won't this look just lovely with all my other cats on the shelf in our bedroom? Thank you, darling.'

'It's a pleasure, Ma.' Nicholas smiled. 'I saw it in a shop window weeks ago and thought of you at once. Glad you like it.'

'I love it . . .' Beatrice was beginning, when Micheál broke in.

'Eat your breakfast,' he urged, knowing full well that his wife would not so much as taste the pancakes and the thin strips of streaky bacon until all her presents were unwrapped. Dympna saw that Micheál's gift, a length of flowered cotton, was to be next and resigned herself to waiting, but after Beatrice had thanked him, passed the material round

46

and held it up against herself she turned to the box of stationery and, once again, thanked both children with what certainly sounded like real delight, and held up the ribbon so that Micheál might tell her that blue was her colour, so it was, and wouldn't she look like a princess with that lovely satin ribbon wound round her hair?

'Now Dympna's, Mammy,' Egan urged, pushing the cake tin carefully towards her. 'Wait till you see!'

'Oh, it's nothing special,' Dympna said gruffly, hanging her head and watching Beatrice's expression through her lashes. 'It's a bit of an extra really, only me and Egan . . .'

Beatrice had undone the string and removed the blue tissue paper. She took the lid off the tin next and gazed inside. The eggs, Dympna thought, looked really lovely, with their mottled colours and their smooth and beautiful shapes. Micheál leaned over and looked into the tin as well, whistling beneath his breath. 'There's a rare lot you found, alanna,' he said admiringly. 'What'll you do wit' them, Bea? Sure an' you could have the biggest omelette in the world, so you could – or will you make a grosh o' cakes an' biscuits wit' them? I'm mortal fond of a slice of your fruit cake, an' it'll keep for ever, shut up in that fine tin.'

'Do with them? I'm sure I don't know,' Beatrice said. She turned to Dympna. 'I suppose you got these yourself, scrambling about on those dreadful cliffs and risking your neck every moment? Well, I don't want your death on my conscience, Dympna, so please don't do such a dangerous thing again – you aren't a boy, you know, for all you try to act like one.'

There was a horrified silence. Nicholas, who had picked up his mug of tea, froze with it half-way to his mouth. Egan and Micheál both stared at Beatrice as though she had grown two heads. Dympna felt tears begin to prick behind her eyes. She had been so sure Mammy would be pleased, and if it hadn't been for the eggs they sold there would have been no writing paper, no satin ribbon. But she swallowed hard and said in a small voice, 'It's not really dangerous, Mammy – I go after eggs every year, you know I do.'

'Yes, but going a little way down for one or two is one thing . . . anyway, I'm not going to argue with you, Dympna. Just don't do it again. It's bad enough that you'll be off on the fishing boat when Dermot goes, without my having to worry that you're sliding down the cliff like any one of the village boys.'

'Well, it's nice that you're concerned, Bea, but I t'ink we ought to start eatin', else we'll still be here dinner-time,' Micheál said in a rather strained, hearty voice. 'There you are, Dymp, your mammy loves you too much to want to t'ink of you on those cliffs, so no more egg collectin' wit'out you ask me first, hey? Pass me the sugar, Egan.'

Everyone ate; quickly, because all of them, except presumably for Beatrice herself, had been embarrassed by her words. Egan began to say something, then stopped and crammed a forkful of pancake into his mouth. Micheál ate stolidly, staring at his plate. Nicholas gave his sister a brilliant smile and started to talk about the work he would be doing when his new term began after the Easter break.

Gradually, the talk became general. Dympna asked her father if she and Egan might have crab lines and go out in the boat with him. Micheál reminded her that he was going over to see Aidan's parents that morning, and added that since the tide was well out they would probably do better in the shallow water around the rocks. 'I'll give ye a scrabbler,' he offered. 'If you paddle round the rocks, where the weed grows thickest, you can often find a big ould crab hidin' up till the tide comes in again. Take a bucket, you might find several, an' I'm mortal fond of crab for me tea, so I am.'

And presently they finished their food and left the table, Beatrice to bustle into the bedroom with her presents, and the boys to help with the clearing away and washing up, even Nicholas lending a hand without being asked. Egan went into the bedroom to find out whether Beatrice wanted any messages and came back, eyes round. 'She's been cryin', though when I asked what was the matter she said nothin', an' why didn't I go an' do what Daddy said. But I think she's sorry about . . . well, about what she said, Dymp.'

'Well, she could have said so to me,' Dympna said crossly. 'I wonder why she didn't like the eggs this year? She's always liked 'em well enough in the past, and I was younger then and likelier to slip.'

Nicholas, hanging the mugs on the dresser, turned and pulled a face at her. 'Oh come on, Dymp, you know Ma! She doesn't think it's ladylike for you to go in the fishing boat with Daddy, but she'd rather that than have me go . . . and I'm no use anyhow, you know I'm not. So I suppose she felt ratty with you over that and . . . and hit out. She doesn't mean it, she'll be sweet as apple pie with you come dinner-time. It just shows how she worries about you, d'you see? Cliffs and fishing boats are dangerous places. So don't take on.'

'I'm not,' Dympna said. 'Do you – do you really think it was worry and not crossness?'

'Sure it was,' Nicholas answered. 'I'd be scared stiff

if I saw you half-way down those cliffs and I suppose Ma, being a woman, has a picture of it in her head that terrifies her. So don't you think about it again. Hear me?'

'All right, Nick,' Dympna said slowly. 'I'll put it out of me mind. And next time I'm thinking of egging, I'll think twice.'

'Don't you dare – I do love gulls' eggs,' Nicholas said. He grinned at her, a flash of very white and well-cared for teeth in his thin, serious face, and came over to where she stood by the washing-up bowl to give her a hug. 'You're a broth of a girl, so you are, and I'm really proud of you. I don't say much, but I think it's grand of you to go on the boat instead of me, so don't let Ma upset you. Why, if she's crying it's because she's sorry for what she said but too proud to say so. Aren't I right, Egan?'

'Probably, Egan replied cautiously. 'Oh, c'mon, Dymp, let's go an' get the scrabbler before Daddy goes off to find Aidan's mammy.'

# Chapter Two

'Jimmy! Hey, Jim!'

Jimmy Ruddock was mooching along Liverpool's Scotland Road, impelling a stone shaped like an egg along in front of him with one bare, dust-coloured toe, when he heard the call coming from behind him. Immediately his shoulders hunched up and he sank his head down on his neck, giving the appearance of a tortoise trying to hide away in its shell. Indeed, he did not attempt to look round to see who had shouted or to slow down so that the caller might catch up. Instead, he did quite the opposite. He began to hurry onwards without so much as casting a glance about him, and the stone, which had skittered ahead after the last kick, found itself overtaken and ignored by its erstwhile companion.

'Jimmy! Aw, c'mon, wack, doncher know y'pals when they's hollerin' for ye?'

Jimmy gave a great, martyred sigh and slowed his pace, then turned to face the small figure running along the pavement, her bare soles flapping and her torn skirt bobbing as she hurried in his wake. He recognised Elsie Taylor, who had recently moved into the house next door but one to his aunt's and uncle's home in Kennedy Court, which was in Gay Street, just off the Scotland Road, though they had scarcely exchanged more than a word or two. He wondered what made her think that he would call any mere girl a pal, let alone one he scarcely knew, but he was not about to add to his enemies by being unkind, so he greeted her with what civility he could muster. 'Oh, it's you, Elsie. What d'you want, queen? Gawd, you near on give me a heart attack, yellin' out me name like that. I thought you was Bertie or Solly. Or even bleedin' horrible Edwin.'

'I doesn't sound like them, does I?' Elsie asked rather plaintively, coming to a skidding halt by the boy's side. 'Where's you goin', anyway? And why d'you think the Blaney boys is after you?'

'Why? 'Cos they always is, that's why,' Jimmy said morosely. 'If you'd lived in the Kenny a bit longer that's one thing you *would* know, queen. Why, I tell you, Els, when I'm a feller growed I'm out o' this. I do me best to help in the house, I run messages an' light the fire an' sweep the floor same's as I did when me mam was alive, but I don't get no credit for it, norra chance! And today Aunt Blaney give me a tanner for to run a message for her, an' that bleedin' Edwin caught me up, screwed me arm up the back of me bleedin' neck, and took the tanner. I *told* him it were to fetch his mum some scrag-end from the bleedin' butcher and did he give a tinker's cuss? Not him, he just sort o' crowed, like, and ran off. So either I prig some scrag-end, which ain't likely since I don't even know wharrit looks like, or I gorra earn meself another tanner. Or I could just run away to sea, I reckon . . . only I reckon I don't look more'n twelve yet, do I?'

His companion eyed him judiciously. She was a skinny waif with matted, hay-coloured hair and a dress so stained and crushed that it took a very keen eye to pronounce it blue, but although very dirty it was clear at once that this was mere surface dirt, the sort that any child who played in the street would attract; she had been clean that morning and would be clean again at nightfall. Though even shorter than Jimmy himself she stood straight, hands on hips, legs straddled, confident and curious, and not afraid to show it. Jimmy, however, knew himself to be a very different case. He might be just as dirty, just as ragged, and only an inch or two taller than she, but he knew that the dirt on him had a settled look, as though it had been there some considerable time and intended to stay there. He wished he could do something about it, but his aunt was indifferent to dirt and though Jimmy had once been clean as a new pin, now he was usually too busy grabbing some food and clearing out of the court to think of dunking himself under the pump. As for clothes, if he managed to get hold of something half decent – and the scuffers often handed out clogs and kecks to kids who needed 'em – he lost them as soon as he got home, even though the Blaney boys were all bigger and fatter than he. And even now, though he tried to appear at ease, he knew his glance slid nervously about him as he talked, whilst he held himself always as though for flight should danger threaten. It's not that I'm yeller, he told himself resentfully, only them Blaney fellers is all bigger an' stronger than me, even Edwin, who ain't as old. And they takes pleasure in beatin' me head in, 'cos they know they won't gerrin trouble, not for hittin' *me*.

'I dunno, I'm not very good at judgin' age,' Elsie said after a moment's thought. 'Why d'you want to look older, though? You *are* thirteen, 'cos you're in me cousin Philly's class and he's the same age as me, give or take a month or two.'

'Course I'm thirteen, you cloth-'ead,' Jimmy said scornfully. 'But it ain't no use runnin' away to gerra job and live by yourself if the first scuffer what sees you takes you back home to your . . . your aunt, 'cos he can see you ain't old enough to be on the loose. But why did you yell at me, anyway? Did me aunt send you after me? Or me uncle?'

'No, course not,' Elsie said at once. 'They's so busy wi' their own affairs I doubt they've ever noticed me. No, I yelled out 'cos it's Sunday, an' I been to mass this mornin', so I'm free for the rest of the day. You looked as if you were goin' somewhere – somewhere definite like. So I thought as how I'd ask if you'd tek me along.'

Jimmy stared at her. This was an offer of friendship and such offers did not often come his way. Indeed, he scarcely mixed at all with other kids, because in order to go to school one had to have boots and his aunt refused to provide him with such luxuries. Once, he had gone to school regularly and with pleasure, had studied his books, had taken boots for granted. But that had been when he had a dad and a mam of his own: ever since his father had been lost at sea, things had been very different. Finding themselves suddenly bereft and with very little money, he and Mam had moved into lodgings near the Blaneys, because Aunt Ruby was her elder sister, after all, and Uncle Sam had said he would help over things like carrying heavy loads or moving the furniture around. And although they had only had one room, which was cramped and pretty uncomfortable, things had gone along all right for a while. Mam had worked at a small milliner's shop, and he had gone to school and been reasonably well fed. But then Mam had started to cough and one night she had been so bad that blood had come, and the doctor had put her into the sanatorium where, he had promised Jimmy, she had a good chance of recovery. Only she did not recover. She got worse and worse, with strangely waxy skin and brilliant pink cheeks. She had kept telling him she would get better, but soon neither he nor she had believed it, and after she died there had been no choice but to move in with the Blaneys when they had offered him a home. And once under their roof, he was completely at their mercy.

Not that they had any mercy. So far as they were concerned, Jimmy Ruddock was just another mouth to feed, and once the boys began to turn on him, it was as though his uncle and aunt, too, wished him gone and no longer made any secret of the fact. Jimmy had been with his cousins almost a year now, and things simply got worse and worse.

'As soon as you're earnin' you'll be off, no doubt,' Uncle Sam had growled only a week ago. 'Oh aye, you won't hang about to hand over your wage packet then, not you! You'll be off, that's what you'll be.'

'Who's goin' to employ a squirt of a kid like him?' his aunt had said derisively. 'Filthy little toe-rag, he don't look ten, so no wonder no one 'ud believe he were past thirteen.'

Jimmy longed to shout that if they fed him better – if they fed him at all – he might well be larger and be able to get a job on a Saturday or after school, but nearly a year's bitter experience had taught him that answering back was dangerous as well as foolish. He had always assumed that his aunt had loved her younger sister, but once Mam had died, he realised his mistake. Aunt Ruby had envied his mam her neat home, her clean and well-cared-for son and the loving husband who brought his money home and rarely took a drink. Uncle Sam Blaney drank like a fish and fought anyone who crossed his path when he was sozzled, as well as hitting the kids and his wife, too, if she got close enough. Of course, Aunt Ruby had never said so outright, but reading between the lines it soon became clear to Jimmy that his aunt took positive pleasure in treating her dead sister's son as badly as she could, as if to show him that things were now very different.

But now Elsie was looking up at him inter-rogatively and he had to stop brooding over the Blaneys and answer her question. He stared down at her, wondering what on earth she had asked him, but fortunately, before he had to admit he had forgotten, she repeated her remark. 'Well, are you goin' to tek me along wi' you?' she asked, a plaintive note creeping into her voice. 'Only I don't know nobody in Kennedy 'cept you and I'm gettin' terrible bored, hangin' around me mam all day wi' nothin' to do.'

'You don't know me so very well,' Jimmy observed, but he felt gratified, nevertheless. And the girl was right; so far as he knew, the two of them were about the only people of their age in the court, though there were a great many kids younger and a good few older as well – namely, his Blaney cousins. 'Anyhow, what about your cousin Philly? And you've got brothers and sisters – I seen 'em when you moved in.'

'Philly lives right down the other end of the Scottie,' Elsie told him. 'Besides, he's in a gang. They're up to all sorts an' they don't want me hangin' round. And if Mam knows I'm at a loose end I'll get landed wi' the kids – me big brothers don't want me with 'em, you know what the fellers can be like. So can I come wi' you, Jim? Can I?'

It was, Jimmy discovered, nice to be wanted, nice to hear someone actually asking for his company. He pretended to consider, however – no point in giving in too quickly. 'Well, I don't see why not,' he said at length. 'I was goin' to the butcher's for me aunt's scrag-end, but now I'd better go along to the market and get me some old orange boxes. Me aunt said as how I were too small to gerra job, but I've got a pal on the market what gives me boxes so's I can chop 'em up an' sell the kindlin'. An' sometimes I go into the posh part o' the city an' carry stuff home for women ... you know, rolls o' linoleum, bits o' carpet, bags o' spuds ... they give you a few pennies for carryin' stuff.'

'Then your aunt must know you ain't too small for work,' his new friend observed, falling into step beside him. 'But will you be able to get the money in time to buy the scrag-end for your aunt's stew? I'll be glad to give you a hand, I don't want the money meself, but I'll help you chop an' collect an' that. Be glad to do somethin', I tell you.'

'Thanks; and as for tellin' me aunt I does a little job from time to time, I don't tell her *anything*,' Jimmy said with emphasis. 'If I did she'd tek the money off of me, and I've gorra *eat*, you know. She puts food on the table, tea-time, but I always gets the tiddiest bit on my plate and half the time me cousins nick wharrever I'm give afore I've had more'n a bite or two.'

'No! Well, ain't they wicked?' Elsie said, satisfactorily wide-eyed. 'You want to come round to our place, Jimmy. My mum's gorra big family to feed, but she'd not let one of us go short and any mate of mine's welcome any time.'

Jimmy was touched by this offer, but did not intend to show it. 'Thanks, but I manage awright most o' the time,' he said gruffly. 'You don't know your way around yet, I dare say? Well, we're luckier than most, livin' in the Kenny, 'cos we're near Paddy's Market, where everything's cheap, and near the fruit market, too. That's where I'll go today, to get me a supply o' boxes.' He grinned down at her. 'I've told you all about me, now you can tell me about your little lot,' he continued. 'A big family, you say? I thought there was several kids when you moved in.'

'Yup. There's eight of us,' Elsie said. 'I'm right in the middle . . . there's Sal, Joe and Alan older'n me and Freddy, Arthur and Mabel younger. Oh, and the baby, she's Suzie and she's just startin' to toddle. She's the one I get landed with, mostly.'

'It must be nice to have brothers and sisters,' Jimmy said rather wistfully. It would be good, he reflected, to have anyone who would stand up for him when his cousins and their parents turned on him as they so often did. He frequently thought of running away, but he knew in his heart that living on the streets would be even more dangerous than dossing down with the Blaneys. He slept in the back bedroom with his cousins and usually managed to wedge himself into a corner and get some sleep, though there were nights, particularly in summer, when the older boys were restless and spent what felt like hours tormenting him. But with luck I'll be out of there by the time the weather gets better, he told himself with groundless optimism. You never knew, though. Sometimes he had wonderful dreams in which his father was not dead but had merely been washed overboard and then picked up by a foreign craft, which was unable to bring him home to England for several years. In the dream Oswald Ruddock came grinning into the house, smiting Blaney heads and shouting abuse at them for the way they treated his son, before seizing Jimmy in his arms and giving him a great big hug. That was a good dream, though he was having it less and less frequently of late.

'I've got some money,' Elsie said presently, as the two of them continued to walk briskly along the Scotland Road. 'It ain't a tanner, but it's a threepenny bit. Do you suppose we could get enough scrag-end wi' that to fool your aunt? Only if she's makin' a stew for tonight's supper you'll be hard pressed to gerrit home in time. An' you could pay me back when you've sold your kindling,' she added.

Jimmy stopped short and heaved a sigh. It was true that Aunt Ruby had told him to get a move on and not to linger in the street else she'd never get the grub on to the fire in time, but he imagined that the difference between sixpenn'orth of meat and threepenn'orth would be noticed at once by anyone as mean as his Blaney aunt. He said as much, but Elsie, it seemed, was a good deal more cunning than he had imagined.

'Ye-es, but suppose we buys somethin' even cheaper than scrag? There's a feller on Byrom Street sells off-cuts for dogs, I reckon if we bought the best-lookin' dogs' meat on the stall you might gerraway with it. Is your aunt a good cook?'

'Nah. She never does nothin', she don't make cakes or pies, they's all bought from the shop,' Jimmy assured her. 'She chucks a bit o' meat an' some veggies into a pot an' calls it stew, that's all she does. Why, when my mam was alive she made all sorts . . . the baker cooked some of the stuff up for her, like . . . but me Blaney aunt don't even bake bread.'

'Right; then the chances are she won't know the difference 'tween dog meat an' scrag end. Let's go.'

Later that evening, loftily accepting that his helping of stew was niggardly, smiling inwardly when Edwin leaned over and began to spoon up what little there was, Jimmy knew that he had been fortunate

59

beyond his wildest dreams when he had fallen in with Elsie Taylor. She was a great girl, with more go in her than in most of the fellers he'd met, and even after a few hours spent in her company he knew she was a good 'un.

The suggestion about buying dogs' meat had been downright brilliant, Jimmy thought, eating as much bread and margarine as he could get down him, whilst his cousins were still gobbling stew, the best part of it being that whether they knew it or not, he was having the laugh on the Blaneys. He had felt a twinge of something very like fear when Edwin had walked into the kitchen and seen the stew bubbling on the fire, but on reflection, he realised that Edwin could scarcely ask where he had got the money for scrag-end without revealing that he had stolen it in the first place. He supposed that Edwin, a regular thief himself, had simply assumed that Jimmy, too, had stolen in his turn.

But the meat aside, Elsie had proved her metal when they had reached the stall of the giver of boxes. Old Mrs Alexander, who ran a fruit stall on the market, had a soft spot for Jimmy and usually saved him one or two of the wooden empties that came to her full of oranges, but after Elsie had admired the stall, said the boxes were the best she had ever come across and pointed out the beauty of a stout length of orange box rope, Mrs Alexander had suddenly handed the rope over to her, telling her to tie it round her waist whilst she wasn't skipping with it or sure as eggs was eggs, someone would try to snitch it off her. Mrs Alex had been kind to Jimmy, but one or two boxes were his lot, yet when he was with this girl everyone they met seemed friendlier somehow. Elsie was so . . . well, so *ordinary*, Jimmy thought, yet she had something . . . and it suddenly occurred to him what that something was. Elsie Taylor was interested in people. She really listened when you talked to her, she fixed her eyes on your face and she felt for you – that was it, she felt for you. Sympathy, interest, amazement, amusement, they chased across her plain little face like dogs after a cat, and you felt you were of consequence to one small person at least. It made you want to help her, though it couldn't be only that. It must be because Elsie made it clear at once that she would like to help you in her turn.

'My, this is a great rope for jumpin',' she had said enthusiastically to Mrs Alexander, stroking it as though it were a favourite cat. 'I bet you could jump rope best of 'em all when you were a nipper, hey, Mrs Alex? I bet you knew all the rhymes, didn't you? You goin' to show us some of the games you played when you was a girl?'

And bless me, just when Jimmy was getting ready to scarper as fast as he could in case a woman so old took offence at this remark, Mrs Alexander had taken the rope in her old hands – for she must be quite fifty, Jimmy thought – and had begun to skip rope in a very professional way, singing as she did so:

> Oh me Uncle Mick
> He had a big stick
> And he took it to the slaughter
> He killed two thousand orangemen
> At the battle of the Boiling Water.

Jimmy had, to be truthful, felt a bit of a fool standing there whilst this old, old woman skipped rope and sang. But Elsie laughed and clapped, and soon other stall-holders joined in and everyone got friendly and a bit silly, and Jimmy found himself given a turnip that was only slightly withered, an onion that wasn't withered at all and a luscious orange, which he and Elsie presently took up a quiet jigger and shared, laughing as the juice ran down their chins leaving white trails amongst the dirt.

'Are people always like that to you, Els?' Jimmy had said presently as they left the jigger and began to walk towards the nearest butcher's shop. 'Mrs Alex is ever so kind, but she never give me an orange before. And that rope's a good 'un.'

'Probably didn't think of it,' Elsie said absently. 'It ain't that folk is mean, exactly, it's more that they don't think, half the time. But if you think of them, like . . .'

She had not finished the sentence, but she did not need to – Jimmy understood. It takes two to make a quarrel, his mother had sometimes said when he and a friend had argued and fought. So did it take two, it seemed, to make a friendship, to make one's mark in any way upon another's consciousness.

'That's the end o' the stew, but there's bread an' jam, if that greedy tyke hasn't ate it all.' His aunt's voice broke in upon Jimmy's thoughts and he stared round the table at his cousins. They had scraped their plates clean and were about to start on the bread and jam. Not that he had had jam, oh no, Aunt Ruby hadn't told him there was any so he had just made do with bread and a bit of margarine. But it didn't matter; hadn't he had half of a huge orange, and hadn't the two of them taken the onion and the turnip back to the Taylors' house so that Elsie's mam could make use of them? He had felt really good, giving something to someone else, and Mrs Taylor, no prettier than her daughter but with a fair share of that warmth and humour which Elsie had in such abundance, had been delighted with his gift and had invited him to come home with Elsie any time. 'And we'll find you a mouthful of summat,' she had said cheerfully. 'We don't have much, but what we do have we shares, eh, Elsie?'

Oh, Jimmy had felt warmth then, and wanted. So now, when his aunt snatched up the plate of bread and margarine as indignantly as though he were a stranger who had been caught stealing it, and pushed the food over to the opposite side of the table, he merely slid back his stool and headed across the kitchen towards the back door.

'Where d'you think you're buggerin' off to, young Ruddock?' his cousin Solly said aggressively. 'You don't just walk out in the middle of me mam's good cookin'. Come back 'ere before I . . .'

'Oh, leave 'im go, it's all the more for us,' Edwin said sulkily. 'Pass the bread, Tom.'

And Jimmy, hurrying along the court, chuckled under his breath. They had eaten dogs' meat, and he was about to start chopping wood so he could pay Elsie back her threepence. But first of all, he must have as good a scrub as he could manage under the pump, because Elsie had said, thoughtfully, that water was free and a feller who was clean would always get treated nicer than one who was downright filthy. Sighing a little, for in Jimmy's opinion the only good thing about Aunt Ruby was her dislike of soap and water, he decided that since Elsie was right over so many things, she was probably right about washing, too. So now he dipped into his pocket for the sliver of soap Elsie had given him and plucked up his courage. He needn't strip, it was just the bits that showed for now, but tomorrow he would either go up the Scaldy and have a proper swim in the water warmed by the soap factory, or he would earn a penny for the public baths.

Ten minutes later, a good deal cleaner on the surface at least, with his skin glowing from contact with the strip of ragged cotton he had extracted from the rags beneath which he slept, Jimmy set off across the court. Whistling gaily under his breath, he skirted a group of kids playing ollies and made for the Taylors' house. He had already noted the scrubbed and redded doorstep, the bright, clean linoleum in the kitchen and the good smell of cooking that the Taylors, no doubt, took for granted. Life, which had seemed so dark when Edwin had twisted his arm and taken the tanner, suddenly appeared bright and hopeful once more. Furthermore, it felt strangely good to be clean, though he guessed that he would not be particularly clean by a mother's standards. Smiling to himself at the thought, he went round the back and knocked on the door, then, upon hearing a bellow from within, cautiously stepped inside.

The room was crowded; eight children ranging in age from fourteen to not yet two sat around the table, eating a stew similar in appearance to the one in the kitchen he had just left. But how differently it smelled. Jimmy swallowed. His hunger, unappeased by his aunt's meagre offering at suppertime, rose within him as he eyed the food. And the faces, though some were stew-smeared, were all friendly. He had no difficulty, either, in picking out Elsie from her numerous brothers and sisters, though all of them had hay-coloured hair and were in varying degrees skinny and smallish. But Elsie's smile was the widest, and she jumped up from the table at once and bade the sister next to her 'shove up, Mabs! Me pal what I telled you about. He's come to help me finish up choppin' that wood.'

Mrs Taylor was seated at one end of the long table and, at the other, a man he had not previously met presided, and turned and grinned at him as he slid carefully into the gap Elsie and Mabel had made for him on the long wooden bench.

'Wotcher, young 'un,' he said cheerfully. 'Want a plateful of scouse?'

'Yes, please,' Jimmy said at once and added, 'Mr Taylor.'

'Aye, that's me,' the man said. He looked round the table. 'Anyone finished? Ah, trust you to git outside o' a meal in no time, our Joe! Hand your plate along and I'll fill it agin' for our Elsie's pal.'

And presently Jimmy was eating stew and drinking hot, strong tea, and soon he found he was talking more freely than he had done for two years – and with no sense of impending doom hanging over his head, either.

'It must be nice, livin' at your place,' he said wistfully later that evening, as he and Elsie trailed home to the court, having gone all the way down to Pier Head to watch the ferries coming and going with the last workers aboard. 'Your mam and your dad are just like mine were.'

'Yeah, it's awright,' Elsie acknowledged. 'Me mam an' dad may yell, an' make out like they'll not let you do what you want, but they's awright too, really. So just you visit us whenever you're feelin' low. Mam and Dad won't mind.'

'I'll do that,' Jimmy said, much relieved. He felt as a prisoner would, when a pal says he'll leave the door unlocked. Life would be so much easier if he had a bolt-hole to make for now and then. But of course you couldn't say so, not to a girl, so when they reached the Blaneys' house and faced towards it, he just waved, then turned back and grinned at his companion. 'See you tomorrer, then, queen.'

'See you tomorrer,' Elsie echoed.

And Jimmy, creeping silently – or as silently as possible – through the house and up the creaking stairs to his corner of the boys' room, told himself that his life had changed very much for the better. Now that he had a pal there would be more point in getting out of the court and having some fun. He wondered why he had not thought of it before, but realised that the numbing horror of losing his parents and the room which had been home to him, plus the misery of being under the thumb of the Blaneys, had simply drained him of ideas and hope.

But the ideas were beginning to come back to him, as though Elsie's friendship and interest had opened a long-locked cupboard in his mind. He would get some boots, so that he could go back to school, and would keep them at the Taylors' place. He would continue to wash himself regularly and would make sure that he ate, and furthermore, he would do it without stealing. And he would go to church with Elsie on a Sunday morning, so that they might have the rest of the day to themselves. I'll start tomorrow, he vowed, curling up very small on the straw pallet which he and Edwin shared. Yes, tomorrow will be a new beginning – and if my mam's watching from heaven, won't she just be pleased!

As a result of Elsie's companionship – and championship, for she would not willingly see him bullied – Jimmy began to enjoy life. He told her of his plans to attend school once more and she threw

66

herself into the acquisition of boots with such enthusiasm that within a month Jimmy, duly booted and in a clean shirt and patched trousers, went daily to school and began, tentatively at first, to fight back when Edwin pounced on him.

'I give him a bloody nose today when he tried to take my apple at dinner-time,' Jimmy told her when they met at the entrance to Kennedy court, for whoever was first usually hung about for the other. 'He weren't half surprised – but he didn't try to thump me again.'

'Bullies are always cowards,' Elsie said wisely. 'You've took off your school togs, I see. Everything awright there?'

'Yes thanks, grand,' Jimmy said, rubbing his bare feet in the dust to get them appropriately filthy before going indoors. He was determined that Aunt and Uncle Blaney should never realise that he was attending school regularly, in case they put two and two together and found out about his clothing and boots. Once they got their hands on his stuff they wouldn't think twice about either pawning it at Fred Francis's on the corner of Horatio Street and the Scottie, where their own respectable clothing spent most of its life, or they might simply hand his boots and good flannel shirt to Edwin. Since Edwin and Tom were both at his school it was of course perfectly possible that one or other of them might mention their cousin's suddenly smart appearance to their parents, but having thought it over, Jimmy considered it unlikely. Tom was nearly fourteen and about to leave school for ever, and since he was a poor scholar and a bully into the bargain he was not exactly popular with his teachers. This meant that he spent as little time as possible in class, and since

Edwin, too, frequently sagged off school, the chances of either brother noticing his clothing and reporting back to their parents were slight.

However, it was clearly impossible for him to walk into Kennedy Court in his decent things without his aunt or uncle noticing, so early on Elsie had evolved a plan. She was fond of planning and after some head-scratching and muttering had come up triumphantly with a solution. 'Look, do you 'member me sayin' I'd a cousin Philly what's your age, at your school? He was in your class, weren't he?'

'That's right,' Jimmy had said readily. He liked Philly Raddles, a small, square, pugnacious boy who had a natural talent for maths and a grin with nearly split his head in two. 'Philly an' me gorron grand, I were sorry to stop seein' him when I couldn't go to school no more.'

'Aye. Well, as I told you, he lives a good bit further along the Scottie than we do, on Bostock Street. That's fairly near St Anthony's, ain't it?'

'Yeah, a couple o' streets further out. Almost in Bootle,' Jimmy had agreed. 'But what's that got to do wi' me decent clobber?'

'Me aunt Raddles is ever so nice,' Elsie had informed him. 'She likes me, what's more. If I go up to her house after school and explain, she'll let you go in and change into your old things there. Only you'll have to gerrup a lot earlier than you need to get there fust thing in the mornin', so's you can change the other way round before class. See?'

'She wouldn't mind?' Jimmy had asked dubiously. 'She don't know me, though, Els. She might think I swiped the stuff.'

'She might, but she won't. I'll explain, I said,' Elsie had reminded him. 'Look, I'm usually up early; we'll go up there together before school tomorrer, an' I'll keep your school stuff now an' hand it over outside Aunt Ethel's house. Well, only if she's agreed to do it acourse,' she added punctiliously. 'Only she will, I'm sure.'

And she had. So even though it meant leaving home very early indeed each weekday morning, Jimmy got himself up and off to the Raddles house to change into his school clothes every day, and was often rewarded by a large plateful of porridge, sitting next to Philly at the kitchen table whilst friendly Mrs Raddles bustled about in a stained pink dressing-gown, doling out porridge and hot tea, with a cigarette attached to her lower lip.

In the evening, the process was reversed. Jimmy arrived in the their kitchen looking trim and left ragged. And all he did to pay something back to Mrs Raddles for her kindness was to keep her permanently supplied with ready-chopped kindling and to run occasional messages for her.

So now here were Jimmy and Elsie under the blackened brick arch, which led from Gay Street into the inner recesses of Kennedy Court, talking over their day.

'Auntie's ever so good, ain't she?' Elsie said as the two of them went under the arch and lingered for a moment outside the Blaney house. 'She likes you an' all, our Jimmy. She told me she'd keep your school stuff over the summer hols if you like.'

'Summer hols? But it can't be nearly time . . .' Jimmy said, sounding as surprised as he felt. Summer holidays? But to him, term had scarcely begun.

'Aye, there's only another two an' a bit weeks of term left,' Elsie said placidly. 'Then you'll have weeks an' weeks to do what you like in. We'll have a good time, though, you an' me. Especially if you can get some work by then.'

'Well, I'd be ever so grateful if Mrs Raddles could keep me good togs,' Jimmy said. 'No one won't want wood chips, though, norrin in the summer. What'll I do, Els?'

Today, as on most school-days, Elsie's hair was in two thick plaits; now she pulled one of them round over her shoulder and put the end thoughtfully in her mouth. 'Oh, there's bound to be somethin',' she said vaguely through her hair. 'It 'ud be nice to find somethin' we could both do, though. It ain't no use either of us goin' for an errand boy, 'cos we can't ride a bike. But we could help in a greengrocer's, an' sweep the floor an' tek the money, couldn't we?'

'Yes, I suppose so, but they don't want schoolkids as a rule, they want girls or fellers who're after real jobs. An' we neither of us look older than we are.'

'Deliverin' newspapers? Helpin' the feller what sells the milk? Or the baker, the door-to-door one, I mean. Carryin' parcels? Only you can hang around Paddy's Market a long time an' not get anything to carry. Oh, I dunno. But there's got to be somethin'. Just think of all the things we could do if we had money. Trips to the cinema, rides on the ferry or the overhead railway, days on the beach, goes on the funfair . . .'

'Yeah, I know what you mean, but there's another three weeks before we've got to start thinkin' about jobs,' Jimmy said comfortably. 'Tell you what, at playtime I'll ask around, see what the other fellers do to earn a bob or two. Does your cousin Philly do a job come the holidays?'

'No. But they've got all the older fellers earnin' and me cousin Dora workin' too, so it's all right for Philly.

70

It's not too bad in our family either, 'cos Sal an' Joe both have jobs, and Alan will be startin' in reg'lar work soon. Only Mam can't give me money for trips and that, so I want to earn for meself.'

'Yes, I'm the same . . .' Jimmy was beginning, when a raucous voice from the house behind him brought his head round sharply.

'Jimmy! Your uncle's on a late tonight, so we're havin' supper early. Go an' get me ten penn'orth o' chips from the corner shop, an' don't linger or I'll see that you . . .' Aunt Ruby, starting to threaten something unpleasant no doubt, noticed Elsie and stopped short. 'Come along, Jimmy,' she added in a voice so dripping with honey that Jimmy felt quite sick. 'Go right away an' I'll give you a penny for yourself,' she finished.

'Awright, Aunt,' Jimmy said shortly. To Elsie he said in an undertone: 'See you tomorrer and if I've thought of anything I'll let you know.'

He took the money his aunt was holding out and turned on his heel, making his way out of the court. What a wretched woman she was . . . but he would have a chip or two on his way home or he knew very well he would never taste them, and chips were easily the nicest thing to appear on the Blaney menu. And all the way to the shop he would rack his brains for the sort of job that a couple of kids could do to earn themselves some money.

Very much later that evening he met Elsie as she crossed the court, heading for the lavatories at the end of the yard. He called her over, beaming from ear to ear.

'Hello-ello-ello,' Elsie said, trotting across to where he stood and grinning back at him, a couple of sheets

71

of newsprint in one hand. 'What's happened, la? Lost a penny an' found sixpence?'

'No-oo, but nearly. I've found meself some work. Oh, not right away, but the feller said I could start on Saturdays whiles we're in school and then do more hours in the holidays. What do you think?'

'I say, you *are* a one! Wharr is it? Newspapers? I suppose you could learn to ride a bike, if you know someone who'd lend you one.'

'Wrong. Try again.'

'Oh . . . the milkman? Or a baker? I wouldn't mind deliverin' for a baker, 'cos you might get to try the cakes an' give me some.'

'Wrong and wrong again. Give up? After all, you aren't out here for the pleasure of me company, are you?'

But Elsie would not tamely give up just because she had urgent business, so she hurried across to join the queue of others waiting for the WC, jumping from foot to foot and making ever wilder suggestions as to Jimmy's job. Jimmy, growing tired of the game, at length blurted out his news. 'It's the last place I'd ha' thought of tryin' – it's the chip shop. They need someone to peel spuds and cut them into chips, and someone to brush and clean the floor every now and then so's the girls on the counter don't slip and break their necks. They even need someone to sell, sometimes, when they're really busy.'

'And they'll tek you on? No kiddin'?' Elsie gasped, wide-eyed. 'Oh, Jimmy!'

'Well, they said they'd try me, which is near as good,' Jimmy said hastily. 'So I'm to go on Saturday morning early and the feller will watch me work and have a word wi' me, he said. I say, d'you think I'd better wear me best things?'

72

'What, to peel bleedin' spuds?' Elsie gasped. 'Course not, you great fool. But you'll need your boots wi' all that hot fat on the floor.'

Jimmy agreed that he would definitely wear his boots and promised to see that Elsie got free chips if it was within his power to do so. Then, as she reached the head of the queue he bade her good-night and returned to the Blaney household, actually feeling so happy that the usual sinking of the stomach he experienced every time he walked within the walls was absent and he whistled a tune to himself as he went across the kitchen to clear away, before going to bed.

There was no washing up – another advantage to buying chips – but plenty of greasy paper which had to be disposed of, so he jammed the rubbish into a brown paper bag and put it on the fire, poking it around with a stick until it lit up and burned. Then, since the fire was mainly ash by now anyway, he riddled it through and raked out the remains, got some clean sheets of paper and a handful of wood chips and laid it ready for morning. Having got a bit mucky doing this he went to wash his hands and discovered – surprise, surprise – that both buckets were empty. Trust Edwin to steer clear of any work that was going, he thought grimly, though his cousin had still been eating stolidly when he, Jimmy, had been sent out to buy a jug of porter and some Woodbines for his aunt and uncle. He had plonked the messages on the kitchen table and gone out again, since the rest of the family were now into bread and jam, and he saw no reason to hang about. But surely they could have fetched water in and taken the rubbish out, just for once?

Still, there were advantages to a chip meal, he

73

reflected, as he clanked the two large tin buckets out to the tap in the court to fill them with water for the morning. They seemed to improve Blaney tempers, for the boys had ignored him all through supper. And what was more with a whole ten penn'orth, even he had found some on his plate, which was a treat, though he had helped himself to a few in the shop before allowing the man to sprinkle them with salt and vinegar, and wrap newspaper round them.

By now it was late, so he was the only person at the tap and was able to fill both his buckets without hurrying. When they were brimful he carried them, not without difficulty, back across the court and into the kitchen, where he stowed them beneath the greasy little table on which his aunt kept the washing-up bowl. Then, yawning, he made for the stairs.

Not a bad day; a good one, in fact. He had found himself a job and one which might well prove to be amusing as well as bringing in some much-needed money. And though he had not mentioned the fact to Elsie, he could not help thinking that if she came along to the chip shop when he knew they would be busy and offered to do an hour or two there, the proprietor, Bill Lumley, would probably jump at the chance of an extra pair of hands.

But she'll have to wash and brush her hair and wear a tidy dress, Jimmy reminded himself as he eased open the door of the back bedroom. No one won't give her a job in a food place if she's mucky and untidy. But by now he knew his Elsie. She would get herself up like a dog's dinner if there was a chance of a job, and once she got her feet under the table she'd charm them into believing she was the best worker in the business. She probably would be good, too, since she enjoyed work and was always bounding with energy.

Jimmy glanced cautiously around the room, but all that met his eyes were the mounds of sleeping bodies and the only sound was that of gentle and not-so-gentle snores. Relieved, he padded softly across the floor to his corner of the straw mattress, slid out of his jacket, got quietly into bed and pulled the jacket over his shoulders. No one stirred, though someone, probably Solly, who talked in his sleep, muttered something about a number eleven tram being no manner o' use to someone after a forty-three.

A job – I've gorra job! Jimmy was saying to himself as he began to relax. The air in here was thick with the warmth and stuffiness generated by half a dozen bodies, but he was too tired to get up and open the window a crack, so he would just have to put up with it. In fact, he was in the middle of marvelling how the cousins could possibly sleep in such a fug when he toppled into dreamland.

# Chapter Three

'Jimmy, be a good lad an' go round to the tater merchant, will ye? We'll be wantin' another sack at this rate . . . my goodness, an' I 'member tellin' our Maisie as the warmer weather 'ud be bad for business, since folk 'ud buy ice-cream instead o' fish an' chips. I'm just thankin' the good Lord that when Eddy King came down from Fleetwood this mornin' I took more'n me usual whack o' fish because they was so good. Never seen cod or haddock like it . . . but Fleetwood fish is always the best.'

Jimmy had worked for the Lumleys in his holidays and at weekends for a year and to his immense relief, now that he was fourteen and had left school, the boss had agreed to keep him on as a full-time worker. 'You never shirk, Jim,' he had said frankly when Jimmy had explained that he had to leave school since he was fourteen and needed proper money now. 'You're strong an' all, an' the customers like you. You can start full-time come Monday.'

But that had been a while ago and now Jimmy was well used to working full-time and enjoyed both the work and having a proper pay-packet of his own at the end of each week. Not that he had it to himself for long; his aunt took a good half, though she could scarcely be said to be feeding him, for he ate at the Lumleys' and only went back to Kennedy Court to sleep.

Elsie, however, had not been so lucky. She had a job

working in a milliner's shop on the Scottie, but she got a miserable little wage and Jimmy was often glad to be able to mug her to a meal or a visit to the picture show in return for all the kindness she had shown him when he had first met her.

But right now, he finished chipping the last of the peeled potatoes, dried his wet and wrinkled hands on a piece of towelling hanging on the back of the scullery door and turned to Bill Lumley. His boss was a big, freckled, fair-haired man who sweated profusely; right now, with the shop full of customers and every fryer going full bore, he looked as though he had just been fished out of the Mersey, Jimmy thought, grinning. Bill's hair was plastered to his wet red face and the neck of his rather dirty off-white shirt was heavy with water.

'That's it, Mr Lumley; Eddy's fish is the best you can get for many a mile,' Jimmy agreed. He liked Eddy, a skinny, fair-haired man who was building up a considerable reputation in the Pool for his excellent fresh fish. Now that Jimmy was working full-time the two of them sometimes ate their midday meal together, Eddy apparently liking nothing better than a piece of fried fish despite being surrounded by them all day. 'I'll get you the spuds – be glad to have a breath of air to tell you the truth. Shall I take the handcart?'

'Aye, 'cos if we ask them to deliver, we'll be out o'spuds long afore they arrive back. Can you manage two sacks, wi' the cart?'

'Yes, easy,' Jimmy said. 'Want anything else whiles I'm out?'

'Ask Mother,' Bill said. He always referred to his wife as 'Mother', no matter who he was addressing. 'I'm fine for fish, but mebbe we could do wi' more butter, only it melts so. An' the meals don't go on long after nine o'clock, it's more carry-outs.'

'Right, Mr L,' Jimmy said again. 'Purrit on the account?'

'Aye. An' after you've got the spuds you can nip up to the Jug an' Bottle an' fetch me some ale; reckon Mother an' me deserve it.'

Jimmy hurried out of the chip shop, where he had been zealously cleaning the floor with an ancient mop soaked in something smelly but efficient, and into the back kitchen where Mrs Lumley prepared for the eating-in customers plates of fish, chips and peas with bread and butter on the side. Her eldest daughter, Minnie, presided over the teapot this evening, constantly pouring out the cups of sweet, strong tea, whilst Maggie, who was only sixteen, brought through the supplies of cooked fish and chipped potatoes from the shop.

'Mrs L, Mr L says could you do wi' some more butter, for the bread n' butter, like. I'm out now to gerrim more taters.'

Mrs Lumley looked across at him and grinned, never stopping for one moment in her scooping up of chips and tipping them onto the heated plates in neat, cylindrical piles. 'Butter? Nay, lad, I don't think we'll be needin' much more, this'll last us.' She pointed with her metal scoop at the big brick of margarine standing on the back counter by the three loaves of bread. 'Besides, the bleedin' stuff keeps meltin'. Afore you go, Jimmy, fetch me up some more ice for it.'

There was a cellar beneath the shop, reached by a flight of steep and slippery stone steps. Jimmy took up the lamp that stood at the head of these stairs and went down carefully, one hand holding it before him, the other, with the empty ice-bucket around its wrist, guiding him against the whitewashed wall. At the bottom of the steps there was a compartment for coal and a large, thick-walled boxlike container for ice. Jimmy stood the lamp down beside the icebox and opened it, holding his face over it for a moment to enjoy the sudden updraught of cold air. Then he fished out several lumps of gleaming ice and dropped them into his bucket. Finally he set off up the steps once more, well laden.

'Here y'are, Mrs Lumley,' he said, standing the bucket down by the margarine and replacing the lamp before closing the cellar door. 'It's quite cool down there, isn't it?'

'Aye. It's awright in the summer, but it's bleedin' freezin' in the winter,' Mrs Lumley said cheerfully, picking the ice out of the bucket piece by piece and placing them as close to the rapidly melting margarine as she could. 'Thanks, young feller. Now get them spuds afore Mr Lumley runs out o'chips.'

'Sure,' Jimmy said. He trotted out of the kitchen, threaded his way between the sweating but cheerful customers eating their fish and chips at the small, white-painted tables, and went out of the front door and into the still warm sunshine of early evening. The handcart, with its front wheel immobilised by a bicycle chain and padlock, stood waiting for him and he unlocked the padlock in a moment, being well used to this task by now, and began to trot along the pavement, dragging the little cart behind him. The potato merchant was not far away, fortunately, since even with the help of the handcart two full sacks of potatoes were extremely heavy, so it was not long before Jimmy had given his order and balanced his sacks carefully right in the middle of the cart.

'Thanks, Mr Jones,' he said. 'Mr Lumley said as how

you was to put 'em on his account; that awright?'

'That's fine,' Mr Jones said. He was a small and canny Welshman who often had a laugh with Jimmy over his once-small stature, though now that the Lumleys fed him whenever they ate themselves, he had long ago lost his rapier-like thinness. 'Why, boyo, I can see the muscles poppin' out on your arms like . . . like *mole'ills* on a mountain. You'll be a prize-fighter yet!'

'Norrif I can help it, Mr Jones,' Jimmy said, lifting the handles and propelling his handcart out of the potato merchant's yard. 'I'm goin' to get me a horse 'n cart an' fetch spuds in from the country to sell 'em to fellers in chip shops, like you do. That's the way to mek your fortune I'll be bound.'

'Why don't you have a chip shop yourself, mun?' Mr Jones called, coming out onto the pavement. 'Or you could be a farmer, 'cos that's where the big money is . . . us fellers what fetches the spuds in are just middlemen, scrapin' a bob or two.'

'Ah, wharrever you say you potato kings is as rich as that feller whose touch turned everythin' into gold,' Jimmy shouted breathlessly over his shoulder, bumping the handcart down the kerb and across the cobbled street, but Mr Jones just laughed, shaking his head, and returned to his yard.

It was a lovely evening, though, Jimmy mused as he turned the corner, knowing that the shop was not far distant now. In fact, it was no evening to be working. But the Lumleys were so good to him and had changed his life very nearly as decisively as Elsie had, so he worked his very best for them – and was well paid for it, too. It had made things easier at home in some ways as well. He had not told his aunt and uncle about his job when it was just holidays and weekends, but when it became full-time they found out, of course. The Lumleys' place was only a stone's throw from Kennedy Court and when Aunt Ruby didn't feel like cooking she frequently sent one of the boys along to Lumley's for chips – for fish as well, if she could afford it. So it was not long before Edwin the tale-bearer carried the news back that his cousin Jimmy was workin' all day an' most of the evenin' in the chip shop, and why couldn't he, Edwin, get a good sort o' job like that?

Naturally, Aunt Ruby and Uncle Sam immediately cornered Jimmy and demanded that he hand over his wages, but by this time, Jimmy was growing wise in the ways of the Blaneys and, looking them both in the eye, assured them that he would give them a fair rent but would not be bullied into parting with more. 'They feed me, which counts as part of me wages,' he said stoutly, if untruthfully. 'You've gorra tek that into account.'

'I'll go round there an' ask 'em what they pays you, you lyin' little tyke,' his aunt screamed. 'Don't you think you can gerraway wi' earnin' good money an' keepin' it all to yourself when I'm feedin' you an' clothin' you . . .'

'You needn't,' Jimmy said, trying to sound friendly and calm, and knowing that he probably sounded sullen and angry. 'Whenever I need new clobber I buy an old shirt or some old plimsolls from Paddy's Market wi' me wages, so you needn't bother yourself. And . . . and the Lumleys feed me, I told you so.'

'Perhaps they'd like to sleep you an' all,' Aunt Ruby jeered. 'You might as well ask 'em if they'd like to tek you on full-time at home as well as at work, like I did when me poor sister upped and died on us.'

'Yes, awright, I'll ask 'em,' Jimmy said with deceptive meekness, but this was going too far and his aunt

81

and uncle immediately forbade such an action.

'You'll stay wi' us and pay for your keep,' Uncle Sam said menacingly. 'Don't try an' bilk us either, young Ruddock, or it'll be the worse for you.'

It annoyed Jimmy very much that he had to hand over some money to his relatives every week after this, because he could see from the hatred in their mean little eyes that if he did not do so they would in all probability beat him senseless and then take whatever they could find. But strangely enough, simply the fact that he did pay them seemed to make him, if not liked, at least accepted by his aunt and uncle. Also, he began to realise that though they would not have fed or clothed him of their own accord, they were equally unwilling to be seen as the sort of people who would turn their own flesh and blood from the door.

'It's weird,' he had said to Elsie only the previous evening. 'Because most people know they treat me real bad and no one interferes, so why won't the Blaneys just turn me out, the way they'd really like to? Folk won't think worse of them than they do already?'

'Oh, that's folk for you,' Elsie had said, shrugging. The two of them were sitting on a broken-down piece of wall, eating the chips which Mr Lumley had given him when he had closed up the shop. 'Folk'll stand so much , then it's mumbles an'mutters an' rumours an' dark looks, an' next thing you know it's the scuffers movin' in an' cartin' off some great bully of a feller to stand trial for . . . well, for wharrever he done.'

'Only I wouldn't *mind* bein' chucked out,' Jimmy had pointed out. He leaned across and took a particularly good, crisp-edged chip. 'Well, norrif the Lumleys 'ud let me sleep under the counter in the shop, or somewheres like that. Why, they feed me like a bleedin' king, or like one o' their own already.'

'But if you lived there you wouldn't get the same good wages,' Elsie had reminded him. ''Cos they'd not be able to do both, they can't wi' their own girls, can they? An' you like bein' a bit independent, don't you?'

'Oh aye, I like it all right. But I like the shop and all. And if I weren't livin' wi' the Blaneys I wouldn't have to give 'em half me wages.'

'Oh, you!' Elsie had said, laughing. 'But you know the Lumleys couldn't have you livin' there, not really. So just keep payin' an' keep out o' the Blaneys' way an' you'll be awright, see if you aren't.'

So Jimmy had put the thought of leaving the Blaneys out of his mind for the moment and now, trundling the handcart over the uneven flagstones, he wondered what he would really do in a year or so, when he was old enough to get a place of his own. The chip shop was a grand place to work, of course, but the truth was he couldn't keep himself even on the good money the Lumleys paid him . . . not if it meant paying out for a room as well as proper meals and proper clothes. The family all wore old dresses and kecks and shirts beneath their smart green and white striped overalls, but on the rare occasions when they weren't working – Sundays for instance – they had decent clothes and lovely shiny boots. They also bathed with astonishing frequency, but Maggie had told him that if a girl wanted to get fellers, she had to fairly soak herself to get rid of the smell of fried fish. Jimmy liked the smell of fried fish, but he could dimly understand that perhaps a girl would prefer to smell of something more . . . more romantic. And indeed, when Maggie was all dressed up to go dancing on her evening off, then the sweet smell of lily of the valley which emanated from her every time she moved was very appealing, and Jimmy found himself inhaling appreciatively every time she passed by.

There were other snags to moving out on your own, too, when you did not have your parents to live with and to support you. Jimmy knew that now he was earning his living he, too, would be expected to have good Sunday clothes and possibly pay for a good seat in the cinema for himself and some young lady from time to time. Elsie, bless her, was his pal and content with the gods, high up against the ceiling in whatever picture palace they frequented. And if he moved out he would have to have a place of his own and rooms were expensive. Folk said it was cheaper to live outside the city – but where would you work? Jimmy knew nothing about the countryside save that potatoes grew there, and cabbages, too, so unless you could grow things, he supposed vaguely, you simply had either to live in the city, near your work, or spend large sums of money travelling from your country home each day.

So all in all, he would do best to save as much as he could against the day when he really felt he could go it alone and leave the unpleasant Blaneys and Kennedy Court behind him for ever.

The handcart actually seemed to be growing heavier, Jimmy thought as he turned the last corner and saw Lumley's ahead of him. Thank goodness! Even though it was back into the thick, hot smell of fish and chips and sweating Lumleys, very soon now he would be able to unload the spuds, lock up the handcart and go along to the kitchen to get going on peeling the spuds and cutting them into chips.

Jimmy turned round to back up onto the pavement and because his hands were greasy with sweat – and chip fat – the handcart slid sideways and before he could stop it one of the sacks of potatoes had catapulted onto the ground. Cursing – he had a good line in curses – Jimmy stood down the cart and went to pick up the spuds. To his surprise, someone lifted the other end of the sack and between them they replaced it in the handcart.

'Thanks very . . .' Jimmy was beginning, then stopped short, his mouth dropping open. 'Oh . . . it's you, Frank!'

'Yeah, thass right,' Frank Blaney said. He looked ingratiatingly at Jimmy, his big, rather handsome head hung down so that he was looking through his lashes, his heavy dark curls falling across his broad forehead. He grinned at Jimmy almost apologetically, as though to show he meant no harm, Jimmy supposed.

Although he did not much like any of his cousins, Frank was not as bad as the rest in Jimmy's eyes; being the eldest boy still at home he usually left his cousin alone. Nevertheless, Jimmy did not want any Blanley to come interfering round at the chip shop, so he scowled at the other boy. 'What do you want?' he said aggressively. 'I'm busy . . . can't you see that?'

'I saw you was strugglin' . . . that ole bugger oughtn't to mek you cart spuds about. You've growed a lot, I'll admit that, since you started work, but you still ain't half my size, nor you don't 'ave my strength . . .'

'I can manage, thanks,' Jimmy said stiffly. 'Me hands were sweaty, so they slipped on the cart handles and it tipped a bit.'

'Oh, I don't mind givin' a hand,' Frank said airily, seizing the handcart and heaving it by main force up onto the pavement. 'D'you go through the shop?'

85

'No, not wi' the cart,' Jimmy said. 'I carry the sacks in over me shoulder – don't you worry yourself, I'm used to it.'

'Well, you tek one an' I'll tek the other,' Frank said, and without pausing for Jimmy's agreement – or otherwise – snatched up the nearer of the two sacks. 'Straight through the shop now, then?'

'No! It's all right, I can . . .' Jimmy said, heaving the second sack up and onto his shoulder where it balanced precariously, feeling like a ton weight. He began to stagger across to the narrow tunnel between the chip shop and the stationer's next door. 'Leave it, Frank, it's my job, not yours.'

He plunged into the tunnel and heard, without surprise but with considerable dismay, Frank following him. He voice boomed and echoed around the tunnel. 'S'awright, Jimmy, I ain't axin' for nothin', I'm just givin' you an 'elpin' 'and.'

It would have sounded churlish to repeat that he did not need a helping hand so Jimmy said nothing but marched on, trying to look as though the sack weighed no more than a feather. In the little cobbled yard he turned left and went in through the back door, which led straight into the scullery, and heard Frank following. As hastily as he could he dumped the sack of spuds down by the old stone sink and then turned to take Frank's burden, but his cousin was already in the room and thumping the sack down likewise. 'Cor, it were pretty bloody 'eavy,' Frank said, sounding breathless. Despite his size he was not used to weight carrying Jimmy realised. 'Wharrelse can I do, Jimmy?'

'You can't do anything . . .' Jimmy was beginning when the door to the kitchen opened and Maggie said: 'You've got 'em then, Jimmy. Coo, you were

86

quick, an' Mam sent you down to cellar first, didn't she? I bet that ice is meltin' fast down there.' She stopped short and stared across at Frank. 'Who's your friend?'

'Oh . . . it's only me cousin, Frank Blaney,' Jimmy said reluctantly. 'He's the eldest one still livin' at home an' he carried one o' the sacks through . . . though I could ha' managed very well alone, given time.'

'That's good of you, Frank,' Maggie said graciously. 'Could you do wi' a drink o' lemonade? I poured one out for Jimmy, I can easily get another.'

'That's very kind o' you, Miss Lumley,' Frank said. 'I could do wi' a wet.'

'Give him mine, Maggie,' Jimmy suggested, but this suggestion was met with a frown and a shake of the head.

'No indeed, you need a drink, Jim, same's we all do. I'll fetch another through for Mr Blaney.'

Mr Blaney! Jimmy stared at Maggie's back view, disappearing through the doorway. It occurred to him then that Maggie was a pretty girl, with her thick, shiny brown hair and big brown eyes. And he supposed, stealing a glance at his cousin, that Frank was not bad-looking either. He was tall, dark and, though he had the heavy, almost sulky look that all the Blaneys seemed to have inherited from their father, he wasn't spotty, like Edwin, or fat and vacant-looking, like Tom.

Still, it did not do to stand here thinking when there was work to be done. Jimmy filled the low stone sink half full of water and tipped several pounds of potatoes into it. Then he attacked them with the wooden spoon, stirring them vigorously until most of the dirt was in the water instead of caked on their sides. To his annoyance, Frank came over and peered

87

into the water, then backed a step or two as Jimmy began, deliberately, to splash.

'Hey, mind me clean kecks,' he said, quite mildly for a Blaney. 'In only put 'em on an hour since, I don't want to gerrem all earthy.'

'Stand back, then,' Jimmy said gruffly. 'I can't clean the muck off these perishin' spuds without splashing a bit. What are you hangin' around here for, anyway?'

'Less of your cheek, you nasty little tyke . . .' Frank was beginning angrily, when the door between the kitchen and scullery opened and Maggie came in, carefully carrying a second glass of lemonade.

'Here y'are, Mr Blaney,' she said, handing him the glass. 'Now we've all gorra drink, perhaps Jim'll finish his own off, too.'

Jimmy, with a bad grace, picked up the glass of lemonade and drank it straight off, then wiped his mouth and heaved a sigh. 'Thanks, Maggie,' he said. 'I needed that. Are you goin' to give me a hand wi' these?'

'Can't,' Maggie said. 'I'm fetchin' stuff through. But I'll come back in about five minutes to chip whatever you've peeled.'

'I'll give the lad a hand,' Frank volunteered. 'Anyone can peel spuds, I reckons.'

'I shouldn't think you could,' Jimmy muttered. 'I ain't never seen you raise a finger in the house. We'll probably end up wi' spuds the size o' walnuts an' peel thick as pig-sh . . .'

'It's all right, Mr Blaney,' Maggie cut in, overriding Jimmy's comment. 'It's Jimmy's job, after all. Better leave it to him.'

'Well, I could just wait until you come back to chip 'em, an' – an' carry 'em through for you,' Frank said rather desperately. 'When does the shop close? Come to think of it, I could do wi' some chips meself . . . will you serve me if I go round to the shop?'

'I'm in the café, tonight,' Maggie said. Jimmy turned to throw a handful of peeled spuds into the bucket of clean water waiting for them and saw Maggie giving his cousin a very come-hither glance. Oh Lor', he thought, dismayed. That's all it needs – for Maggie to go takin' a shine to a bad 'un like Frank.

'Then I'll come into the café,' Frank said with what he no doubt thought of as gallantry. 'Then I could 'ave a nice cuppa tea an' all, I dare say.'

Frank probably had the money, Jimmy knew that, because his eldest cousin had once worked at Cammel Laird's shipyard and even after being sacked he always seemed to have plenty of dosh in his pockets. Jimmy imagined that he did some sort of trading with his old workmates – buying cheap and selling dear – because he had heard his cousin Solly talking about Frank's money-making activities in a way that had seemed half proud and half ashamed, but now it occurred to him that Frank might be doing something more actively dishonest in order to keep himself in funds. Though his eldest cousin gave his mother as little money as possible he was always buying himself new clothes and going to a steam-bath where he had his nails manicured and his hair splendidly oiled. What was more, he frequented expensive restaurants and went off for days at a time sometimes, coming home with stories of sea trips and coach trips, which made the other boys complain bitterly that Frank was a miser who only spent money on himself.

But what mattered right now to Jimmy was to get Frank out of the scullery so that he could get on, so he saw him go with real relief – mingled, however, with apprehension. He could scarcely expect Frank to keep his mouth shut, he would go home tonight and find his aunt and uncle demanding more money, saying that he was clearly being paid a real wage . . . possibly tying to extract from him just what he *was* paid . . . Jimmy could see his hard-working but pleasant life changing, and through no fault of his own.

To make matters worse, when he took a bucket of prepared chips through to the shop Mr Lumley said accusingly: 'You should know better, young 'un, than to 'ave your friends an' relatives in me scullery during shop hours. I ain't never said it weren't allowed 'cos I thought you'd a bit more sense, but we don't 'ave folks what don't work wi' us in there, any more'n I'd let customers come be'ind the counter in the shop.'

'I didn't let him, he came,' Jimmy said. 'He's me eldest cousin, Mr Lumley, but I don't have anything to do with any of 'em if I can help it. I kept tellin' him to gerron out of it but once Maggie give him a lemonade . . .'

'Oh, so that's how it was,' Mr Lumley said. 'Now Maggie should ha' known better. I'll 'ave a word.'

'I wonder if you'd not tell me cousins or me aunt and uncle, if they ask you, what I'm paid,' Jimmy said desperately as his employer took the bucket of chips from him and began to throw hissing handfuls into the bubbling fat. 'You see, they don't much like me, any of 'em, an' though I give me aunt money I have to keep some back for food an' clothes an' that. So if you wouldn't mind, Mr Lumley . . .'

'Ah, so that's the way of it,' Mr Lumley said, nodding as if well satisfied. 'Mother said as 'ow you looked 'alf-starved when you first come 'ere, but she's that soft . . . Now what was the name again?'

'Blaney, Mr Lumley. Me cousins is all fellers and

the one that come in here was Frank, he's the eldest what still lives at home. Could you . . . could you say me money varied, an' that I had a deal of it in food? Only if they find out . . .'

'Don't worry, young 'un. Not only won't I tell 'em a bleedin' thing, but they won't ask, I'll mek sure o' that,' Mr Lumley said cheerfully. 'Just you tell your aunt, from me, that if 'er lads come round 'ere makin' trouble you'll lose your job an' she'll lose the money you give 'er. I've often found that bullies don't tek to a bit o'bullyin' back, some'ow.'

'Thanks, Mr Lumley,' Jimmy said fervently. He glanced uneasily towards the doorway through which the workers in the shop could see into the restaurant. 'Umm . . . Is Frank in there now? He said he'd go round and get hisself a meal, and I don't fancy him hangin' round until I finish here and then comin' home wi' me.'

'No, he's gone. Went when I telled that young madam o' mine that she knew full well I wasn't havin' no fellers pantin' after any of me girls whiles they're a-workin'. An' come to think of it, young Maggie never lerron as how he'd follyed you into the kitchen, which she might ha' done, in fairness. But afore your cousin went he said you'd axed him in . . . which I now know wasn't the truth be a long chalk. You carry on wi' your work, young 'un, an' don't worry your head about them Blaneys. They won't interfere wi' you unless they wants to explain theirselves to me, that's for sure.'

'Thanks, Mr Lumley,' Jimmy repeated. He picked up his empty bucket with his heart suddenly as light as it was. 'I'll go and get started on the next batch of chips, then.'

Standing before the sink in the dark, low-ceilinged

little scullery, scrubbing away at the next batch of potatoes, Jimmy told himself that he was a lucky feller. The Lumleys were a close-knit and united family, yet it seemed as though they had taken him to their collective hearts, for he was the only person working in the Scotland Road shop who was not a relative. And Mr Lumley had just now believed his version of events rather than that of Frank, who was a man grown, or even Maggie, who was his favourite child.

Digging out eyes and other blemishes with the sharply pointed knife, Jimmy thought about his employer's family and his three thriving shops, the two largest both with fish restaurants attached. The eldest Lumley girls, Myra and Marianne, and their husbands, whose names he did not yet know, ran the other two shops, but Jimmy was naturally most concerned with the Lumley's on Scotland Road, where he worked himself. They did very good business, it was easy to see that, for there were queues from the moment that the shops opened at noon until late at night, when they closed. But it was not just the good business, it was the goodwill that seemed to surround the Lumleys, whether it was towards their customers or each other and the one member of staff who was not family. Even the girls seemed to like Jimmy, giving him extra helpings at mealtimes and seeing that he always had a big parcel of chips to take home with him when the shop closed. Before Elsie had got her job and was still at school they had been good to her as well, paying her for doing their messages when they were busy in the shop and handing over oddments of feminine adornment such as a necklace which needed mending – Elsie's nimble fingers soon had it as good as new – and stockings with only one or two runs in them.

'She might as well have 'em as chuck 'em out,' Minnie said. 'She's a good kid, that Elsie. Dad always says if you find someone what's honest an' hard-workin', you freeze onto 'em fast, an' I reckon you two youngsters both come from that category.'

But that had been when Jimmy and Elsie had been at school; now, the Lumleys did not see so much of Elsie, though she usually managed to come round of an evening, once her work was finished for the day. Then she gave a hand with the cleaning up, and she and Jimmy walked home together, talking quietly and eating chips out of newspaper.

Jimmy finished the next batch of spuds and began to chip them into the empty bucket, working auto-matically now, for the evening was drawing to a close and he was suddenly aware of his tiredness. Thank goodness it's not far back to the Kenny, he thought, slicing away. At least I don't have to go catching a bus or a tram like some fellers do. But he knew that tonight he would go home by back ways, and with caution. Frank had not bothered him before, but there was no guarantee that he was not just like the other Blaneys at heart and would be waiting up some dark alley to give Jimmy a pounding for not somehow letting him infiltrate into the Lumley household. But I never said he was light-fingered or not to be trusted, Jimmy reminded himself. And I could have, easy as easy. After all, Solly said the other night, when they thought I was asleep, that Frank was so sharp he'd cut himself one of these days, and that, surely, could mean dishonest?

Jimmy finished the last potato and lifted up the bucket in order to drain out the water. It was heavy and for a moment he felt the room spun round him as he supported the weight over the sink, which made him realise that he had not had his usual supper. That bleedin' Frank had really got to him, but when he took the chips through he'd ask if he might take a few minutes off and someone would feed him as they always did.

And presently, in the kitchen, he was sitting down, with Minnie and Maggie, to a grand supper. A large piece of haddock, his favourite fish, a mound of chips, several rounds of bread and margarine and a cup of well-sweetened tea were before him and Jimmy, elbows out, was eagerly tackling them.

'It's good grub, ain't it, Jimmy?' Maggie said, with her own mouth full. 'That feller . . . your cousin . . . d'you like 'im?'

Jimmy looked at her cautiously through his lashes. What should he say? Jimmy knew enough about girls to realise that if she had a soft spot for Frank she would not take kindly to hearing the harsh truth. But on the other hand, he did not fancy lying to the girl, who had always been nice to him. He glanced uneasily at Minnie, who smiled back at him. She was eighteen and engaged to be married to a sailor, though her father kept teasing her that he would have to give up the sea once they were wed.

'Can't 'ave a son-in-law what doesn't work in the business,' he had told her. 'It ain't as if 'e was workin' on a fishin' trawler, either. He's a bleedin' officer on a transatlantic liner . . . too high an' mighty for the likes of us.'

But Minnie did not mind. She laughed and told her dad that Eifion – for her fiancé was a Welshman from Snowdonia – would make a good chip shop worker when he decided to make an honest woman of her.

'Well, Jim' Maggie said impatiently. 'Do you like your cousin? No need to go so red; I only met the feller this evenin', it ain't likely I'm particularly interested, is it?'

'I don't like him much,' Jimmy said, making up his mind. 'He doesn't set on me like the others do, though. But I . . . I don't think he's a trustable chap, like.'

'No-oo,' Maggie said thoughtfully. 'But is he a good dancer, d'you know?'

Jimmy gaped at her, bottom jaw dropping so low that he would not have been surprised had it struck him in the foot. 'A *d-dancer*?' he stammered. 'I dunno, Mags. I've never heard any of me cousins talk about dancin'.'

'Has he asked you out?' Minnie said, far more worldly wise than Jimmy. 'If so, you want to watch 'im, queen. He's got sly eyes an' snake-'ips, if you ask me. Not the sorta feller to go out with more'n once.'

'Who said anything about more than once?' Maggie said, her eyes dancing. 'Anyroad, I just thought I'd ask.'

Jimmy, shrugging, started to eat again, and then it was time to clean down and close up, and soon it was near on midnight and he was so tired it was all he could do to get into his ragged coat and go out into the cold, crisp night air. On the pavement he thought about heading for the back alleys just in case Frank was lying in wait for him, but a moment's reflection told him that this was extremely unlikely. After all, he had not queered Frank's pitch with Maggie, since Frank had found the opportunity to ask her out. And if Frank really did intend to make a play for his employer's youngest daughter, then he was surely too worldly wise to go beating up a worker whom the whole family seemed to like.

Accordingly, Jimmy went straight along Scotland

95

Road, passing shops either already closed or about to put their shutters up, until he reached Gay Street, where he turned right and then right again, into the court. At this time of night, Jimmy thought uneasily, going under that brick arch was like entering hell. It was pitch dark and a close, foetid smell hung about it from both the number of bodies packed into each house and the stench from the privies at the far end of the paved space between the houses. What was more, cats, or rats, or both, were investigating the piled-up rubbish waiting for the dustmen and Jimmy could see a great many small eyes, glowing red, green, or yellow, turning towards him as he stepped cautiously across the flagstones.

But it was no use hanging around wondering whether any of the eyes' owners was about to pounce. Jimmy went briskly up the steps into the Blaney house, making as little noise as possible. In the smelly hallway he stopped for a moment to get his bearings, then mounted the stairs with the utmost caution. But no one stirred and when he went into the boys' room, apart from the awful stuffiness and the smells of so many people squashed into so small a space, he immediately felt that no one was lying awake. They all slept. And very soon after he had laid down and pulled his ragged bedding over him, so did Jimmy.

'Well, now we've sat down at last, I've got summat to tell you, Elsie. I . . . I think you'll like it; it's certain sure that I do.'

Jimmy and Elsie were sitting side by side on the iron railings at the top of Everton Brow, looking down on the city spread out below rather as two monarchs might survey their kingdom. They had been to mass, had enjoyed a Sunday roast with Elsie's family and all the time Jimmy had kept within his own breast the news that he had to tell. Because in church there had been people all around them, at dinner-time there had been Mr and Mrs Taylor and her brothers and sisters, and until they reached Everton Brow they had been with Joe Taylor, accompanying him to the home of his sweetheart, Louisa Albertson, who lived in a large house on Rupert Hill and had invited Joe to Sunday tea. Joe had thought it only right to buy Mrs Albertson a large bunch of red roses and fragrant pink lilies, the sort sold by the old women who congregated in Clayton Square and had some of the finest blooms one could find in the city. But having bought the flowers on Saturday morning, Joe seemed to have spent all his time since then in moving them around the house, changing the water in which they stood and shouting at anyone unwise enough to walk too near them.

'They cost me all me beer money for a fortnight,' he kept saying. 'I don't want so much as a petal to fall whiles they're in this 'ouse, so watch it, all of you.'

And then, when the great afternoon came at last, he had wrapped the flowers carefully in beautiful blue and white paper . . . and discovered what anyone could have told him, Elsie said scornfully. The lilies, beautiful as they were, were also the possessors of the sort of pollen which dyes everything it touches deep, iodine yellow. Poor Joe's shirtsleeve bore the brunt of a too-close encounter and his right hand had fingers so deeply stained that he looked like a nicotine addict.

'If I carry this lot up Everton way I'll be yaller as a bleedin' Chinaman be the time I'm at Louisa's house,' he had moaned pitifully. 'Tell you what, Els; if you an' young Jim there will come wi' me, an' carry them

97

perishin' flowers, I'll . . . I'll give you a threepenny joe, I swear it.'

'Each?' Elsie had said suspiciously. She knew her brothers. 'Threepence each would be picture money, but threepence between us wouldn't gerrus far.'

'Threepence each,' Joe had confirmed, heaving a deep, dramatic sigh. 'Oh, Jim, don't you never go courtin' a gal, else you'll be penniless in no time, same as me.'

'What do you want to tell me?' Elsie asked now. 'I thought as 'ow something was up, Jimmy, 'cos you're a bit like a firework what fizzes and fizzes, and then goes off unexpected with a great huge whoosh. Don't say your uncle's gone and give some o' your money back.'

The previous week Uncle Sam had actually told Edwin off for taking money out of Jimmy's jacket. He had not made Edwin give it back, but he had told his youngest son that at least Jimmy was earning, which was more than Edwin looked like doing, so he could keep his thieving hands to himself. This was, of course, because the money in Jimmy's pocket had been what he now handed over to Aunt Ruby each week, but it had still been a considerable surprise when his uncle had actually behaved as though Jimmy had some rights in the household. Now, however, Jimmy shook his head.

'No, I didn't say I were goin' to tell you there'd been a miracle, just . . . just . . .'

'Oh, spit it out,' Elsie said impatiently. She dropped down from the iron bar on which she had been perched, then heaved herself up onto it, wriggled into a comfortable position and turned a somersault. Still hanging upside down she said commandingly: 'Tell me right now, Jimmy, or I won't give you your share o' the sixpenny bit Joe 'anded over just now.'

'Yes, you will,' Jimmy said, quite unperturbed by this threat. 'Though I wouldn't mind if you didn't, queen, 'cos I get better paid than you do. But I'm going to tell you anyway, so don't go in a takin'. Elsie, how would you like to come on a day trip to Blackpool, in a charabanc? It's next Sunday and there ain't no charge, it's a treat for the Lumleys. I told you about it weeks ago, when Maggie an' Minnie kept talkin' about it, only I didn't think the Lumleys would ask me, because they've always called it the family trip, but now Mr Lumley tells me it's for everyone who works there, and . . . and he says to tell you you can come along o' me, if you'd like to.'

Elsie swung herself upright and clambered back onto the bar. She stared wide-eyed at Jimmy, whilst a slow smile spread across her face. 'A day trip to Blackpool? Oh, Jimmy, I'd live it more'n almost anything. I'll ask me mam to put us up some snappin' and a drink o' cold tea in a bottle, and I'll gerra bathin' suit off me friend Susie . . .'

'You won't need no snap,' Jimmy said proudly. 'Maggie told me it was ever such a posh do, wi' a proper hot dinner in a big restaurant, an' a good tea, wi' sandwiches and cakes and fizzy pop or tea or whatever you want, then a real supper in another restaurant, and they stop on the way home at pubs, only Mr Lumley says you an' me an' the boys what work in the other shops is too young for the pubs, so they'll bring us out lemonade an' crisps an' sandwiches, if we want 'em after eating all day.'

Elsie heaved a sigh of deepest satisfaction. 'Coo-er!' she said reverently. 'Just you tell Mr Lumley you wouldn't catch me missin' a do like that. When do we start?'

'It's awfully early,' Jimmy admitted. 'The charabanc leaves at six o'clock in the morning, and Maggie said it's usually midnight or past be the time we gets home. But the followin' day's Monday, and we shan't open till tea-time so's we all gerra a good long lie-in. I wondered if you might tell your old Andrews you were sick, so's you could lie in as well, an' go in late. What d'you think your mam will say?'

'She'll say go and enjoy yourself,' Elsie said readily. 'Mam's no spoil-sport. As for work next day, I'll see how I feel. What happens when we reaches Blackpool, then? Is it straight on the sands, or along to the pleasure beach, or up to the Tower? I want to see the Winter Gardens and all . . . Oh, and the lifeboat, and the new Waxworks – as good as Madam Thingamybob's in London they are – and . . .'

'You've been there,' Jimmy said, secretly disappointed. He had thought to give Elsie such a treat and she had been there already.

But Elsie, thus challenged, shook her head. 'Nah, but me mam and dad went there on their honeymoon and they're always on about it. Oh, and Sal went too, when she were goin' out wi' that awful Malcolm O'Donnell, only she said he tried it on so she come home early. But she loved it – Blackpool, I mean, not wharrever it was Malcolm tried on – and keeps on sayin' she'll go back again one day. I say, wharrif I beat Sal to the draw and gets there first? That 'ud be one up for me, eh?'

'Yes, it would, only you aren't like that, Els,' Jimmy said shrewdly. 'So you'll come, then? Will we go home now and ask your mam, so's I can tell Mr Lumley for sure first thing tomorrer?'

Elsie slid down from the bar and dusted her hands briskly on her short grey skirt. Then she set off down the hill by Jimmy's side, chattering as she went. 'Oh aye, we might as well go and get Mam's permission, though she'll not say no, I promise you. Oh, we'll need some money though, Jimmy, 'cos we've got to have a go on everything. Me sister went on the Big Wheel when she were there, only they've took that away, an' then there's Blackpool rock – you have to buy it to tek home to the kids what didn't go – and there's paddle steamers what tek you out for a sail and they sell special doughnuts, all hot, what no one makes as good, and . . .'

'I know. I'm takin' some cash out of me savings,' Jimmy assured her. 'I'll give you half of whatever I take, so that's fair, ain't it? And I bet your brothers will cough up somethin' good when it comes to the point.'

'You're right,' Elsie agreed. 'Shall we run downhill, Jimmy? Only I'm too excited to walk.'

Jimmy said nothing to his cousins or aunt and uncle about the Blackpool trip. So far as he knew, Maggie had not met up with Frank since the dreadful evening when his cousin had insisted on carrying the sack of potatoes into the scullery, so the news of the treat was unlikely to get back to them by a roundabout route.

But it was all that he thought about the whole week. In his imagination he soared up the Tower in the magical lift and viewed the wonders as far afield as America. As he cleaned potatoes, peeled them, chipped them, watched his contribution tipped into the sizzling fat, he was seeing the vast stretches of golden sand, the brilliant blue of the sea and himself gambolling into the waves and showing Elsie how good a swimmer he was, for he had learned to swim when he was no more than eight or nine. As he walked home, tired out after work, he climbed aboard the Big Wheel, the roundabouts and swingboats and cakewalks which, the Taylors and the Lumleys assured him, were around every corner in Blackpool. It only crossed his mind once that it might rain, for August had been a marvellous month, with almost constant sunshine, but when he asked Minnie what they did if it rained she beamed at him and heaved a sigh of utter contentment. 'We spends more time in the Tower, an' the Winter Garden,' she said. 'We takes longer over our meals an' we dances the night away. But it won't rain; it never rains on the Lumleys' day out.'

As the day grew nearer he became too excited to sleep and spent the first couple of hours of each night lying staring at the ceiling and imagining what he would eat for his hot dinner at the big restaurant. Then there was the tea; sandwiches the like of which he had never tasted, Maggie assured him, and cakes so bulging with cream, so smothered in whirls and twirls of icing sugar, that they were more like dreams than down-to-earth cakes. And when he slept he dreamed of the Blackpool he had never seen, and the food he had never eaten, and the wonderful rides and amusements he had never aspired to enjoying before he had known the Lumleys.

Once, he must have cried out in his sleep, babbling something or other that woke his cousin, for Edwin had shaken him and said: 'Where? Where is it?'

'Wha . . .?' Jimmy had croaked. 'Where's what?'

'I dunno,' Edwin had mumbled, settling down on the mattress once more. 'You said somethin' about tables loaded wi' jellies and ice-cream, an' all the food a feller could eat. You're mad, Jimmy Ruddock, that's wha' you are.'

But Jimmy, settling down to sleep again also, had smiled to himself. Even if the trip to Blackpool was cancelled tomorrow, he realised, he had had such a good time anticipating all the fun they would have that the disappointment would not be so great. Besides, now he had an aim in life. When he was old enough he would go to Blackpool and get a job. Then he would work hard on the pleasure beach or in one of the numerous wonderful restaurants until he had enough money to buy the Waxworks, or something equally impressive. And then he would come back to Liverpool, rich as . . . as Mr Lumley, and treat all his friends and rattle the cash in his pocket and buy ice-creams for urchins such as he himself had once been.

By the Saturday, however, his cousins were beginning to view him with deep suspicion. Edwin had clearly confided in his brothers that Jimmy had been having strange dreams and shouting out in his sleep, and Frank, who was hardly ever at home except when he wanted his washing done or a meal made, came to tea and kept quizzing him as to why he was so bloomin' happy that he had a permanent grin on his face.

'Who says so?' Jimmy said quiet mildly, for his good humour had even spilled over to include his cousins. 'You aren't here often enough to know whether I'm happy or not.'

'Edwin says so. An' so does Tom and Solly,' Frank replied. 'You can't go round grinnin' like a Cheshire cat without someone remarkin' on it, young Ruddock. I've heard tell there's a treat comin' up in the Lumley fam'ly. But that won't include a cheeky young tyke like yourself, that's for sure.'

'No, of course not,' Jimmy said, immediately suspicious. Mr Lumley had said that they didn't advertise the trip to Blackpool, because it didn't do to tell some folk that the whole family were away for a long day out, and Jimmy had no intention of letting the Blaneys into his secret. 'But me an' me pal's been savin' up for a ride on the overhead railway, down to Seaforth. We'll mebbe go tomorrer. If me pal's gorrenough money, that is. Else it'll be next Sunday, I s'pose.'

'Oh aye?' Frank said, then seemed to lose interest in Jimmy. He stuck his elbows on the table and shouted: 'Pass the bleedin' loaf, Solly, or I'll come up there an' tek the whole lot for meself.'

'That you won't,' Solly said, grabbing the loaf and beginning to carve himself another slice with the big green-handled bread knife. 'You don't live 'ere no more, Frank, so if you want bread, go out an' buy yourself some.'

'That's your brother you're talkin' to, Solomon Blaney,' Aunt Ruby said crossly. 'Frank's norra a bad lad – he brung me as nice a joint of pork as I've ever laid eyes on for tomorrer's dinner. I'm goin' to do roast taters an' a nice big cabbage to go with it, an' apple sauce an' all, so just you button your lip.'

Jimmy smiled to himself, but only inside his head. He would not be hanging around hoping for a little slice of pork and a smear of apple sauce, he would be in Blackpool, living like a king.

'Well, Elsie? Ain't this the bee's knees? Ain't it just the best thing you ever done in your whole life, just about? Oh, look at that sea!'

Jimmy and Elsie and the boys from the other shops were all sitting on the sand in the sunshine, gazing out across the beach at the little waves which barely seemed to caress the shore. They had done most of the things they had planned to do already, for the charabanc had deposited them just outside the pleasure beach shortly after nine o'clock and they had made straight for the beach. Mrs Lumley had given them five shillings each, a fortune, for what she termed 'amusin' theirselves', and they had enjoyed donkey rides, ice-creams, a brief venture into the waves to see who could swim the furthest and a lot of larking around.

'Yeah, it is grand,' Elsie agreed. 'Is it always like this, Wally?'

'It always is when we comes,' Wally said. 'I ain't never known it bad, have you, Ivor?'

Ivor shook his head. 'Nah, it's always just right is Blackpool. Whassa time?'

'Dunno,' Elsie said, but Jimmy strained round to see a clock which he had noticed earlier.

'Near on half past twelve,' he announced after squinting at it for a few moments. 'What time do we have to meet up wi' t'others, fellers?'

'A quarter to one o'clock, outside the Tower ballroom,' Wally said. 'It's always the same; charabanc will be waitin' there, an' we'll all gerrin and go off for us dinners.'

'Well, we might as well make our way back now, then,' Jimmy said, reaching for his black and sandy plimsolls and his shirt and trousers, for he had stripped to his underpants to go in the sea. 'I know we had ices not so long ago but I'm just as hungry as if I'd had nothin' at all.'

The others agreed and everyone began hastily dressing, whilst Elsie, who had declined haughtily to remove any clothing but had paddled with such enthusiasm that her skimpy little dress was soaked to the waist, tried to shake the clinging sand off the still

105

damp material. 'I'm goin' to look a rare sight,' she wailed as they began to stroll up the beach. 'Wharrif Mrs Lumley won't tek me into a posh restaurant, all sandy like this?'

'She will; you won't be the only one what's sandy,' Ivor assured her. 'Anyroad, we'll give you a hand wi' shakin' it off before we leave the beach.'

'I'm goin' to tell Eddy all about this trip, come Tuesday mornin',' Jimmy announced as he sat on the edge of the promenade and brushed vigorously at Elsie's sandy skirt. 'I told him he ought to ha' come with us, but he said Blackpool an' him were no strangers, they knew each other well. Odd sort o' thing to say, I thought, only Maggie told me that Fleetwood's only another ten mile further on, so I suppose he meant it ain't anything special to him. Hey, Elsie, me skin feels sort o' tight over me nose, and you look a bit red in the face, too. Does it hurt?'

'Aye, an' so does mine. It's the sun. We ain't used to it, bein' in the shops most o' the time,' Wally said as the small group regained the promenade and began to walk in the direction of the Tower. 'Best keep out of it for the rest o' the day, or you'll burn.'

'We'll be out of it whiles we has us dinners,' Ivor said lazily. 'And as the day goes on the sun gets weaker . . . anyroad, you don't burn so easily. Come on, there's the charabanc – last one there can't sit on the back seat!'

'All aboard? Everyone satisfied? It were a grand supper, weren't it? Who asked for fish an' chips, then?'

There was a lot of loud laugher at Mr Lumley's question, for not one of the party had feasted on fish and chips. They had had steak pie, or roast chicken, or lobster mayonnaise, or a great baron of beef basted in the pan with mustard and served with Yorkshire puddings so fluffy that they might, Minnie said, have been made in heaven. And they had eaten their fill, even the small children, for the married Lumleys had between them no fewer than six kids, ranging from a tot of barely a year to a lusty little lad of seven.

'I likes eatin' fish an' chips, Grandad,' a small boy of four or so said loudly. 'I likes it ever so much. Only Mam wouldn't let me, she said us could have fish an' chips tomorrer.'

More laughter, even better natured this time, for they all knew that Mr Lumley was proud of the quality of his fish and chips, and got quite cross when one of his daughters complained that the smell of them lingered for hours despite the heartiest of washes, and that they were ashamed to go to dances at the dear old Grafton Ballroom when the attar of roses or the lavender water fought all evening against the strong and clinging pong of cod.

'Well, Austin, so we can,' Mr Lumley said, throwing out his chest. 'Best fish an' chips in the Pool, though I mebbe says it as shouldn't. Anyone want to 'ave a jimmy riddle afore we leaves?'

'Dad!' 'Oh, Bill, you are too bad!' 'You'll gerrus hung, Mr Lumley!' The comments came amidst more laughter, but apparently no one needed to avail themselves of his offer.

'Right? Anyone not bought their rock, then? We can stop off outside the pleasure beach if anyone's forgot their rock for old Aunt Emma or little cousin Percy.'

But it seemed that everyone had remembered their rock, too. Even the driver, an old friend of Mr Lumley's called Alf, waved a couple of sticks of the stuff and Elsie, indeed, had a shipping order, for it seemed that every member of her family and all her friends would be expecting a present from this wonderful day out. So Jimmy, feeling generous after such a marvellous day, had bought rock for his aunt and uncle and smaller sticks for his cousins. 'They'll mebbe not pester me if I give 'em somethin',' he said with rather doubtful optimism. 'I'll hand 'em over tea-time tomorrer, before I go off to the shop.'

'All ready to leave, then? Right. Now we'll 'ave a bit of singsong. I'll start off wi' a good old sea shanty, then someone else can tek over.'

'No rude songs, Dad, there's kiddies present,' Mrs Lumley cautioned, whilst old Mrs Lumley senior, a frail eighty-year-old with the most piercing voice Jimmy had ever heard, stated firmly that her son never sang rude songs until he'd had a skinful, which hadn't happened so far today, though it would doubtless occur before they got back to the Scottie.

'Ain't it been lovely, though?' Elsie murmured into Jimmy's ear as they settled down on the warm, tobacco-scented upholstery of the charabanc. 'Look at them stars, old Jimmy. They're nothin' like as bright as that in Liverpool.'

'They're the same stars, cloth'ead,' Jimmy said, putting his mouth close to her ear to make himself heard against a rowdy rendering of *Bobby Shaftoe*. 'But at home, there's the street lamps in between – it makes the stars look smaller and not so bright. Want a humbug?'

'I don't mind if I do,' Elsie said sleepily, taking a sweet from the crumpled white bag Jimmy proffered. 'Oh, Jimmy, I'm glad you asked me to come. It's been the best day of my life so far.'

'And mine,' Jimmy said, sucking his sweet. 'And to

think Els – whiles I work for the Lumleys, this happens once every single August. Mind, I don't reckon to stay a spud peeler for ever, though they pays me fair for what I does. But I reckon when I'm earnin' a proper wage, a man's wage I mean, not a boy's, I'll save up and come to Blackpool meself every summer, no matter what.'

'So'll I an' all,' Elsie said. 'I'm goin' to come here for me honeymoon, just like me mam did, years back. An' . . . when me an' me husband gets us some kids, we'll bring 'em along an' all, because it's the best place in the world, ain't it, Jimmy?'

'Easily the best,' Jimmy said.

In front of them, Maggie turned in her seat and grinned at them. 'How d'you know it's the best place in the world?' she enquired, raising her eyebrows until they nearly reached her hair. 'You ain't been anywhere, neither of you.'

'So what?' Jimmy said. 'We knows a good thing when we sees it, don't we?'

'I bet there ain't nowhere like the pleasure beach, anyway,' Elsie said stoutly. 'We went on the Pleasure Beach, Maggie, an' screamed like anything! Well, I did,' she amended. 'I dunno whether Jimmy did 'cos I were screamin' too loud to hear anyone else. It were prime, I'm tellin' you.'

'I know,' Maggie admitted. 'But I'm goin' to the Isle of Man next summer, wi' me mates. There'll be a crowd of us an' we'll find ourselves a good boardin'-house an' some fellers – oh, I can't wait I'm tellin you.'

'Why didn't you go this year, then?' Elsie said. 'I bet you didn't because you wanted to come to Blackpool, wi' your mam an' dad an' the rest of us.'

Maggie's pert little face looked rueful for a

moment. 'Me dad won't lemme go till I'm seventeen,' she explained. 'Still an' all, you're right; Blackpool's pretty grand, for a day.'

There was a commotion at the front of the charabanc and then the vehicle slowed and Mr Lumley stood up. 'We're comin' up to our first stop,' he shouted. 'Kids, when we stop come an' tell our Maisie what you want an' someone'll bring it out to you. The rest of you, get ready to fight your way to the bar . . . gents, take care o' the ladies. Kids, be good whiles we're gone, or you won't have no more lemonade.'

As Maggie had prophesied, the charabanc did not roll into Scotland Road until well after midnight and by the time Elsie and Jimmy got back to their homes, both houses were apparently in darkness.

'Thanks ever so much for takin' me wi' you, Jimmy,' Elsie whispered, as they stood outside her home, which was pitch black as were all the rest. 'You're the nicest feller I know . . . I love you, I does.' After this startling remark she stood on tiptoe and kissed Jimmy's cheek and, much touched, Jimmy took her gently by the shoulders and kissed her, too, then held her away from him.

'There's no one I'd rather have wi' me than you, our Els,' he said honestly. 'It has been a grand day, hasn't it? But we'd best get some kip, else we'll not be much good in the mornin'.'

'Awright, Jimmy,' Elsie said, and headed for her darkened house, but as she opened her front door Jimmy saw a light shining under the kitchen door and knew that someone, either her parents or a brother or sister, had sat up for her, and was glad. Elsie had so much to tell that she'd never sleep with it all busting to get out. Now, with someone to talk to, she'd be able to sleep soundly once she got to bed.

As for himself, the thought of a light would have been more frightening than comforting, but he need not have worried. The house was dark and remained so as he went silently up the stairs and into the back bedroom. He was terribly tired, but managed to get his plimsolls and outer clothing off before creeping into his usual corner on the mattress and pulling some of the bedding over him.

And now I suppose I'll be too excited to sleep, he thought crossly – and slept immediately.

# Chapter Four

Dympna came up from the boat with Micheál, the big reed creel of fish slung between them. It had been a good day, better than they had had for some while, and the catch was big enough for a good deal of it to be taken in to Clifden to be sold, leaving sufficient fish left over for Mammy to salt down and cook for them all week. It was also heavy enough to make Dympna's arms begin to throb, though she took no heed of that. She could not do so, for she had had to earn her place in the fishing boat and having done so, was not likely to jeopardise it just for a bit of arm-ache.

She glanced down at herself as she crunched over the stones and rocks of the beach. Big seaboots, canvas trousers tucked into them, a man's grey working shirt and a thin, well-holed fisherman's jersey. On her head she wore a greasy old cap pulled well down, a protector from the sun, which did its best to burn her very white skin, and also a help when the wind blew strongly or the cold bit into any exposed surface. Her hair was tied back with a length of string and though she hated to give in, she had been forced to let her mother provide her with a pair of tough canvas gloves because otherwise her hands blistered and split with the constant salt water and hard work, so that when hauling the catch and handling the sheets she had been in agony, particularly when the raw skin had gone septic and driven her half demented. But provided she wore the gloves when handling the boat and the catch she remained whole, so she had taken to them willingly in the end, and so far as she knew no one ever remarked on the gloves or thought less of her for wearing them.

Now it was October, which meant she had been working with her father for nearly eighteen months, so her job was not longer a sort of secret. But last year, when she had wanted to start work so that Nicky could be relieved of all fear of being taken aboard, she had had to consult Mr O'Neill, for it was only with his connivance that she could miss her last six months or so in school.

At first, Mr O'Neill had frowned at her, this thick, gingery brows drawing together over his large nose, his enormous moustache seeming to bristle with disapproval. 'Girleen, you're my brightest pupil since your elder brother started at the village school,' he had said reproachfully. 'I'd set my sights on seeing you at a convent school in the town, so I had. And now you're telling me you'd rather catch fish? I can't bring myself to believe my ears.'

'It isn't that I want to exactly, sir,' Dympna explained. 'But my daddy can't manage the boat and fish as well without some help – no one could. When the weather's bad it needs one to see to the sail and another at the tiller, and when it's good and the catch is heavy, it takes two to heave it aboard. Then, when the wind's light . . .'

'It's all right, girleen, I know all about the fishing,' Mr O'Neill said a trifle reproachfully. 'Did not my own father and two of my brothers take to the sea like three guillemots, and did they not have me educated so that I might have a better life than theirs? But your father has managed right well with Dermot, has he not?'

'Yes, sir. But Dermot's got engaged to marry Eileen McCarthy from Roundstone, and her father's got a fishing boat bigger than ours and he's only daughters, poor feller, so he's relying on Dermot to help in his boat now he's going to become part of the family. And you can't blame Dermot, sir, for bettering himself – that's what my daddy says.'

'I see,' Mr O'Neill mused. He had pulled at one side of his long moustache, the frown still in place but no longer, Dympna saw, was it an angry frown. It was a thoughtful one. 'And your brother Nicholas, who will be studying for a scholarship to go to university in Dublin to study medicine, no less, cannot be asked to give up his big chance for a fisherman's life. Is that it?'

'It is, sir,' Dympna had admitted, glad to have the matter put so succinctly and understood so well. 'Egan's a good wee boy, but he's only eleven. He doesn't have the strength, yet, to be of much help, even if he could get out of going to school, which I don't suppose he could, could he?'

'No indeed, for I take leave to tell you, girleen, that your young brother does not have the brains of a . . . lobster. It takes me all my time just to get simple arithmetic and a bit of reading and writing into him, so he can read a newspaper and fill in a form. Ah dear, and it's yourself I'll be losing, who seemed like a certainty for the convent school, and Egan I'll be nagging instead. It's no life, girleen, being a schoolmaster, indeed it is not.'

'You like it though, sir,' Dympna had said, made bold by the conviction that things were going her way. 'I thought I might like it, too . . . because when Egan's old enough to work with my daddy then I'll be free to study again.'

'Aye. But you'll be sixteen by then. A bit long in the tooth for the school work, particularly in a school where the next-oldest pupil will be coming on fourteen.'

'I know. But couldn't I take a job like Ann . . . I mean Miss Ennis does, sir? A pupil teacher? They go on to college afterwards, don't they, sir, and become real teachers, like you? Couldn't I do that?'

'It's a possibility,' Mr O'Neill had admitted, slowly nodding his head. 'Suppose I give you work each week, girleen, and you promise me to do your best to keep up with your lessons in the evening? Oh, I know you'll be out late in the summer, but in winter, when the evenings are long and dark, suppose you were to come to me a couple of times a week for coaching and the rest of the time you'd study at home? What d'you say to that?'

She had agreed, of course, and had stuck to her agreement, though at times she cursed both herself for agreeing and the schoolmaster for suggesting that she should continue with her school work. But it'll pay off one day, she told herself, though as the months passed she had become less and less sure that she would ever leave the fishing. She loved the freedom of it, the sense of achievement when the catch was good and the quiet companionship of her father.

And he was quiet; a quiet man. He never chatted, Dympna thought. If he wanted to explain something to her, he did so in the minimum of words needed to get the facts across. If he was pleased with her he smiled his slow smile and maybe patted her shoulder. If he was annoyed about the way someone else kept crowding his boat, or disappointed about the turn the weather had taken, he would quietly move away and take up a different position or shrug philosophically and turn up the collar of his coat and pull his cap lower over his eyes.

Yet the normal father-daughter fondness that had always been between them had deepened into something very much stronger. There was reliance in it, because each now knew the other to be totally dependable, and on Dympna's side, at least, deep admiration for a strength of body and spirit upon which she, and the rest of her family, leaned almost without realising it. Micheál was the backbone of the body family, Dympna often thought. Mammy cooked and cleaned and mended for them, and she helped them with their work and listened to their stories of failure and success and loved them, Dympna supposed, in her fashion, but she was not a demonstrative woman. To her knowledge, Beatrice had never kissed or hugged any of her three children once they were past school age. Nor did she ever, in public at least, so much as squeeze Micheál's hand.

Daddy, on the other hand, never attempted to interfere with their school work because he was too thick to understand it, or so he said. But he fished and grew vegetables, and mended their boots when they had any, and kept the house thatched and the walls from letting in wind and weather. Yet when she, or Egan, or Nick, was unsure, or sad, or felt helplessly inadequate, it was to Micheál they went. They did not have to put their feelings, or woes, into words. Micheál would put a heavy arm about your shoulders and say you were the cleverest kid he's ever come across, so you were, and what call had anyone to argue with that? Even Nicky would unburden then, explain what had happened, ask, without words, for comfort and reassurance. And get it, accompanied by

116

a hug, which sometimes said more than words. Mammy might be bracing, or tell you that worse things happened at sea, or simply say it was a small matter and not worth breaking your sleep over, let alone your heart. She might have been right, yet you went away uncomforted, the inadequate feelings stronger, the longing for understanding deeper.

'Will we take a wee rest now?' Micheál said, interrupting Dympna's thoughts. 'It's been a long day and there's enough fish here to keep your mammy busy for a week or more. Let's put the creel down in the grass for a moment.'

The tide had been out when they got back, which meant a long walk across the stony beach before they even reached the quay, so now, though they had only a short way to go, Dympna was vastly relieved that her daddy had made the suggestion before her arm simply dropped off. She staggered with him to a patch of grass and heather, and let go her side of the creel with great relief. 'Phew!' she exclaimed, straightening her back. 'When did we last have a catch like this 'un, Daddy? Won't Mammy be pleased!'

'Aye, she'll be pleased sure enough,' Micheál said rather cautiously. 'But your mammy's not the one to show her pleasure – still, she'll be pleased. Wit' the winter comin' on, and the pig we're killin' next week not a specially big one, she'll be wantin' all the salt fish she can get by the time we're celebratin' Christmas.'

Dympna sighed and collapsed onto a nose of grey rock surrounded by the thick, heathery undergrowth, which flourished wherever no plough had turned the earth. She looked around her, at the thicket of gorse and hazel and wild fuchsia and delicate, wind-moulded birch trees that grew against the top of the cliff, their leaves every shade from primrose to deep gold, and thinning now like the hair on an old man's head. The sky was a pale, almost wintry blue, and the last rays of the sun reddened the thatched roofs and white cob walls of the fishermen's cottages. Isn't this the most beautiful place on earth now? she thought wonderingly, the breath catching in her throat. It's lucky we are to live in a place so beautiful, even if the living is hard. She turned to Micheál, squatting on his heels in the heather at her feet, filling his old pipe, then tamping the black tobacco down and fetching out a box of matches to light it. She watched him puffing hard, until the red glow at the heart of the tobacco steadied and grew bigger and a thread of pale blue smoke arose, and let him have his first proper puffs before she spoke. 'I sometimes wish Mammy was better at being pleased, Daddy. It . . . it's hard to do as you should when you get no word of praise for it.'

Micheál took his time answering, as he always did. He went on puffing at his pipe and squinting up his very dark blue eyes against the smoke, smiling at her as he caught her gaze on him. Isn't my daddy the best-lookin' feller in the whole world now? Dympna asked herself, admiring his face, brown as the mahogany table in the schoolmaster's house, and his straight nose and square, strong teeth. And my mammy's pretty as a picture, she added fairly, thinking of Beatrice's smooth hair the colour of well-ripened barley and her figure still trim and neat, and her broad, unlined white brow.

'Your mammy is English, alanna,' he said at last, having given the matter long and serious thought. 'Maybe the English keep their feelings bottled up in a way we Irish cannot. I t'ink your mammy was

118

brought up never to let out a good shout when she was hurted, nor a good hooray when she was pleased wit' life. So now it comes hard to her to show us that she's pleased when we bring in a grand catch.'

'Ye-es, but she shows when she's annoyed with us, though she doesn't slap, like Finola's mammy,' Dympna argued. 'Many's the tellin' off I've had from Mammy when I've not brought in the spuds quick enough, or wasted my time on workin' at my books when she'd rather I was mendin' torn shirts or knittin' a new woolly hat for the winter fishin'.'

'You have to work at your books; surely Mammy's never said otherwise?' Micheál asked in a shocked tone. 'Sure an' wasn't it an agreement between yourself an' the schoolmaster, now? Your mammy wouldn't want you to break an agreement.'

'No . . . she never tells me to put my books down, but sometimes when she's busy and needs a helpin' hand her lips go tight and she looks at me as though . . . well, as though she'd like to grab the book I'm readin' and hurl it t'rough the nearest window,' Dympna said and saw her father's lips twitch.

'Ah well, alanna, that's because she's been brought up to believe it is the women who do the domestic chores. There are you, her only daughter, out on the fishin' boat most o' the day and even up at the potato patch, cultivatin', while she's doin' the work o' t'ree women all by her lonesome.'

'I know . . . but she could ask Nick to give a hand, or even Egan. Why does it have to be me, when I'm workin' like a feller?' Dympna asked, getting up from her perch on the rock and going over to the big creel of fish. 'It's no manner o' use sayin' that they're real fellers and I'm just pretendin', because that isn't true at all at all.'

'No, of course it's not. But the mammy's afraid, alanna, that you'll forget how a woman should work. She wants the good t'ings of life for you – a man, a home of your own, children. She doesn't want you to forget how to mend, or cook, or knit.' He stood up on the words and came to take up his handle of the basket. 'That's all it is, alanna, I promise you.'

'Little chance I have of forgettin' such t'ings, when she reminds me at every turn,' Dympna muttered, but low enough for her father to pretend he had not heard. After all, there was no point in blaming Micheál for Beatrice's failings, if failings they were. And besides, with every day that passed, Dympna was getting more independent, better both at the fishing and at her books, and even at her hated domestic tasks. Out loud she said: 'Well, Daddy, in another year Egan will be wantin' my place on the boat and I'll be applyin' for a pupil teacher job wit' Mr O'Neill. Then, mebbe, Mammy won't want me darnin' socks.'

'Aye, in another year,' her father agreed. He stood up, stretched, then took hold of the creel. 'He's a good lad, Egan, but the brains of him he's got straight from meself, so he has. Lucky that you and Nick have your mother's intelligence and quick mind. Now here comes Rosa to see what we've caught – isn't she a clever dote, that donkey? I've brought her a nice apple, so I have.'

Dympna watched as the donkey came cautiously down the steep bank from the common land where she grazed and nosed her father's pocket until he put their burden down and produced a couple of little pink-fleshed wild apples and fed them into her small, velvety mouth. Micheál loved Rosa and made a point of gathering pocketfuls of the sharp-sweet little apples for her from a tree which overhung the lane that led to the farm, producing one every night as they walked home. Rosa seemed to know by instinct when they were about and always came down to greet them. 'She's a dote, so she is,' Dympna agreed now as the little beast fell into step behind them. Beatrice used Rosa in the little cart, which she drove to market when they had any produce to sell, and Micheál used her when he was carting seaweed up from the beach to enrich the soil of his potato patch, but though she and Egan fed her, brushed her down and harnessed her to the cart they had never attempted to climb onto her back. 'For she'd kick up her heels and duck down her head and toss you to kingdom come,' Micheál had warned them when they were small. 'She's been broke to harness but she never could abide man, woman or child gettin' astride her. That's why we got her so cheap.' So now Dympna watched Rosa chumbling away at her treat until every fragment had been swallowed and then they picked up the reed basket and set off once more for home with the donkey walking alongside Micheál so that he might stroke her long, pointed ears and talk softly to her.

The cottage looked all white and gold in the last rays of the sun, and Micheál ducked his head to go in at the back door and called out: 'Anyone wantin' fish hereabout? We've been after gettin' some fine cod, haddock and coley, so we have. Where's the mistress of the house?'

And then they both went indoors to the empty kitchen and stood the fish creel down on the big wooden table, and waited for Beatrice to come in and examine the contents.

*

With Egan in school, Micheál and Dympna out in the boat and Nicholas in Dublin learning to be a doctor, Beatrice was often lonely. It was odd, this, because her days had largely been spent alone for many years now, yet it was only when she knew that Nicholas would not be coming whistling over the threshold each evening, knew, too, that Dympna and Micheál had each other's company all day, that the feeling of loneliness had come.

She was certain that letting Dympna go off in the boat had been the right thing to do because it had freed Nicholas – she never even thought of him as Nicky – for the work that he was now doing at the university, yet she frequently regretted what had happened. She told herself now, as she scrubbed a great pan of potatoes for their main meal of the day, that she could not possibly be jealous of Dympna for what woman of sense would be jealous of her own daughter? What was more, she had never, right from the start, pretended to be in love with Micheál, which meant that she could scarcely envy Dympna Micheál's constant company.

She hardly ever let herself remember those early days now, when she had lived in a big house in Liverpool as of right, with four sisters older than she, and another three years younger. She had been pretty, then and vivacious – the most spirited of the Campion sisters who were renowned throughout Liverpool for their prettiness and their lively ways. But when she was fifteen she had met Millicent Reid at a dancing class and they had speedily become bosom friends. Millicent, like herself, was one of a big family, but she had brothers, godlike creatures who played golf and sailed boats and rode to hounds. Beatrice had not come into contact with many young men and she had formed a deeply secret but passionate attachment to Rupert Reid, the eldest – and most godlike – of the brothers. He was pleased rather than otherwise to find himself the recipient of such adoration, but nothing came of it and Beatrice had known, really, that nothing could. Rupert had been paying gratifying attention to her sister Elinor, who was to inherit their uncle Samuel Badger's considerable fortune and estate when their bachelor relative died. Her parents talked of the possibility of a marriage with bated breath, and Elinor preened herself on getting such a handsome and desirable *parti*.

So when Mrs Reid, in conversation with Mrs Campion, had mentioned that she was taking her family over to Ireland for the summer and that she would be most grateful if Mrs Campion would let little Beatrice accompany them, as a companion for their daughter Millicent, Mrs Campion had been eager to accept. She was a faded, blue-eyed blonde, who had very little to do with her children, did not, in fact, like children very much. She was ruled by her husband, a quick-tempered, domineering man who had made a fortune out of coal in his native Derbyshire before moving to Liverpool and buying an interest in the shipping firm which he now owned. Mr Campion longed for sons and had never quite forgiven his wife for giving him six daughters, but when asked, timidly, if he would mind Beatrice going on holiday to Ireland with the Reids, he had been happy to accept. The Reids were old money; Mr Campion thought it would be a very good thing if his daughter Elinor were to marry into the family, and who knew what might come of a friendship between Millicent and Beatrice?

Only unfortunately Beatrice and Millicent, despite

being of an age, had been brought up very differently. Millicent seldom read a book and disliked outdoor pursuits. She was afraid of animals, even the dogs her father kept for the shooting were monsters so far as she was concerned, and though she liked shopping, clothes and dancing, she did not consider the shops in Galway to be of any particular interest and as for the coast, the ponies in the stables and the wonderful countryside, such things bored her to tears.

So Beatrice was thrown very much on her own resources, for she was a vigorous, athletic girl who played tennis, sailed a boat and rode. At first, she had felt rather let down, simply wandering around the grounds or taking a pony out by herself, but then Rupert Reid arrived on the scene and everything changed. Beatrice rode with him, cantering beside Lough Corrib with gentle hills misty on the horizon, promising further adventures when they had the time for a longer expedition. Rupert had a sail boat and he taught her to crew for him, and he took her down to the beach at Salthill and encouraged her to show off her swimming – and her new swimming costume, as well.

Beatrice had admired Rupert from afar ever since she had first met him, but now that admiration became something more. She had a blue bathing costume, the same blue as her eyes, and noticed that when she wore it Rupert was more attentive than ever. She was too young and inexperienced to realise it was not the bathing costume, but what it revealed, which attracted him, so she continued her daily trips to the beach for a swim.

And all the time, on the beach, the fishermen were in the background. Young men who had never seen a girl in a bathing costume, let alone a daring one like

Beatrice's, sauntered along the beach as though merely out for an evening stroll, eyeing the lovely golden-haired girl as they did so. Eyeing her as hotly, she realised later, as Rupert.

But at the time she scarcely thought about the fishermen. They were just an audience, albeit an admiring one. And when Rupert was busy about the estate or with his male friends she started to go along to the fishermen's quay to talk to them. One was nicer than the rest: Micheál Byrne, who had blue-black hair and dark-blue eyes, and who spoke a soft and gentle brogue and made it plain that he would do anything in his power for her. But he was only a fisherman and, though Beatrice liked him well enough and often singled him out, sitting down on the edge of the quay and chatting, liking his looks and his adoration, she never thought of him as someone she might one day marry, any more than she would have considered one of the servants in the Reids' big, rambling house a possible suitor.

Then one afternoon the family had gone off in a motor car to Limerick to do some shopping. Beatrice was asked if she would like to accompany them, but although she knew that Millicent would go, she had no desire to waste a splendid, sunny day looking at shops. So she took a packed lunch down to the beach and prepared to have a quiet day all by herself, meaning to return to the house when it was time to change for dinner.

It was a golden afternoon and the sea splashed invitingly at the edge of the flat rocks, which sloped gently down to the water. Beatrice had changed into her bathing costume and played around on the edge of the waves for a bit by herself. She slid into the water and swam for a while, then she began to walk along the shore, intending to sit down presently and eat her picnic, for the fishermen would all be out in their boats and although there were one or two other groups on the beach they were all young families with small children and, as such, of no interest to herself.

She had not know that Rupert, too, had stayed at home until he came up beside her and put an arm about her slim, tanned shoulders. He had told her to put her picnic out on the rocks for the gulls, for he would take her somewhere nice for luncheon. 'You'll have a much better time with me,' he had said, his eyes glowing, his mouth full of mischief. 'Oh, come on, Bea, don't be a spoil-sport.'

She could not possibly allow herself to be thought a spoil-sport, so she had obediently scattered her sandwiches to the gulls and gone with Rupert, not even changing out of her costume but wrapping her striped towel round herself and hurrying beside him, wondering where they were going to go, for he had said there was no need to dress.

He had taken her back to the house. 'It's quite all right, they're all in Limerick and Mrs Cuffin, the housekeeper, has given the servants a day off. We'll make ourselves a nice little feast in the kitchen – I'm a dab hand at cooking bacon and eggs.'

Even now, Beatrice could not remember that afternoon without a flutter of excitement in her stomach. Rupert had been so wonderful, had seemed so kind. And back at the house he had led her upstairs to her own room, telling her that he would sit on her bed and look out of the window whilst she got into something more comfortable.

At this point, she had tried to resist what she knew to be an unwise suggestion. She had said – truthfully

– that her bathing costume had dried on her, that she could easily slip a skirt and jumper over it, that he could wait for her in the kitchen. 'You might start cooking the bacon and eggs,' she had said, smiling up at him, and he had smiled back and led her upstairs without another word, as though he knew how excited she was at the prospect of . . . of being alone with him.

They had gone into her room and Rupert had closed the door. Then he had taken her in his arms and begun to kiss her. His hands invaded the top of her costume, making her gasp, sending extraordinary feelings arrowing through her as he began to caress her breasts. She had jerked her face away from him, feeling her heart begin to pound. 'Rupert,' she'd said in a small, shaking voice. 'Rupert, don't, you mustn't . . . it's . . . it's wrong!'

But wrong though it was, it had seemed less wicked than daring, a grown-up and interesting way to behave, for Rupert, so much older and wiser than she, had merely replied: 'You don't want to catch a chill, my darling. Don't worry, I'll soon have you warm as toast, then we can go back down to the kitchen.'

He had rubbed her hard with the towel, so hard that it had seemed he really was just trying to get her warm, and she had protested, laughing, that he would have the skin off her body at this rate. Then he had stopped rubbing and opened the towel and taken the straps of her costume and pulled them down over her arms, then lower, lower, gazing at her all the while as though – well, as though he was seeing, not little Beatrice Campion, his sister's friend, but something much more awe-inspiring.

She had protested – well, she thought she had, at

any rate – but he had gone on pulling the costume down until she was bare between his hands. Then he had laid her down on the soft double bed she and Millicent had reluctantly shared and put his arms round her . . .

She had not known about babies. That was to say, she had not known what actions made babies. She had been frightened at one point, had tried to push him away, but it was not because she was afraid she might have a child. He had hurt her, she had cried out . . . and then she was pulling him closer, muttering that he was the nicest boy she had ever met, that she loved him, loved him . . .

They had still been naked, entwined, when the door had opened. Mrs Cuffin, the housekeeper, had come in, given a startled gasp and backed out, shutting the door behind her with a slam which had almost stopped Beatrice's heart.

Beatrice had sat up, hands flying to her breasts, but Rupert had pushed her back again. 'No point in getting in a state,' he had said. 'I'll deal with old Cuffin – we've known one another for years. Just forget it – she probably didn't even recognise you, down flat in the feathers like that.'

It had spoiled everything, but it soon became clear the Mrs Cuffin had not told the Reids, for they treated Beatrice with all their usual friendliness, though for several days afterwards Beatrice avoided Rupert.

It did not last, of course. She had told herself severely that she had done wrong . . . but the next time Rupert had sought her out, taken her riding, stopped the ponies near a little wood, tied their mounts to a tree and led her amongst the trees, she no longer wanted to resist. He had assured her they were safe here, that no one would see them . . . and even after all the terrible things which happened later, Beatrice could still look back on that second time with delight, remembering how Rupert had thrilled her, making her as keen as himself for more secret meetings, more love-making.

Then Mrs Cuffin must have said something to Mrs Reid, or possibly even to Mr Reid, for it was he who called her to his study one morning, a week before they were due to return to Liverpool and their respective homes. 'Miss Campion, what I'm going to say may surprise you, but it certainly won't shock you. From what I've heard you're a hardened young person, quite beyond being shocked by anything I might say. But I'll not have you going back to your parents and filling their heads with tales about my son, no indeed. So I just want to make it clear . . .'

'I . . . I don't understand,' Beatrice had stammered. 'How could I tell tales about R-Rupert? I d-don't know any tales to tell.'

'No, you won't,' Mr Reid had said thoughtfully. 'Because I'm going to write to your parents. I'm going to tell them that I'm sending you home a week earlier than we had planned because you're a bad girl. I shall say it's known that you've been playing fast and loose with one of the local fishermen, and I dare not keep you in my house any longer now that my decent son is staying here.'

'B-but Rupert's been here for weeks,' Beatrice had said, tears standing in her eyes. 'You know he has, Mr Reid. And I-I've not p-played f-fast and loose with a-anyone! I don't know what you mean by it.'

'I think you do,' Mr Reid had said grimly. 'So you'd better get your bags packed, young lady. I'm a man of my word and you'll be leaving us tomorrow morning just as soon as I've bought the necessary tickets.

That's all I have to say to you. You may go – and don't mention the matter to Millicent or I'll make sure you regret it.'

Beatrice, stunned, had got up out of her chair; this was a nightmare, it could not be happening. She and Rupert had done a wrong thing, she knew it in her heart, had always known it, but was that enough for Mr Reid to punish her by telling lies to her own family, by sending her home in disgrace? 'It was Rupert as well as me,' she had said in a small voice, turning back in the doorway. 'My father will be very angry that you've told lies about me.'

Mr Reid had come out from behind his desk like a whirlwind and grabbed her by the shoulder. Then he had shaken her, hard, and slapped her face. It was a cruel blow, her head had rung with it and the tears which ran down her face had seemed to excite him, for he hit her again, ringingly, then turned her and marched her across the hallway to the bottom of the stairs. 'Go to your room,' he had said between gritted teeth. 'And don't you ever let me hear you telling lies about my son again, you . . . little whore!'

She had gone to her room, sick at heart and terrified, and had lain there for hours, trying to tell herself that it would not happen, that they might indeed send her home in disgrace but they would not lie about it as well. But it was true; he had done just as he threatened. He had sent her home virtually under guard, with a long-faced elderly aunt who carried a letter addressed to her parents. And the Campions had read the letter and held long, worried conferences at which she was not even expected to be present. Her mother had reproached her, had reminded her that Elinor was to marry into the Reid family. 'We cannot have you ruining Elinor's chances of happiness because you behaved – well, *misbehaved*, I should have said – with a poor fisherman,' she had said accusingly. 'The wife of a young man like Rupert Reid must be above reproach, there must be no scandal about her family.' And when Beatrice had told her that Mr Reid had lied she had not been believed. Then her father had called her into his study and after raging at her for several minutes, had abruptly asked the name of the fisherman who had had carnal knowledge of her.

She had stared, confounded. Carnal knowledge? Wasn't that something out of the Bible? But when he had persisted, rushing across the room at one point and slapping her, twice, across the cheeks, she had given in. 'It . . . it was Rupert,' she had said, rubbing fruitlessly at the tears which streamed down her face. 'He . . . he said he liked me, he . . . he did things . . . I d-didn't know it was wrong.'

'Rupert? Your sister's fiancé? No, no, you can't mean Rupert Reid, Mr Reid said that it was . . . so who is this Rupert?'

'It *was* R-Rupert Reid, father. The . . . the only son. Th-the one who was paying court to Elinor. Only it must be me he loves, or he wouldn't have d-done . . . what he d-did.'

Her father had stared incredulously for a moment, and then she could see by the look on his face that he had believed her. He had said nothing more, had told her to go to her mother, and for three whole glorious days Beatrice had thought that the misery and bullying would now be over. She had gathered from what her parents had said that if a man did – that – to a girl, they had to marry. Well, she would be very happy to marry Rupert, because he was handsome and kind and very clever, and all her friends would envy her. It was a pity that he had been Elinor's young man, but he clearly preferred herself, so that was all right. And soon she and Rupert would have a wonderful wedding, with herself in white tulle and satin, and then they would move into a nice little house in Crosby or Formby or even Southport, and live happily ever after.

Now, of course, she knew that she had been living in cloud-cuckoo-land, that her father, hand in glove with Mr Reid, had only one thought in mind, to keep her disgrace from the neighbours and to get Elinor and Rupert respectably married as soon as might be. Mr Reid wanted to keep what had happened between herself and Rupert hidden for all time, and what better way of doing it was there than to enlist her father's help and co-operation? She even appreciated, now, that she had put everyone in a very difficult position. A gentleman's daughter like herself should never have allowed any man, especially not her sister's intended, to make love to her. Not so very many years ago, girls had been packed off to nunneries for such sins. But because they did not want any fuss, they were forced to take advantage of her innocence, to let her believe that everything was going to be all right.

When her father had told her to pack some thing because he was taking her round to the Reids' house, she had actually been happy. Happy! She had not expected her father to abandon her there, nor to tell Mr Reid that he might do as he liked with her, provided he got her respectably married before . . . well, as soon as possible.

But she had not known that at the time, of course, and even if she had, she would have made no fuss because she thought it was Rupert who would marry her. She had made no objection to going back to Ireland with Mr and Mrs Reid and Rupert for the same reason. He was a very hangdog Rupert, what was more, who could scarcely bring himself to look at her, though she tried very hard to be as near to him as possible, because she had still thought that they were to be man and wife, assumed that they would marry in Ireland, quietly, because it would upset Elinor to learn that her younger sister was married before her. Wiser now, Beatrice had also thought that they must never tell Elinor what she and Rupert had done before their marriage, so she went willingly off with the Reids and Rupert with no thought of their possible deceit crossing her mind.

The household had been astonished to see them. Mrs Cuffin had given her sharp looks, but had been unexpectedly kind. She had come to Beatrice the day after they had arrived at the house and advised her to choose someone who would look after her properly when the time came for marriage. Beatrice, pathetically grateful for a kind word after what felt like years of punishment and disgrace, had said she would. Yet even then it had not occurred to her that Mrs Cuffin was trying to warn her Rupert was not the bridegroom the Reids had in mind.

She had only learned afterwards what Mr Reid had done. He had gone down to the quay when the fishing boats came home and had questioned the men, asking which of them remembered the young lady who had been staying down here a few weeks back – a young lady with golden hair.

Old Mr Byrne had said, cautiously, that he seemed to recall someone wit' golden hair who had talked to his son, sometimes, when Micheál was cleaning down the *Aleen* after a fishing trip. Micheál, listening, had come forward at once. Yes, he had seen the young lady down on the beach, usually alone but occasionally with a young gentleman, and had talked to her on several occasions, telling her stories about the fishing and the local people. Yes, he had liked her, thought her both beautiful and clever. Mr Reid had taken him to one side and asked him straight out if he would consider marrying her. If he would consent to such a marriage, Mr Reid would undertake to pay him the sum of five hundred pounds.

Micheál stared at him for a long moment while Mr Reid had taken a couple of steps backward and seemed on the point of speaking again – he opened and shut his mouth like a cod fresh out of water, Micheál had actually said – when Micheál had made his decision. 'I'd marry her for love, so I would,' he had said. 'Sure and isn't she the most beautiful t'ing ever to come to our village?'

But of course Beatrice had known nothing of this until long afterwards. All she knew was that suddenly things had started to move. The Reids seemed to be forever whispering in corners and looking at her with sly expressions. Rupert went off early each morning and did not usually return until after she was in bed at night. Mrs Reid told her that she was to be married, but still said nothing about the bridegroom, though Beatrice had thought it odd when her hostess bought her a number of truly horrible print dresses and thick, hand-knitted cardigans. She also supplied her with large canvas aprons and woollen vests and knickers which would have reached well below Beatrice's knees had they been intended for her personal use. But she assumed they were for her maid, as were the stout boots and white cotton nightdresses, the long black cloth coat with a rabbit fur collar and the black woollen dress for best . . . it must be for a servant, otherwise it was the most peculiar trousseau that Beatrice had ever imagined. Did Mrs Reid think she ought to clothe our *housekeeper*, she asked herself despairingly, viewing the harsh, hard-wearing materials with some unease. No mention had been made of where she and Rupert were to live, but she assumed that these clothes meant Ireland and an Irish staff. But once she was married no doubt everything would be different. She would be able to choose her own things and would put away, once and for all, the strange, ugly garments her future mother-in-law had provided for her servants, buying in their place light print dresses and cotton aprons, with dark-green cloth for best and dainty lace caps for servants actually waiting on the family, as they would one day.

The priest who was to marry them had been to the house and talked about her wedding, her future life. She had scarcely listened, so embarrassed was she. His brogue was thick and though he was a Catholic, as she was herself, she did not like the way he looked at her, not his apparent assumption that she and Rupert would stay here in Ireland once the knot had been tied.

She had scarcely seen Rupert, but on the day before her wedding he had suddenly appeared as she was walking in the gardens. He was lurking in a thick shrubbery and called softly to her, and as soon as she saw him she began to smile and went to him with a wildly beating heart. Now, at last, she would be able to talk to him, to ask him about the peculiar clothes and his mother's strange assumption that they should remain in Ireland after the wedding.

But she got very little pleasure from the encounter for Rupert might just as well not have listened to a word she said – indeed, she thought he had not – since all he did was to keep saying he was sorry, explaining that if it were just himself the story would be very different, telling her that she would be happy, she would not regret her decision. Beatrice had not known what he was talking about and just smiled and smiled, and held his hand and told him how she was looking forward to being a married lady at last.

It was not until her wedding morning that Mr Reid had explained. Rupert could not marry her because he was engaged to her sister, and it was important that he and Elinor should be married without a breath of scandal. But clearly she, Beatrice, must marry too, because of what she had done. Her parents quite understood how things were and had agreed that provided she married someone, they did not much mind whom. A local fisherman, a good, religious man with a boat of his own and a comfortable little house, had agreed to make her his wife. She must be grateful, because she could not possibly marry Rupert. Surely she would not want to break her sister's heart, as well as ruin Rupert?

Beatrice had stared at him, wide-eyed, slow to take in the import of his words. 'But I don't want to marry anyone if I can't marry Rupert,' she had said in a very small voice. 'It . . . it was Rupert who . . .'

'Yes, that's what you say,' Mr Reid had said, and all at once his reasonable tone changed and became hard and spiteful. 'But it won't be what I shall say – nor your prospective husband, my dear. We shall tell a very different story and we shall be believed, I can promise you that. So you must just put a good face on it.'

If she had known that Micheál would have told the truth, backed her every inch of the way, she must have protested. But though she had talked to him, even flirted a little, she had never learned more about him than his name. As it was, she had tried to run away and was brought back by Mr Reid only a few minutes before her wedding was due to take place.

It had been a nightmare, that wedding. She had stood beside Micheál – she did not think she looked at him once until it was all over – and felt cold, cold, cold. Cold as death. A poor, terrified creature, caught in an inescapable trap. And afterwards, when the local people had gathered, staring at her and at Micheál with friendly curiosity, she had simply wanted to hide, to run and bury herself somewhere quiet until she could undo the dreadful thing which had been done to her.

But Micheál had been kind, and when he had tried to take her in his arms and she had drawn back, shaking violently, he had sighed and kissed the back of her neck and moved away from her. And for a long, long time he had never tried to persuade her to let him touch her, for she knew, now, that what she and Rupert had done was what made the babies come and turned you from a girl into a woman.

And after their wedding night, which was not a wedding night at all but a parody of what she had believed a wedding night should be, she had woken up next day feeling very ill. And when she swung her feet to the floor she had been most dreadfully sick and had kept to her bed in the simple, crowded house for weeks, whilst her mother-in-law looked after her and tried to tempt her non-existent appetite and her brothers-in-law, deeply embarrassed by the whole affair, gave her little presents, told her stories and tried to make her happy.

But it was Micheál who had brought her through it,

who told her about the five hundred pounds which, he said, she might have for her very own since he did not want it. He had told her, very kindly, that she was going to have a baby and never intimated, by word or look, that he knew he was not its father. Beatrice had supposed, dully, that he was too ignorant to realise that simply sleeping in the same bed was not enough to make her pregnant, that therefore, since she was pregnant, she must have been possessed by another man. She had not cared. She had simply wanted to die, because it was no use, planning to run away home: her home was lost to her. Her parents wrote, sending her some money, saying that it was all for the best and describing Elinor's happiness now that the date of her forthcoming marriage to Rupert was fixed. She had ignored the letter, never acknowledged the money, which she handed to her mother-in-law, and that wise woman took it and tucked it away and never mentioned it again.

And once Nicholas was born, Beatrice began, slowly and gradually, to accept her lot, because from the moment she saw his small fair face, she knew that she had got Rupert after all. For the baby was in his image. From the light-brown eyes to the toffee-coloured hair he was exactly like his father. And there were no two ways about it, she adored her little son. She carried him about with her, tied into her shawl, and sang to him and told him stories. Micheál, who had been kind to her, was always kept at a distance, because she was determined never, as long as she lived, to have another child. Certainly she did not want to repeat the pleasure and pain which Rupert had given her with anyone else. Or, indeed, with Rupert himself. For from that one unguarded moment had come her downfall.

So she had given all her love to Nicholas and she had worked in the house with her mother-in-law, whom she soon grew to respect, and on the land with her brothers-in-law, quiet young men who seldom allowed anyone to know what they were thinking. And she had slept each night in the narrow box-bed with her husband Micheál and they'd respected each other's space, and Micheál kissed her on the brow each night and then settled down with his back to her and slept.

After they had been married for three years, Micheál's brother Geralt brought a girl home and said he and Maura were going to be married. The little house was crowded enough, with Micheál's mother, her two younger sons and Micheál and Beatrice and their small son, without adding another soul to the mix, and it was soon clear that Maura was already pregnant. Mrs Byrne looked round her at her sons and their wives, and then she sat in the chimney corner and wrote a letter. She had said nothing to Beatrice, but she and Micheál had gone off by themselves one evening, going out for a walk as dusk was falling and not returning until late.

The letter, it later transpired, had been Micheál's uncle Fergal, a solitary soul who lived in the small cottage down by a sea lough in Connemara where Micheál's mother and all his aunts and uncles had been brought up. Fergal was the oldest now, in his late seventies, and wanted to go and live with his daughter Maeve in Cashel. Old Mrs Byrne had written to her brother, telling him that his nephew, Micheál, was willing to take the place on and she had received a reply after a couple of weeks, indicating that Fergal would sell them the cottage and the bit of land he owned, but wanted to take his curragh with him, since he hoped to do a bit of fishing from his daughter's place.

'Micheál and meself talked about the possibility of such a move,' old Mrs Byrne told her daughter-in-law when she had received Fergal's letter. 'It's a nice little place, so it is, and the folk roundabout are friendly. For meself, I'd be happy to go there, but I'm after t'inkin' that you and me son Micheál could do wit' some space an' time to yourselves, so I'll be bidin' wit' me younger sons and Maura. What d'you t'ink of the idea, Bea?'

Beatrice had jumped at the chance of moving out of the cramped little house where all the neighbours knew that there was something strange about their marriage, something which the Byrnes were keen to keep quiet. But the practicalities were not so simple. 'Micheál's a fisherman,' she had said doubtfully. 'How will he fish, without a boat?'

'We've t'ought it out,' Mrs Byrne had assured the younger woman. 'He'll take the *Fair Aleen*; he's me oldest son after all. He'll pay Fergal for the cottage an' he'll put a bit more towards a craft for Geralt an' Murdoch, if it's a fishin' boat they're after gettin'. But it wouldn't surprise me if the two of them took some other course one o' these days.'

And so it had been arranged. She, the toddling Nicholas and Micheál had piled all their small possessions into the *Fair Aleen* and sailed round the coast until they reached the sea lough, which Micheál had visited many times when he had been small. Uncle Fergal was at the house, but all packed up to leave, with his possessions in the little donkey cart and the kettle on the fire, ready to welcome them. It was the first time he had met Beatrice, and the fact that she had gasped with pleasure at the sight of the white, rush-thatched cottage at the top of the little bit of cliff, with the stone quay and the beach below, and the sloping green hill above, was a good introduction.

'You'll tek care of me little home, so you will,' he had exclaimed, taking both her hands in his. 'Aye, it's been a good little home to our family time out of mind, and it'll be a good home to you an' me nephew, for isn't he a Donahue in all but name? Now there's peat still on the pile, for I'll not be carryin' it across Ireland like some poor tinker, and I've left you me four old hens – they still lay, from time to time – an' there's a basket of praties be the fire an' as fine a cod as you'll see in all of Connemara sittin' in the stone sink, just waitin' for you to put him over the fire.'

'You are good,' Beatrice had said earnestly, giving the old man a spontaneous hug, and had seen her husband's eyes widen, for she was not a demonstrative woman. 'We'll be happy here, as happy as you've been, I'm sure. And if you'd ever like to come back for a stay we'd be proud to welcome you.'

So the Byrnes had moved into the cottage by the sea lough and the neighbours had come crowding round to see the pucan, exclaiming over its size, the beautiful lines of it, the great canvas spread of its brick-red sail. And quite soon Beatrice was digging in the tiny patch of garden, climbing up and over the hill above the cottage with Nicholas in her arms to plant potatoes and cabbages, and searching for eggs that her four old hens still laid so that she could cook one for the child's tea. The work was hard, but Micheál was soon bringing home good catches and then they bought a little handcart so that he could push it into Clifden to sell fish when they had some to spare, and she salted the fish, too, as she had done when she lived with her mother-in-law, and she began to be content.

Micheál missed his family sorely at first, she knew that, particularly the youngest brother, Murdoch, who had sailed the boat with him. Was that why she had not run, screaming, from the cottage the night that he decided to make a real wife of her? She thought, now, that she must have grown complacent, thinking him as satisfied with their relationship as she herself was. And knowing how gentle and good he had been with her over so long a period, perhaps a tiny thread of generosity, a qualm of conscience, had prevented her from fighting him.

And from that night had come Dympna, the child she resented. Now, scrubbing the potatoes clean in the bowl of water and dropping them into the pan, she acknowledged that she resented Dympna for the most unfair reasons: because she felt that Dympna had been a little living chain, tying her to the cottage, to Micheál and to her life here.

Secretly, in her heart, she had lived with the bright hope that one day she might go back to England, with Nicholas, and confront Rupert. She no longer deluded herself that he would marry her: she knew better than that. Her sister Elinor had given Rupert a little son and they had a good life together, a successful life. Elinor entertained and Rupert was something important in the shipping company and was well regarded in the city. Beatrice knew these things because although she no longer corresponded with either her parents or her elder sisters, she sometimes got a letter from her little sister, and she always replied to those letters, as if she were reluctant to cut herself off for ever from the family to which she had once belonged.

She had dreamed of going back with her fine, handsome little son and persuading – did she mean blackmailing? – Rupert to set them up in a little house somewhere. She had parted, rather reluctantly, with a little of the five hundred pounds which she was saving for when Nicholas might need it, but she told herself that she could always spend some of it on her escape.

That was, until Dympna was born. Beatrice had had a hard time with Dympna, which was strange, considering she was her second child and not her first, but Dympna had come into the world feet first – a breach birth – and at one point the elderly woman who had agreed to help with the birth for a small sum had called Micheál to the door, telling him in a breathy whisper that he had best make all speed he could over the Clifden and fetch the doctor, for his wife did not seem able to deliver the child and since she could not feel the head, she feared that something was very wrong.

Micheál had not panicked or laid blame, Beatrice thought now. He had hurried up to the Sullivans and asked them to send someone across for the doctor, then he and Mrs Sullivan had come breathlessly into the cottage – into the very room where she lay labouring – and had told her not to worry, to lie quiet and try to relax whilst they saw to things. 'For if the baby is the wrong way up then haven't I delivered forty or fifty lambs and calves in just that position?' Mrs Sullivan said practically. 'Micheál says there's not much different between one baby crittur and the next, so between us, we should be able to help you, alanna.'

Then she had advised the elderly neighbour to go and make them all a nice cup of tea and heat some

143

water for to clean the baby up when it came, and to find a pair of scissors and some clean cloths. And once the woman was out of the way Mrs Sullivan had stripped the bedclothes off and begun the delicate task of manoeuvring the baby into a position that made it possible to birth her quickly, so that the child should not be in the birth channel too long.

And Micheál had helped. It was not work for a man, to see a woman giving birth, she knew that he should not even have been allowed in the room, but he did not seem to mind. Indeed, when the little creature had been hauled into the world, blue in the face and apparently lifeless, he had snatched the child up, dangled it upside down and smacked its small bottom until it gave a great gasp and began to scream, and then he had plunged it into the warm water which the neighbour had supplied, dried it on a piece of towelling and plonked it into her arms whilst Mrs Sullivan dealt with everything else.

'There you are, me darlin' Bea,' he had said breathlessly, smiling down at her. 'Your wee daughter's after comin' the awkward way, like all women. Give her to suck now, so she knows she's alive and in a good place.'

Afterwards, Mrs Sullivan told her frankly that it was very likely Micheál had saved her life. 'For that foolish woman, who had only seen five or six babes born and thought she knew it all, would have wrung her hands and wailed while the child stuck in the birth channel and you and it died,' she said frankly. 'You've a good man there, Beatrice Byrne, and isn't it time you admitted it?'

So how could she possibly have left Micheál with the poor, skinny little baby, to manage as best he could, whilst she and her fine son made off back to

England? No, no, it was out of the question, for she owed him her life as well as that of her girl-child. Even to herself, at that time, she could not admit that she was beginning to appreciate Micheál for himself, for his gentleness, his many small kindnesses and his strength, which supported her when she felt she could go on no longer.

So she had stayed, but resentment of the new baby had grown and grown. Dympna had been a sickly child, difficult to rear. She did not sleep well, waking fractious and crying after an hour's fitful slumber, and she did not seem hungry, either. Beatrice fed her for a couple of weeks but then her milk dried up and she was forced to wean the child. The baby did not like the bottled milk and would weave her head fretfully from side to side, refusing the teat. Beatrice frequently lost patience with her and gave up, sighing that if the child wanted to starve herself to death . . . but many and many a night Micheál walked up and down with the baby in the crook his one big, muscular arm, the bottle held to her small mouth, patiently persuading her to take a sip more and a little sip more, until she had fallen asleep, with most of the milk drunk.

It was the same when Dympna began to eat solid food. Beatrice would put the dish before her and take it away again, almost untouched. Micheál would spend hours playing games which involved the baby opening her mouth at the approach of the spoon, loaded with food, and although it took time, at the end of it the dish was empty and the baby full. She's not a bad gorl, she's me little angel-child,' he would say when Beatrice got angry and tried to take Dympna down from the table and throw the food to the cats. 'She'll eat up for her dadda, so she will . . . you watch this, Mammy!'

And he taught her to walk, to talk . . . only in the end he had persuaded Beatrice to do a bit more towards the talking. 'For you'll not want a little gorl wit' a brogue as thick as me own,' he observed. 'So you have a crack wit' her when you've a mind – she's quick, the wee monkey, she'll learn soon enough.'

And so she had, Beatrice had to admit it, though grudgingly. What was more, she had turned from a skinny, sallow little creature into a striking, if not beautiful child, with Micheál's blue-black hair and very dark-blue eyes in a small, flowerlike face. Her body was straight and her movements quick, and when she smiled her mouth tilted up at the corners and her eyes narrowed into shining slits.

Nevertheless, Beatrice preferred her sons, both of them, to her daughter. When she had known she was expecting another baby she had prayed that it would be a boy. She was sure she could never manage to bring up another sickly, difficult daughter. And indeed, she had loved Egan from the first, though never in quite the same way that she loved her first-born. Egan was brown-haired and grey-eyed, a sturdy child with a loving and generous nature. He was not clever, even Beatrice admitted that, but he tried very hard and was good-tempered about his own failings. 'Sure an' I've not got a brain in me head worth tuppence,' he was apt to say cheerfully. 'But who needs a brain if he's got muscle? I'm goin' to be a fisherman, like me daddy, not a teacher or a doctor or a priest.'

And then there was the way Micheál had continued to treat Nicholas; he did not favour him above the others, that would never have been Micheál's way, but he loved him and made sure Nicholas knew it. Why, when those flying men, Lieutenant Arthur

Whitton Brown and John Alcock, had crash-landed in Derrygimla, where the Marconi wireless telegraph station was, Micheál had put the small Nicholas on his shoulders and walked him a good seven miles over rough country, through bog and briar, to see the plane. ''Tis the forst crossing of the Atlantic by air,' he had told Beatrice. 'And me little lad's not goin' to miss out on seein' a t'ing like that. Why, it'll be somethin' for him to boast about to his own little'uns, when he's a man.' Micheál, Beatrice reflected now, had far too big a heart to behave ungenerously towards any of her children.

Beatrice dropped the last potato into the cauldron and picked up the bucket of fresh water. She tipped it onto the cleaned potatoes, then put the bucket back under the wooden draining board and fetched a handful of salt from the crock by the fire, tossing it into the cauldron. There was a hook over the fire and she heaved the cauldron up in her arms and hung it from the hook, so that the flames licked at its base. Then she went back to the draining board and began to clean the two big cabbages, which the girl had fetched down from the field before she left for the fishing. In her head, Beatrice often referred to Dympna as 'the girl', finding it easier, for some reason, than using her name. She wondered where Egan had got to . . . school would have finished by now, but she knew her youngest son. He would be wandering along the lanes with little Maria Sullivan, telling her stories, teasing her, sometimes pulling playfully at her plait of hair – but never allowing anyone else to take liberties with his small friend. Maria, Mrs Sullivan was fond of saying, would be safe with young Egan, for he'd allow no one to bully her but himself.

Beatrice got the big frying pan down from the shelf next, and cut a chunk of the pork dripping into it. They would kill the pig soon, which would mean they would be eating fresh meat for a little while, but until then she liked to cook the fish in the pork dripping. It gave a delicious flavour to the small cod, or haddock, or huss, for the biggest and best fish went to market, leaving the family to eat up the smaller, less attractive part of the catch. She put the pan by the fire, then began laying the table, clattering the tin plates and the thin, bendy knives and forks onto the bare wood. They used the table-cloth on Sundays, but weekdays did not matter and the cloth, which had been most beautifully embroidered all over by Micheál's grandmother, would not last for ever.

Presently, with the meal on the go, Beatrice sat herself down by the fire for a moment and put another turf onto the flames, waiting to see it catch and dreaming into the golden heart of it. She thought about Nicholas in Dublin, surrounded by beautiful and gracious buildings, by educated, literate people. Once, she would have known bitter, gnawing envy, but now she simply thought that it would be nice indeed to have him back when the Christmas holidays came. He could tell them so much, explain so much, and he would enjoy doing it, she just knew he would. And then there was Egan: when school broke up he would be at home with her all day, though he would doubtless expect to go out with his father and Dympna from time to time.

The thought was enough to bring the bitter taste back into her mouth. It was so unfair! Dympna would have it all – she was smart as paint, the schoolmaster said so, she was going to be beautiful in an unusual, slightly fey way, and her father adored her. It was indecent, the way he looked at her, with such loving pride. It would never have happened had she done as Beatrice had wanted and gone into service somewhere far away from the village. Yes, there was no doubt about it, Dympna would have all the things that Miss Beatrice Campion, for all her wealth, had never managed to acquire. She would use her brains and become a teacher when Egan was old enough to take her place on the fishing boat. Thus she would still keep Micheál's love and admiration, because he would think her a very clever girl, to go to teaching college and get herself a good job. And he would continue to love her because Micheál was like that: loyal. He would not cease to love her just because she was no longer living at home. One day, no doubt, she would also get herself a good husband . . . not a fisherman, struggling all the time to make ends meet, to feed and clothe his children, to . . .

Hastily, Beatrice jumped to her feet. She went over to the piece of polished tin which was propped up on the mantelshelf and was all the mirror she had. She smoothed her hair, still as dark a gold as on the day Micheál had first met her, and ran her hands down her smooth sides to the curve of her hips. She was still good-looking, she still had a slim, supple body. It was wrong and wicked to feel such burning jealousy, such bitter envy, and towards her own daughter, too. Dympna was a good girl, it was not every girl who would have gone on the fishing boat so that her elder brother might take his place at university and become a doctor. Besides, Micheál had always admired her, Beatrice. Indeed, she thought that he had loved her, too, from the first moment that they had talked, down by the fish quay. He had married her, had he not, given her children? She was his wife, of course he loved her. Her own feelings were so jumbled and mixed that she preferred not to question them. And all Micheál felt for Dympna was the natural love of a father for a pretty, intelligent daughter. She really must stop behaving as though she and Dympna were rivals for the love of Micheál Byrne.

Shaking her head at her own foolishness, Beatrice took off her calico apron and walked towards the door, picking up the bucket as she passed the draining board. She would go to the spring and refill it, and presently she would move the cauldron to one side of the fire and put the kettle over the hottest part of the flames so that the could have a cup of tea when everyone was home. She opened the back door and glanced towards the beach – and froze. Her husband and daughter were crossing the strip of sand, heading for the cottage. They were holding the big, dripping creel between them and it was sagging with the weight of the catch. They were laughing, looking at each other, laughing again . . . they were happy, happy, happy! They did not look like father and daughter, they looked like a couple of friends who were sharing a joke and teasing one another. Micheál never looks at me like that, Beatrice found herself thinking as she bent her head and trudged towards the spring and the old tin bath. How dare they – how *dare* they laugh like that? Oh, she's a brazen hussy, to laugh like that when she's nothing but an awkward, black-haired monkey of a girl, her clothes covered in fish scales, her hands red-raw from handling the fish and the ropes and the flapping, brick-red sail. She should have more respect, more . . . more . . .

But she did not want to be caught spying on them. She went to the spring, filled her bucket, then stepped behind a convenient hazel bush. She waited until she saw them turn the corner of the cottage, then followed, trying to look surprised as father and daughter turned towards her with identical expressions of pleasure and excitement on their faces. Beatrice crossed the room and peered into the creel. 'You've had good luck,' she said, smiling up at Micheál. 'There's a grand lot of fish there – will I cook some for our supper?'

'Aye, there's enough to salt down some, sell some in Clifden, eat some fresh and still have one or two to give to a neighbour,' he said, turning to beam at Dympna. 'And why were you after fetchin' water when you've a strong daughter an' a great lump of a husband to do it for you?' He walked over to her and took her hands, his eyes smiling down into hers. 'Come along, alanna, you go and sit be the fire for a change, while we're after showin' you the size of the catch. There's the finest cod we've seen since last winter, and coley wit' flesh as white as your own clean sheets, an' huss, fiddle fish, weavers, rokers . . . what do ye fancy for this evenin's supper, alanna? Say the word, an' I'll start to clean it an' fillet it for ye.'

'I've done the spuds and the cabbage, but a good fat piece of cod would go down a treat,' Beatrice said longingly. They did not often eat fresh cod, it was too desirable a fish in the market place. 'I've got pork dripping melting in the pan . . . clean us a cod then, Micheál.'

'I will so,' Micheál said sturdily, picking out one of the biggest fish and reaching for the long gutting knife, which he kept in his belt. 'It'll be ready be the time you've heated the pan, alanna. Dymp, me darlin', you can have first wash.'

# Chapter Five

Mr Lumley had arranged for the chip shops and fish restaurants to close all day Monday to give his staff a chance to recover from the excesses of the previous day, but of course Aunt Ruby knew nothing of this and when she came upstairs at about ten o'clock and saw, when she popped her head around the back-bedroom door, that Jimmy still lay there, she rushed into the room and cuffed him awake.

'What's up wi' you, you lazy little tyke?' she said, righteously wrathful, though Edwin still lay with his mouth open and his eyes sleep-encrusted. 'You keep tellin' us as 'ow you like your job but you're goin' the right way about losin' it. Get your arse out o' them covers or I'll fetch you a belt across the ear.'

'The shop's closed till this evening,' Jimmy said in a sleep-blurred voice. In fact, he had had no idea where he was or what was happening to him when his aunt had first addressed him, and even now was only beginning to come to himself. 'We was out so late that Mr Lumley said no one need come in until after tea.'

'Out? Oh, so you did go to Seaforth wi' your pal. I told Frank that you'd ha' been here else, stuffin' yourself wi' the roast pork an' the apple sauce. But I dunno what it's got to do wi' Lumley where you go or what you do.'

'No, you've gorrit wrong,' Jimmy said wearily, sitting up and rubbing his eyes vigorously. 'The

Lumleys went out too . . . but it don't matter, I'm gettin' up now, anyroad.'

Aunt Ruby snorted but left the room and presently Jimmy thundered down the stairs and popped into the court, ostensibly to use the privy but actually to fetch in the rock he had hidden away in Elsie's mam's log pile. When he went back indoors he handed over the two largest sticks of rock and put the others in the dresser drawer. 'It's for me cousins,' he mumbled when he saw his aunt staring. 'We went to Blackpool, everyone brought rock back. It's the best, is Blackpool rock.'

'Well, I won't deny I'm partial to somethin' sweet occasionally,' Aunt Ruby said in her society voice, which she usually saved for the landlord whom she considered a cut above herself. Now, she eyed the rock with unabashed greediness and peeled back the paper, taking a bite off the end. 'It's not bad,' she mumbled through a mouthful. 'I'll give Sam 'is when he comes in for 'is dinner.'

'Right,' Jimmy said. He had not expected thanks, which was just as well, he told himself, leaving the house and wandering across the court to the Taylors' place. He wondered whether Elsie was still sleeping or whether she, too, would have been awoken, but guessed that, because she had decided to take a day off work, Elsie would have been making the most of it to have a lie in, though she would probably have woken of her own accord by now.

He went to the Taylors' back door, but here a disappointment awaited him. Yes, Mrs Taylor said, Elsie was up, she had gone up Everton way with Mabel and Suzie, to see the school dentist on the corner of Mill Street.

'She's a good gal, our Elsie, tekin' her little sisters to

the dentist. Mabel's proper teeth, the grown-up sort, come afore the milk teeth ha' dropped out, so she's got two sets, like,' Mrs Taylor explained. 'The dentist wants to see whether he should tek some of 'em out, an' he said as how he'd check on the baby's at the same time, in case she's goin' to have awkward teeth an' all.'

'Never mind; mebbe I'll go up along Everton way then, see if I can find 'em,' Jimmy said, having given the matter a moment's thought. 'The thing is, the shop's closed till five o'clock so I've time on me hands for once and it's a shame to waste it doin' nothin'.'

'Well, if you misses 'em an' they come back 'ere, I'll tell 'em where you've gone,' Mrs Taylor said vaguely. She was making bread, bashing away at the dough as though it was a personal enemy, whilst Freddy and Arthur played ollies almost under her feet. 'Come back 'ere for your dinner, Jimmy. It's bakin' day, so there's plenty.'

'After yesterday you wouldn't think I could eat another mouthful; only I can, of course,' Jimmy said. 'Thanks, Mrs Taylor. See you later, then.'

The way to hell is said to be paved with good intentions and certainly Jimmy set out with the best of all possible intentions – that of joining his friend and helping her take care of her small sisters.

The trouble was, because of his job Jimmy could not usually roam the streets whilst the shops were open, since the school holidays were no longer his free time, and naturally he wanted to have a look at everything, particularly as Monday was as sunny and pleasant as Sunday had been, weatherwise. So he chose the most interesting route. He crossed Comus Street and dived into Peover, which housed, as it happened, several of his pals from school. They were playing out, or at least some of them were, and had to be told why he wasn't around much during the daytime. Most of them promised to come and get a penny twist of chips and told him to make sure they had good measure, and then he crossed Rose Hill and began to thread his way along the smaller streets until he came to Village Street, where the best toffee in all Everton was sold. This shop had to be passed with resolution, otherwise Jimmy knew he could easily have spent all the money in his pocket on their delicious wares.

After the temptations of Village Street had been bypassed, he emerged onto Everton Road itself, where there were interesting shops with goods out on the pavement and housewives pinching tomatoes and searching apples for bruise marks, and clacking away to each other at the tops of their voices.

Jimmy walked slower now, fingering the change in his pocket. It was left over from yesterday and could be spent in any way he wished, and he was still wondering whether to get himself an iced bun and a bottle of gingerbeer or whether to blue the lot on sweets on his way home when someone hailed him.

'Hey, what you doin' in our neck o' the woods?'

Jimmy turned and saw that it was Wally, who also worked for the Lumleys, with a toffee apple in one hand and a bulging string bag in the other. He grinned stickily at Jimmy, then beckoned him. Jimmy would have had to cross the road anyway since the clinic was on the further pavement, so he shrugged and crossed, deliberately lingering to make an approaching tram ring its bell at him before leaping for the pavement.

'Hello, Wally,' he said as they met. 'Me pal's gone to Mill Road to see the toothie so I thought I'd walk along and meet her. Only there's a good few roads hereabouts she might of took, so we might of missed each other.'

'Oh, is that it! I though per'aps you was comin' up to talk over what happened yesterday.'

'Yesterday? Oh, the Blackpool trip,' Jimmy said. 'I can tell you I ain't thought of anything else – weren't it just prime?'

'Yes, it were . . . but I weren't meanin' *that*,' Wally said scornfully. 'I meant the burglary . . . don't say you haven't heard?'

'What burglary?' Jimmy said, with a sinking sort of feeling in his stomach. 'Oh, not the shop!'

'Not just one shop. All three of 'em,' Wally said, his voice almost awed. 'Mr Lumley reckons it were a gang, an' we've had the scuffers round an' everything. They even took our dabs,' he added with some importance. 'So's they could reckernise staff fingerprints from burglars', I reckon.'

'Was much took?' Jimmy asked. 'Oh, lor', I suppose I should have gone round to the Lumleys this mornin', only how were I to know? Come to that, how did you know, Wally?'

'Scuffers,' Wally said briefly. 'They come round right early. Wonder why they've not been to your place?'

'I dunno,' Jimmy said, puzzled. 'Mr Lumley knows where I live, but I dunno if he knows which number, Kennedy Court. Look, Wally, I'd best be gettin' back. Will you walk along o' me for a bit, tell me what's been took and that?'

'Well, awright, only I'm doin' me mam's messages, so I can't be too long,' Wally said righteously. 'They took all the Sat'day takin's, that's for sure. They hide 'em up, but the burglars found 'em, which was makin' the scuffers think it were an inside job.'

'An inside job? Does that mean one of us?' Jimmy said incredulously. He felt his face grow hot and wondered just what he had given away to Frank on the Saturday, when he had hinted he would not be in on Sunday. 'Well, that means you, me or Ivor, 'cos all the rest are family.'

'Aye, but they know *we* didn't do it, 'cos we was in Blackpool,' Wally reminded him. 'They think someone told someone else it were the family day out, an' where the spondulicks was kept. Only I don't know, does you?'

'No, haven't a clue,' Jimmy said thankfully. 'Oh, Gawd, I'd best go round to the Scottie shop as fast as I can.'

'Well, I would if I were you,' Wally agreed. 'Now you knows what's been goin' on, at any rate. See you some time, Jim.'

'See you some time,' echoed Jimmy. He waved to Wally and began to trot down the road in the direction of the Scottie.

The shop, when he reached it, was in an uproar. Police were everywhere, and so were Lumleys. Maggie saw him and beckoned him over to where she stood, just outside the shop. 'Oh, Jimmy, it's been awful,' she said in a hissing whisper. 'Someone broke in through the back . . . that scullery door's as old as the hills, an' so it wouldn't have took much . . . and ransacked the place. Why, they even went into our flat, an' took bits an' pieces. Me wireless set what Dad bought me for last birthday, an' Mam's fur coat what she's hardly ever worn, an' all the Sat'day takin's, of course. The scuffers say that's what the thieves were after, the money. The other was just spur o' the moment.'

'Do they want to talk to me?' Jimmy asked

nervously. 'Ever since I met up wi' Wally and he told me what was up I've been wonderin' if it were something I'd said . . . only I were real careful 'cos your dad telled me not to blab.'

'Aye, they'll want a word,' Maggie said and caught hold of his hand, shaking it and then pulling him towards the shop doorway. 'Oh, Jimmy, don't look so scared, wack. Me dad telled 'em you was as honest as the day, they ain't goin' to think you took nothin'.'

'No, b-but suppose I lerrit out that we was off to Blackpool?' Jimmy said, hanging back. 'I didn't tell you, Maggie, but me cousin Edwin said I talked in me sleep last week, somethin' about a great big party an' havin' all the food I could eat, he said.'

'Well, I doubt it were your cousin Edwin; the scuffers said it were a professional job, a gang, likely,' Maggie reassured him. 'Come on, let's gerrit over.'

So Jimmy went with her into the shop and a tall policeman with a bushy moustache and very bright blue eyes asked him questions and then said they would go round to Kennedy Court later for a word with his mam, but it was just routine and nothing to worry about.

'Aye, only I don't have a mam, she died more'n a year ago,' Jimmy said, wishing that he did not go so red whenever he was nervous. He could feel his cheeks flaming just as if he'd been hanging over the chipper all morning. 'I live wi' me aunt and uncle . . . they're the Blaneys, at number eight.'

'Blaney, Blaney . . . I've heard that name before, and recently, too,' the policeman said thoughtfully. 'Right, Jimmy. Is Blaney your name, then?'

'No. My mam and Aunt Ruby were sisters; I'm Jimmy Ruddock,' Jimmy explained. 'Shall I go now, mister?'

'Aye, all right, unless you're going to stay and help the Lumleys to clear up. There's a deal of mess about,' the policeman said. 'It would be a kind act, Jimmy.'

So Jimmy went into the shop and began to help in the clearing up, which was considerable, for the thieves seemed to have taken a positive pleasure in turning things upside down, breaking plates and cups and dishes, and emptying the contents of any drawers or cupboards out upon the floor. Mr and Mrs Lumley, grimly tidying up and throwing out articles which were too badly damaged to be used again, welcomed him kindly but distractedly. 'Hello, lad,' Mrs Lumley said. 'Come to gi' us a hand, have you? Well, anything what's broke beyond repair purrin me sack, that'll be a great help.' She was filling a potato sack with broken china as she spoke, working automatically, and her eyes were red and puffy. Jimmy was sure she had been crying and felt deeply embarrassed. Grown-ups did not cry, that was for kids. But when he saw that Mr Lumley's eyes were red too, he supposed that anger makes the eyes red as well as tears, and felt a bit better.

Side by side, the family and Jimmy laboured. They stopped for a quick meal of ham sandwiches and cups of tea, then started again, and by four o'clock Mr Lumley said the place was as right as it was ever likely to be and told Jimmy to get off home and not to come in again until seven o'clock.

'Eddy brought the fish an' the potato merchant brought the spuds, so once we've ate some tea ourselves we'll start a-fryin',' he said. 'We'll soon be back to normal workin', an' that'll be good for us all.'

'Yes, 'cos we're goin' to have to work for almost nothin' until we've earned back what have been stole,' Maggie said quietly. 'Never mind, eh? It's a

159

challenge, that's what me dad'll say tomorrer, when he's feelin' more himself.'

So Jimmy went home. The family were squabbling over who should peel spuds and go up to the shops for meat pies but once his face appeared in the doorway that, at least was no longer a bone of contention. 'Go an' get a dozen big mutton turnovers from Walton's, an' then come back an' peel me some spuds,' Aunt Ruby ordered. 'Where've you been all day, anyroad? I thought you was off till this evenin'.'

'Oh, just out wi' me pals,' Jimmy said airily, taking the money his aunt held out to him. 'A dozen mutton turnovers. Right.'

Making his way back along Gay Street he wondered why he had not told her where he had really been, for Aunt Ruby was fond of a nice bit of gossip, but decided that innate caution had kept him quiet. She would be bound to show pleasure that the Lumleys had been robbed, for his aunt grudged anyone who had a ha'penny more than she herself possessed and had often grumbled that the Lumleys were only ordinary folk and had no right to be so rich.

The baker's had only been able to supply ten mutton turnovers but he bought two pork pies for the same price and set off again, back to Kennedy Court. He felt rather guilty over Elsie, though, and decided that he would dump the pies in the kitchen and would then rush over to the Taylors to tell them what had happened. If no Blaneys were in the kitchen, that was; if they were they would not see him leave it again until he had peeled, panned and put onto the fire the great mound of spuds at present waiting in a bucket by the back door.

He went into the kitchen and no one was in there, so he stole across to the table and laid the string bag very gently down on the wooden surface. He was half-way back to the door again when he heard sounds from upstairs; heavy feet climbing across the back bedroom and then voices, his aunt's and someone else's, someone strange. They were standing at the head of the stairs now, so Jimmy got the back door open and prepared to sprint for it. Indeed, he was half-way out when words came floating down to his ears, suspending him where he stood as though turned to stone.

'How d'you account for the fact that it has been found in your house then, Mrs Blaney? It's on the list of stuff stolen from the Lumleys and it's got Mr Lumley's initials inside . . . you say you know nothing about it? Where are the boys that sleep in that room, then? I'd like to have a word with them.'

'Stole, you say? Well, officer, I should ha' guessed it. As you know, me nephew works for the Lumleys on the Scotland Road, an' I've not had him livin' here long enough to teach him right from wrong, you might say. It'll be him, that's for sure.'

'Your nephew was in Blackpool with the rest of the workers when the theft occurred,' the man's deep voice said mildly. 'Are you suggesting that he's a member of a gang which did the burglary? He's around fourteen or fifteen, isn't he? A bit young for that sort of life, especially as he's been working in the shop six days out of the seven.'

'I don't know about that,' Aunt Ruby said sullenly. 'I only know none of me own lads would touch what weren't theirs, officer. Oh aye, it'll be Jimmy, that's for sure. He's took money from me purse, food from me cupboard . . . the boys have lost all sorts since he's been stayin' wi' us. Why, the bleedin' wallet were under his mattress.'

Jimmy felt as though his feet were stuck to the ground. What to do? Where to go? He had liked the policeman who had talked to him earlier, but this voice was strange to him and if his aunt told everyone that he was a thief, and stuck to it, they would be bound to believe her. She was an adult and as such much more believable than a boy, even if he had actually worked on the wrecked premises.

'Where is he now? Your nephew?'

'Gone off to do me messages,' Aunt Ruby said. 'I give him the exact money he'd need, so's he couldn't pocket me change. Oh aye, that's another of his nasty little tricks, officer. But he'll be back any minute, I dare say, an' you can arrest him then.'

Jimmy did not wait to hear more. He slid out of the back door, across the yard and round the corner into the court. It was the work of a moment to run across it and gain the open street. It did occur to him that when he had left the house several of his cousins had been mooching round the kitchen, but they seemed to have disappeared before the police arrived. He supposed, morosely, that with their experience of scuffers, just the sight of one would be enough to scatter them, even if they had done nothing wrong. The wallet he could not explain, save that there had been nothing under his corner of the mattress when he had climbed off it this morning, but he could well imagine that Edwin might stuff a stolen object out of sight before making for the hills.

Does that mean that *Edwin* did the burglary, though, he asked himself, hurrying down Gay Street in the direction of the Scottie. No, of course he didn't. He's a horrible feller, but he doesn't have the skill to burgle all three shops like that, nor the friends to help him. No, it would have been Frank. He had wondered about Frank, but now he realised he had stopped wondering long since. No one who did not work could do the things that Frank did, unless he was up to some sort of skulduggery.

Jimmy was passing Mrs Duffy's shop when he stopped short and pretended to stare into the window whilst he thought. Frank had followed him into the Lumleys' place that night; then he had gone round to the restaurant and ordered himself a fish supper. After that, from various things she had said, Jimmy was pretty sure that Maggie had met his cousin and probably gone dancing with him a time or two. If she had said *anything*, if she had refused to go out with him on that particular Sunday, Frank was quite bright enough to put two and two together and guess that it was the day of the Lumley outing. Come to that, Jimmy told himself, continuing to walk, it was a bit simple of Mr Lumley to think that they could all go off in a charabanc at the crack of dawn the way they had in complete secrecy. Dozens of kids would have seen them depart, all the neighbours, used to this annual migration, would guess where they had gone and would have known how long they would be away. The field was wide open really – anyone who was dishonest enough and clever enough could have done the three burglaries.

He glanced almost without seeing it at the window display, then suddenly focused. Purses . . . wallets. The wallet! He could image all too well what had happened, but how on earth could he possibly convince anyone else? They would think he was trying to get his cousins into trouble if he said that Edwin had likely been given the wallet by Frank, and told to slip it under his, Jimmy's, part of the mattress if the search looked like landing Frank in trouble. It had probably had money in it, Jimmy thought bitterly, so Edwin would have been bribed to do what he liked doing best – getting Jimmy into trouble.

But what am I to do? Jimmy asked himself helplessly. He realised now that hurrying out of the court the way he had not been the sensible thing at all. They would know he had come back by the shopping on the table, and would assume that he had heard their voices and realised his guilt had been discovered. And run. What he should have done was to go to the Taylors at once and explain the whole thing to someone who would listen and believe him. And then he would have had someone to speak up for him, someone the police would trust.

But he had not gone to the Taylors, and it was too late to do so now. Maddeningly, he also realised that all his savings were at the Taylors' house, hidden away under a loose floorboard on the landing just outside the girls' room. He and Elsie had chosen the spot together and since his first visit he had given her several nice little sums to add to his hoard. But no use thinking of that; he could not get back to the court without being caught, either by the police or by the Blaneys, so he had better get as far away as possible from the scene of the crime and decide just what he meant to do.

It was growing dark when Jimmy decided that he would leave the city, for a while at least. He was sure that if he stayed he would be convicted of a crime he had not committed, and worse even than the thought of prison was the dreadful fear of the Lumleys' dismay and hurt, that someone they had trusted and seemed to like should repay them in such a manner.

So flight, for now at least, was the only answer.

Jimmy remembered the many times he had longed to run away in the past, when he had first moved in with the Blaneys, and realised how much his life had improved since Elsie, and the Lumleys, had entered it. Now, he had a purpose in life and a goal, and what was more, he had grown a good deal and got sturdier since his circumstances had improved. At nearly fifteen he no longer had any fear of being spotted and arrested as a child who should still be in school, should he try to get a job in some other town. It was a dreadful shame that he must leave under a cloud, and through no fault of his own, but leave he must.

With this thought in mind he retraced his steps until he was at the Pier Head, with all the buildings and the jumble of huts and shacks amongst which to hide. He found a pile of sacks and carefully made himself a little nest down the side of a leaning wooden shack, then curled up and pulled the sacks over him. The night was balmy, the scent of the river a good deal pleasanter, he thought sleepily, than the smell of the frowsty, unwashed Blaneys all crammed into the boys' little room. Now, when he looked up, he could see the big stars, seeming to twinkle down on him out of the blackness of the sky. I'm going to go because it's the best way, he told the stars, but I'll write a letter to the Lumleys, explaining, and when I've got an address I'll write again and ask Maggie to get in touch with me when the burglary is cleared up. Oh no, I can't do that, because if the scuffers were still searching for me they would come down on me and drag me back to prison. But you can get letters addressed to post offices, I'm sure you can, or perhaps it's little shops. Then you go and pick up the letters for you when no one's about and . . .

He slept, only to dream of being pursued by

policemen, huge and menacing, whilst Edwin squeaked that his cousin was there, in them sacks, and Frank put on his most innocent expression and told a judge in a big white wig that he and his mam had long known that Jimmy Ruddock was the worst sort of thief.

Escaping from the nightmare for a moment, Jimmy wondered once more whether Maggie was fond of his nasty cousin and decided that she had too much sense. So when it was safe, he could tell Maggie that Frank was almost certainly mixed up in the affair . . . only, of course, if he waited until it was safe, the scuffers might have arrested the wrong person . . . suppose they picked on Elsie and slammed her behind bars, and he was the only person who could possibly save her . . .?

But before he could sort out in his mind what was best to be done to save Elsie he had fallen asleep again and the next time he woke it was morning.

Jimmy was extremely hungry on waking and soon very glad that he had not spent all his spare money on sweets. Instead, he went to a workmen's canny house and bought a plate of hot soup and half a loaf of bread. With these inside him he went out once more into the crowded street and found a tap where he slaked his thirst. Then he decided he would walk out of the city and set off, trying to keep in a straight line, for otherwise, he realised, he would simply go round in circles and probably find himself, by nightfall, walking straight into Kennedy Court once more.

I'll go to Wales, he told himself at one point. That'll be grand, all them hills and mountains and sheep. But the city did spread itself out a long way, that was for sure, and he knew that there was the great river to cross before he could reach it. People went by ferry, or they caught a train which went under the river, but for that you needed money. Jimmy still had money, but he did not intend to waste it on train fares or on the ferry. He remembered one of the boys at school saying that he sometimes crossed on the ferry for free, by tagging along close to an older person and pretending he belonged to them. So at around lunch-time Jimmy made his weary way down to the Pier Head once more, intending to get himself aboard the ferry somehow and then to tramp to Wales.

He might have done it, too, but for something that happened when he decided to go into a bakery and buy himself a ha'penny bun. He was actually standing outside the baker's shop, deciding, with watering mouth, which one to purchase, when in the glass of the window he saw a reflection he recognised. He spun round, mouth opening to shout . . . then shut it again, but he had been right. It was Eddy King in his big blue lorry with his name on the side and he was slowing down . . . there was a fish and chip shop further along the road and Eddy was delivering there.

The sight of such a good friend was almost too much for Jimmy. He very nearly gave in and ran up to Eddy to explain the situation, but at the last moment, prudence held him back. Eddy was a friend and a good one, but he was Mr Lumley's friend too and had known the Lumley family much longer than he had known Jimmy. By now, everyone would be aware that he had run away and they would be sure of his guilt. Later, when they had thought things over, he hoped they would realise . . . but for now, approaching anyone who knew him was just too dangerous.

But seeing Eddy was such a treat that Jimmy sauntered up to where the lorry had disappeared and saw it, parked, in a small yard to the rear of the fish and chip shop. Even as he loitered, Eddy came out, picked up a pile of boxes from the rear of his vehicle and went with them into the back of the shop, pulling the door carelessly to behind him.

Jimmy ran over to the lorry. He was not really thinking, he was simply reacting to the lorry being parked there, with the back open. He looked inside and it was full, so far as he could see, of empty fish boxes. Which meant that Eddy would be heading home any time, probably after he had had a meal of some sort with the folk in the fish shop.

Scarcely knowing what he did, Jimmy hauled himself up into the lorry and tiptoed over to the very front of it, hard up against the cab. He eased the boxes out of the way so that he was in a little cave of boxes, crouched against the metal wall, then he made himself comfortable, or as comfortable as was possible. The smell of fish was overpowering and it was warm and rather stuffy, too, but it felt almost homelike to Jimmy. He sat very still and presently he must have dozed, for it seemed no time at all before he heard voices and Eddy came clumping out of the shop.

'Thanks for the meal, Mrs Richmond,' he called. 'See you tomorrer. My, but it's a warm day – wouldn't be surprised to 'ave thunder before night.'

Then there was the sound of more empty boxes being slapped down on the rear of the lorry and pushed so that they slid up towards Jimmy's end, then footsteps and the slam of the cab door – then the engine roared into life and they were off.

It was a terrible journey. The fish boxes were quite amenable until Eddy put on his brakes abruptly, which he seemed to do rather often. Then they came sliding and squeaking and jostling across the metal floor of the lorry, to pile up against poor Jimmy in his cave. By the time they had been travelling for half an hour he was a mass of bruises – or at least he supposed he was – and his muscles ached from the strain of trying to prevent himself from following the boxes' lead. But several times, caught off balance, he rocketed across the metal floor and crashed against the – fortunately – tightly locked rear doors. Also fortunately, he told himself grimly after one particularly noisy crash, Eddy was clearly used to the frolics of the boxes on his homeward journey and did not notice the odd yelp which was forced from poor Jimmy's throat.

But the journey ended at last. The lorry slowed, turned sharply in at, Jimmy imagined, a gateway and stopped. Jimmy just had time to arrange himself behind a pile of boxes when the door opened the dim light streamed in. Peering between two of them, Jimmy saw that a strange young man stood there and was presently joined by Eddy.

'Want to start at once, Ed?' the boy said and Jimmy saw that he carried a coiled hose-pipe over one arm and realised, with real horror, that he was about to hose down the lorry bed and to get out the empty fish boxes. Jimmy took a deep breath and wished he were small enough to climb inside one of the boxes, then prepared, miserably, for discovery. But he was saved by Eddy's thirst.

'No, leave it till I've had meself a drink an' some grub,' Eddy said. 'Me mam's got t' beer in, I dare say? And some supper? Well, tis dark now, so it won't get no darker. We'll do it after I've had me grub, Gus.'

To Jimmy's immense relief they moved away, out of view, and after a few very tense seconds Jimmy slowly made his way, on all fours, to the end of the lorry and glanced cautiously around him. The vehicle was in a smallish cobbled yard surrounded by high brick walls. Large double doors, still propped open, led into what looked like a jigger. Certainly it was not a proper roadway.

Jimmy dropped noiselessly off the lorry and padded across the cobbles. He glanced behind him once and saw what he supposed must be Eddy's house, a tall brick building with a light gleaming dully behind one of the downstairs windows. But then he was across the yard and out into the jigger, and making his way along it as fast as he could. This was Fleetwood, he supposed. Well, Fleetwood was seaside, he knew that because Eddy collected his fish fresh each day from the trawlers tied up at the fish wharves; he had told Jimmy so himself. So he would try to find somewhere, perhaps on the beach, to curl up for the night and in the morning he would decide what to do for the best.

When he reached the end of the jigger he found himself in a wide, pleasant street, tree-lined and as straight as a ruler. He half expected to find shops and other commercial premises lining the pavement, but in the faint lamplight he saw that these were private houses and rather large, grand ones, too, when compared with those in the centre of Liverpool. For a moment he stood stock still, wondering if he had somehow managed to get into the posh part of the town, where all the toffs lived. But the house Eddy had gone into had not looked at all posh, but just like any other large mid-terraced dwelling. This road was so wide and straight, however, that it must lead somewhere important, Jimmy told himself, and set off along it. He smelled of fish pretty strongly himself, but sniffed the breeze anyway, hoping to smell the sea. He could only smell his own noisome fishiness, however, so he continued to walk, convinced that he would find the sea without too much trouble, and then he could decide what best to do. He guessed that discovering it would mean the docks were not far distant and everyone knew that cheap lodging houses abounded in such a neighbourhood. But he had very little money and only a moment's thought convinced him that he should save what he had for food. Unless he landed a job pretty soon he was going to need every penny he had just to survive.

The road did indeed lead straight to a pleasant promenade, beyond which he could both hear and see the waves rolling restlessly, their crests white as snow in the moonlight. The beach, however, was narrow and although there were a couple of small rowing boats pulled up close to the promenade he suddenly remembered Eddy telling him that at high tide the water hid most of the sand, and decided that he had not found a suitable spot to kip down for the night after all.

Accordingly, he set off along the promenade, a solitary figure in the black and silver of the moonlight, to find himself somewhere safe for this first night's sleep.

As he walked, Jimmy looked hopefully abut him. To his left, large buildings – hotels he guessed – lined the promenade, but to his right there was just the strip of beach and the sea. Then, ahead of him, he saw a building. Since it was on the sea side of the promenade he doubted if it was a dwelling and sure enough, when he reached it, he recognised the big doors and the slipway which denoted a lifeboat house. Prowling around it, he soon discovered that it was locked up and offered little hope of entry to a would-be sleeper. There was, however, a porch which faced landwards. He circled it again, then noticed, even further up the promenade but again on the sea side, what looked like quite a range of buildings.

Sighing, and glancing up at the moon whilst wondering how much of the night remained – most of it, he guessed – Jimmy plodded on and at length came to a number of seaside bungalows, too small for permanent occupation he decided, but ideal for a family intending to spend a day on the beach.

Some of the bungalows had verandas, and one had a pile of what appeared to be canvas up one end, but when Jimmy examined it, he realised that it was a perfectly respectable hammock, with the hooks to hold the ropes driven in firmly to the veranda posts. In addition, when he pulled out the hammock he found on the board floor beneath it an elderly beach umbrella with all its spokes broken. Clearly, the owners had intended to throw it out, but to Jimmy it was a useful covering against the wind and weather.

Jimmy got to work. It was easy to sling the hammock, then to climb into it, covering himself with the heavy cotton of the old umbrella, and in less time than it takes to tell, he was stretched out, with the cotton umbrella pulled up to his chin, enjoying the soft sound of the waves on the beach and rocked by a gentle breeze.

He lay there for a few minutes, watching the stars in the dark sky overhead, then, whilst still congratulating himself on his luck, he feel deeply asleep and did not wake until dawn crept across the sky next morning.

The small trawler bobbed like a cork on the grey-and-white water and Jimmy, sitting in the thwart with two ropes which he was splicing together, looked over the side at the choppy little waves in the harbour and wondered whether, when they upped anchor and made for the swing bridge, he would presently cast up his accounts, for he had not, previously, sailed in anything like really rough weather. But there was no reason why he should be sick, after all, for he had been sailing with the *Maid Margery* for almost nine weeks now and, apart from his very first voyage, when he had hung over the rail for the first half-hour watching his breakfast reappear, he had not again disgraced himself. He had even retained his hold on the indigestible hunks of home-made bread and mutton pasties which Mrs Totteridge packed up for them, as well as the inevitable slices of cold lardy cake which had had stronger stomachs than his, old Abel said, up-chucking on a choppy day. So I'm not a bad sailor, Jimmy comforted himself, as the *Margery* slid smoothly towards the Wyre Dock. I dare say I'll be all right.

It was a great misfortune for all their stomachs, his thoughts continued, that good skipper though Abel might be, and charming though his wife undoubtedly was, she was no cook. The house was always shining bright, meals were there on the table when they returned from the fishing, but Mrs T had no gift for the pastry and cakes which she loved to make and insisted on supplying when the men were fishing inshore. Accordingly, when they were only going to be out for a day or so she insisted that the trawler should sail each morning laden – and the term really meant what it said – with her home-cooked goodies. The other crew members, elderly men like the master of the *Margery*, teased him sometimes about Mrs Totteridge and her heavy hand with pastry, but it was comfortable, familiar sort of teasing and Jimmy took it in the spirit in which it was meant and continued to work as hard as he possibly could for Abel and to eat Mrs Totteridge's indigestible lardy cake and her bread, which seldom rose in the tin but skulked flatly somewhere at the bottom of it, without a word of complaint. So now Jimmy's stomach, once shrunk from lack of food and later stuffed with the best fish and chips in Liverpool, was growing accustomed to very different fare.

Jimmy, however, took it all in his stride because above everything else, he was a realist. He knew how lucky he was to have a job at all, for with winter coming on work in Fleetwood was scarce, and even luckier that Abel had given him a chance on the *Maid Margery* when his own ship's boy had been caught breaking into a small jeweller's shop in Lord Street. What was more, Abel had let Jimmy sleep in the little back bedroom of his neat terraced house in Abbot's Walk. Once, it had been his son Bertie's room, but Bertie had gone up to Liverpool in twenty-seven, at the time of the great hurricane which had brought the sea crashing into the town so that most of the streets had been under ten feet of water, and according to Abel, great tree-length logs from the sawmills had come roaring down amongst the houses, creating havoc and doing considerable damage to the trawlers in their dock.

Whilst the trawler was being refitted, therefore, Bertie had signed on as a deckhand on a timber boat which plied between Africa, Sweden and Liverpool, bringing mahogany, cedar wood and quantities of pine back to Britain. He sent long letters home and money as well whilst the trawler was being refitted, but since Jimmy's arrival he had not appeared in Abbot's Walk, though Mrs Totteridge spoke wistfully of his eventual return – and spoiled Jimmy in every way she could in memory, so to speak, of her absent son.

By the time Jimmy arrived in Fleetwood, of course, the trawler was herself again and going to sea regularly, so Jimmy now had a berth both at sea and ashore, and was happy, because he had speedily discovered that he loved the outdoor life, the sea and even the hard and punishing work of the fishing. No one could enjoy gutting, mind you, stuck down in the hold amongst the ice with your hands numb and aching, and your feet almost as bad, but it had to be done and Jimmy did it willingly. The *Maid Margery*, Abel's command, was a sailing trawler at a time when the docks were full of steamships, which Abel called, disparagingly, either coal gobblers or up-and-downers, which Jimmy thought was a strange way of describing them at first, until Luke, the mate, explained that the engines of such monsters had vertical pistons which moved constantly up and down. Coal gobblers spoke for itself and was an old Suffolk expression, for Abel had originally sailed from Lowestoft, only moving up to Fleetwood upon meeting and marrying his wife.

They were a happy little crew. The permanent crew members, Luke, the mate and Norm, the third hand, shared lodgings on Dock Street, and the cook who came with them on a long trip was a large black man called Sam Swift who had retired, being at least seventy – he claimed to have passed his century, but no one believed him – and signed on as a favour to Abel whenever the *Maid Margery* was going to sea for a good spell.

'Once, we sailed right up to Iceland as a reg'lar thing,' old Abel told his new ship's boy. 'But not any more, young feller-me-lad. That's too far for three old feelers an' one what's still wet b'hind the lugs, to say nothin' of a cook what thinks he's Methuselah.'

Jimmy thought that one day he would sign on with a coal gobbler and see for himself all the wonderful sights that Abel and the others described – huge icebergs, penguins diving into the sea and being pursued by great black-and-white killer whales, seals riding on the bow wave and then falling back to stare at the crew with great, inquisitive eyes – but for now, the *Margery* was good enough for him. However, he could sympathise, though secretly, with Bertie Totteridge's desire for more adventure, for more distant voyages, even though he himself was so happy at present.

It was lucky for Jimmy that Bertie was mostly at sea, too, because Mrs Totteridge said she was glad of another young fellow about the house and Abel seemed to be of the same mind. The Totteridges took in summer visitors whenever Mrs Totteridge was able to find holiday-makers she could squeeze into the tiny back bedroom, but that was strictly seasonal. Jimmy had wondered a trifle apprehensively at first whether he would be asked to move on when the summer came but Mrs T said sentimentally that Jimmy reminded her of Bertie, and fussed over him like a mother hen, assuring him that he was far less work than the visitors and even letting him borrow any clothing of Bertie's that fitted him and insisting that Jimmy was as good as one of the family.

'Our Bertie'll be home one day, when he's decided to settle down wi' some nice young woman,' she often remarked. 'And then it'll be your turn, our Jimmy, to go sailin' off into t'wide blue yonder. But for now, it's real nice to have you here.'

As for the trawler, Abel considered that with himself in his mid-fifties and Luke and Norm in their sixties, a lad like Jimmy balanced their slowness and made them into a decent and effective crew. He was confident that Bertie would come home one day and want to join his father on board the *Margery*, but in the meantime a youngster such as Jimmy was just what they needed. 'We've got experience enough betwixt the three of us to bring in every fish in the Irish sea, but it don't do no harm to have a quick-thinkin' ship's boy aboard,' he had told Jimmy, when he had first taken him on. 'You'll have keener eye-sight than us old 'uns, an' quicker reactions too. When we come into harbour to tie up you'll be able to jump like a cat from ship to shore. Us three's a bit stiffish in our joints to go leppin' across the side with a rope's end in our teeth.'

So the strangely assorted little group had settled into working together and Jimmy learned a great deal, both about fishin and about the vessel in which he sailed, for the *Margery* was driven only by her brick-coloured sail, whereas all the modern trawlers were powered by steam. He became adept at leaping out of the way as the boom swung over, hauling the halyard to set the sails, splicing rope, mending net, helping to cast out the trawl and bringing it in again, laden with a silvery cargo. He enjoyed himself and was proud of his new knowledge, but naturally enough he did have pangs of homesickness for Liverpool and for the Lumleys, and often longed to get in touch with Elsie, for he could image how intrigued she would be learn of his new life.

By now it was the end of October and autumn was definitely beginning to blend into winter. Abel told him that he did not intend to take the *Maid Margery* out far in bad weather once he reached sixty, but Jimmy had only grinned and said that perhaps someone else would have given him a berth by then, since he was useful in a fishing boat already. Abel had grinned too, reminded Jimmy that his sixtieth birthday was still more than five years away and had continued to set a course.

So here they were on this wet and windy day, having taken on ice, sailing the *Margery* out into the Wyre Dock and then into the lock. All their food and gear was aboard and so was Sammy, checking over his stores and doubtless planning the meals he would prepare, for Sammy was an excellent cook and enjoyed the challenge of feeding the crew. Several other smaller trawlers were lining up to leave, for the tide was full and the wind set fair for a voyage out to the west coast of Ireland and the Porcupine Bank, where good fishing might be found when their own coastal shoals were thinning.

The *Margery* surged out of the lock and into the area of the River Wyre, known as the Tiger's Tail because of its bends, and the wind hit them full force, flattening Jimmy's hair into his eyes so that he was forced to push it under his cap. Abel, as skipper, was at the tiller and Luke and Norm were chatting in the tiny cabin whilst Jimmy, layered in ragged jerseys that had once contained the young Bertie, with canvas trousers over his own thin, patched kecks, handled the sheets, whilst Abel roared instructions, and kept warm despite the cold. Abel, not only layered in jerseys but topped off with oilskins, must have been even warmer, but Jimmy was constantly moving and Abel was not, and when, presently, Norm came up and took over from him, advising him to go below to help Sammy get them a meal, Jimmy went into the cabin reluctantly, for after the violent pummelling of the wind it felt stuffy and he was aware of a certain lurching sensation in the area he had frequently heard described as one's bread-basket.

On the small mess deck Luke looked up from his

perusal of a game of patience, only just begun by the look of the cards. 'Cold out there?' he enquired. He pulled a face at the game and began to shuffle the cards back together again.

Jimmy shrugged. 'A bit rough,' he acknowledged. 'But she's not tippin' about too much.'

Luke smiled and put the cards back into the drawer from which he had taken them. The cabin had a tiny galley opposite the mess deck, but the mess deck was where they ate, chatted, wrote letters home or played games when they were not actually sleeping, fishing or on watch. Jimmy like it there; he had listened to many a tale when the wind was light and the others in a yarning mood, and had played many a game of cards, too, despite a tendency to lose every hand. The galley, however, was another thing altogether. The heat from the stove and the smell of the cooking food could sometime make him long for the deck once more, though once he got accustomed he knew he would be happy enough, helping Sammy with the preparation of food.

'This is the first time we've been on a long-haul trip since you joined us,' Luke said now, slamming the drawer on the pack of cards and turning back to Jimmy. 'You'll be glad to see land agin if we're ten or a dozen days or more at t'grounds. That'll test your love o' the sea, boy! Now off wi' you, Sammy needs a hand.'

Sammy's black face split into a grin as Jimmy sidled into the galley. 'Tek a look in the store cupboard, boy, and then you'll be able to mek suggestions when I run out of ideas for our grub. Go on, then when I ask you for a tin o'summat you'll know where to look and won't waste time searching.'

Jimmy opened the food store rather self-con-sciously. Since he had been told it was his duty to help the cook he had paid more attention than usual to Mrs Totteridge's preparations and had been glad to see flour, a tub of margarine and a tray of eggs coming aboard beside a large piece of fat bacon, a sack of potatoes and another of cabbages, though the tins of condensed milk and the blue bag of tea which had accompanied the other things had reminded him that if he didn't make an effort and get to like the cups of very strong sweet tea, which he brewed most days for the other men, he would go thirsty on this voyage. Abel kept a bottle of rum 'to keep out the cold' for himself and the other men, but Jimmy, being too young for spirits, usually drank water or waited until they got ashore for such treats as lemonade or ginger beer. But the weather made him think with much more longing of hot drinks, so perhaps he would develop a taste for strong tea.

Right here and now, however, he must get going on the preparations for a proper hot meal. There were potatoes to be peeled and a cabbage cleaned. He was seeing to the potatoes when Sammy announced that he was going to make pancakes for afters. Jimmy loved pancakes and had got Norm, who usually cooked on short runs, to give him a few lessons. Tossing them in the small, low-ceilinged cabin would not be wise and he was not yet sufficiently sure of himself to flip them over with the fish-slice, as Norm did, but he could cook both sides by standing the pan off the gas and carefully rolling the pancake other side up, which seemed to do just as well, in the end, as the more flamboyant methods.

'I'll make the pancakes, if you like,' he volunteered. 'Norm often lets me make the puddin'.'

'What's we havin'?' Luke asked, poking his head into the galley as Jimmy got out the makings of the meal. 'You aren't cookin', are you, Jimmy? Hey up, you aren't a-goin' to attempt a duff, are you, young feller?'

He sounded horrified; a duff, even in expert hands, would take the best part of two whole hours to cook. Jimmy contented himself with a mysterious smile and went back to peeling potatoes. Here, at least, he was on familiar ground. When they were ready he shot them into the pan and stood the steamer on top, then chopped a cabbage and piled that into the steamer whilst Sammy was beginning to mix batter.

'I don't fancy all them caterpillars you've jest put aboard,' Luke muttered, still peering into the galley. 'You're supposed to wash cabbage – didn't you know that, young 'un?'

'I will wash it,' Jimmy said, remembering guiltily that one was supposed to wash vegetables before using the water to peel the spuds into. But it was seawater, not the precious stuff they used for drinking. 'I'll just nip up an' fill a pannikin.'

He accordingly nipped, and was shocked by the strength of the wind and the way it whipped rain into his face as he climbed out on to the deck. But Abel actually had his old pipe going, though the smoke streamed away so fast he could barely see it, and Norm was hanging onto the sheet and apparently carrying on a conversation with his skipper as though this were a mild and sunny day in August, and the *Maid Margery* in her most compliant and easygoing mood.

Jimmy leaned over the side and waited until the *Margery* heeled, then dipped his pannikin into the nearest wave top and returned across the deck to plunge below once more. Once there, he began to wash the tough, leathery leaves of the cabbage, saying idly to Sammy that it was really awful out there now, but adding that he did not feel even slightly ill.

'Awful? Ye don't know the meanin' o' the word,' Sammy growled, lighting up one of the tiny Wood- bine cigarettes which Abel, a pipe smoker, told his crew contemptuously were a landswoman's smoke.

'Well, I didn't feel ill, anyhow, and the sea's comin' right over the rail when we heel,' Jimmy said defensively. He began to wash the cabbage, reflected that the sea was a good deal rougher than it had been on his first voyage and he still had not felt the awful uprush of agony which presaged seasickness. That first time have been unbelievably painful and Jimmy had wondered, for a day or so, whether he would ever be able to go to sea again. But he had grown accustomed, as his shipmates had prophesied.

Sammy, beating batter, laughed a trifle derisively. 'Awful?' he repeated. 'It's rough out there, that I grant you, but we're running before a stiff northerly so she's all but sailing herself. Wait till we're tacking wi' the wind against us and the sea building up into crests high as mountains, and see how ye feel then.'

'Well, I feel awright,' Jimmy muttered, but too low for Sammy to hear. He found it difficult to believe that the weather could be rougher than it was now, but there was no point in saying so. Luke and Norm had been proved right in countless ways regarding the sea; no doubt Sammy was the same, for the crew of the *Margery* seemed to know most things about wind and weather. They had been trawling these seas all their lives, from what he could make out, and were justifiably sure of themselves.

When the meal was cooked, Jimmy was handed the steaming bacon joint on a large white serving plate and took it onto the mess deck. He began trying to slice it, endeavouring to keep his body between the joint and Luke in order that his extreme ineptness should not be seen. But Luke craned his neck, then got ponderously to his feet and surged over to him.

'Here, you're supposed to *carve* that bacon, not hack at it like bleedin' Sweeney Todd,' Luke objected, firmly removing both the bacon and carving knife from Jimmy's slippery grasp. He stared at the bacon, his thick, curly grey eyebrows rising until they almost met his equally thick, curly grey hair whilst his dark eyes sparkled with amusement. 'Ugh, what've ye done to this here knife, hey? Fetch me a cloth, boy, or I'll fetch you a clip round the lug.'

Jimmy, grinning, got the cloth and watched whilst Luke cleaned the knife handle and then began expertly slicing the bacon. It looked easy, but . . . 'Gi' me a go, an' tell me where I'm goin' wrong, Luke,' he pleaded presently, when Luke had cut five thick slices from the joint. 'I'll never learn, else, an' I'm norra lorra help to you if I can't cut meat.'

So Luke, who despite his growls was really very good-natured, showed Jimmy how to handle the big knife and at what angle to attack the joint, and under his tutelage Jimmy presently managed to cut another four slices which, though somewhat uneven, were, Luke said, at least passable. Jimmy watched through the half-open door and as soon as Abel, Luke and Sammy were served – Norm was on watch – he seized the big wooden spoon and beat the batter one more time, then stood it by the stove and hurried through onto the mess deck to take his own place at the long wooden table. The warm glow of contentment which always came over him after a job well done filled him now. That thief what took the money from the Lumleys did me a good turn, I reckon, he told himself as he picked up his eating irons and began to dig into the food before him. Before, I were a nobody, just a feller workin' in a fried fish shop, doing a job which any lad of my age could ha' done. But now I'm a deckhand on a trawler and a galley cook, and I can help rig sails and dodge the boom, too. Then I can mend net, and ride out a gale, and . . .

At this point a head appeared in the cabin doorway, a grizzled head, but this time the face wore a sad-looking walrus moustache and the eyes were blue; Norm, upside down with the Woodbine still clinging to his lower lip, said affably: 'She's reefed and holdin' steady. What's that grub like, eh?'

'Capital,' Abel said, 'Gi' me five minutes and I'll take over from you myself. What's for afters, boy Jimmy?'

'Pancakes. I'm makin' 'em,' Jimmy said, casting a professional eye over the almost empty plates of himself and his companions. He shovelled potato and onion sauce into his mouth and spoke thickly through it. 'I'll be puttin' the batter into the pan in another couple o' minutes, Skip, then I'll serve you first.'

Norm disappeared and Abel cut himself a thick slice of bread from the loaf which stood in the middle of the table and wiped it round his plate. 'Right, lad,' he said affably. 'Mebbe Sammy had better give you a hand, eh?'

But to Jimmy's delight, the big negro shook his head. 'T'young feller will manage,' he said. 'Off wi' you, Jimmy, and show us what you can do.'

Sammy had been right about the weather, Jimmy reflected a few days later, as he helped the men to heave the great trawl inboard and rejoiced with them at the size of the fish caught in the net and flapping in its folds. The shrieking wind had worsened a good deal before they had reached the fishing grounds, but now it was almost pleasant, with a fresh breeze but a calm sea and with the Irish coast, on their starboard bow, looking so green and pleasant that it could have been spring instead of late autumn.

Jimmy said as much to Abel, who told him that he would probably get a chance to look at it even closer in a day or so. 'I usually come round to this partic'lar part o' the coast, cos' years ago I were in a bit o' trouble an' a feller from this little village, he got me out o' it. Now th'Irish don't hold much wi' English fishermen, 'cos some of 'em goes into the Irish waters to get the fish. The locals ain't got deep-water vessels, you see, they're inshore fishermen an' go back home, nights. But I keep to my own waters, an' they 'preciate that. An' I visit me pal now an' then . . . and fill up my water tanks an' all.'

Jimmy nodded. Water, he knew, was always a worry when you were at sea; no matter that some skippers were fonder of rum than water, they still couldn't do without it and jealously guarded their supply. But Abel always did his best to see that they had enough to drink and Jimmy knew they were lucky, furthermore, that Abel was equally generous with the food. 'You need your belly well lined for haulin' on the trawl,' he would say. 'No point in expectin' work from hungry men.'

Jimmy knew, from talking to other deckies who doubled as cooks' helpers, that some skippers actually slept on the food lockers, even though they were padlocked and the skippers always held the key. And they growled and fought over releasing so much as a tin of corned beef or one of condensed milk more than they needed, saying that if they ran short the men would blame them. But the men knew full well that skippers provisioned the boats and if they could manage to save on food, the food so saved would stay aboard and the skipper would not need to take on so much for his next voyage.

So now Jimmy slumped down onto the seat next to Abel and asked curiously: 'What did the Irish feller do for you, then, Skip? Was he aboard the *Margery* when he got you out o' trouble?'

Abel laughed. 'No, nothin' like that, lad. It were in the Great War when we were both in the navy in a manner o' speakin'. We were haulin' King George's trawl, as they said then, an' I didn't have the old *Margery*. I were first mate aboard a steam trawler, the *Get Going* out o' Lowestoft at the time, an' Paddy Sullivan, he were third hand. The trawler were armed, like – we had gun, a twelve-pounder, an' three real gunners from the navy, an' we'd sunk a submarine an' were out lookin' for another. Only acourse we was fishin', too, 'cos they needed the fish worse'n ever wi' the war on.

'Now it were just about at this point that the Huns realised we'd got armed trawlers, because afore then their strategy, if you could call it that, was to board us, put the whole crew off the trawler into the little boat, take all the fish we'd managed to catch – an' it weren't easy, 'cos we couldn't use lights an' sometimes that meant haulin' in the pitch black – an' then blow up the trawler. Well, that were why the navy agreed to arm the trawlers, so's they could defend theirselves. Then even armed the little smacks . . . I reckon they must ha' given the Huns food for thought, when a little old smack blasted off wi' her gun . . . so acourse the Huns didn't want to come up alongside for to steal the fish an' blow up the boat, it were too dangerous. Instead o' that they started torpedoing us . . . and on this partic'lar day it was just

186

what some frigate done to the *Get Going*, only by then she were renamed the *Mabs & Lucy* . . . an' the poor little ole boat disappeared in about five minutes an' there we were, tryin' to swim, only there weren't nowhere to swim to, if you understand me.'

'I do. But why was the boat renamed?' Jimmy asked curiously. He looked at Abel with a good deal of respect and also rather doubtfully. The Great War had ended ages ago, so if the skipper had been in his forties then they would scarcely had conscripted him into the navy, would they? But Jimmy's ideas of the past were vague; he had heard of pressed men who were virtually kidnapped, so if that had happened in the Great War, perhaps Abel had been pressed? He was about to ask Abel when the skipper began to answer his last question.

'They renamed the trawlers an' smacks whenever they got a submarine, to put the Huns off the scent,' Abel explained. 'Remember, not all the trawlers were armed, be a long chalk. They didn't want to advertise that this little ship were armed to the teeth an' had already accounted for at least one submarine, so they changed the name. Savvy?'

'Ye-es,' Jimmy said, still sounding doubtful. 'But Skip, why were you taking a job on a trawler when you were . . . well, you weren't a boy to be ordered about, were you.'

'No, I were in me thirties, but I didn't have my own boat,' Abel said patiently. 'I got the *Margery* from my prize money after the war. We done well, we sank three submarines an' took five prisoners. Now d'you want to hear why me an Paddy Sullivan is friends or not?'

'I do, I do,' Jimmy said hurriedly. 'Go on – and I won't interrupt again.'

'Right. Well, the *Mabs & Lucy* had sunk her second submarine an' taken five prisoners. We'd picked 'em out o' the drink an' taken them back to port wi' us, which were more like savin' their lives than takin' prisoners, but there you are, that's what they called it, you see. An' the very day we set out from port again, we was hit. It were a grey old day, cold an' kind o' spiteful, wi' a wind on our quarter which cut into you like a perishin' knife. We'd gone out again without bein' renamed, but we planned to do it ourselves as soon as we could – we had paint aboard – and were discussin' what name we'd choose this time when the skipper hollered us. We raced up on deck, me an' me pal Paddy, thinkin' about the prize money if the truth were told, for they paid us a thousand pounds a crew for a sunk submarine, an' we'd been lucky so far.

'The bloomin' U-boat was on the surface, chuggin' along as innocent as though no one on board had eyes in their heads, but by 'eck, she was well armed. Someone said after that she had a four-inch gun trained on us, but we didn't know that at the time, acourse. So we crept across the water, feelin' mighty clever, hopin' to get in range afore she noticed us. Only all of a sudden there was a dreadful screamin' noise an' a splinterin', tearin' sort o' crash, an' we realised she *had* seen us, an' though she were still out o' range o' our twelve-pounder, we were within range o' her guns.

'After that, all hell let loose on board the *Mabs & Lucy*. Our gunners got our little ole pop gun trained, but our shells were fallin' well short an' the skipper he screamed out: "Get closer, fellers, or turn tail. No use sittin' here whilst they blow us to matchwood!"

'We turned tail, or tried to, but they were comin' nearer to us now, an' comin' fast, what was more.

They could see we weren't a match for 'em, I dare say, an' they must have realised by our actions that we was armed, but not with a sufficiently high-calibre weapon to reach 'em. I were standin' by the skipper at the wheel, an' so were Paddy when the submarine started approachin' an' just as skip give the order to skedaddle a shot carried away our mast an' mains'l, an' the skipper told me to go below an' bring up his sealed orders. We had to scuttle 'em, we all knew that, if there were any danger of 'em fallin' into enemy hands, so I hurried, you can guess, an' I heard him tell Paddy to fetch a pigeon. We kept a couple o' birds in wicker cages down below when the weather was bad an' on deck when it were good . . . they were homin' birds, see?

'Well, as I come up the companionway I heard another shot strike an' saw the superstructure go . . . and just as I got out onto the deck half of it were blown away and one o' the gunners – Eversley his name was – staggered an' went down on one knee. He'd been hit through the shoulder it turned out later.

'"Give us the papers," Skip said, and snatched the handle off the winch, roped the envelope to it, an' handed it back to me. "Chuck that over the side," he said. "An' see it goes to the bottom."

'I ran over to the starboard side of the ship, which was a task in itself, since it were higher out o' the water than the port side, dropped the winch handle an' its burden over the rail, an' saw it go straight down. Then I went back, tellin' the skipper that it had gone all right an' tight.

'"The poor ole *Git Going*'ll soon be the *Git Gone*. She won't be afloat herself much longer," one of the deckies said in a quiet, matter-of-fact sort o' voice. "Are you goin' to get the boat out, Skip?"

'It weren't a big boat, because it didn't do to change your appearance overmuch, but it would hold all eight of us. The skipper looked round, and just then up come Paddy, wi' both pigeons. "I t'ought we'd better let the pair of 'em go, Skip," says he. "The first one might get picked off by some sharpshooter on the sub. If we send the same message wi' the pair of em . . ."

'Course, I knew it were really because we'd treated them birds like pets, Paddy an' me as well as the rest o' the crew, an' there didn't seem much point in lettin' one of 'em drown for no good reason, but the skipper never said nothin', 'cos he were writing a message on one of them little thin cigarette papers – you know the kind of thing. When he'd finished – it just give our position an' said the poor old *Get Going* was sinkin' an' we'd an injured man aboard – he told Paddy to let both pigeons go just as the other fellers released the boat an' it hit the water wi' a considerable smack and the old man . . . I mean the skipper, o' course . . . told us to jump quick, 'cos the trawler wouldn't last more'n a minute or two.

'Well, I know I jumped, but just as I did another shell came screamin' through the air an' holed the ship below the water line an' down she went, quick as quick, so my jump went all anyhow, an' plump, I hit the water an' went gugglin' down. I panicked then, tried to lash out wi' me legs an' arms, came up into air for one second and then felt something strike me a hard blow on the back o' the head.'

'Cor, Skip, then you din't swim?' Jimmy said, astonished. Coming from a city on the waterfront, he had been encouraged to learn to swim by his parents and, whilst they were alive, had gone to the baths in Margaret Street whenever he had a few pennies to spare.

But Abel looked astonished and slightly shocked. 'Swim? No fisherman ever swims,' he said reproachfully. 'We don't intend to git into the bloody sea, young feller-me-lad, we intend to stay on the surface. Which, bar that one accident, I done before an' since.'

'My Dad taught me to swim when I were six,' Jimmy said. 'He thought all young fellers should be able to swim. Liverpool's a port, same as Fleetwood, so I thought . . .'

'Well, we does things different up here,' Abel assured him. 'But the point is, I were hit on the head an' as good as a goner, an' you promised not to interrupt no more.'

'Sorry,' Jimmy said contritely. 'Go on, Skipper.'

'Well, I don't 'member much else, only that I came round to find I were floatin' in the sea wi' me head held up on something, and someone was tellin' me to keep still an' trust him. I do believe I thought it were the Angel Gabriel himself, or some such, because I did just as I was told an' never struggled nor shouted out, an' presently I heard other voices and my shoulder bumped against something, an' it were the boat from the *Get Going*, wi' all the other fellers aboard her, 'cept for me an' Paddy. It were Paddy who'd dived in an' hauled me out o' Davy Jones's locker and dragged me to the boat, an' once we was alongside the other fellers helped my good friend and myself aboard. An' that's why I goes into the quay in one o' the sea loughs off the Connemara coast, an' has a word or two wi' old Paddy an' refills me water tanks there.'

Abel tamped down his pipe and began smoking once again, eyeing Jimmy ruminatively through the thin veil of blue smoke that surrounded him. Jimmy grinned. 'You can't leave me high an' dry there, Skip,' he objected. 'What happened to you all? Did the pigeon get through? Was you captured by the submarine? What about the mate's wounded shoulder? You've only told me half the story.'

'Oh, so you're interested in war stories, eh? Well, the submarine didn't want us, not without no fish, so they just turned away . . . but they took a couple o' shots at the boat, only I reckon it were too small a target an' the shots just whistled by over our heads. We sat in the bilges, me wi' Paddy's jacket round me, for they'd stripped off my soaking clothes an' rubbed me as dry as they could wi' the skipper's pea-jacket, an' we watched the pigeons. Fool birds! They just circled round for a bit, an' kept trying to land amongst us, only we drove 'em off – we had to, o' course – an' all of a sudden, like, they set out towards the English coast, flyin' fast an' lookin' like angels to us. They'd go home to their loft, see, an' the feller that owned 'em would see the message strapped to its leg an' get it to the navy as quick as he could.

'Then we settled down as best we could to pass the night. The fellers took turns at the oars, but as it got colder, young Eversley got hotter, an' he began to talk an' jabber, an' truth to tell he weren't makin' no manner o' sense. He were delirious, talkin' to fellers that weren't there an' throwin' himself around an' then screamin' out when he knocked the bullet wound. By the time day dawned we were real worried about him. The rest of us were awright; we'd got a barrel of water an' some ship's biscuits stowed away in the stern an' we shared some of the food round an' had a cup o' water each. Some of 'em leaned over the side an' washed their faces an' hands in sea water, but I didn't. I'd seen enough o' sea water for the time, I told 'em. But the gunner looked really sick an' though we hoped we'd run into the fleet somewhere – for we'd all left Lowestoft together, four or five of us, an' there were a deal more'n that fishin' somewhere on the banks – we weren't lucky. An' presently a bank o' fog came rollin' up an' the skipper said we'd got no choice. He'd have to dig the bullet out o' Eversley or else we'd lose him. He asked the other two gunners whether they fancied the job – they were regular navy, see, not exactly under the skipper's command, though of course they were on board the trawler – an' they told him to go ahead, so when it was really light he an' myself took a good, strong hold o' Eversley and took his shirt off an' began.

'One of the lads had a hip flask full of rum, an' though I dare say he didn't much like doin' it, the skipper an' me we held the Eversley boy down an' Paddy poured rum into him. We knew it were bad for the fever, but we didn't know what else to do. Eversley were a strong young chap, he could have throwed himself over the side . . . so anyway, we got rum into him until he stopped shoutin', an' then our skipper dug the bullet out wi' his gutting knife, then bound the wound up wi' some lengths o' Eversley's shirt-tail.' Abel shuddered briefly. 'Skip done the right thing, they told him so when we got the poor young feller ashore, but it's not something I'd like to have to do, I tell you straight.'

'And the pigeon? Did it get back to its loft, or did you run into the fleet, or . . .?' Jimmy began, only to be impatiently hushed.

'I'm tellin' you, aren't I? Both pigeons got back to their loft, an' the feller what owned 'em read the message an' took it straight to the naval commander at the port. An' they sent out a frigate to bring us in, an' a couple o' days later they picked us up, not all that far from where we'd first taken to the boat.'

'I bet you were glad to see 'em,' Jimmy said fervently. 'I bet young Eversley were, an' all. Did he get well again, Skip?'

'Oh aye, he recovered, but he left the navy. He had a stiff arm afterwards, you see. I believe he took an office job, an' did well. Come to that, we all did awright. I bought the *Maid Margery* wi' my prize money an' a bit I'd put by, as I told you, an' Paddy went back to Ireland an' bought himself a little ole farm. Done well, too, has Paddy. Married wi' two daughters an' three sons . . .' He chuckled. 'Oh aye, an' his wife's the prettiest young 'oman I ever did see.'

'There's a lot of Irish in Liverpool,' Jimmy said reminiscently. 'Me bezzie were a girl, name of Elsie Taylor. She's got Irish in her, same's most of us.'

'Oh aye?' Abel's grizzled eyebrows rose and his eyes twinkled down at Jimmy. 'Sweet on her, are you? Goin' to mek her the happiest woman on earth one o' these days?'

'What, marry her?' Jimmy asked, wrinkling his nose at the repulsive thought. 'Not me, Skipper, I ain't a-goin' that way, I'll not get weighed down wi' a woman to keep an' then a parcel o' kids. No, I shall be like you, an' skipper me own trawler. Or mebbe I'll be like . . . like someone else I know, an' have a big fish an' chip shop, an' lots of workers an' heaps an' heaps o' customers.'

'That's what you say now,' Luke said, coming over to where the two of them were sitting on the thwarts watching the sun sinking slowly in the west. 'But you've not got a mother to cook your meals an' wash your clothes, who'll do it better – or cheaper – than a wife? A bachelor may not have the responsibilities, but he don't get looked after an' fed an' cuddled o'

194

nights like a married chap does.'

'Nor he don't have the money to keep in comfort in his old age,' Abel said equably. 'Oh ah, you married fellers have it good sometimes, but you can't beat a nice little nest-egg for to keep you in your old age. And how many wives let a feller save his money, eh? None as I know of.'

'Mine *insists* I save my money, she don't give me no choice,' Norm put in. 'She teks it off me soon's I'm paid an' I seldom see more'n a few bob till next payday. One of us is goin' to have a comfortable life when I'm too old for the sea . . . I just don't like to say which one.'

'You're henpecked,' Abel said, making Jimmy go off into a squeal of laughter. 'You should stow your money away an' let her have just a little at a time, so's she has to ask. As it is, you're the one who earns the money an' the one who has to ask, an' all.'

'I don't see why he's grumblin',' Luke said. 'You always have your glass o' stout an' your pint o' shrimps when we goes out together – an' some change to jingle in your pocket.'

'Oh aye, but that's because I put me wages in me right-hand pocket an' me bit o' cash for jollies in me left-hand one, an' she's not discovered it, yet,' Norm said dolefully. 'Don't you go tellin' on me, young Jimmy – and no more gigglin' over me misfortunes, either.'

'It's about time you did some work, an' cooked a meal,' Abel interrupted. 'Go on down to the cabin, boy, an' cut up that loaf. We'll fry some of the mackerel we caught this afternoon. You'll be givin' Sammy a break, which he could do with, being over a hundred years old like he claims. Then when that's done you can sling your hammock. It'll be a long day tomorrer.'

# Chapter Six

Jimmy was on deck, coiling rope, when he noticed the fleet of little boats. One minute, he thought, they were alone on the sea with the land looming, sweet-smelling and colourful, on their port bow. The next he happened to glance over the side and the sea was alive with small, black-tarred fishing boats, most of them with two men aboard, one of whom propelled the craft along with his heavy oars whilst the other heaved in the nets so that the small craft could make for the sheltering harbour. 'What's them?' he asked the mate, who was only a few feet away, heaving their own nets into a neatish pile, for they were too far inshore for legal fishing. 'Look, Luke, at all them cockleshells!'

Luke glance overboard. 'Inshore fishing fleet,' he said briefly. 'They've been after mackerel, I dare say. Well, they'll fish for anything they can get, poor blighters, to fill themselves. Ireland's not a rich country, nipper, so they have to work real hard just to keep their bellies full. That's why the skipper's so agin any English fishin' in the limit. What's more, though the rowin' boats are sturdy enough the others – the cockleshells you called 'em – are what they call curraghs, just made wi' canvas on a frame an' then tarred over. Light enough, I'll grant you, but not much use in a rough sea, an' they're real inshore craft. I know we're all grumblin' that the fish is being taken by too many people', an' sayin' that there won't be a

196

livin' for any of us at this rate, but at least we can get out after the fish. We dunna go up to Iceland or Greenland or other distant waters, but we could if we'd a mind. As 'tis, we go out to Porcupine Bank, whereas these fellers have to stay within sight of land. There's one sail boat comes out o' this part o' the world, he's a fellow from Galway what come into property in Connemara an' brung his boat with him when he moved up here, an' he can go further out an' get back faster. But 'tis a hard life and if you want to see fellers work, nipper, you keep your eyes skinned on them little cockleshells.'

The *Margery* was edging her way inshore now, under only one sail, with Abel at the tiller and Norm handling the sheets, for the wind was fitful, now gusting briefly, then failing them altogether, and what with the gathering of the little boats and the difficulty of sailing inshore with such an unhelpful breeze, everyone was concentrating hard on their own particular job. Jimmy, however, was not wanted, except as cook, so after another glance at their accompanying craft he went down the companion-way and began to look over his ingredients. They would not make harbour until the sun had set, so they would eat as soon as they had anchored; he had better be prepared.

However, it was not a difficult meal, tonight. On Abel's advice he had concentrated on a beautiful treacle duff, which would be preceded by corned-beef sandwiches. That meant no potatoes to peel or cabbage to prepare, and this was as well, since they were almost out of potatoes and completely out of cabbage. But Abel had explained that he always came out short on vegetables when he was bound for the Irish coast. 'Paddy charges me a fair price; a good deal less than I'd pay in Fleetwood,' he had explained. 'He likes the business and I like the fresh food. At this time o' year we might get some apples, too. I'm powerful fond of a nice apple pie.'

'If we'd come ashore earlier in the year we could mebbe have picked some blackberries,' Luke said wistfully. 'Or young Jimmy could have; I'm even fonder of blackberry an' apple pie than a plain apple one. Still an' all, we do awright.'

'If Paddy's wife has bottled any blackberries I'll buy some off her,' Abel said handsomely. 'Can't say fairer than that, can I?'

So now, in his miniature galley, Jimmy cut thick slices off one of the long loaves of bread which Mrs Totteridge had baked for them, spread margarine thinly on each slice and then hacked off good big wedges of corned beef. When the sandwiches were made he put a jar of pickled onions on the table and climbed the companionway. Up there, he leaned on the rail and began to study the small boats once more.

Most of the Irish craft had two occupants, usually a grown man and a stripling, and it did not take much watching for Jimmy to take Abel's point. These men worked incredibly hard. Their nets were hauled in hand over hand, without any help from winches or other mechanical aids, and their catches, from what he could see, were not large. In addition to their nets, several of the boats had one member or the other of the crew with a mackerel line over the side, which would be jerked inboard every so often and the fish removed one by one from the line.

One boat in particular, which was right under their bows as they made their slow way inshore, caught Jimmy's attention. A big man was at the oars but Jimmy could see the long, rakish mast and the lowered sail, and he guessed that it must be the boat owned by the Galway feller who had come up the coast and brought her with him, and because he knew a little more about it he stared with some interest. She was called the *Fair Aleen* and was crewed by a man in his mid forties, Jimmy supposed, aided by a very young boy. The boy wore canvas trousers rolled up above his knees and a long, flapping shirt covered in fish scales and by no means clean. But hard though all the men worked, this boy seemed determined to work harder than any. He fairly flew about the boat at his father's command – Jimmy assumed them to be father and son – and although so small he was wiry and tough, taking his turn at the oars when the older man wanted partially to pull in the net to see what sort of catch they had made and manfully heaving at the clumsy, heavy oars as though anxious to prove that size was not everything.

As the boat fell behind them, Jimmy got an even better view of the boy and his cry of surprise brought Abel's head round.

'What's up, lad?' the skipper said quickly. 'I've not grazed a boat, have I? I've not run one down?'

'No, you're well clear . . . but Skipper, the boy in that boat – that one there, just falling astern of us – is a girl!'

'Nay, not in a fishing boat, lad,' Abel said, but he stood up as he spoke and craned his neck to see over the rail. 'They don't tek their women to sea . . . it'll be a young land wi' hair what needs a bit of a cut, like.'

'No, it's a girl – see her? She's got long black hair. It were tied back so I couldn't tell her from a feller from the front, but now she's more or less alongside . . . see, Skip?'

'Can't be a girl,' Luke said. He, too, came to the side

for a brief moment. 'Nay, lad, it'll be a young feller what needs a haircut.'

'It's a girl,' Jimmy said obstinately, but the little boat was falling astern fast and now even Abel, who had been in the best position to confirm Jimmy's suspicions, was shaking his head. 'Nay, 'twon't be a girl, Jimmy. Fisherfolk the world over is superstitious, none more so than the Irish. It'll be nobbut a lad, come out wi' his da instead of an older brother. How's the supper comin' on? We'll be tied up at the quay in ten minutes an' I'm hungry as a hunter.'

'Supper's ready,' Jimmy said. He knew better than to argue when all three of the older men were against him, but that did not mean he thought himself mistaken. He had had the best view of all into the little boat, and the boy had been a girl, he was sure of it. I'll ask around when we get ashore, he told himself. I'm certain she's a girl. And then he remembered that Ireland must have a postal service and this would be a very good place, none better, to send off letters to Elsie and the Lumleys. He hated to think that either his best friend or his kindly employers might think him a thief, but he had not dared to write from Fleetwood; it would be too easy for the police to come up and drag him back to stand trial for a crime he had never committed. And since leaving Liverpool, he had either been at sea with Abel or ashore in Fleetwood itself. But now, far from that town, it would be perfectly possible to post letters home – and everyone would assume that he had fled to Ireland, which was as good as a foreign country since the king no longer ruled there.

Immensely elated by this thought, Jimmy took himself off to the cabin, removed a pad of writing paper and a stub of pencil from the table drawer and prepared to write. I'll start with Elsie, he told himself, licking the stub and tracing a wobbly *Dear Elsie*, on its clean surface. Then I'll do the Lumleys. And when we get ashore I'll cadge a few pennies from Abel as an advance on my wages, and post them as soon as can be.

It was fortunate, perhaps, that by the time they had made their way cautiously through the inshore fishing fleet and tied up at the quayside, darkness had fallen and Abel decided that it was too late for paying calls. 'We'll have us some breakfast tomorrer, an' then we'll go visitin',' he decreed and they were happy enough to obey, particularly Jimmy, who needed to finish his letters.

They were not easy letters to write, either. He wanted to tell Elsie and the Lumleys that he was safe and well, and that he had not touched a penny of the missing money, but of course they knew that, because he had been with them. No, his aunt had been trying to make the scuffers believe that he had colluded with a gang, giving them the information that had led to the break-ins and then sharing in the goodies which had resulted. And a letter saying all this was terribly complicated. And he would have to tell them that he had overheard his aunt's words, and because the wallet had been found in the boys' room he had a strong suspicion that one of his cousins, probably Edwin, had been involved.

Only that was clat-telling in a big way, because he had absolutely no proof, and yet he might get Edwin into as much trouble as his aunt had tried to make for him. So he sat at the cabin table with the writing paper in front of him – whilst all around him the men played card games, wrote letters home and chatted –

and agonised over his letters. It would be easier to come clean with Elsie, he decided in the end, so he wrote her a long, rambling letter in which he told her what he had overheard his aunt saying and gave it as his opinion that one of his cousins must have planted the wallet.

The letter to the Lumleys, in the end, was far simpler.

*Dear Mr and Mrs Lumley and All* [he wrote].

*You must of wondered why I ran off, and I only hope none of you thought it were a sign of guilt, because it were not. I heard my aunt telling the police she'd found something of yours hid away under my bed, so I ran off. But I never put it there, and I never told anyone we was off to Blackpool, though my eldest cousin might have guessed. You see, he brought home a pork dinner and when they were talking about I said I might not be there, since a pal and meself was off to Seaforth for a day out. I thought Frank seemed not to believe me, but I might of been wrong. I am truly sorry if anything I said caused the break-ins, but it were not me, honest.*

*One day I will come back when it is all settled and the thieves found and I hope then you may forgive me for running, which seems a daft sort of thing to do now.*

*Your friend Jimmy.*

Once the letters were written Jimmy put them in two small blue envelopes, addressed them carefully and stuck them on the table with the rest of the mail. No one commented except for Abel, when he asked Jimmy if he'd like to post the letters whilst he was ashore. 'Yes, please,' Jimmy said at once. 'I've – I've just been tellin' me pals wharra good time I'm havin'.' He hoped that this would stop any enquiries, but he soon realised he need not have bothered. All the men knew he hailed from Liverpool, and took it for granted that he had been writing regularly to his friends and relatives there. Not once had Abel or his wife asked an inquisitive question as to why Jimmy had suddenly turned up in their midst; they simply accepted him as a useful lad willing to work for his living. Which is about right, Jimmy told himself, getting into his hammock that night. And one of these days I'll go back to Liverpool, to Kennedy Court, and ask Elsie what happened about the Lumleys' break-ins and whether it would be safe to come home.

Lying in his hammock, however, just rocking in the slight swell which slapped gently against the quayside, it occurred to Jimmy that there was no need for him to go back to Liverpool ever, if he did not wish to do so. He liked Fleetwood, he loved his job and could see no reason ever to return to the city, though he would be a deal more comfortable, he realised, if he knew that the police were not looking for him. Just before he slept he tried to remember his job at the fish and chip restaurant, and his life in the court. The job had been all right, though there have been quite longish spells of boredom, when he had been alone in the vegetable kitchen, peeling and slicing mound after mound of potatoes. But life in his aunt's home had been pretty dreadful, really. No, he definitely preferred the fishing fleet and old Mrs Totteridge to anything that he had known whilst at Kennedy Court. And with this comforting thought in his mind he slept at last.

Morning dawned cold but bright, with the sun climbing over the low hills to the east and pouring in through the small window of the cabin as Jimmy set out breakfast. It was bread and jam, strong tea and a hard-boiled egg each. The eggs, Sammy told them, were the last they had.

'Tomorrer we'll have fresh eggs,' Abel said. 'If the Sullivan hens is layin', that is. But winter's not upon us yet, not judging by the warmth of that sun on my back. Want to come up to the farm wi' me, Jimmy?'

'Yes, please,' Jimmy said at once. 'Will you want me for cartin' water first, though, Luke?'

Luke and Norm grinned at each other. 'We've managed in the past, we can manage today I reckon,' Luke said. 'You go up to the farm – you'll be cartin' spuds an' cabbage, that's enough goodness for one day.'

'Right. Will I post all the letters, then?'

'Aye, might as well,' Luke said. He always wrote to his wife when they made a landfall; he had told Jimmy so the previous evening.

'Is there a shop here?' Jimmy asked. 'I'd like some more peppermints.'

There was a guffaw from the men. 'Shop? There's not even a pub, me boy, which is why Abel lets us put in here,' Norm said. 'No danger o' the crew goin' off and gettin' drunk as newts. That's right, ain't it, Skipper?

'Oh sure,' Abel said, grinning. 'You'll not get your mints here, young 'un. Unless you want to foot it to Clifden, that is. Clifden's a grand town, you'll find all you need there.'

'I don't suppose there'll be time,' Jimmy said ruefully. 'You'll take on water and veggies and go, won't you?'

'Oh aye, but it teks the best part o' the day, you'll find,' Abel told him. He finished the food on his plate and slammed down his knife and fork, drained his mug and put that down too. 'Who's on clearin' and washin' up today?'

'Jimmy,' Luke said, straight-faced. 'Luke an' me'll start gettin water.'

So Jimmy clattered the cutlery, tin plates and mugs into the bowl, poured boiling water from the kettle onto them, rubbed everything clean with the dish-cloth and bundled them back onto the table. Then he dried them quickly with the piece of towelling kept for the purpose and got himself up on deck. Abel was leaning against the rail, smoking his pipe. He turned as Jimmy scrambled up the companionway. 'Ready, young 'un?' he asked. 'Right; then here we go.'

The pair of them descended on to the quay and Abel led the way along it and then up a short lane and onto an area of rough grass, gorse and heather, upon which a couple of donkeys and a good few geese were grazing. Jimmy, looking around him, saw that to his left were a number of thatched and white-washed cob cottages. He noticed that they had bright gingham curtains at the windows and that the nearest one had a geranium plant, still bravely flaunting its scarlet flowers, in the middle of the window-sill – and saw, vaguely, a face, framed with black hair, the eyes wide and dark, looking out at them.

'Who lives there, Skip?' Jimmy asked curiously, indicating the nearest cottage. 'Do you know any of 'em? Only someone's a-peekin' round the curtain at us.'

'Them's fishermen's cottage,' Abel said, still puffing his pipe and clenching it between his teeth in order to answer so that his voice came out sounding slightly odd. 'The fellers we saw fishin' last night mostly lives around here. But it's a small place an' they don't have many visitors, I reckon. It's just curiosity, boy; just curiosity.'

'Yes, I suppose . . . only it looks a bit familiar, sort of . . . a bit like someone I've seen before,' Jimmy muttered. 'Take a squint, Skipper.'

But when Abel swung round the face promptly disappeared, though the gingham curtain swung for a moment from the speed of that departure.

'It'll be one o' the fellers we saw last night,' Abel said. 'They would look familiar to you, seein' as how you'd only just set eyes on 'em. Come on, lad, we goes straight across here an' up that thar lane . . . see it? Atween banks wi' hazel trees atop it?'

'Yup,' Jimmy said. 'Skip, it wouldn't surprise me if it were that gal I saw . . . you know, the fellers said it must be a boy wi' longish hair only I were certain-sure it were a female.'

'Well, if so perhaps she'll show herself, prove you right,' Abel said good-naturedly. 'Only the fellers will say it'll be her brother you saw . . . you know them. Come on, best foot foremost.'

He strode off across the rough grass and Jimmy had no choice but to follow, though he kept glancing back as he walked. I'm sure it was that blamed gal, he was saying to himself. Just like a gal to peek out an' then dodge back – but I'll find her before we leave this place an' then the fellers will have to admit she exists.

But he said nothing more and began, as he walked, to glance about him. Before him, the hills were clothed in the whitening grass of autumn and the perennial gorse and heather, but the lane, as they proceeded along it, was hedged with well-grown trees and these were beginning to lose their autumn-tinted leaves. As they walked they passed fields and meadows, too, cultivated for the most part though

206

the gold of gorse was still much in evidence, as were the little streams which came rushing and chuckling down the hills towards the sea. Jimmy found himself walking as quietly as he could, almost tiptoeing, because you could have heard a pin drop and he found he did not want to break the silence. Not that it was silence, not really. Birds sang and twittered, a cock crowed loudly and he could hear animal noises which, he realised, he had never actually heard before, yet nevertheless recognised. A cow lowed, making the very 'moo-oo' noise which had been written in one of his early primers, and a sheep baaed after its lambs. Behind them, someone was cutting wood and the wind stirred the leaves of the autumn trees to a soft rustling.

'Ain't it quiet, though,' Jimmy ventured as they walked. 'I dunno as I'd feel very easy, livin' where there ain't no sounds.'

'You don't find the sea quiet, do you?' Abel enquired. 'You've never complained aboard the *Margery*.'

'There's always noise at sea,' Jimmy pointed out. 'There's other fellers shoutin', one to the other, and the creakin' of the riggin', and the sound of the wind in the sheets. And there's the waves, 'o course. They make a deal of noise.'

'I reckon, if you lived in the country, you'd hear country noises soon enough and wouldn't think it that quiet,' Abel told him. 'Here's the lane – not far to go now.'

It was a good walk up the lane, however, to the Sullivan's farm, which was reached by going through a five-barred gate and up a dusty track across more of the rough, tussocky grass and heather where several wicked-eyed goats grazed and more geese set up a honking and a hissing at the sight of them. 'Tek no notice,' Abel hissed out of the corner of his mouth. He looked, Jimmy noticed, rather red about the gills, as if he had suffered from the geese in the past. 'Just keep walkin', an' kick out good an' hard if you feels . . . ouch! Why, you snakey bastard you . . .'

The largest goose had marched forward like the captain of a fighting force – which, it seemed, he was – and had pecked with considerable force at Abel's canvas trousers, and judging by the way Abel swore and bounded forward, the peck had not stopped at the canvas, either.

Abel turned, but too slowly; the goose had moved out of range and now it lowered its head to within an inch or so of the ground and began to advance once more, hissing like a kettle on the boil as it came. Jimmy took a swipe at it and the goose promptly whacked at him with its wing, then a slightly smaller goose came towards him, and another and another, and he found himself attacked on all fronts.

'I said kick, young feller, not smack it's bleedin' wrist,' Abel snarled, kicking out with his seaboots but making sure, Jimmy noticed, that he was nowhere near the geese when he did so. 'Oh gawd, here come the dawgs!'

The dogs rushed down on them, snarling and threatening, but at least they succeeded in scattering the geese, Jimmy was glad to see. He said, 'Good dog then, good old feller,' but kept his hands cautiously in his pockets – this little outing was turning out to be more like an offensive into enemy territory than a marketing expedition.

However, Abel was being attacked by a large black-and-white animal with its tail going like a windmill and its huge ears flapping wildly, and

Jimmy was about to go to the rescue – or so he told himself – when he realised that this was friendship on both sides. And the silence, which he had found so uncanny, had disappeared with the presence of the dogs and the geese, which was one good thing, for the dog which was making much of Abel was doing so to the accompaniment of little yelps and whines of pleased recognition.

'Well, if it ain't Whiskey, me old pal Whiskey,' Abel was saying trying to hold the dog off and ruffling its ears affectionately. 'Now you tell your pals it's only old Abel and perhaps we'll be able to git up to the farm all in one piece.' He turned to Jimmy. 'Whiskey's me pal Paddy's best sheepdog, they ain't usually far apart so . . . Paddy, call your ole feller off before he licks me to a jelly an' terrifies me new deckie-cook into next week.'

Jimmy turned and saw a middle-aged man, with a round, ruddy face, bright blue eyes creased at the corners from constantly gazing into the sun and wind, and hay-coloured hair, standing just beyond the circle of the excited dogs. 'Sure an ould Whiskey wouldn't hort a flea, young feller,' the man said in a curiously high, softly accented voice. 'Come on, you dogs, show some manners will ye when I've pals a-visitin'.' The dogs immediately drew off, until they were in a half-circle of bright eyes and lolling tongues. Abruptly, they no longer resembled a wolf pack but merely looked like household pets. Paddy Sullivan grinned all round, then held out a hand the size of a shovel. ''Tis grand to see ye, Abel, grand! An' whose the young feller-me-lad, eh? Any friend of the skipper's is a friend of mine, young man, so you're welcome here. What do they call ye?'

'Jimmy. Jimmy Ruddock, Mr Sullivan,' Jimmy said.

He liked the look of this bluff, friendly man who still seemed more like a seaman than a farmer to him. 'Your dogs scared me, but not as much as your geese.'

'Oh, the geese won't do you much harm, 'tis the old gander what'll have a bite out o' ye if he feels in the mood,' Mr Sullivan said, indicating the largest of the geese. 'That thar's the father of all me goslings an' the husband of all me geese, so you can't blame him if he gets a trifle hot-tempered from time to time. Imagine yourself wit' seventeen wives, young feller, an' I'm sure you'd feel like takin' a chunk out of anyone handy. But they're grand watchdogs, geese . . . though as you can see I've plenty dogs, an' all. Now let's be makin' for the house. Biddy always puts the kettle on an' gets out a bottle of the good stuff as soon as we see the old *Margery* hovin' to down by the quay.'

'And I dare say one o' your lads gets up to the potato patch?' Abel enquired hopefully as the three of them strode along the track towards the house, which Jimmy could now see clearly ahead of them. It was thatched and whitewashed like the cottages down by the quay but it had an upper floor; bedrooms looked out of the thatch like bright, surprised eyes and a late rose climbed the small front porch and spilled frilled pink flowers over the green-painted front door. 'An' another goes to dig cabbage? For I've brung the sacks up, all ready.' He indicated the pile of sacks beneath his arm. 'An' some extry, in case you're in need of 'em. Only Jimmy can fetch 'em down to the quay this time, whiles you an' meself talk over old times.'

'Your lad an' mine can take the donkey cart, so they can,' Mr Sullivan said. 'But come in, come in . . . here's me lovely Bridget, an' hasn't she put the kettle on just as I said, an' got out a little jug of somethin' rare an' special?'

Bridget was plump, dark-skinned, smiling. She wore wooden clogs, a dark-blue homespun dress and a spotless white apron, and her eyes rested on Abel with affection and on Jimmy with kindly curiosity.

'The top o' the mornin' to ye, Mr Totteridge,' she said in a warm, singsong voice. 'And to your young friend.'

'This is Jimmy, Mr Totteridge's deckie-cook,' her husband said. 'He's come for the spuds an' the cabbage, so's me an' Abel here can have a bit of a crack an' a taste o' your poteen. Where's Seamus? An' . . .?'

'Where d'you t'ink?' his wife said, smiling at him. 'They're after liftin' the spuds an' cuttin' the cabbages, so they are. And our little Maria's took a basket round the hedges, findin' up any hens what's layin' astray. Sure an' you'll have a grand basket of eggs to tek back wit' you to the *Margery*, so you will.'

'Good, good,' Mr Sullivan said. 'Will ye wet the tay now, Biddy? A nice hot cup o' tay's what the young feller will be wantin', afore he goes up to the field.'

'Thanks very much, Mr Sullivan, a cuppa tea would be real welcome,' Jimmy said politely. It was in his mind to cross-question the Sullivan young about the fishergirl, and he felt that it would be best done when the skipper was elsewhere and could not start to laugh at him for his fancies. 'Do . . . do I have to go through the geese an' the dogs to reach the field, though?'

Mr Sullivan laughed. 'I'll send Maria wit' you, Jimmy,' he said kindly. 'I see her makin' her way across the farmyard this minute, so I do. She's a good wee gorl, she'll take you there an' willin'.'

So Jimmy took the proffered cup of tea and the crumbly, treacly oatcake and was putting away both with a lively appetite, for the climb up the to farm had made him forget his earlier breakfast, when the back door opened and a child came into the room. She could not have been more than nine or ten, he thought, with short, dark hair and a pert little face. She stumped across to the kitchen table, accompanied by an indignant-looking speckled hen who had entered with her, clucking around her feet and looking anxiously up at her as though expecting to be fed. The child stood down her basket on the table, then lifted a bare and very dirty foot and kicked the speckled hen as though it had been a football, so that it soared, with an indignant squawk, out of the still open doorway. 'Get out, you,' Maria said crossly. 'She says how she's broody, Mammy, an' she bited me when I took her eggs out from under her. I don't like that hen, Mammy.'

'Well, if she's broody . . . yes, she must be,' Mrs Sullivan said as the hen, apparently undaunted by its abrupt and unplanned flight, came bustling into the kitchen once more. 'Just give her her eggs back, alanna, so she can sit on 'em and turn 'em into fluffy little chicks. No, don't kick her again, there's a dote.'

'But she bited me,' Maria said, holding out a small, dirty hand with several angry-looking peck-marks upon it. 'She'll do it again if she's not kicked.'

'Not if you take the eggses back to her nest, alanna,' Mrs Sullivan said. 'Now which are the ones you took from her, can ye tell me that?'

Jimmy looked into the basket, sure that Maria would be unable to do so, for though there were brown eggs, white eggs and speckeldy ones, they all looked very similar to him. But the child put her head on one side consideringly and picked up two of the eggs. 'These two was the ones I tooked up last,' she announced. 'They came from under her – they're still warm, Mammy. An' – an' the other one over there wit' the mucky footprint on it.'

'I see it,' Mrs Sullivan said. She took the egg indicated carefully out of the basket and picked up a handkerchief, which she knotted so that it formed a sort of carrying sling. 'There! Put the eggs in it and take 'em back to the nest on your way to the taty field wit' this young gentleman. Can ye do that, Maria?'

'Sure I can,' the girl said sturdily, taking the handkerchief and its burden. She glanced doubtfully around the room. 'Where's the young gentleman, Mammy? I only seed a boy wit' sailor's trousers.'

Everyone laughed and Mrs Sullivan said smilingly: 'This is a young gentleman, Maria. He's called Jimmy. It's just another way of sayin' boy really, but a more polite way. Now off wit' the pair of you and be sure you pick the best taties, Jimmy.'

'Good,' Maria said. 'C'mon, Jimmy.'

She led him out of the room with the hen fluttering at knee-height now and then, showing a spirit and determination which Jimmy had thought entirely lacking in poultry. He was certainly learning something today, however. Geese and ganders were to be approached with caution and even a motherly-looking hen could inflict damage if she thought her eggs were being misappropriated.

'Speckledy were on a nest in the barn,' Maria informed her companion as they crossed the farmyard. 'That one, there. See? The nest's in the hay, a right good spot she's chose, ould Speckledy. Can ye take a holt o' the eggs for me, an' pass 'em up when I's climbed the manger? Only that buddy hen'll likely have another go at me once I'm near her nest and Mammy would be cross if I dropped the nasty crittur's eggs.'

'I'll hold 'em,' Jimmy said, considerably amused. 'Or would you rather I put 'em back for you?'

Maria gave him a long, considering look as they crossed the barn floor, scattered with hay and straw, then nodded decisively. 'Yes. You'll not drop 'em,' she decided. 'Tell you what, I'll grab Speckledy whiles you put th'eggs in the nest. Awright?'

'Fine. So long as she doesn't bite you again,' Jimmy said gravely. 'I wouldn't want that to happen.'

Maria shrugged small shoulders, handed over the egg-filled handkerchief and pounced on the speckledy hen, which first squawked a protest and then began to peck vigorously at any part of her attacker she could reach, kicking out strongly as she did so with long, scaly yellow legs. Jimmy saw that her feet were clawed, but Maria merely tightened her hold and Jimmy hastily transferred the eggs from the handkerchief to the nest of hay in the manger and then, before Maria could squeeze the erring hen any tighter, he took the bird from the child – it pecked him as hard as it could – and plonked it down on the nest. 'There you are, you bad-tempered bird,' he said breathlessly. 'Don't you come at us again, you wicked old thing.'

But the bird immediately settled itself on the eggs, uttering little crooning noises in the back of its throat, and Maria turned away, taking his hand as she did so. 'She'll be fine now, so she will,' she said decidedly. 'She'll be sittin' now till the baby chicks come, an' I'll not come near her again when I'm collectin' eggs for me mammy. Now we'll go to the taty field, where me brothers is.'

As they walked back across the farmyard and then up a sloping meadow, Jimmy decided to ask Maria about the girl she had seen on the fishing boat. To his pleasure she did not so much as raise an eyebrow at him, but nodded firmly. 'Oh aye, that'll be Dympna, so it will. She works wit' her daddy, he's a grand man he is, an' she's as good in a fishin' boat as any feller, so she is. I heered me daddy say that,' she added. 'She's a Byrne, an' sure an' they're a strange family. There's a big boy, Nicky, he's away in Dublin, at a – a sort o' school, an' then there's Dymp, she's the one who helps her daddy, and Egan, he's still at school, only in the village, not in Dublin. He's me favourite, is Egan. I'm goin' to marry him when I's growed up, d'you know that? An' there's a daddy an' a mammy too. D'you know somethin', Jimmy? The mammy's English. She is so, honest to God.'

She stopped, apparently breathless, and Jimmy said: 'I'm English meself, Maria. And if there's two boys in the family, why does a girl go fishin'? It's hard work fishin' – I should know, because I'm on the *Margery*, with Mr Totteridge.'

'*I* don't know, do I – I'm only a child,' Maria said immediately. 'I don't know why they're a strange family, either. I've just heered peoples say so.'

'Would it be because the mammy's English?' Jimmy suggested as the two of them crossed a piece of wild ground where gorse bloomed and rocks thrust their blunt granite noses out of the tangled mass of heather underfoot. 'I don't suppose there are many English people in this village, are there?'

'Well, there's one, I telled you so,' Maria pointed out. 'See that hole? There's a coney warren here; if we'd brought Titus we could have mebbe cotched a coney.'

'Then I'm glad we didn't bring Titus,' Jimmy observed. He had no idea what a coney was but decided he had no desire to catch one. 'Where's the field, Maria?'

'There – see, t'rough that hedge? That's Kieran, that is, diggin' spuds like a machine, so he is. Come on, let's run.'

Back on the *Margery* that evening, as she beat her way out of the bay towards the fishing grounds, Jimmy mulled over what he had learned during the day: that living in the countryside, which he had only read about in books and had assumed to be idyllic, was not all it was cracked up to be. The silences, he felt, would get him down. And then there were the geese, the dogs and the odd way that a hen, that bird which he had previously believed to be the most placid of creatures, had turned into a fighting fury when her precious eggs had been taken, yet other hens seemed positively glad to get rid of the things.

Then there were the countryside dwellers. The Sullivans had all proved to be friendly and forthcoming, from old Mr Sullivan down to little Maria, but the same could not be said for that wretched fishergirl – and he had done his very best to be diplomatic and friendly, even though he had got off to a bad start. But was she forgiving? No, indeed!

The two of them had met on the quayside, when he had been unloading the sacks of potatoes from the donkey cart on to the *Margery*. He had not been aware of her at first in the small knot of people, but then one of the Sullivan boys – they were so alike he had difficulty in telling Kieran from Seamus or Seamus from Kieran – had called out: 'Are ye goin' to give us a hand now, Dympna? Wit' your muscles behind us sure an' won't we be rid of the taties in less t'an no time?'

Dympna! He had realised who it was at the sound

of the name and had swung round . . . to stare incredulously at the most beautiful girl he had ever seen. She was quite tall, only a couple of inches shorter than he, and slim with the sort of whipcord slimness he had never before seen in a girl. She wore a thick fisherman's jersey, very much too large for her, and a long, dark skirt with an uneven hem, which almost dragged on the ground, yet even so whenever she moved he could see how supple she was and graceful.

Her hair was black, almost blue-black, and fell in heavy, silken waves around her shoulders, whilst her eyes were such a dark blue that he thought them black too, at first. Her face was broad across the brow, tapering to a tiny, determined chin, and her mouth was firm, the scarlet of her lips in vivid contrast to her very white, clear skin.

For a moment he simply stared at her, unable to believe that a girl like that could work on a fishing boat. Then he moved away from the cart and his companions and said, stuttering a little: 'So you're the girl I saw on the fishing boat as we came through the fleet. Well, I never thought to see a gal heavin' at the net like you did, and bringin' the catch ashore.'

She did not seem to take this as a compliment, though that was how he had meant the words. She smiled at him, however, then brought her soft brows together in a frown. He saw that her eyebrows were very fine and dark, like birds' wings, and tilted, so that they gave her face a lively expression even in repose. 'Irish girls are stronger than English ones, I expect,' she said, and her voice was soft and clear, the brogue nowhere near as pronounced as that of little Maria Sullivan. 'We make nothing of hauling on a net, nothing at all at all.'

'Oh . . . but you're only half Irish, aren't you? Someone said you've an English mother,' Jimmy said, and saw the beautiful face change in an instant from vivacious interest to outrage. Poor Jimmy realised he must have said something to offend her, but had no idea what was wrong with saying that her mother was English, for had he not been told as much, scarce an hour ago? 'But I don't think I've ever seen a girl with the fleet before,' he finished lamely.

Dympna's eyes flashed and she ignored his last remark. 'Who told you I was only half Irish?' she demanded hotly. 'My mammy may have been English born, but she's lived here for nigh on twenty years, which makes her Irish in my eyes. As for meself, you won't find anyone, anywhere, who's prouder to call herself Irish than Dympna Byrne.'

'Oh, and you're very right, I'm proud to be from Liverpool meself,' Jimmy said hastily, much flustered. 'And anyway, most of us scousers is of Irish descent, you know. I'm sure my gran came from Ireland – her name was Eileen Kelly – and I believe my grandad had an Irish mother as well.'

'Irish descent, wit' an accent on you the like of which I've never heard before,' Dympna said, her cheeks flushing a delicate shade of rose. 'There's no doubt in my family that we're Irish, we don't have to look into the past to find our . . . heritage.'

'Oh! Well . . . I don't want to argue,' Jimmy said lamely. 'But would you be good enough to tell this feller just comin' ashore to pick up the spuds that it *was* you I saw with the fishin' fleet yesterday? Only the rest of the crew didn't believe me, they thought I'd gone soft in the head.'

Dympna had been standing near him as they talked but now she stepped back and laughed scornfully.

'Sure and if it's not just like an Englishman to expect a woman to do his dirty work for him,' she said. 'Tell 'em what you please, I'll not lower meself to so much as exchange the time o' day with 'em. Good-day to you.'

'Hey, hang on a mo,' Jimmy called as she turned away from the quay with her head held high and her nose in the air. 'You ain't got no call to . . .'

'Get on wit' your work, young man,' she called over her shoulder, as loftily as though she were the queen, Jimmy thought wrathfully. Sure, she was pretty as a picture, but that didn't give her the right to be so horrible to him.

But he had one more try, anyway, because she was so very pretty, and he had thought her sweet as well until he'd gone and offended her in some way. 'Awright, Dympna,' he said coaxingly. 'You don't have to say anything about being a fishergirl if you don't want. I 'spec' someone's teased you about all Connemara women havin' webbed feet, but . . .'

She turned back then, all scarlet cheeks and blazing eyes, looking so angry that Jimmy actually fell back a pace. 'Go home, English,' she hissed. 'And don't you dare mention webbed feet again, unless you want me to smack your silly turnip of a head for you.'

Jimmy stared. What on earth was the matter with the girl? What was wrong *now*? But he did not intend to take such rudeness lying down. 'I'm goin' home pretty soon, and I'll be glad to shake the dust of your dirty little country off me feet,' he said furiously. 'As for smackin' heads, if you carry on bein' as rude and nasty to everyone as you've been to me, someone'll knock your silly head right off your silly shoulders and serves you right.'

He hoped she had heard – he had shouted the last

219

words loudly enough. But it was clear that she did not intend to remain on the quayside any longer, swapping insults. She fairly flew across the cobbles, her black hair bouncing on her back as she ran back up the steps and was out of sight before he had come to the end of the sentence.

Much humiliated, Jimmy turned back to the cart. His brief exchange of words with the girl had taken only a few minutes and Kieran and Seamus were still unloading the sacks of potatoes and cabbage whilst Luke, rowing the little boat, was only half-way between the quay and the *Margery*. He felt tears of anger in his eyes and rubbed them furiously, then turned to take another sack off the cart and realised, from the incurious glance which one of the Sullivan boys gave him, that neither boy could have heard the humiliating exchange of insults between himself and their countrywoman. Well, that's one good thing, Jimmy Ruddock, he told himself as he began to carry a sack across the quay. At least they won't think me a poor sort o' feller to be worsted by a bleedin' girl.

So now, back on the *Margery*, with a big bowl of pancake mix awaiting his attention and bacon sizzling in the pan, he was able to look back on his first trip to Ireland with a certain amount of complacency. He had got on fine with the Sullivans, he had learned a thing or two about life in the country – namely, that he wouldn't like it – and apart from his encounter with that horrible Dympna girl, it had been a useful experience.

Jimmy picked up the plates, which had been heating on the side, and arranged them round the mess table, then began to scoop slices of well-browned bacon out of the pan onto the plates. He still did not really understand what he and Dympna had quarrelled about, except that she was overly sensitive about being half English. But facts is facts, he told himself, adding four or five, floury potatoes to each plate, and the fact is the girl's only half Irish whether she likes it or not.

'Come an' gerrit!' Sammy shouted through the hatch and the crew came thundering down into the cabin and attacked their food with all their usual gusto. But as he ate, as he cleared away and washed up after the meal, and as he got himself into his hammock later that night, he still felt vague regret over the sheer stupidity and unnecessariness of the quarrel. She was so beautiful – but beauty, he reminded himself, was only skin deep, and what was the good of looking as lovely as a fillum star if you'd a tongue like an asp and were so touchy no one dared talk to you?

So it was all the more annoying that, when at last he slept, he dreamed abut Dympna Byrne all the night long and she was a good deal sweeter to him in his dreams than she had been in real life. Which made it hard, next day, as he helped to cast out the trawl and, later, to heave it aboard once more, to tell himself firmly that she was just an ignorant Irish bog-trotter who needed a good hidin' and he pitied the man who married her because no one likes a scold.

I hope I never dream about the spiteful ole girl again, he told himself that night as he tumbled, exhausted, into his bunk, for they had half filled their fish holds with large fat cod. And for once his wish was granted, to his vague disappointment.

Dympna turned away from the boy who had tied up at the quay with the English fishing trawler, fairly boiling with annoyance. She had always thought the

English were a strange lot, for all her mammy was one of the them – perhaps because of it – but now she knew she was right. First off, the boy had called her half English, which was a rich old insult in itself, so it was, to one who considered herself Irish through and through. It made her feel like a poor mongrel dog, neither one thing nor the other, a real betwixt and between. And then, as if that wasn't bad enough, he had called her a fishergirl – a *fishergirl*, as though she were one of those Scottish floosies who followed the herring fleets, gutting the catch on the quayside so fast that the barrels were tight-packed in no time, and never losing a chance of screaming out a coarse joke or a crude phrase to amuse the men around them.

What was worse, he had seemed totally unaware that he was insulting her. And then to expect her to confirm to his wretched crewmates that she was the girl who worked on one of the fishing boats with her daddy! As if she had nothing better to do than hang about until his fellow fishermen came ashore. But there was no point in thinking about anyone so downright infuriating; she had best put him right out of her mind and concentrate on getting indoors before Mammy wanted to know why she had not come in with her father and started nagging at her the way she so often did.

But the cottage, when she reached it, was empty. She knew Micheál would have gone on up to the potato patch and would be digging a basketful for her mammy, and she guessed that Beatrice was in the dairy still. For the past couple of months Mrs Sullivan had been paying Beatrice to work there because she herself had so much extra to do in the autumn, when crops were harvested and fields ploughed up, that she could not manage all the dairy work herself.

Patiently, Beatrice trudged up to the farm as soon as she had done all her own chores, arriving there by midday. Then she would start the long process of pouring the tall cans full of milk into the big, shallow cream pans, bringing them to blood heat and skimming the cream off the top as it thickened. She then transferred the cream to the butter churn and patiently turned the handle until the cream began to become butter, when she added a judicious amount of salt. Finally, when the butter was made, she took it from the churn, rolled it into a long sausage shape, cut it into pound-weight pieces and patted them with the two carved butter pats until they were in oblongs, with the picture of a cow on one side and the legend *Sullivan's Best Butter* on the other.

Mrs Sullivan was generous, too. Many a misshapen pat of butter came their way now, and she often passed on oddments of clothing that might fit either Dympna or her mother, or a pair of trousers outgrown by Seamus or Kieran. In the summer she had given her helper four pullets and a young cockerel, and the pullets had actually begun to lay. The eggs were dark brown, small and very sweet, but Beatrice said that as the hens grew, so would their tiny eggs.

'I'll ask if I can have a borrow of one of her broodies and put a few eggs under, so we get ourselves some little chicks, come the spring,' Beatrice had said only the previous evening as the family sat round the newly kindled fire, for one did not light a fire in the autumn to burn turves all day when there was no one at home to sit by it. In winter it might be different, but right now it was lit by the first member of the family to get within doors. Sometimes it was Egan, but not tonight. He had probably been kept in again,

Dympna thought ruefully, knowing how her brother liked to chatter in class and how low an opinion of such behaviour was held by Mr O'Neill. She waited a few moments, but no one else arrived so she got the matches down from the mantel and after some rearranging of the neatly laid driftwood and turf she struck a match. A couple of tries later, the fire began to look as though it might live, after all.

When it was clearly going to keep burning she moved over to the window to see whether Egan was coming up from the schoolhouse and got an unpleasant shock. A tall, burly man was coming along the bit of a lane towards her with long strides, accompanied by that rude English boy – and he was staring at the cottage as though he'd the second sight and knew she was in the dark little room behind the greenish contorting glass. Crossly Dympna dodged out of sight, then went across to the piece of polished tin on the mantel and took it down to examine her reflection. Damn! She had a smear of wood-ash across one cheek and although she had taken off her cap she had not tidied her hair, which hung round her face in witchlocks, making her look disreputable, to say the least.

Still. Past experience told her that he would not have seen much, what with the glass and the dark interior and all. Just a quick glimpse of a face, perhaps, but he could not possibly have recognised her. Comforted by this, she went back to her fire, checked that it was burning steadily and transferred her attention to the rest of the room. Beatrice had got water in and cleaned round generally, but she had not laid the table nor done anything towards the evening meal, so Dympna got the plates and cutlery out and began to chop salt off the big block and to grind it with the back of the knife. If Micheál came in soon with the potatoes they could have the meal started before Beatrice got back.

But even as she worked, Dympna's annoyingly shallow mind – she told herself – kept returning to her encounter with the young fellow off the trawler. He had been rude, but so had she, and he had not, she thought, meant to be quite as rude as he had been. He had not, for instance, realised that she was extra-sensitive about her mother being English because Beatrice used the fact to make her daughter feel – oh, somehow foolish and inadequate, Dympna supposed.

But it was no use dwelling on what had happened. He had been rude and she had been rude too, and very likely they would never meet again, which was a happy thought to go to bed on. But presently, she knew, the boy would be passing across the green, this time with sacks of potatoes or cabbages to slow him down. She could, and probably should, go out then and apologise for her rudeness. But she would see the flicker of movement as he came down the lane, there was no need actually to peer out, so she went on with her work in the cottage and did not go to the window again even when Egan, dashing through the back door and slinging his bag of books onto the table, told her in ringing tones that she should go down to the harbour right now, so she should, for several English trawlers were in and sometimes the fellers aboard gave kids biscuits, or a handful of raisins. Or, which was better, they might let you go aboard and take a look at the living accommodation and the part of the trawler where the crew slung their hammocks.

'I know they're in; I saw them,' Dympna said briefly. 'You go, Egan. I'm getting supper.' She had no wish to apologise to *anyone* with her brother as audience.

Egan's eyebrows rose until they almost disappeared into his hairline. 'You're gettin' *supper*?' he said incredulously. 'And when's gettin' supper been more important than havin' a nose round an English trawler?'

'Ever since I grew up, which I did a year or more back, unlike some,' Dympna said icily. 'Go away, Egan, I've told you I'm busy and so I am indeed.'

'Oh, so you're the little English Miss today, are you?' Egan said nastily. 'Too grand for the likes o' me an' me pals, too grand . . .'

Dympna leaned across and flicked him with the piece of towelling they used to dry the crocks. The towel cracked like the mains'l in a gale, and Egan gave a roar and clapped a hand to his cheek, where a red mark testified to his sister's accuracy. 'Ouch, that hurt! Aren't you the nasty one, Dympna Byrne. Just you stay there till I give you one back.'

'You shouldn't be after hitting a girl,' Dympna told him smugly, but she withdrew strategically behind the old wooden rocking-chair which stood to the right of the hearth. 'Besides, you were very rude, so you were. And I'm warning you, if you come near me, Egan, you'll get another clack, for I'm a good marksman with this bit of towel and I don't mind having another go at you.'

'Do what you like, you English snob,' Egan squeaked. He had picked up the dishcloth and was aiming it at his sister's head. The cloth was still soaking wet from the breakfast dishes and inclined to be smelly, and Dympna, who had been holding the towel in the usual pre-flicking position, relaxed somewhat. She had no desire to find herself with a gob full of dishcloth.

'Wait on, Egan, you called names first, and if this is a proper fight we'd best . . . Ugh!'

The rag, impelled at speed, caught her full in the face, unfortunately with her mouth open. Egan gave a squeak of triumph and came hurtling round the chair whilst she was still disentangling herself from the missile. He grabbed her wrists and held them hard, and Dympna, having tried to kick him without success – the rocking-chair was very much in the way – decided that it would be prudent to give in. Egan might be only thirteen, but he was as tall as her and every bit as strong. Indeed, in the school holidays when he came with Micheál and herself to the fishing, she had an easy time, for Egan did all the hard work and did it willingly, furthermore.

'Pax, pax,' she said now, laughing. 'I shouldn't have flicked your face, Eggy, and it's sorry I am, but you did call me an English Miss and indeed, indeed I am no such thing.'

'Nor you are, Dymp,' Egan agreed, letting go her wrists. Like his father, he was a placid and good-tempered fellow, difficult to annoy. 'Well now, let's be gettin' this table set or the daddy will be back wit' the tatties and there'll be nothin' else done. Now will you be comin' down to the harbour wit' me when the supper's ready?'

'No, no, but I'll not stop you goin' with your pals,' Dympna said. 'Don't you waste time here, Eggy, you go off. I'll be quick as a flash, you see, and when I've done the tatties I'll most likely come down to the harbour, take a look around.'

'It's not fair to leave you to get on alone. You've been workin' on the boat all day whiles I was sittin' on me bum in school,' Egan said, but he glanced longingly towards the back door. 'What sort o' catch did you have?'

'Quite good; but there were a grosh of boats out, including the English fleet,' Dympna explained. 'Daddy cleaned and gutted earlier, so Mammy will have some fish to sell tomorrow. He saved us enough cod for Mammy to make a decent meal, though, so we shan't go hungry.'

'We'll never go hungry whiles there's a good spud in the ground,' Egan said a little gloomily. When times were hard and the fishing poor, potatoes were just about all they did get. Then he brightened. 'But we've had either fish or pork most nights, since Dermot went and you started to fish wit' Daddy,' he remembered brightening. 'Are you *sure* you'd as soon stay here, Dymp?'

'Sure I'm sure,' Dympna said patiently. 'Off with you, Egan.'

It was only after her brother had left that she remembered, with a shock, that she had intended to watch for the English boy so that she could go and apologise to him for her bad temper, earlier. And now she realised that she must have missed the feller, because she had been too busy fighting with Egan to keep a look-out.

She was still berating herself when her father passed the cottage windows and presently came round to the back door with half a sack of spuds, which he threw onto the wooden draining board. 'There! If you'll clean them for the pot, Dymp, I'll chop the greens an' put the fat in the pan. Mammy's almost finished up at the dairy; what a surprise for her to be sure that we'll have made the supper before she's over the threshold.'

Dympna tried to summon up some enthusiasm at the thought of surprising her mammy, but it was uphill work; she was still wanting to kick herself for missing the English boy. But then she told herself that she would go down to the harbour when the meal was over and possibly he would be hanging round the quay, the way boys did, and she could have a quiet word with him.

So she worked with a will and made no demur when Beatrice sent her down to the harbour to fetch Egan up for his supper. She ran all the way until she reached the slope from which she could see the quayside, then slowed to a walk, casting her eyes down and trying not to peer too obviously through her long lashes.

But she could have saved herself the bother. The *Maid Margery*, it seemed, had sailed.

# Chapter Seven

'November's no month for fishing, especially with
the weather turning nasty. I can scarce sell what fish
you catch now, folk eat enough fish later, when the
pork's all gone and the potatoes are running short.'
Beatrice glared at Micheál, who looked hangdog,
much to Dympna's annoyance. Why could her daddy
not stand up to her mammy, and tell her what she
knew very well already; that though fish did not sell
so well in November they salted down just fine, so
they did, and it might be the only thing a good few
people had to eat, barring the ever-present potatoes,
during the lean months when the weather was often
too bad for a foray, even into the relatively sheltered
waters of the bay.

'But later, the weather won't let us out at all,
alanna,' Micheál said almost pleadingly. 'And you
must know as well as I do meself that the November
mackerel, if we find a shoal, will be the best fishin' of
all. 'Tis a fine, oil-rich fish, the mackerel. Why, if we
have a good catch today you'll sell every mackerel an'
scarce go out o' the village, an' any white fish we
catch can be salted and eaten weeks from now, if you
an' Dympna here work hard, as I know you will.
What's more, salt fish sells well in the New Year, if
you've enough salted down to spare some to market.
Now don't go tellin' me not to sail, for that would be
bad luck indeed, so it would.'

Bad luck. That was fishermen's talk. Dympna had

heard her mother say the words a dozen times, in a scornful tone, but when you were at the mercy of wind and waves even the most sensible, down-to-earth man would probably think twice before failing to keep in with the gods of chance. According to others, her daddy was taking a risk in allowing her to sail with him, for many fishermen thought that a woman aboard a boat was bad luck. But so far, she had proved her worth. They had had good catches, the fish had sold well and the boat was in good condition thanks to Micheál's constant care, so after a year which had been more prosperous than most, the other men who sailed with the fleet no longer eyed her askance.

'I wouldn't want to put bad luck on you,' Beatrice said grudgingly. 'If you're set on taking the *Aleen* out, then . . .'

'It's me work, alanna,' Micheál said simply, getting his oilskins down from the hook on the back of the kitchen door. He had invested in some second-hand oilskins for himself and for Dympna after a particularly good catch a month back and she felt privileged every time she wore them, for most of the men made do with a couple of extra jerseys and a sack over the shoulders to keep off the worst of the rain. Not that it did; you got soaked both with rain and the constant salt spray, but with the oilskins it was a different story. Spray and rain simply slid off them, leaving you warm and dry beneath. 'An' a man has to do his work as you know right well. I'd not go – certainly I'd not take Dympna – if I didn't have to.'

Beatrice snorted and gave Dympna a chilly glance. She's jealous because I go out with Daddy and she cannot, Dympna thought, astonished. As though Daddy cares a jot for me when Mammy's around . . . no, that's not right, but he loves her so much and wants to be with her . . . why can't she see that?

'Oh, I'm sure you'll take good care of the girl,' Beatrice said, her voice heavy with sarcasm. 'So go then, if you must you must, you've got your oilskins, thanks be to God.'

'If you get any sharper you'll cut yourself,' Micheál said drily. 'We'll be off now. And if we find and there's a good few, we might be late back, so I've took the dark lantern.'

Dympna saw that her mother was about to start nagging about staying out late, so she made a great business of taking her own oilskins down off the door and picking up the bottles of cold tea and the thick slices of her mammy's home-made bread with fat bacon sandwiched between them. 'We'll be glad of the food if we're going out to the bay,' she observed, smiling at her mother. 'And we'll try to get home before dark. I hate being out in the dark, so I do.'

She waited, almost braced, for her mother to find something wrong with this remark, but instead Beatrice smiled at her, with something close to fondness in her eyes. 'There's a sensible girl,' she said in a softened tone. 'It's worry for the pair of you makes me seem cross. I . . . I look out at the water, and it's so wide and angry-looking, and I'm afraid. The sea's so big and deep. You're out there, fighting it, but I'm alone, imagining awful things. So do try to get in before dark.'

'We will, Mammy,' Dympna said when her father did not reply but continued to fold a mended net into a manageable burden. 'Wish us luck, now.'

'Oh . . . good luck, then,' Beatrice said resignedly. 'If it falls dark and you aren't back me and Egan will bring a lantern down to the quay.'

'T'anks, me darlin',' Micheál said, slinging the

bundle of net over one shoulder. He crossed the room in a couple of strides and gave his wife a kiss. 'See you tonight.'

It was cold in the boat. The wind had a bitter nip to it and very soon Dympna had pulled her red woollen cap as far down over her ears as it would reach, put her sou'wester on top of it and tied it tightly under her chin. She thought she probably looked odd, but what did it matter so long as she was warm and dry?

Not that she looked like being warm and dry for long. She and Micheál had set out with four other boats, but the water was choppy, the wind changeable and very soon the *Aleen* had left the other three behind, for Micheál had set the sails as soon as they were in deep water and had turned the *Aleen* to catch the wind just right, gusty though it was. The result was a voyage which resembled a race, with the sail stretched tight and puffed with wind, and the boat ploughing through the waves so fast that they were soon out of sight of the other boats. Micheál grinned at his daughter. 'Like it?' he shouted against the scream of water under the hull and the roar of the wind in the sail. 'We'll start out deep, an' if we don't find fairly easily, we'll keep castin' further and further inshore. Suit you?'

Dympna grinned back and held up a thumb to indicate satisfaction. Daddy knew she loved the way the lean black boat could tear through the seas, though it was not, she suspected, anywhere near as safe as the round, beetle-shaped craft favoured by most of the fleet. But her grand-daddy, who had crewed for a rich man on a private yacht when he was young, had built the *Aleen* for speed, and Micheál and

Dympna were proud of her and had long used her speed to get him out to the fishing grounds before his fellow fishermen.

When they were no longer in sight of land Micheál chose what he suspected would be a likely spot, brought the *Aleen* head to wind and started to cast out the net with its bobbing corks. Then he handed the rest of it to Dympna and brought the boat back into the wind, easing her gently ahead whilst Dympna continued to cast slowly over the side. When the net was cast Micheál brought the *Aleen* back up head to wind and lowered the mains'l. Then he sat back on the thwarts, picked up one of the bottles of cold tea and took a long draught. Dympna followed suit, for the voyage had been exhilarating – and tiring, too – and she was thirsty. There would be time, now, for talk, or conjecture, or idleness, until Micheál felt that the net had been out long enough to catch something and they began the slow – and hopefully heavy – task of hauling in.

'Wind's risin',' Micheál said after they had been sitting in companionable silence for twenty minutes or so. 'Gusty. I'm not over-fond of a tricksy wind.'

'Nor me,' Dympna said. 'Even in summer I like a steady wind.'

'Aye,' Micheál replied. There was a long pause, during which he fished a small clay pipe out of an inner pocket and an equally small amount of black shag which he smoked when outside the house. Beatrice was not a lover of tobacco; she said that the smells inside the cottage were powerful enough without adding burning weeds to the rich mix. 'Women don't like a gusty wind – your mammy's always curt in a gusty wind. I wonder why?'

'I hate having me hair blowed into me eyes,'

Dympna said, having thought it over. 'Mebbe Mammy's the same.'

There was another long pause. Micheál nodded and struck a match, holding it to the shag, which he had tamped firmly into the bowl of his clay pipe. It was an old pipe, smoke-blackened, and Dympna knew that it was replaceable; should it go overboard Micheál would be annoyed, but not upset. His cherished cherry-wood pipe, which he kept in one of the niches at the side of the fireplace, was a different matter. He would, she knew, be heart-broken if anything happened to that pipe, because Beatrice had bought it for him years ago, when Dympna had been a toddler and before Egan had been born.

'Women don't like their hair bein' mussed,' Micheál said in a musing tone. 'Aye, you're right there, alanna. Your mammy once got mad at me, when I mussed her hair . . . yes, I reckon she hates the old wind for meddlin', same as you does.'

'*You* mussed her hair, Daddy?' Dympna said, unable to keep the astonishment from her voice. 'What for? I wish my hair was barley-gold, like hers,' she added. 'Then I would get mad at the wind for blowing it all over me head all right.'

'Aye. It were after you were born . . . she was so scratchy-like wit' me that I lost me temper, so I did.' He puffed at his pipe, his eyes fixed on the tipping horizon but not seeing it at all, Dympna guessed. 'Oh aye, your daddy lost his temper, which mebbe I ought to ha' done a long time since. And – well, that was long ago,' he added rather guiltily. 'But it put me in mind of this mornin', so it did. Tellin' me not to take the boat out.'

Dympna fished a striped peppermint ball from her pocket and popped it into her mouth. It was an understood thing between them that whenever Micheál went in to town to buy himself some tobacco, he would get two ounces of peppermints of one sort of another for Dympna. It was only fair, he told her, that she should have something to suck whilst he smoked his pipe, and she had been happy to agree. After a few sucks, however, she wrinkled her brow. 'Mammy worries about the sea,' she said, almost apologetically. 'She once told me she loved it when she was young, but living by it day after day, she'd grown to hate and fear it.'

Micheál nodded. 'Aye. I 'member well when she came down to Salthill as a girl. Pretty as a picture she was, an' swam like a fish, so she did. I were a young feller then, mebbe twenty-five, twenty-six, an' your grand-daddy had told me over an' over that fishermen shouldn't go dippin' in an' out o' the sea like seals, else mebbe they'd need to do it for real. Well, when I talked to your mammy I told her why fishermen don't usually swim an' she t'ought it were just about the silliest t'ing she ever did hear. So I watched her, an' I watched the young fellers who came down to the beach for a swim, an' when they'd all gone I practised an' practised, which is why I'm the only strong swimmer in the fleet today.'

'Egan swims, Daddy,' Dympna pointed out. 'Most o' the young fellers do now.'

'Oh aye. When I said I were the only one I meant the only one o' my age or older who could swim. You swim a bit yourself, don't you, Dymp? I 'member tellin' your mammy I'd not have let you come to sea, only you swam an' Nick doesn't.'

'I'm not as good as Egan,' Dympna admitted. 'But I can get by, Daddy.' She wondered whether she should tell him that Nicholas swam a great deal

236

better than any of them, but decided it would not be tactful. He had learned late, to be sure, when he went to the big school in the town, but perhaps he had not mentioned the fact in Micheál's hearing, and since her father clearly believed Nick to be a non-swimmer it might be better to forget that she knew differently. 'Did Dermot swim, Daddy?'

'Oh aye, he swam. The t'ing is, Dymp, that when I were a kid it were school all term time, and at holidays you had some free time to be sure, but a lot of it was spent sellin' the fish your daddies caught or doin' messages for your mammy or cultivatin' your potato patch. We give the young 'uns more time to theirselves these days, which is very right an' proper. An' acourse my daddy – your grand-daddy – was often away, an' I was the eldest, so I were, which put a deal of weight on my shoulders one way an' another.'

'I see that,' Dympna nodded. 'Even now it's all shinty an' football in the winter, an' cricket in the summer, on the green. But Mr O'Neill says he'll teach anyone to swim who can't, which means giving up some of your time in the holidays or after school, and that's enough to make all the fellers and most of us girls decide to learn off our own bats.'

Micheál nodded and chewed. The fat bacon was good and the home-made bread flavoursome and satisfying, but the cold still bit and the constant rocking of the small boat, though it no longer made Dympna feel odd inside, did make her keep one hand on the thwarts to steady herself. The weight of the net, dragging against the water and, hopefully, getting heavier as it filled with fish, made the boat behave as if it were an anchor in the choppy sea, so every now and then even Micheál found himself grabbing for a handhold to steady himself by. Both of them had finished their first packets of food – Beatrice always made them two packets each – by the time the net had been in the water long enough, and Dympna wedged the creel with their food in below the thwarts and began to shuffle forward. She seated herself in the bows, ready for action when Micheál gave the word, but he was still stowing his own food, still thoughtfully chewing. It was unusual for Dympna to finish first so she guessed that her father was thinking deeply and, presently, he cleared his throat and spoke. 'This mornin', alanna. When your mammy told me not to get the boat out.'

'Yes?' Dympna said promptingly when the silence began to stretch.

'Aye, she were worried about us, the pair o' us,' Micheál admitted after more thought. 'She's mortal fond o' you, so she is.'

This was going a little too far. 'Well, she doesn't act fond, Daddy,' Dympna said.

'Wait on a minute, I'm . . . I'm t'inkin' how to tell you this.' There was another silence, then Micheál cleared his throat again. 'When Nick was beginnin' to learn his letters an' toddle about a wee way,' he began. 'I t'ought . . . I t'ought t'would be good to have another child. I telled your mammy I wanted another son an' . . . an' we had a bit quarrel, like. She had a bad time wit' Nick an' wasn't keen to go through that again.'

'Oh,' Dympna said rather dubiously. In her experience, most women had a hard time with their first child, often with the rest, as well. But this did not mean that they held back from producing more children. Mrs Sullivan had birthed eleven children, though only seven of them had survived, the O'Reagans had four girls and three boys and most of the children she had known in school had been members of large families. She glanced at her father; his face was looking a little red about the gills but determined. Plainly, whatever story he had commenced on he meant to finish it no matter how little he relished the telling of it. She looked hopefully at the net again; surely it was nearly time to begin to haul it in? But once Micheál got started on a story she knew from past experience that he would finish it come hell or high water and anyway, she was fascinated by what he was saying. 'Does it take some women like that, Daddy? Make them want no more children?'

'Aye, it does. Only . . . only I knew in me heart that it would do us all a power o' good to have a proper family – Nicky was in a fair way to bein' spiled rotten, atwixt us two – so I argued wit' your mammy, an' when she persisted . . . I gave her a little shake an' telled her the second babe would come easy, no trouble. And I were wrong. She had a hard time wit' you, just as she'd had wit' Nicky, an' sometimes I t'ink she holds it against you, just a tiddy bit, you know.'

'Really, Daddy?' Dympna breathed, forgetting to glance at the net in her fascination with this revelation. 'But it's still unfair, so it is, to take it out on me. You can't help how you're born.'

'True,' Micheál said. 'I t'ought you might find it easier to understand . . . just remember your Mammy loves you awright, she's just . . . just t'inkin' back.'

'I'll try,' Dympna said rather grudgingly. 'But I wish . . . I wish she didn't always pick on me.'

'Good,' Micheál said. He looked relieved and Dympna realised that he must have been waiting to tell her the story for some time now. Probably whenever Beatrice was particularly cross and unfair, she thought ruefully. But she had spoken no more than the truth when she had said Beatrice was being unfair. 'Now I t'ink it's time we hauled; I've a good feelin' about this catch, so I have.'

Dympna pulled on her canvas gloves, seized hold of the net and turned to grin at Micheál. 'I'm ready,' she declared. 'I'll start heaving when you tell me, Daddy.'

The catch was every bit as good as Micheál had hoped. Fish came up with almost every foot of net until the bottom boards were hidden beneath a squirming, kicking mass and Dympna's oilskins were covered with silvery scales.

'Not much point in stayin' out here no longer,' Micheál said with satisfaction, bundling the net under the stern thwarts and glancing up at the sky, which was darkening ominously. 'We'd best get back before the weather turns bad on us. We've been lucky today. Never push your luck, me old daddy used to say.'

So they turned the boat shorewards and despite the weight of the fish they had taken Micheál hoisted the mains'l and soon they were scudding homewards, with the light rain in their faces and thoughts of a good peat fire and a hot meal adding to the pleasure they felt in their catch.

The Byrnes had a good Christmas for the pre-festival fishing had been good and Micheál insisted that everyone should have a present. Nicholas came home and lorded it over them because he was no longer a first-year student but into his second year and doing well what was more. He had his own rooms in Dublin, a grosh of friends of both sexes and a great many fascinating books, some of which dealt with his work as a medical student and some he had bought for pleasure. His mother and father listened indulgently whilst he described the pranks natural to young men away from parental influence for the first time in their lives; Dympna and Egan listened enviously. Such goings-on! Such drinking and boasting and playing of tricks! Such placing of toilet articles upon steeples, such cheeking of teachers – only Nicholas did not call them teachers but lecturers – and such gargantuan meals served in the room of one young man or another whilst the rest crowded in and drank beer and sang very rude songs! And it appeared that the prettiest girls in Dublin, according the young Mr Byrne, wanting nothing more than to be in the company of the medical students.

Dympna expected her mother to be outraged by these cheerful and probably inaccurate descriptions, but Beatrice behaved like a young girl herself, giggling, blushing, telling Nicholas that he was dreadful, really he was, and that naturally young women would be attracted to him, but hoping devoutly that he would not allow himself to be led astray by any of them.

Despite his warm welcome and the presents he was given, however, which included a fine fountain pen, writing paper – not that he wrote home – and an embroidered waistcoat that Beatrice had made with her own hands, he did not stay home until the sixth of January to share the joys of Little Christmas with his loved ones. No indeed, for would not all Dublin be *en fête* and waiting for the life and soul of the party, the popular Nicholas Byrne, to return to lead their revels?

'I don't understand it at all at all,' Ruan Sullivan muttered to Dympna as the two of them were pushed out of the warm living-room into the chilly hallway so that the rest of the gathering might concoct a charade. Ruan was the same age as Nicholas and had been despatched by his father to learn estate management on a big estate not far from Dublin. The Sullivans' famous party, which was in full swing, had not been sufficient to tempt Nicholas to stay another day, but the rest of the Byrne family were there and greatly enjoying themselves. 'Where does your brother get the money, Dymp?' Ruan continued. 'I can't spend like he does and my daddy's a warm man, by local standards anyway.'

Dympna shrugged. The same thought had crossed her mind, but she had decided that her brother probably hung about on the fringes of a group of monied young men and that half his boast were just that – empty boasts. She said as much to Ruan, who looked doubtful. 'Maybe you're right,' he said slowly. 'But sure an' wasn't there a ring o' truth in some o' the t'ings he told us? All that drinking and womanising . . . he might have made that up, I suppose, but what about the parties? I spend time in Dublin meself and you don't get asked to that sort o' party unless you're pretty well-to-do yourself.'

'Well, Nicky isn't,' Dympna said, after some thought. 'And why go back if it isn't to parties and fun? Because we have such fun here, at home, over Little Christmas.'

'Sure we do,' Ruan said, dismissing Nicholas from his mind with an airy wave of the hand. 'Sure and haven't I got the prettiest girl in Ireland all to meself for five minutes and aren't I wastin' me valuable time?'

And with these words he put both arms round her, strained her to him, and kissed her very thoroughly and excitingly, making Dympna decide that she *would* marry him after all, for she had vowed to do no such thing only the previous day when he had come down to the harbour and, stealing her nice red woollen cap, had flung it to the top of the *Aleen*'s tall mast and dared Nicholas to climb up and get it back.

'What's goin' on out here?' demanded a voice just behind Dympna, making her leap like a salmon and drag herself free from Ruan's embrace. A grinning Egan nudged her in the ribs. 'Kissin' like ... like a *gorl*,' he whispered in her reddening ear. 'And you workin' wit' Daddy on the fishin boat – shame on you!'

'Egan!' Dympna gasped. 'Oh, you nearly gave me a heart attack, so you did. If Mammy had come out ...'

'Well, she didn't. And she'd look pretty foolish naggin' away at you, Dymp, considering all the t'ings she's been laughin' over wit' Nicholas,' her brother said severely. 'So come on, watch our charade and tell us what word we're actin', because me an' Maria's the next couple to guess, an' we want our turn out here, so we do.'

Ruan and Dympna laughed and Dympna teased her younger brother about his fondness for little Maria, then she and Ruan went back into the warm room and Nicholas, as a subject of conversation, was dropped. But somewhere in the back of Dympna's mind a little worm of worry nagged and niggled away at her, because if Nicholas was borrowing the money, or ... or taking it in some way, wouldn't that just about break the mammy's heart now? She asked Egan what he thought, but Egan was more interested in his own future than that of his brother. 'Sure and Nick's not got the spunk to rob a bank, an' what other way would he have for gettin' money?' he asked scornfully. 'He'll be hangin' on someone's coat-tails, that's for sure; someone wit' money, if you ask me. When I want some I'll work for it, so I will, so's me and Maria can get wed an' have a farm of our own.'

Dympna laughed at her young brother and his insistence that he and Maria would marry one day, and when the festivities finished and life went back to normal she forgot about Nick's stories and became more interested in her own doings. She liked Ruan and enjoyed riding on the pillion seat of his newly acquired motor bike, though this treat finished – for the time – when he returned to the estate outside Dublin. Indeed, her own life was too hard to allow her much time for speculating about Nick – or dreaming over Ruan, come to that.

The worst of the winter passed as most of the other winters in her life had passed. She and Micheál went out in the boat when the weather was sufficiently clement, and when they could not fish they mended old nets or made new ones, dug for bait on the beach or put out shore-lines from the rocks. Her hands grew calloused and her nails broke off short, for it was gruelling labour in winter, and when Micheál was working on his potato field Dympna had to help Beatrice in the house and garden, as well as doing her overdue school work. In the back of her mind, the idea that she might one day teach in school kept her at her books, for she was determined to better herself once Egan was old enough to take her place in the *Fair Aleen*. Indeed, she was beginning to realise that her fishing days were numbered; Egan would be fourteen in June. His school-days had not been distinguished and he was desperate to start working on the boat. It would not be fair to try and deny him his right once he left Mr O'Neill's classroom.

Once, when the two of them had been baking all morning, Beatrice had looked at her consideringly across the table piled with soda bread and brack and potato cakes, and had suggested, not for the first time, that she might consider taking a domestic post at one of the big houses in the nearby town. 'The money isn't particularly good,' she had admitted, passing a floury hand across her hot forehead. 'But such work is what they call "all found", meaning you are fed, clothed and so on, which means the wage you get is pocket money, to be spent on such things as ribbons and underwear, or to be saved for your wedding trousseau. What's more, you would learn a great deal about keeping house. You would stand a much better chance of meeting suitable young men in the town than you would in the village here.'

It had sounded like a rehearsed speech to Dympna and she had given her mother a quick, hostile glance. 'I don't want to do domestic work,' she had said slowly, trying to keep her tone light, uncommitted. 'I like to be out of doors, Mammy, you know I do. And though you say I won't meet people here, what about Ruan Sullivan? We get on well, so we do.'

'Oh, Ruan's a nice boy, but he'll never be more than the son of a farmer, even though the Sullivans are increasing their holding on the land,' Beatrice had said. 'You're a pretty girl, Dympna. You could do better, I'm sure of it.'

Dympna had picked up two tins of well-risen dough and walked over to the wall oven with them. 'Well, I'm still with Daddy for a while, yet,' she said pacifically. 'Time enough to consider what I'll do next in a few months, when Egan leaves school. But remember, Mammy, Mr O'Neill said I could go in for teaching if I worked at me books, and I've been working, you know that.'

Beatrice had sighed but changed the subject and Dympna, having made her point, was happy to leave it. But she had a strong feeling that the topic was not

245

closed; Beatrice would revert to it again many times.

March arrived, with its gales and sudden sunshine. The bit of garden Mrs Sullivan had made in front of the farmhouse came into bloom and the great bush of fuchsia, which half-hid the peat pile to the side of the Byrne's cottage, began to cover itself with tiny, pale-green leaves and long, pointed, purplish buds. The hens, which had laid rarely throughout the winter, began to search out nests in the thickening hedges and the old sow in the sty on the end of the cottage swelled with the happy results of her visit to the Sullivan boar.

Beatrice seemed easier in her mind, less liable to tighten her lips and criticise. She's softer, somehow, Dympna thought, as though the imminent spring had got through her mother's iron reserve and made her gentle. Catches, which throughout the winter had been poor, suddenly improved and when Beatrice drove to market in the donkey cart, with her fish laid out on cabbage leaves, she began getting good sales. Micheál invested in some lobster and crab pots and said confidently that when summer arrived the folk who came holidaying in the big houses would be glad of shellfish, which they seldom saw fresh at home.

But though life seemed to have taken a turn for the better, it was still important to work hard. Dympna sat an examination in the local town and came home quietly confident. She might not go to university, as her brother had, but she thought she could well be offered a place as a pupil teacher once the results of the exam were known. Of course she would not be earning a proper wage at first, but it would mean better money in the long run, if she continued to work at her books.

'Not long to the Easter holidays now,' she said to

Micheál one windy March morning when they were preparing the *Aleen* for sea. 'I wonder, will our Nick be coming home this time?'

Micheál, folding nets shrugged. 'That's anyone's guess, so it is, alanna. He writes home, of course, and your mammy reads me the letters, but he hasn't said he'll be comin' home. Does he get a holiday, then?'

'Of course he does, Daddy,' Dympna said a trifle impatiently. 'He came home for the Easter weekend last year and Ruan, who seems to get similar holidays, only shorter than Nick's usually, will be home in ten days' time.'

'Aye, but Ruan doesn't have a job,' Micheál pointed out. He finished with the net and began coiling rope. 'Nick's workin' in a pub, so he is.'

'Oh?' Dympna said, rather surprised. In all wonderings as to where her brother had got his money it had never crossed her mind that he might have earned it. Nicholas was so – well, so superior, she supposed – that it never occurred to either Ruan or Egan or herself that he might have got himself a job. And certainly Nicholas had never mentioned such a thing in her presence. 'I didn't know that, Daddy.'

'No, nor me. But the other evenin' your mammy mentioned it. Said he was earnin' good money servin' customers in a Dublin pub. So you see, though he may have a holiday from college, that doesn't mean to say he can get away from the pub – and keep his job, like.'

'I see that,' Dympna said. She felt vastly relieved. It was wonderful to know where Nicholas got his money from – but how odd that he had never told them, never boasted a bit about not only being top of the class, but of having to work, evenings, as well. 'But perhaps he'll be coming home for a day or two, Daddy. Pubs don't open over the holiday weekend itself, do they? Over Good Friday to Easter Monday, I mean.'

'No, you're right there, I doubt they open then,' Micheál admitted. He started to hoist the brick-red sail and Dympna scurried about as she always did when the boat began to put to sea. 'Mebbe we'll be seein' the boy for a few days, then.'

In the harbour and with the boat still by the quay it had been possible for them to converse without undue difficulty, but once they cleared the harbour and headed out into the open sea it was a different story. Micheál, used to making himself heard in any weather conditions, could shout loudly enough when he chose, but Dympna, though her voice rose to a scream, sounded more like a gull than a human being and was difficult to hear at all clearly. However, she took a deep breath and shouted. 'Wind's getting up, Daddy. Will we be going out of the bay?'

Micheál shrugged. 'If we find in the bay well an' good,' he shouted. 'If we don't, we'll go further out. Your mammy will want us in before dark, so we won't go further than we have to.'

Dympna nodded and settled down to do her share of sailing the boat.

As the day wore on, the wind increased and the great, pillowy clouds turned from white to grey and from grey to nearly black. The *Fair Aleen* butted on against the waves, but when Micheál finally decided to cast the net the catch was small, the fish mainly under-sized bass and ling, with a few hake thrown in. Not a catch to make one turn at once for home, Dympna decided rather sadly. The wind, she thought, was rapidly reaching gale force and she would be a good deal happier once they were in the somewhat doubtful shelter of the bay.

But it was scarcely half-way through the afternoon and Micheál, having taken a long, frowning look at the sky and another at the size of the waves, apparently decided to give the fish another chance. 'We'll cast once more,' he said optimistically. 'If it's after comin' on to rain, which seems likely, that'll mebbe bring the fish up. Look at the clouds, alanna.'

Dympna looked, without much enthusiasm. She thought that her father was right and it would rain, presently, but somehow doubted that the rain would calm the sea enough for the fish to rise. Still, he was a man wise in the way of fishing and knew what he was talking about. So when he gave the word and brought the *Aleen* head to wind she was ready with the net, refolded after its first attempt.

'Here we go,' roared Micheál as the boat jerked and plunged on the increasingly violent waves. He cast out his end of the net from the bows, then Dympna took over as Micheál dealt with the boat. And presently, as they sat themselves down in the thwarts to wait, the rain started. Heavy, soaking rain, carried on the gale so that it slashed into their faces and beat about their oilskinned figures. Before she could do anything about it a particularly violent gust seized the sou'wester from Dympna's head and ripped the string which tied under her chin, carrying the hat off on the gale, further out to sea. Dismayed, she stared after it for a moment, but then the wind blew strands of hair into her eyes and mouth, and she clutched the thwarts and stared up at the black and bulging clouds, letting down the deluge of rain upon them, and wished – how she wished – they were safe ashore.

But wishing is never much help and presently Micheál pointed over to the horizon. 'Look,' he said, his voice almost quiet. 'That's torn it; we'd best haul right away.'

Dympna followed the direction of his pointing finger with her eyes and saw that far away but coming closer, lightning jabbed great golden forks from the black clouds overhead to the black sea, and this was accompanied by the growl and crack of thunder, which she could hear even above the rush of wind and rain. Taking her lead from him, she got quickly to her feet and the two of them began to haul the net.

It came easily, which would have been a bad sign on most days but today, Dympna thought, they were both grateful for the lack of resistance, even though it meant a poor catch, or none at all. She and Micheál seized great armfuls of net and bundled it into the bottom of the boat, and she began to disentangle fish from its folds, throwing them into the stern of the boat which was inches deep in water, whilst Micheál folded the great, wet stiff net into a bundle. Then he hurled himself at the mast and began to prepare the *Aleen* for her next move whilst Dympna, without being told, knelt on the bottom boards and started frantically to bale, hurling the mixture of sea water and rain over the side and then, when the boat seemed less like some sort of aquarium, with the fish actually beginning to swim around their feet, she went back to the tiller and watched Micheál as he fought to get the mains'l hoisted with a couple of reefs in, for the wind was coming strongly off the land and that meant they could not turn and run for shelter but must take their way laboriously back to the bay.

Micheál sat down with the main sheet in his hand and glanced over to where she waited at the tiller for instructions. 'The storm's comin' this way, alanna,' he roared above the crash of the waves, the howl of the wind, and the creaks and groans of the poor *Aleen*, desperately struggling, or so it seemed, to keep all of them dry and afloat. Not that they were so very dry; Dympna's hair was drenched, hanging like rat-tails around her face, and the rain channelled off her head and down her back in a long, slithering icy river of water, which the oilskins were powerless to keep at bay. 'We'll make the best time we can . . . Jay, but it's awful dark, it's all I can do to see the harbour.'

Dympna, straining to hold the tiller steady and to move it as and when Micheál told her, looked ahead and could not see anything; what with the rain sheeting down and the wind blowing her eyelashes into her eyes, and the darkness, which seemed, if anything, worse than it had done five minutes earlier, she could not even make out the curve of the bay. But then Micheál shouted at her to concentrate on the house lights and she peered ahead and saw them at last, tiny stars of brilliance against the blackness.

It was a slow, laborious business, however. They tacked and Dympna did her very best to keep the tiller in the right position, but she was not strong enough and several times Micheál looped the main sheet round one brawny wrist and came to help her. But at last he shook his head, dashed the rain out of his eyes and decided to change his approach.

'Sure an' were not gettin' anywhere like this,' he bellowed. 'We'll not reach the quay until the storm eases, an' it looks fit to blow all night, so it does. We can't put out a sea anchor because the waves are too high an' gettin' higher, so we'll have to run for the beach. Once we're in the shelter of the cliffs the *Aleen* will be easier to handle, but we must keep her off the rocks.'

Dympna nodded; she was too tired to speak. She tried to see the sandy little beach in her mind's eye. It was to their left and was a bite of white sand guarded on either side by two long arms of black and wicked rocks, which reached out well into the sea and kept it calmer there than it was in the main bay.

'See it?' Micheál roared presently. 'It's still to port of us; stare hard, alanna, for it'll help if you can see where we're headin', so it will. Look up, to the top of the cliffs; the land is darker than the sky, just about. See?'

Dympna stared and presently she was able, despite the rain and hair in her eyes, to make out the long reef of rock nearest them, and she could see the cliffs, a thicker darkness against the black of the storm. 'I see it,' she shouted back. 'What'll I do, Daddy?'

'Go onto the port tack,' Micheál shouted. 'If we can get a bit further in, alanna, we'll be sheltered from the worst of the wind. Can you manage?'

She was putting her full weight on the tiller and the reefed sail was bearing them rapidly, but not too fast, into the shelter of the little bay, when something, a freak wave or perhaps a blast of wind made tricksy by the nearness of land, grabbed the *Aleen* and spun her round, so that her stern crashed into the black rocks with an awful tearing, grinding sound, which Dympna heard and recognised even above the noise of the storm.

'We've hit,' Micheál shouted. 'Is it bad? Can you see if she's holed, alanna?'

'I don't know . . .' Dympna began, when she noticed a cod give a wild wriggle and disappear. She saw that they were indeed holed and that water was coming in and fish were going out at far too fast a rate for her baler to help. 'Yes,' she shouted. 'We're badly holed, Daddy. The water's coming in . . . she's going down . . . what'll we do?'

Micheál reached up and pulled the mains'l down, then leaped across the boat and tore off his oilskins. He tried to push them into the hole, then seemed to realise that it would be a fruitless gesture and grabbed an oar. With the boat already low in the stern he yelled to Dympna to go up to the bows and began desperately pushing the oar against the rocks, and she realised he was trying to manoeuvre the boat around them.

Dympna followed his example. She, too, took an oar and began to fend them off as well as she could. The harder they worked the more the *Aleen* seemed to understand what they were about and presently, though they were now up to their knees in water, Dympna realised that the worst was over. The waves were still buffeting them, but they were smaller and the shore was no more than fifteen or twenty yards away.

'Stay where you are, Dymp,' Micheál shouted. He was struggling out of his sea boots and Dympna, with a vague memory of being told once at school how sea boots could drag you down to Davy Jones's locker, kicked off her own, and watched as he jumped over the side.

Dympna screamed; she couldn't help it, but she realised almost at once that her father was doing the only thing left to them. He was going to swim until he could wade and he was taking her, and the dear old *Aleen*, with him. He had the painter wound round one wrist and began to swim strongly towards the land, and the boat, the stern now completely beneath the waves, followed him like a reluctant dog put on the lead for the first time. But she did follow, and Dympna wondered whether she, too, should jump over the side to lighten the weight.

She was dithering in the bows, with the oar she had

grabbed earlier still in her hand, knowing that the sea was running too fast for her own weaker swimming efforts but hoping that the oar would help to keep her afloat, when she saw that Micheál was wading. The waves were up to his chin, every now and then one larger than the rest completely enveloped him, but when the water retreated there he was, standing sturdily foursquare to the shore, with the painter across his shoulder now to ease the weight of it, towing the boat to safety.

She jumped out when the water was only waist-high on Micheál, and immediately regretted it. For a start, there must have been a hole where she jumped, because the sea, icy cold and surging in huge waves still, simply did not stop at sand when she expected it to, so that before she knew what was happening it had closed over her head and the undertow was spitefully dragging her down. She kept her head, however, and her mouth closed, too, and before she had had a chance to panic, she felt a hand close over the bundle of oilskins and jersey at her neck and found herself dragged to the surface like a drowning kitten.

'Keep a hold on me, Dymp,' her father gasped. 'I dussen't let go of the *Aleen*, but you hang on to me jersey. If I go into a hole you'll feel me go down . . . stay by me, I'll see you safe ashore. Not long now, girleen, an' t'three o' us'll be safe, if not dry.'

But it seemed a long time to Dympna, during which she struggled on, forcing one icy leg in front of the other, the toes feeling fearfully for the bottom, in case the sand sloped down and she plunged over her head once more.

But they were gaining. A little at a time, but gaining, nevertheless. Dympna felt the water gradually grow lower. The waves which beat at her back and sucked at her, first trying to smash her to the ground and then endeavouring to pull her back into the deeps, were dragging, now, only just above her knees. But the water seemed rougher, the waves were coming at her from all directions . . . she stared, trying to understand what was happening, then a wave at about waist height thundered down on her, knocking her off balance. She clutched Micheál, then saw him stagger . . . and fall.

The shock was unbelievable. Her big, strong father, knocked flat by a wave against which she had staggered, then remained upright? It did not seem to make sense . . . then as she went to help him, her foot was stubbed agonisingly against something as sharp as a knife and she, too, fell forward . . . her knees immediately giving her the answer to what had happened to Micheál.

Rocks. The tide was right in and as they neared the shore, the reef of rocks had spread out into the tiny rock pools and loose stones which, at low tide, were scattered half-way up the beach. Micheál had stood on one of the sharp ones just as the big wave came and it had knocked against him as he was already beginning to fall. She, too, had trodden on sharp rocks . . . and now she knew they were probably in greater danger even than when they had first holed the *Aleen*.

It took less than half a second for these thoughts to flash through Dympna's head, of course, and all the while she was groping for her father, trying to find him, to pull him upright. And just as she touched his shoulder she was hit by something a good deal harder than the wave, and went down on top of him, sprawling half on his body and half on the knife edges of the little rocks.

It was the *Aleen*. Micheál must have let go of the

boat for a second and now the waves had her. Whilst the tide continued to come in they would hurl the boat against the shore until she was matchwood. Once it turned and began to go out, they would carry the *Aleen* with them and they would see her no more. But more important than any boat was her daddy, lying under the water, drowning.

Dympna felt the wave recede and lay still, with only her nose above water, until the boat had swept past her, without hitting her this time. Then she got to her knees and braced herself back against the next wave, praying that the boat would not knock her cold so that the pair of them would drown. The wave hit, but she did not fall forward. It's the seventh wave that's the worst, Dympna told herself, struggling upright and trying to ignore the pain in her torn and bruised feet. That was the second or third since the one that knocked me over, so I've got a bit of breathing space, so I have. But I must get Daddy up first before the next seventh wave or it's as good as dead he'll be.

She bent and grabbed for her father's shoulders, or where she believed his shoulders would be. Nothing. Then she remembered the drag of the retreating waves and tried behind where she stood . . . and felt the weight of him, moving at the water's whim, a dead weight.

She sensed a soundless, terrifying scream building up inside her and bent to her task, telling herself that she must not waste a second nor an ounce of energy, but must simply use all her strength to get Micheál out of the water before he drowned. She heaved with superhuman strength, the strength of total despair, and got him, swaying and sagging, to his knees. The water poured off him and his head lolled, senseless still, if not . . . but she would not let herself think that he was anything but unconscious. She groaned beneath her breath, then she caught hold of him by the hair and began to drag him, inch by painful inch, towards the dry sand. And with every inch gained her confidence returned, though the pain from her cracking arm muscles was so severe that had the situation been less desperate she thought she would have had to rest, just for a moment. As it was, however, she simply ignored her body and continued to strive with all her strength. She *would* get her father out of the sea's grip and up the beach to safety! She *would* bring him back to life just as soon as they were safe ashore. And she would, somehow, get him home before he died of cold and exposure.

In the struggle towards the beach the boat came up twice more on the crest of big waves and beat them cruelly hard, forcing Dympna to crouch over her father and take the worst of the *Aleen*'s weight upon her back and shoulders, but as the water grew shallower so did Dympna's strength increase, and after what felt like hours of struggle she realised they were out of the last of the creaming surf. It should have been easier, she thought petulantly as she heaved and tugged, for though the sand beneath hands and knees was cold and wet still, it was beach and not sea bottom upon which she crawled but without the incoming tide to help her, the great, sea-sodden weight of her father seemed more than she could possibly drag up the sloping beach. Yet, somehow, with tears blinding her and pain tearing at her, with the breath rasping in her throat and her body nothing but one great, enormous ache, she suddenly realised that they had gained the beach itself. And when they were both high, if not dry, she got shakily to her feet and faced the sea.

The *Fair Aleen*, fair no longer, was thundering

towards the beach, sideways on, the water within almost level with her gunwales, and Dympna's heart quailed at the thought of going into the surf again to try and grab the painter or some other part of her to tow her ashore. But what would they do with the boat? A fisherman without his craft was neither good to man nor beast, she thought confusedly. But damn the boat, it was Micheál who mattered. Was he breathing? She bent over him and for a moment it seemed to her that he was drowned, and if it was so, what was the point of going on? No Daddy, no boat . . .

He was on his side. Dympna rolled him onto his stomach and began to heave at his shoulders, remembering vaguely some lectures on life saving which she had attended one summer long ago. She struggled and heaved at Micheál, with her arms round his stomach, and suddenly he made a horrible sort of gurgling sound and sea water poured from his mouth mixed with something which smelled very bad indeed, and as it spewed out onto the sand Micheál gave a cough and a gasp . . . and began to breathe.

Dympna screamed in a thin, wavering voice: 'Oh, Mary, Mother of Jesus, thanks be to you and to God the Father and all the saints . . . me daddy's alive! He's alive!' She smacked his back as hard as she could a few times and heard his breathing continue, though bubblingly. Then she ran down to the sea again, screaming over her shoulder as she went: 'I'm goin' fishing, Daddy – I'm fishing for the *Aleen*, so just you wait where you are, so.'

Micheál made no reply, but Dympna steeled herself to run once more into that wild and foaming sea. The poor *Aleen* was bottom up now, but at least that way she was floating, and as she was hurled into the shallower water Dympna lurched forward, so weary that she hardly knew how to put one foot in front of the other, and grabbed wildly at the rounded hull, running her hands down the rough wood and feeling for something to tow the boat ashore with. At her second attempt, her searching fingers found a rope which could have been the mainsheet or the painter, or indeed any other rope which was still attached to the *Aleen*. She caught hold of it and heaved and struggled and wrenched, and felt the blood begin to run down her hands, making them slippery . . . and suddenly the boat was digging into the sand, and Dympna sat down abruptly and knew she had won. The boat was ashore though the tide had not yet turned, and even if she could get no further, she should be safe here for a while, for several hours at least. And in that time, Dympna told herself wearily, making her slow way up the beach to where her father still lay, surely I can get help?

Beatrice sat in front of the fire, staring dumbly at the flames. Every now and again she got up and went to the window, framing her face with her hands and putting it close to the glass so that her fingers would keep the light back and enable her to see out.

'They'll have gone ashore further up the coast, Mammy,' Egan said every time she did this. 'They'd never get back into the harbour wit' the wind a-comin' at them from the land the way it is. So don't you be worryin', sure an' they'll be laughin' at us when they come in wit' the catch tomorrer mornin'.'

'Micheál knows I worry,' Beatrice said each time. 'He'd come ashore and then he'd come home, or send a message. He'd not leave us for hours and hours, with a storm the like of this one battering at the cottage and driving me half out of my mind with fear. I wonder, should we go down to the quay again? I'm afraid the lamp I stood out will have run out of oil by now, if it's not blown out.'

'I'll go if you like,' Egan said patiently to his mother's back. 'But wit' the sea so high an' terrible, they'll not see that little light until they're almost safe, Mammy. They'll be seein' the lights from the cottage first. But if they were well out, wit' other boats, they'll all head for the nearest harbour an' it'll mebbe tek time before they can make for home.'

Beatrice sighed and came away from the window. 'Is the storm still as bad, would you say?' she asked, sitting down by the fire once more. 'D'you think it's lessening, Egan? Which harbour would you run to with the wind coming off the land the way it is.'

'I don't t'ink Daddy would make for the harbour, unless he was wit' the fleet, he'd head for somewhere nearer home, so he would. I know, he'd go for the little bay opposite the quay that's like a bite o' white sand wit' two curves o'black rock, like arms,' Egan said after a moment's thought. 'Look, Mammy, I'll go over there as soon as the wind drops a bit, but in the meantime, you'd best go to bed. You'll be no manner o' use tomorrer unless you get your sleep.'

'I couldn't sleep,' Beatrice told him. 'I'll mash the tea again.'

Egan watched whilst his mother warmed the pot and made fresh tea. She poured them both out a mug, then hurried over to the window once more, peering through the glass into the blackness beyond. 'It is lessening,' she said, turning back into the room. 'Earlier, I could scarce stand against it. Now . . . yes, I fancy I could walk along the coast.'

'It's black as the darkest night out there, Mammy,' Egan pointed out. He stirred a spoonful of sugar into his mug. 'You'd mebbe fall an' break your leg before you'd gone ten yards. And it's a long way round the head o' the sea lough to that little bay, even if they make for it and not'ing's certain. If you're hurt it'll only make t'ings worse for Daddy an' Dympna. You'd best stay here. I'll go, if it'll make you easier in your mind.'

'It won't,' Beatrice said bluntly. 'I need action, Egan, I *need* to go out, dark or no, windy or no. I've waited all evening for some sign, but now I'm tired of waiting. I'm going out.'

'I'll go for you, Mammy,' Egan insisted. 'I can nip along the coast path in no time and be back before you know it. You watch from the window an' you'll be able to see the light of me lantern, so you will, a-bobbin' along the cliff path.'

Beatrice crossed the kitchen and took her long, dark coat down from the hook on the back door. She slipped into it and muffled her head and neck in a thick, hand-knitted scarf. Then she went over to the dresser and took a lantern off it. Whilst her son, muttering, got into his own outdoor things she calmly filled and lit the lantern, then turned to him. 'I'm not going down to the quay again, Egan. There's very little point if you don't think they'll try to come on with the wind blowing against them. I'm going round the coast, to that little bay you thought was a possibility, and I'll keep a look-out in all of the little bays as I pass them. Don't you think it's likeliest that Daddy would do his best to come ashore nearer home? Unless he was very far from this part of the coast when the storm struck, of course.'

'Ye-es, it's probably likeliest,' Egan agreed. He had donned his sea boots and his patched jacket. Now he wound his own scarf round his head and neck, and opened the back door, raising his voice against the wind. 'Awright, Mammy, if you're determined . . . tek my arm and duck your head when you feel the wind on your cheek.'

His mother complied and the two of them hurried out, Egan slamming the door behind them, and set off along the winding lane which would lead, eventually, back down to the coast and across to the little bay.

Outside, the darkness was complete at first, the light of the lantern probably making it seem darker than it was. But as his mother had said, the wind was dropping. Egan let Beatrice hold the lantern at first, but when they reached the little lane that wound along between its banks of hazel and gorse, he took it from her. 'Hang on to me, Mammy, and save your energy for when we need to get down onto the beach,' he shouted. 'I'll manage the light. If you need help, you just tell me now. Off we go.'

And indeed, it was tough going for Egan as well as for Beatrice, though before they had gone half a mile he became aware that the rain which had hurled itself so spitefully into their faces seemed to be lessening too. Presently they reached a place in the hedge where Egan remembered pushing through the last time he and Dympna had gone swimming there, and he heaved his mother through the small gap and they set off across the meadow.

'Not far now, Mammy,' Egan told her. 'Can you feel how we've turned ourselves so's the wind's at our backs? That means we're above the bay . . . here, this is the cliff edge. It's not a long drop, but you'll need to go careful.'

Before she had gone more than a few feet his mother let of him and began to grab at the wiry, tussocky grass, which was the only plant to survive on this part of the cliff. 'Suppose we've made a mistake, Egan?' she said breathlessly as they descended. 'Suppose we're wrong and this isn't where they've come ashore? Where do we try next?'

'Don't meet troubles half-way, Mammy,' Egan shouted, because in truth he did not know how to answer her question. Out of the dozens of tiny bays and inlets and sea loughs, how could they possibly search each one? But as soon as they reached the sand he knew their search was over: the bulk of the *Fair Aleen* was before them, dark against the whiteness of the wave-crests and there was something else . . .

Heart in mouth, Egan abandoned his mother to her slower descent and set across the wet sand at a gallop. He yelled above the sound of wind and waves, yelled in fear and horror . . . and saw a movement from what looked like a huddle of rounded rocks just above where the boat had been stranded.

'Dympna! Is – is that our daddy?' He reached her and fell to his knees, grabbing her hands and squeezing them hard. 'Oh, Dymp, you're alive, so you are! But what's happened to Daddy? Is he . . . he can't be . . .'

'He's alive,' Dympna said, her voice hoarse and small, her hands, in Egan's warm clasp, cold as death. 'He's breathing, but oh, Egan, I can't make him talk to me, or move, or . . .'

Her mother's shriek made her jump and she turned to the older woman at once. 'Mammy! He's not dead, but he's hurted bad. I think his head must have struck one of the rocks . . . he fell as he was wading ashore, dragging the *Aleen*. I've got him as far above the water as I can, but the tide's not yet turned . . .' Beatrice was keening over Micheál, not wasting a glance on her daughter, so Dympna turned back to her brother. 'Egan, the three of us won't be able to move him – we must get help.'

'You're not in a very brave state yourself, Dymp,' Egan said. 'Dear God but you're cold as death, so you are – colder. Look, you take my jacket and wrap it round you and run to the nearest cottage. Tell 'em to bring a door and as many strong men as can come to carry Daddy.'

'Right,' Dympna said. She got to her knees as slowly as though she had been sixty instead of sixteen, then hesitated. 'Wouldn't you go faster than me though, Egan? I could wait here wit' Mammy while you fetch help.'

'Yes, that would be wiser,' Beatrice said, her voice still high and strained. 'Go on, Egan, you go. We'll manage with your daddy. I'm going to wrap him up in my coat for a start.'

'No,' Egan said with a firmness he had not known was in him. He lowered his voice. 'Dympna's cold as deat', so she is, she needs to keep movin', Mammy.' He turned his head to address Dympna, who was getting laboriously to her feet. 'You go off now, Dymp, an' keep movin', then you'll be back all the sooner.'

'All right, Egan,' Dympna said. She took off her own soaked jacket and let Egan help her into his, then set off into the darkness at a slow and stumbling walk. Egan waited until she was out of earshot and then turned back to Beatrice. 'Come on, then, Mammy, gi' me a bit of a hand to get Daddy out of his wet t'ings. He's too big to get your coat onto his shoulders, but we can lay it over him.'

'She'll be too late,' Beatrice said, her voice sullen. 'She'll not hurry herself like you would, Egan. Why wouldn't you go?'

'Because Dymp's got to keep movin', to get herself warm,' Egan said promptly. 'Mammy, she used most of her strength up draggin' Daddy out o' the sea, she'd be no manner o' use in gettin' him out of his wet t'ings, but if she's set to runnin' for help she'll do it fine. Now let's see what we can do for me daddy.'

Beatrice dragged Micheál's wet upper clothing off and she and Egan wrapped him in her long black coat. Then she wound his head lovingly in the long, thick scarf she had been wearing. And then, because he insisted, she took Egan's scarf and draped it round her own shoulders. She began to chafe Micheál's hands and to rub his face vigorously with a corner of her long skirt, whilst Egan rubbed at his feet and chattered inconsequentially, telling both of them that his sister would soon be back, so she would, with several strong men who would soon have them safe home.

But all the time she worked on the inanimate body before her, she struggled with an agony of regret. Why had she never told Micheál how she felt about him? Indeed, she had never acknowledged how she felt until this very moment, though she now realised that the love had been there all the time, for many, many months . . . nay, years. Cool, self-controlled Beatrice Byrne had loved Micheál dearly and deeply for at least ten years, and not once in all that time had she showed him, by word or sign, how she felt. But I'm not an Irishwoman by birth, I'm English, and cold English at that, she tried to excuse herself. Besides, he must have known how I felt . . . surely? Why did he think I slaved at the work of the cottage if not for his sake? Why did I sell fish from the donkey cart, break my back over our vegetable patch, spend hours and hours bottling apples and making blackberry jelly and salting down the rest of the catch, if not for love of Micheál?

But it was no excuse and now she knew it, now that he lay there, unconscious of her presence, his eyes closed and his mouth firm, stern even, so that he reminded her of a man she had seen once who had been drowned just off the shore. Grim, the man had looked, as though he had given death a good run for his money and had gone down to him angrily at the last, furious that his life should have been taken and he with a use for it for a long while yet.

But Micheál was not dead, not yet; she still had a chance to tell him to explain. He might be able to understand her if she spoke to him – she had heard many times that hearing was the last of the senses to desert a man. Maybe he was lying there this minute, with her coat warm about him, listening to all the sounds, the crashing of the waves on the shore, the shrill of the wind . . . and her own teeth, chattering in her head from the cold and from fear that he might never open his eyes again, never speak to her . . . never understand that now, seeing him lying on the sand like one dead, she could acknowledge, for the first time, that she loved him more than life itself and would willingly die for him.

Egan was busy, chafing his father's feet, taking off his own worn woollen socks and putting them lovingly on Micheál's long, pale feet, then the skin of his father's ankles, calves, knees . . .

Beatrice bent low over her husband and began, for the first time in their married life together, to try to tell him what he meant to her, how much she loved him, begging him not to leave her, not to die. She kept her voice low, so that Egan would not hear, but she continued to talk, almost to whisper, into Micheál's ear while she went on rubbing his hands, arms, face, hoping to bring back the warmth, the life-force which hovered behind that still, pale face.

# Chapter Eight

It was a long run back to the cottage, but Dympna soon realised that Egan had been right; left to hang about any longer on the cold beach she might well have simply given up. As it was, she ran her hardest, which wasn't very hard to start with, but as the warmth came up from her pounding feet to the rest of her body she began to feel that she might live. It was, indeed, the anxiety for her father which drove her so well that she forced her weary legs onwards, over the rough grass and through gorse and bramble patches, until at last she reached the lane. She neither paused nor queried her direction, but simply turned for home and ran as she had never run in her life, with the result that she was banging on the door of the Brannegans' which was the first cottage she reached, before she was completely exhausted. But leaning against the doorpost, feeling as though any moment she might simply sink to the ground, she wondered, for the first time, whether she had been right to go home, to fetch people she knew, rather than to head in the other direction when she reached the cross-roads and go on to the schoolhouse, or even further, to the nearest farm, but it had been instinct which had driven her and instinct, in the end, had not done so badly by her.

She did not have to stand outside the cottage long. The door shot open, Mr Brannegan gave an exclamation of horror, and before she knew what was happening she had been picked up bodily and dumped in the big chair nearest the fire whilst the family stood around and fired questions at her. What had happened to her? She was wet as a seal, had there been an accident? It was a wild night, so it was, the curraghs and the black Connemara boats had fought their way back to their various harbours as soon as the storm began . . .

'We got the *Aleen* beached in the bay opposite our quay,' Dympna said through rattling teeth, for reaction was setting in and she was shaking like a sail in a gusty wind. 'Me daddy towed us in . . . fell on rocks below the water . . . must ha' hit his head . . . can't make him speak . . .'

There was no need for further explanations. Mr Brannegan got his two big sons and they set off at once for the bay, whilst Mrs Brannegan went to the next cottage and the next, spreading the word. And when she came back she made Dympna drink a cup of hot cocoa and without further ceremony pulled off her soaking clothes right down to her long woollen socks, until she was bare as a babe, and she helped her dress again in a worn greyish shift, an old black skirt stiff with age and none too clean, and a pair of her husband's woollen socks. Then she put on her own coat and announced that the men had taken a door off its hinges no doubt, but it was a long way to bring a poor feller, so it was, and would it not be better to get Rosa and the cart?

Dympna immediately saw the sense of this and wrapped herself in the thick woollen shawl, which Mrs Brannegan lent her, and pushed her feet into a pair of boots several sizes too large, the property of another son who was off courting a girl in Clifden, clad in his best. Then the two women went round to the sheltered side of the Byrnes' cottage and sure enough, there was Rosa, contentedly chewing a mouthful of dried grass. She looked up in surprise as the lantern light fell on her, but Dympna and the older woman fetched out the cart and together managed to get the little donkey between the shafts and harnessed up without any problems.

'She's a dote, so she is,' Dympna said breathlessly as they turned donkey and cart into the lane. 'You get aboard, Mrs Brannegan, and I'll lead her, in case she stumbles in the dark.'

'Are you sure you'd not be better stayin' at home and keepin' yourself warm?' her neighbour asked. 'For 'tis mortal cold you were, alanna, when you come to our door.'

But Dympna had been warmed and refreshed as much, she thought, by the kindness and the immediate offer of help as by the cocoa, and told the older woman that she was fine, so she was, and the better for keeping on the move. And when, presently, they met the men with her father lying on the door they had used to carry him, she was glad she had not stayed at home. Egan was supporting Beatrice, who was weeping hysterically, and the donkey cart proved to be just the thing, for they put Beatrice aboard it and then Micheál, and Beatrice held him so that he did not fall and seemed calmed and reassured simply because she was doing something useful, whilst everyone else set about getting back to the little settlement as quickly as possible.

Once there it was hot cocoa for everyone and bed for Micheál – a bed as close to the turf fire as they could make it without scorching him, for he was cold still and neither moved nor spoke. Mr Brannegan wanted to know what had happened and nodded wisely when Dympna explained, saying that they were lucky that the boat was ashore and not tossing out somewhere in the mid-Atlantic.

'And now you go off to bed yourselves,' Mrs Brannegan advised kindly, pausing in the doorway after she had shooed her menfolk through it. 'I've put your clothes to dry by the fire, Dympna. Come for them in the morning – but not too early, mind. You'll need your sleep this night.'

Dympna thought she would never be able to sleep, not with Micheál lying in his fireside bed, so cold and grim and different from the man she knew and loved, but she undressed and got into bed . . . and slept at once, and dreamlessly.

All next day, Micheál lay in his bed. Beatrice was half out of her mind with worry and Dympna and Egan hovered, anxious that when their daddy did wake there should be someone near him, but Micheál neither came round nor seemed aware of their presence. At noon Egan went in to Clifden and told the doctor what had happened, and later in the day he visited them. He took Micheál's pulse, listened to his heart-beat, then told Beatrice reassuringly that she had a fine, strong man, so she had, who would be none the worse for his ducking once a day or two had passed.

'I'll make him a nice little custard with some of the eggs if you'll fetch some milk from the farm,' Beatrice said to Dympna, and Egan had to remind her, as kindly as he could, that Dympna, too, had need of rest. 'But I'll fetch the milk, Mammy,' he added reassuringly. 'And Dr Doyle says he needs rest more than anything else, so don't worry too much. He'll be right as rain in a day or so, just you see.'

Towards evening of the day following the accident,

Dympna began to worry as well, though she did not intend to let Beatrice know and continued to speak soothingly of daddy's sleep being a natural one, but she went to bed convinced that she would not sleep a wink. If only Daddy would stir, say something. Yet such was her weariness that as soon as her head touched the pillow she fell asleep and slept soundly all night.

Next morning, early, Egan woke her. He must have called her several times without response and got worried, for she awoke to find him shaking her sharply and almost shouting her name. 'Dympna! Oh, Dymp, will you wake up! There's t'ings to be done . . . Mammy needs the both of us, so she does.'

Dympna stared round her wildly for a moment, then sat up. 'Egan? What's happened?' she said groggily, trying to push rough rat-tails of hair out of her eyes and wondering whether she had argued with a gorsebush the previous day. 'Mammy needs us? For what . . .' Recollection came flooding back and she pushed off the blankets and swung her feet onto the floor. 'Oh Egan, how's Daddy? Is he awake yet?'

'No, but Mammy wants us to go to Clifden to get the doctor again. She's a bit wild this mornin', Dympna . . . she wants Nicholas fetched from Dublin an' all sorts. And when I said I t'ought she ought to have some breakfast, I t'ought she was goin' to hit me.'

'I'll come,' Dympna said, scrambling to her feet and dragging the Brannegans' borrowed raiment over her head. 'If she wants Nick – does that mean Daddy's . . . worse?'

'Dunno. Hurry, Dymp.'

Dympna did not bother with socks or boots, but

ran barefoot into the kitchen. Micheál lay as before, wrapped in blankets and unmoving. Beatrice was kneeling beside him, with a cup full of something white and thickish in her hand, clearly about to raise him. She glanced up as her daughter and son entered the room. 'Ah, good. Give me a hand to lift your daddy up so he can take some nourishment, Egan. Dympna, you must go in to Clifden – take the donkey cart – and fetch Dr Doyle, not that I've much faith . . . but never mind that. Then you must go to the post office and send a telegram to Nicholas. He must come home at once.'

'I'll get the doctor,' Dympna was beginning, when she saw her father's eyelids flutter. She clutched Beatrice's arm. 'Mammy, he's waking.'

Beatrice had been looking at Dympna but with her words she swung round and stared at Micheál, slopping some of the drink out onto the floor as she did so. 'Micheál, my dearest?' she said in a low, crooning voice. 'Can you hear me now? It's Bea and I'm going to give you some gruel . . .'

Micheál groaned and moved, then sat up on his elbow, swaying dizzily, and looked around him. 'Where'm I?' he said thickly. 'Whyfor am I on the floor, now? What's goin' on, Bea? Gruel, did you say?'

He sounded so disgusted that Dympna and Egan laughed, partly with relief, for only moments earlier their daddy had looked as though he were on his deathbed. But Beatrice put the cup carelessly on the floor and flung her arms round her husband's neck. 'Oh, Micheál, you're going to be all right,' she said, and Dympna saw there were tears on her cheeks, although her voice was heavy with relief and love. 'We thought . . . but you're going to be all right.'

'So I am,' Micheál agreed. His voice, Dympna realised, was slurred and strange. 'Where's this stuff then? It's starvin' I am to be sure.'

He tried to take the cup but could not grasp it, and Dympna knelt on the floor as well and put her arm round him whilst Beatrice carefully held the cup to his lips. Micheál took a couple of swallows, then pulled a face. 'I don't like it,' he said thickly, his tone accusing. 'Why can't I be havin' some dacint grub?'

'Dr Doyle said a light diet,' Beatrice said uncertainly. She looked across at Dympna, her eyes appealing. 'Gruel's a light diet, isn't it?' She turned back to Micheál. 'Do you fancy one of my egg custards, dearest? I made one yesterday, but you didn't fancy it.'

But Micheál, heaving a huge sigh, had lain down again. 'Later,' he said, his voice still slurred. 'I'll have me an egg later.'

Dympna and Egan exchanged worried glances. It was not like their daddy to refuse food when he had fasted for so long. But Beatrice heaved at her husband's shoulders and Egan ran to help her and presently, though he sighed and tried to push the spoon away, he managed to eat most of the despised gruel.

'It's a good t'ing, so it is,' Dympna said as she and Egan walked up to the farm together to fetch more milk and to ask Mrs Sullivan if she had any ideas for tempting Micheál's appetite. 'I know he grumbled, but he could have simply shut his mouth and refused to eat, and he didn't do that. He's better, I'm sure of it.'

'I hope so,' Egan said. 'But it's early days. Mebbe tomorrow his voice'll be more like it should be.'

Dympna shot a quick look at her brother. He might not be the brightest at his lessons, but he had a good head on him for all that. He had noticed the change in their daddy's speech, as she had. 'He took in a deal of water,' she reminded him. 'It'll take time, Egan, but he's on the right road, I'm sure of it.'

Two days later, days in which Beatrice had had Dr Doyle out from town once and had nagged the children to fetch him again, had insisted on trying to get in touch with Nicholas and had been constantly at Micheál's side, the change which had been promised came at last. With Beatrice beaming at them, Egan and Dympna were ordered to stir themselves and make their daddy a good breakfast, for Micheál had an appetite on him like a donkey, he said, and would eat thistles if all else failed.

'Should I be going for the doctor again, Mammy?' Dympna said, smiling. 'Daddy sounds more himself now, so he does.'

'The doctor?' Bea said as though it was a totally new idea to her. 'No, no. But go and fetch a couple of hen's eggs and boil them – lightly, mind – on the fire. And Egan, you butter some bread to go with eggs.'

The two young people scurried around doing their mother's bidding and presently, with the first egg eaten and the second about to be tackled, Micheál looked around him once more. 'It was a storm,' he said, his brow furrowing. 'I was towin' the boat into the bay, but I must have been further to the left than I thought for. I'd took me seaboots off . . . I landed me foot on rocks like devil's teeth, couldn't keep me balance, fell . . .'

'And I dragged you ashore, Daddy,' Dympna said encouragingly. 'Mammy and Egan came, and I went and fetched the neighbours, and we brought you home.'

'That's right,' Micheál said. He heaved a sigh. 'I'm that sore . . . but I'll mend, I'll mend. Where's me breakfast?'

After that, each day brought some slight improvement, until the day when Micheál asked a question which the rest of the family had been too worried to consider. He was in bed still, but although pale and weak, he was noticeably better, and was tackling a plate of salt pork and potatoes when something suddenly seemed to strike him. He called Dympna over, gave her his only half-empty plate and told her what was on his mind. 'It's me boat, alanna,' he said, his brow furrowing. 'What came to me lovely pucan?'

'We got her ashore, as high as we could,' Dympna said as reassuringly as she could. She could have kicked herself for not checking before, but with her daddy so ill she had simply forgotten the *Fair Aleen*. 'She'll be all right there until we can get her seaworthy again so that we can sail her back to the quay, Daddy.'

Micheál sat up straighter and stared across at Dympna. His eyes were dark and his face, which had begun to regain something of its former health, seemed to grow paler as Dympna watched. 'Go down to the quay, Dymp,' he said. 'See if she's still high an' dry in the bay opposite. Then come back here as quick as you can.'

Dympna did not waste a moment. She ran out of the cottage and all the way down to the quay, then stared across the water at the little bay which, four nights ago, had been the scene of such a life-and-death struggle.

There was the bay, with its bite of white sand, its reef of sharp-topped rocks. Dympna's heart missed a beat and she stared until her eyes watered. But of the *Fair Aleen* there was no sign.

It was a whole week before they were forced to acknowledge that they had lost the boat. Their main means of making a living, the craft that had been the pride of the Byrnes' hearts and the envy of all the local fishermen. Micheál had explained, when Dympna returned to the cottage with the awful news, that the tide had not been at the full the previous night, though it had seemed to be so. After they left, it had continued to creep up the white sand and had crept far enough to wash the poor injured boat back down with it when it turned.

'But we'll find her, no doubt,' he had said then. 'Someone will have seen her, will have brought her safe in.'

Only he was wrong. No one had seen her and the only news they had of her was of planking, washed ashore, one particular piece with her name carved lovingly on it.

'Good t'ing I came round before you'd wasted money on bringin' a doctor all the way from Clifden,' was just about all Micheál said in front of the children, but this was disaster, and both Dympna and Egan knew it. Beatrice knew it too, though she said nothing and continued to feed Micheál on the best she could offer and to tend him lovingly, more lovingly than she had ever done before, to Dympna's knowledge. But Micheál was getting stronger day by day, and soon, very soon, they would all have to face up to their changed circumstances. Another boat must be acquired – but how? A curragh would have been possible; Dympna supposed that they might eventually even manage to get enough money together to buy – or make – a Connemara rowing boat. Yet after the first shock, her father did not seem worried. Perhaps, Dympna reasoned, he knew more than he was letting on. Perhaps he knew very well where another pucan was to be acquired and for a price he could afford. And until Micheál was well enough to tell them what he planned to do, she and Egan worked harder than ever before up on the vegetable patch. And waited.

'Bea? Are you awake?' Micheál's deep voice, coming out of the thick dark, sounded almost shy.

Beatrice turned and notched herself comfortably against his broad chest, then put up a hand and rested it against his cheek. 'Yes, I'm awake. Are you not feeling well?'

'I'm fine, so I am. But I've got to talk seriously to you, darlin' girl.'

'Oh,' Beatrice said. Even to her own ears her voice sounded both small and guilty, for she had guessed what he was about to say. 'Are you sure you're well enough, Micheál? I don't want you distressing yourself, getting ill again.'

'Now why should I do that?' Micheál sounded amused now. 'When we must both know what I'm goin' to ask you. Bea, we'll need some of your money for a new pucan.'

'You know I'd give you every penny, Micheál . . . or every penny . . .' Beatrice said. Her voice died away and she cleared her throat a couple of times. 'Only . . . only there's not quite – quite as much as there was.'

'But there'll be enough for a pucan? I'll work on it meself if the fellers what build boats will let me, but it'll be made in Galway, because they're Galway boats. I t'ought we might get one cheaper buyin' outright . . . an old boat, see? I'm tellin meself they wouldn't ask so much for an old boat.'

'How much will a pucan cost, Micheál?' Beatrice said baldly as his voice, too, died away. 'The oldest, cheapest you could buy.'

He named a sum. There was a painful silence. Beatrice found her throat was stiff and dry; she could not speak.

'Bea? In God's name, girl, what have you done wit' all that money? Oh, I'm not denyin' it was yours, I gave it to you to put it in a bank or an old sock against a rainy day, but you've never been a spendt'rift, you're a careful woman, anyone would say so.'

There was another long silence. Beatrice broke it at last. 'Nicholas. Micheál, he needed money. Oh I know he got a scholarship to the college, but he needed money for – for other things. He needed a skeleton – have you ever heard the like? – and it cost . . . it cost a great deal. Then there were other things . . . he has nice rooms, so he can ask other students back, take a girl out now and then no doubt. And – and I never dreamed that you might need it too. I swear I never dreamed it. There's – there's a bit left, maybe Nicholas has got some, too. He took a job working in a bar of an evening when I told him the money was running out, he may have some which we . . . we could b-borrow.'

She finished speaking on a little sob and felt Micheál's warm lips against her cheek for a moment. Then there was silence for what seemed a dreadfully long time, until he spoke again. 'We'll send for Nicholas, see . . . see how much money he's got to spare. Because we can't exist wit'out it, Bea.' His voice, which had been soft, hardened. 'I'll not have me two good little kids an' me wife starve to keep Nicholas in silk socks.'

Beatrice did not smile. She, too, had been rather distressed when Nicholas had come home for a few days and had given her a pair of thin, very fine socks to wash.

'They're silk, Mammy, so treat 'em careful,' he had said. 'They're a terrible price, so they are.'

Now, Beatrice swallowed the sobs which fought to rise in her throat and spoke again, albeit rather unsteadily. 'There's me younger sister Maude, Micheál. We've kept up a correspondence all these years and . . . she's often said she'd like to see me, to help me in some way. She . . . she offered to have one of the children, only I knew . . .'

'One of my children?' Micheál almost growled it. 'She wanted one of my children? Dear God, for why?'

'She thought it would a help, Micheál, if she brought one of them up. She . . . Maude had no children of her own, then. That was when she was married to Mr Oakham, but after he died she married again, to a Mr Ditchling, and now she's got two stepsons, both older than our Nicholas, and three kids, all quite young, of her own. Micheál, we c-can't afford to be proud. If she'll help us, lend us some money . . .'

'A loan,' Micheál said eagerly. 'Aye, that's it – a loan. We could repay it somehow . . . perhaps when Nick's doin' the doctorin' he might give you back the money he's spent. Would you be after askin' her, Bea? Oh, I know you'll hate to do it – I hate it meself, so I do – but I can't t'ink what else to do, save beg in the streets.'

'I'll ask,' Beatrice said quietly. 'I'll write first thing tomorrow and explain what's happened. She knows Nicholas is learning to be a doctor – she seemed very pleased that one of our sons was doing so well – so if I say we'll repay later . . .'

'If only they'd thought of high tide,' Micheál said, almost on a sob. ''Tis a desperate t'ing, to beg money from your family, after all that's been between us . . . but it's only a loan, alanna.'

'I'll tell her that,' Beatrice said. 'And . . . and I'm so sorry, dearest Micheál, that I've let you down, because I have, haven't I?'

'No, no,' Micheál said soothingly. He kissed her brow, then the tip of her nose, then her mouth. 'You have feelin's for the boy which I can't understand, that's all. And now we'll put it all out of our minds and forget the bleedin' money. Awright?'

Beatrice gave a watery chuckle. 'That's the first time I've ever heard you swear, Micheál,' she said. 'We'll get your boat if I have to go down on me knees to me bleedin' sister.'

They laughed a little, cuddled a little, then settled down to sleep. But Beatrice could not help wondering what her sister would say. She knew that, if she and Maude met face to face in the street it was unlikely that they would immediately recognise each other. Nineteen years would have changed the child she had left into a woman and God knew those years must have left their mark on me, Beatrice thought. But what else could she do? She had given the money to Nicholas and now, when it was too late, she saw that she had had no right to do such a thing. The money had been Micheál's and though he had handed it straight over to her, she had always known he had meant it to be spent in an emergency for all of them and not just for the oldest and, she acknowledged now, the most selfish of her children. So she lay, regretting uselessly, until at last she slept.

The boat had been lost in March and it was past

Easter before the letter came. Dympna saw her mother holding it as she turned from the doorway and assumed, not unnaturally, that it was from her elder brother. He had not been home for Easter; too busy, he had said, and he had been invited to spend the actual holiday with a friend in Dublin. Mammy had pretended that she didn't mind, but Dympna saw her sad eyes and felt truly cross with Nicholas. He was unbelievably selfish. He was Mammy's favourite by far, he would be treated like a crown prince should he honour them by coming home for a few days, yet he could not even write Mammy a letter telling her what had happened. Another picture postcard of the university had been delivered a few days before Easter, to be added to Mammy's brave little line of similar cards, tacked up on the back door, above the pegs for coats, and on the card Nicholas had scrawled laconically that he would not be home but would see them in the summer, probably. Not a word about the loss of the *Fair Aleen*, though Dympna knew that Mammy had written to him about it, nor about Daddy's state of health. No, nor would there be a present for anyone, not so much as a length of ribbon for Mammy or a bit of pipe tobacco for Daddy. It seemed to Dympna that Nicholas had cut loose from them and did not intend to jeopardise his freedom by spending a moment more than he had to in their company.

'Is that a letter from Nick, Mammy?' Dympna asked casually, since her mother just stood by the back door, staring straight before her, a dishcloth in one hand and the letter in the other, not attempting to put either one down. 'I thought he'd write once Easter was over. He missed New Year and Little Christmas as well, poor Nick.'

'Twelfth Night, you mean,' Beatrice said almost absently. 'No, I don't think . . . but the letter isn't from Nicholas. Finish the delft, Dympna, and put it away. I – I'll go into my room and . . . read the letter quietly, I think.'

Egan was back at school and Micheál was labouring up at the farm, being paid by Mr Sullivan to help himself and his sons to build a stone cottage for their eldest boy to move into when he married in the spring. It was kindness rather than need that had made Mr Sullivan offer the work, and it was need rather than any skill in building which had caused Micheál to agree to do it, but even that would soon be over and then what will Daddy do? Dympna asked herself, stacking dishes in the dresser and putting the knives and forks into their own special drawer, lined with green baize. Mammy had bought the dresses at an auction and had lined the drawer herself, telling the small Dympna that in the house she had grown up in all the cutlery drawers were lined with baize, just like this one. Dympna had thought then, and she thought now, that the lovely mossy green baize was far too splendid just to line a drawer with; it should be set out somewhere where it showed and brightened the room. But she had always known better than to say things like that to her mother. Beatrice would have crushed her with a pitying look or even a laugh, and Dympna hated to be made to feel small.

Right now, however, she finished clearing away and began to lug a bucket across from under the sink to the fire; Mammy had used most of the hot water in the kettle, now it must be refilled and set back over the fire, for there were a number of housewifely jobs which still needed doing such as scrubbing the stone slabs of the kitchen floor and rinsing through the rough linen tea-towels, and Beatrice would not be too pleased if she found Dympna doing such important tasks with cold water.

She had finished the floor and the tea-towels, and was collecting the buckets to take out to the spring to refill, when someone knocked on the back door. Dympna went across and opened it, tiptoeing over the clean floor. She put her head around the edge of the door, then smiled and slipped out into the icy yard. 'Kieran! What on earth are you doing here? Aren't you busy helping them to build Ruan's house, like my daddy is? I thought your daddy said it was all hands to the pump today to get the work finished.'

'Aye, but it's too perishin' cold for whitewashin', which I was meant to do,' Kieran said, grinning. He was a handsome, dark-haired boy with a slanting, mischievous grin, and was generally acknowledged to be sweet on Dympna, though she was careful never to commit herself. She liked Kieran all right, who did not, but she knew very well that Mrs Sullivan had her eye on a girl for her second son and her name was unlikely to be Byrne. 'I'm goin' down to the quay to take the curragh out an' see if I can't find fish. Your daddy t'ought you might come, wit' your own lines, like, an' see if we manage to strike lucky.'

'Ooh, that 'ud be grand,' Dympna said longingly. She pushed the door open behind her. 'Look, I've just done the floor, but it'll be drying well by now I dare say. Come in, Kieran, and sit by the fire whiles I go and sound Mammy out. She . . . she's in her room. She's had an important letter . . . but she'd be really glad of some fish, I can tell you. Spuds and cabbage are all very well, but . . . look, I'll go and ask her.'

'I suppose the letter's from your Nicholas,' Kieran said, lounging over to the fireplace and sitting on the arm of the larger of the two armchairs. 'My mammy couldn't believe he wasn't comin' home after he'd missed Christmas. She said a t'ing or two, I can tell you.'

'Yes, so did we,' Dympna admitted, with a hand on the door which led through to the bedrooms. Family loyalty was strong, however. 'But he's workin' hard, so he says, and he's got a job you know, servin' in a bar in the evenings. I bet he was miserable, missing our Christmas and Easter. But he'll be home for the summer hols. Almost sure to be,' she finished as she left the room.

Her mother's bedroom door was ajar, but Dympna knocked anyway, then went in, talking as she did so. 'Mammy, it's Kieran, he's taking their curragh out – it's cold I know, but it's a very still day, the lough's like a mill-pond and the sea will be calm, too – so he thought he'd try for a few fish. Daddy said to ask if I might go along. We could do with some fresh fish, after eating so much of the salt stuff,' she ended.

Beatrice was sitting on her bed, with the letter spread out across the lap of her coarse calico apron. Her head was bent and Dympna saw tears on her cheeks. Immediately she went straight into the room and put an arm around Beatrice's shoulders. 'Mammy, don't cry,' she said. 'Was it bad news you've had in your letter?'

Beatrice sat up straight and gave a little shake. She didn't exactly push Dympna away but it was a gesture of repulsion, and Dympna let go of her at once and stepped back. Mammy was not someone to kiss or hug, or to expect a daughter to give her a cuddle now and then. Indeed, Dympna could not remember ever being hugged by Beatrice, though doubtless, when she had been small . . .

'Bad news?' Beatrice said now, her tone cool to the point of iciness. 'Certainly not; indeed, it's rather good news. But . . . I need to discuss it with your father and I'm rather afraid . . . he may make . . . difficulties.' Suddenly she swivelled round so that she faced Dympna and looked hard at her daughter. 'Dympna . . . you know we've lost the boat, but we're hoping to . . . borrow some money from a . . . a member of my family, so that we may replace it?'

'No, I didn't know that,' Dympna said uneasily. Her mother must be aware that neither she nor Micheál had discussed the devastating loss with either of their children. Beatrice might have told Nicholas, but if so, he had not thought it worth writing so much as a word of pity for their plight. 'Does . . . does the letter say you can have the money?'

'Ye-es. Well, in a way. You see I asked my sister Maude, who is married to a rich man, whether he – or she – might . . . might manage to loan us some money. I wrote as soon as I could after Daddy recovered his strength, but all I had back from her until now was a little note inside her Easter card, saying that she would do her best. And now . . . well, now she's written and said we can . . . we can have the money.'

'That's marvellous,' Dympna said encouragingly. 'Isn't that good news now, Mammy?'

'Yes, it is. But she has set out conditions. You see, my dear, she has pin-money which is paid into her bank account quarterly, but she . . . she spent most of it over Christmas. So she has to apply to her husband if she needs more and whilst he . . . he is the soul of generosity, she says, he will still want to know why she needs such a large sum.'

'Can't she explain that it's a loan to her elder sister?' Dympna said, thoroughly puzzled by the whole affair. What was more, the endearment which her mother had used was making her extremely uneasy; Beatrice never called her love names – why should she suddenly start now? What was more, although she knew that Beatrice did not have anything to do with her family, she had always assumed it was because her mother had married beneath her. Indeed, what else was she to think when neither parent had ever mentioned the matter? 'Surely if she explained about the pucan then he would realise it was a good investment and lend the money willingly?'

'No,' Beatrice said baldly after a short silence, during which she stared at Dympna as though seeing her for the first time. 'No, that will not do. But she says if she explains to her husband that we need to have money for the boat at once, but that you will work for nothing for the family for three years, then that would be a solution which would satisfy him. It seems,' she went on desperately, 'that servants are hard to get at the moment and Maude – Mrs Ditchling – would be happy to employ someone she could trust. And there would be no need, then, to repay the money, because you would have worked off the loan,' she added. 'Poor Nicholas . . . money runs through his fingers like water, I'm afraid. When he becomes a doctor he'll need every penny he earns to set himself up in a practice somewhere. But I can't tell your daddy that, of course.'

Dympna stared. She could feel her eyes getting rounder and rounder as her colour rose higher and her heart sank lower. Surely her mother could not be serious? To prevent Nicholas from having to help his family by paying back the money he had taken from Beatrice, she must go away from the village, from Connemara, from Ireland itself, to live as a servant in a strange land? Why, she would not even be working for wages, because she would have been bought, like an ass or a cow. Did her mother truly mean to let her slave her life away in a house, in a town, instead of working on the fishing boat, digging in the vegetable patch, helping Micheál or Beatrice herself in all their multitudinous tasks?

'Well?' Beatrice said impatiently as Dympna said nothing. 'What's so wrong with that, may I ask? You'd be fed, clothed and given a little pocket money in return for work which would seem almost a pleasure compared with what you've been doing here. And you would have bought your daddy his boat, which you helped to lose, you know,' she added.

Dympna began to say that she had done her best to get the boat above the high-water mark, that she had not realised the tide was going to be higher than usual, but Beatrice interrupted. 'Perhaps I shouldn't have said that,' she said quite kindly. 'None of us thought about the boat, we were all far too worried over your father. But Dympna, this is our last chance. If I tell my sister that you won't agree then the matter will be closed. Micheál will never get his pucan and you'll have to go into service anyway, because there will be nothing for any of us, here. Oh, I dare say Micheál will make himself a curragh and go long-shore fishing in it, but he won't need much help from Egan, and what's your brother to do, whilst you're living like a queen in Dublin, working for some rich woman who has no care for you whatsoever?'

'What will Daddy say?' Dympna blurted out as her mother sighed and began to dab the tears from her cheeks with a small square of linen. 'Will . . . will he want me to go?'

'I don't want to worry him with the full details,'

Beatrice said quickly. 'My dear child, it isn't for ever, remember. Nicholas will certainly give you some money back when he's a doctor. Surely, surely you can be a brave girl and do your best for us all for three little years? Is it so much to ask?'

She stood up and took Dympna's hands in hers, holding them firmly. Then she bent down, kissed her daughter's forehead and stood back, smiling encouragingly. 'I knew you'd not let your father suffer,' she said triumphantly. 'Dympna, Daddy may not know at first what he owes you, but in time he'll be truly grateful to his girl. Now you run off with Kieran and I'll tell Daddy the good news when he gets back from the Sullivans.'

Dympna thought of a great many other things she should have said, but somehow she gave voice to none of them. It would be horribly selfish to deny Daddy the money he needed for his new pucan just because she hated the thought of domestic service anywhere, but particularly in England. And it was all very well for her mother to say it was only for three years, but how did she know Nicholas would ever pay her a penny? He had shown very little inclination to help them so far, he had not even alluded to the poor *Aleen* in his brief postcards home. And how was she to get home at the end of the three years if Nicholas did not pay up? Her mother said she would be given pocket money but she supposed that there would be things she simply had to spend that on. She knew very little about domestic service, but thought, from what she had heard girls at school say when referring to members of their own family at present working for one of the big houses in Clifden, that such things as bus fares and toiletries had to be supplied out of one's wages.

Of course she could wash with a piece of red scrubbing soap and walk everywhere, she supposed. But surely, no one, not even Beatrice, would expect her to remain at her mistress's beck and call for three whole years? She would get time off and she could scarcely spend that in her room – even if she had a room of her own. Most lower servants shared, she knew.

All these thoughts had flown through her head in the time it took her to leave her mother's room and go back to the kitchen and Kieran. He stood up as she entered, his face eager. 'Are you comin' wit' me, alanna?' he asked. 'Did your mammy say you could do wit' the fish now?'

'Yes, I can come,' Dympna said. 'I'll fetch a couple o' lines from the sheds.'

And when, presently, the two of them walked, side by side, down to the little stone quay sticking out into the sea lough, she found herself telling Kieran a little of what her mother had been saying to her. Not the whole story, that was too shaming to be put into words to anyone but family. No, she merely said that her mother had managed to get her a good job working for a relative in Liverpool and, in return for her help, the relative would lend Micheál the money to buy a pucan.

'You're goin' over the water?' Kieran said, stopping short. 'But you can't, Dymp! We can't get along wit'out you here – have you t'ought of that? What'll I do wit' no girl to dance wit' at the monthly hop and no one to canoodle wit' behind the peat pile of a summer evenin'?'

'You'll manage,' Dympna said shortly. 'It's not for ever, Kieran. I'll be back soon enough.'

'But . . . but we're courtin', aren't we?' Kieran said.

He caught her shoulders and pulled her to a halt. 'I . . . I t'ought we'd an understandin', Dymp.'

'Oh, did you?' Dympna said. 'And what would your mammy say to that, may I ask?'

'Oh, mammies are all the same, they say their boys are too young to t'ink of marryin' anyone,' Kieran pointed out truthfully. 'But the mammy likes you, Dymp. She t'inks you're a grand girl, so she does.'

'That's very nice of her. But even grand girls aren't always good enough for the second son who works like a good 'un on the land an' has a grand way with' a net and a boat,' Dympna said, half laughing. 'Your mammy's just about to lose her eldest son, don't forget. She won't want to lose you as well.'

'Well, I'm not sayin' I'd planned to marry this year, nor mebbe next,' Kieran admitted, looking a trifle self-conscious. 'You're not seventeen yet an' I'm only eighteen meself. But when I'm twenty-one – that's a good age – I t'ought I'd pop the questions, alanna.'

'Well, when you're twenty-one go ahead,' Dympna advised him. 'If you're still of the same mind, that is. But if I've a been away a year or two, mebbe you'll not be so keen on gettin' involved with a Byrne.'

'I shall,' Kieran said fiercely and promptly began kissing her. After five minutes of this he breathed huskily into her ear: 'Oh, Dympna, let's . . . let's go somewhere quieter than this. 'Tis likely we'll be interrupted just as we get to the nice part and I do want a bit of a cuddle wit' you, so I do.'

'I think we'd best not, Kieran,' Dympna said gently, withdrawing herself from his embrace. 'Come on, let's get down to the curragh. I've got an awful lot of thinkin' to do.'

April was over and May was warming the trees into

blossom and starring the lanes with bluebells when at last Dympna set off for England. She had confided a little in Egan, who had been horrified by the sacrifice she was making, but she had not even told her favourite brother the whole story. How could she, when Beatrice had made her promise not to let Micheál know the arrangement? So far as her daddy was concerned she had offered to go over to her aunt's to help her a bit around the house after she had been kind enough to give the family a generous loan.

'The money will buy a pucan and new nets, and it will reseed the vegetable patch for the spring and buy clothes for the lot of us,' Micheál had said jubilantly. 'Why, there's no need at all for you to go over there, alanna. I'll have Egan in the boat wit' me, so you can go to the teacher training college an' get yourself a teachin' certificate same as you've always wanted to do. Then between us we'll pay back the old loan in no time at all. My, won't I be proud of me girl, teachin' children to read and cipher and do sums and such.'

'I'll mebbe do that, Daddy, when I've spent some time with me aunt,' Dympna said diplomatically. 'But Mammy would like me to go, wouldn't you, Mammy?'

The family had been gathered around the fire, having great potato roast as a celebration of the money which had arrived that morning and now Beatrice looked up, her face red from bending over the fire, and nodded vigorously. 'Yes, I'd like her to go, Micheál,' she said. 'My sister's a nice person, she'll see that Dympna enjoys herself while she helps out with the children and so on. There'll be time enough for her to go to college later in the year.'

'Well, don't you stay longer than the summer, then,' Micheál said in a lordly manner, the manner of one who sees his future suddenly bright ahead. 'We'll want you back home be then, me darlin' Dymp.'

It was hard to pretend, to know that she was being sent away and would not be welcomed back here until Nicholas had begun to pay back the money. If he ever did, that was. Harder, even, to leave Kieran, who wanted to marry her and keep her in Connemara for the rest of their lives. But she had to keep faith. Mammy had written to her sister saying that Dympna would be with them in Liverpool just as soon as they could arrange her clothing, passage and so on, and Maude had been generous. A ticket had been sent – a single ticket – all the way from Clifden to Liverpool, the passage on the ferry boat and everything, and Maude had enclosed enough money to buy Dympna respectable travelling clothes, a neat suitcase and even galoshes and an umbrella, objects which Dympna had never even seen, let alone dreamed of possessing.

So she and Kieran had had a rather tearful goodbye the previous evening, in Rosa's shed amongst the sweet-smelling marsh hay, and today she had said her own goodbyes. Lightly, because Daddy had to believe she was coming back by the end of summer, and Egan, who knew it was unlikely, though he thought she would be back by the following spring. Only Beatrice knew the whole story and she behaved as she always had: with practicality, advising her daughter to buy herself some bread and cheese and some apples before she got aboard the ferry, for by then the food she herself had packed that morning would be long gone.

'I'll do that,' Dympna said calmly. She kissed everyone, even Rosa, standing patiently between the shafts outside the Clifden railway station where her journey was to start. 'Do write to me, Egan – and I'll write to you, of course. Take care of yourself, Daddy, and buy a real good pucan – I'll be longing to see it when I come home. Goodbye, Mammy – you'll write?'

'Of course I will; every week,' Beatrice said. She kissed Dympna's brow and then her cheek. 'Now this is a big adventure for you, Dympna, so be sure to take care of yourself and be good.'

'I will,' Dympna said rather drily. Her mother's parting words had been, as usual, more of an admonition than a farewell. 'Ah, that'll be me train. Goodbye, goodbye!'

She climbed aboard and leaned out of the window, waving vigorously until her parents and Egan were no more than dots. Then she sank back in her seat and looked out at the sweet summary countryside rushing past the windows and began, very discreetly, to weep.

Beatrice was very cheerful all the way home and, once there, made a specially good meal for everyone, because she said she knew they would miss Dympna very much. 'But we'll make the best of it and the time will soon go,' she said cheerfully, laying the table. 'Why, when she comes back you'll be so used to the new pucan that it'll be like the *Fair Aleen* all over again. And very likely Egan here will be courting on his own account – think of that, now.'

'Egan, courting? But he'll barely be fifteen,' Micheál said. 'Have you run mad, Bea? You make it sound as though the girl was goin' away for years an' years.'

'Now wasn't that silly of me, when she'll be back before the cat can lick her ear,' Beatrice said in a marvelling tone. 'I've cooked a good stew now that we can afford a scrape of meat now and then, with herb dumplings – can you eat three, Micheál?'

'I could eat a dozen,' Micheál said jovially. 'I need to build me strength up, wit' a new boat to buy an' the money to buy it to hand at last. But it was hard to see Dympna go; she's been more help to me than most daughters. Aye, she's a grand girl, so she is, and I'll miss her sore.'

'So shall I,' Beatrice said rather grimly, but in her heart she was thinking: Maybe she'll meet some lad in Liverpool and marry him, maybe she'll never come back. And I'll have my darling Micheál all to myself at last, for he's never looked at another woman save Dympna. And it never occurred to her for one minute that this was a strange way indeed for a mother to think of her daughter, and a stranger way to think of the man she so dearly loved.

All the way across Ireland in the railway train, waiting on stations and in Dublin itself, Dympna tried not to think about the time to come. What's three years, when all's said and done, she asked herself from time to time, but the truth was that when you're not yet seventeen, three years seems a lifetime. What was more, when she came back she would be almost twenty, and that was old, old.

Then there was Kieran. Would he wait for her? He had sworn to do so, but he did not know that her stay might be as long as three years and she would no doubt change in that time, as would he. She would be a woman by then and he positively middle-aged. He would be twenty-two, a man indeed! She acknowledged, of course, that people in Connemara did not usually marry young; in fact, the opposite was true. She had once asked Beatrice why this was and Beatrice, having thought the matter over, said that firstly, folk who lived by fishing and working on the land could not afford to get married young and secondly, that if couples got married when they were both in the their thirties, the chances were that they would not have families of fifteen or sixteen children.

Fifteen or sixteen! Dympna had been both shocked and intrigued, but Beatrice apparently thinking that she had gone too far, had refused to elaborate. It was not until recently that Dympna had seen and understood the truth of both her mother's statements. The vast majority of people in Connemara were poor, and the poorest were those who had married young and raised large families. It was a wicked thing indeed to limit the number of babes you had, everyone knew *that*, but if you married late it stood to reason that your child-bearing days would be numbered, which was no very bad thing, for what was the point of bringing mouths into the world which you could not feed?

However, it was one thing to agree to a principle, Dympna discovered, and another to be forced into practising it. She wanted to marry young so that she could enjoy her children and the companionship of her man for as many years as might be. Beatrice had been scarcely eighteen when she had married Micheál and, though their life had not been easy, Dympna thought they were happy. Whether Kieran was to be her chosen mate she did not know, but if she was in England and he in Connemara their chances of finding true love seemed remote. And he was so good-looking, she agonised as the train carried her further and further from him. He was bound the be snapped up by some likely girl – there was red-haired Bridget, the eldest daughter of their neighbours – she was a nice young woman. And then there was pretty, disdainful Siobhan from the cottages over the mountain with her smooth, chestnut-coloured hair and her big, melting brown eyes. And that was just near at hand. If Kieran cared to look further afield Clifden was full of pretty girls – oh, she knew he would not wait for her, she just knew it.

But very soon she had other things to think about. She reached Dublin, and she and her one suitcase managed to find their way to the lodging house Beatrice had booked for her. It was owned by a distant relative of the Byrnes and, though it smelled very strange and seemed oppressively dark and gloomy to Dympna, she was so tired that she fell into the small white bed and slept soundly until roused by her landlady next morning. Then she had a quick breakfast and made her way down to the quays and aboard the steamer for Liverpool. She had barely got aboard, what was more, when she met someone she knew – a young woman who had left the village school for domestic service some years before. Her name was Lily Donaly and she recognised Dympna at once and beckoned her over.

'Come an' sit be me, then we can talk,' she said cosily, squeezing Dympna's arm and pointing to a row of wooden seats against the rail. 'So you're off to England, eh? Well, you'll find it quite a change, believe me. Is it a kitchen maid you're goin' for, or have you sumpen else in mind?'

'I don't really know. Just domestic service,' Dympna said. 'I don't know whether you heard, but Daddy lost the *Fair Aleen* – that was his pucan – in a tremendous storm last March, so we're all going to work as hard as we can so he can get another one.

There's not much a girl can do except go into service,' she finished.

Lily's thin, arched eyebrows rose. 'Well, it's mebbe a start,' she conceded. 'But I got out of it long since . . . I'm a sales lady in a big store, now. The money's better an' you meet a better class of person, so you do.' She looked Dympna up and down. 'Why don't you try for a job like mine?' she asked. 'You look smart and you talk nice – I dare say your mammy made you speak good – so there's no reason why you shouldn't land a better job than skivvyin'.'

'My . . . my employer sent me ticket money and these clothes,' Dympna confessed. 'I couldn't not turn up. I'll have to work for her until . . . until I feel I've paid me debt.'

The older girl snorted. 'Good servants is hard to get – and harder to keep,' she observed. 'Stay wit' her for six months an' you'll have paid your debt, if you like to call it that. Where's your position, anyway?'

'I'm to be taken to Devonshire Road,' Dympna said. 'They're sending someone to meet the boat, thank goodness. I'd never get there, else.'

Lily snorted again. 'D'you think they don't know that?' she demanded. 'They'll see you get to their house all right and start you workin' straight off. But you get fed pretty well in service,' she concluded. 'It's not good food, but there'll be plenty of it. You'll need it when you're up at dawn scrubbing floors and lighting fires, and still there at midnight waiting for them to go to bed so's you can follow suit.'

'You make it sound terrible, like slavery,' Dympna said tremulously. 'It can't be that bad, surely? Are you – are you anywhere near Devonshire Road?'

'No, but nowhere in Liverpool's that far off. Look, I'll scribble the name of me store and me lodgings address on a bit o' paper, an' when you have time off you can some an' visit me. How's that? Either at the shop or if it's an evenin', at me lodgings. We'll keep in touch, an' then when you've had enough o' skivvyin', mebbe I can help you get another job.'

'That's kind,' Dympna said, much encouraged. 'I'll be glad to see a friendly face after a few days I reckon.'

'Well, mebbe I painted it all a bit black,' Lily said, looking rather self-conscious. 'Mebbe it won't be as bad as all that. Just you do your best to please 'em, an' it'll probably be awright. Now how about goin' below? It's gettin' chilly up here.'

Dympna agreed, though to her the freshness of the breeze in her face was welcome; she had felt like a lobster in a pot in the lodging house, but here, on the open deck, it was not so very different from being aboard the dear old *Aleen* and she would have liked to stay out on deck if possible. However, Lily was clearly anxious to be friendly so Dympna followed her meekly below decks and sat in the saloon sipping very strong coffee and listening to her advice and comments on those around her.

'It's a long voyage,' Lily said at one point. 'I usually tries for a snooze when I've 'ad me coffee. Could you do wit' some shut-eye?'

Dympna did not think she could possibly close her eyes with so much going on around her, but presently, to her surprise, she felt her lids getting heavy and almost without realising it she slipped into sleep.

The house was huge. Dympna had been astonished at the size of Liverpool, so much . . . so much *higher* than Dublin even, which had been astonishing enough.

She had felt like a very small mouse amongst very large cats as she stood on the quayside, wondering how her employer would recognise her, forgetting that the lady in question had bought the very clothing in which she was dressed.

It was not her employer who met her, however, but a large woman with marvellously white skin and small, tightly buttoned mouth. She had thick grey hair cut and waved fashionably beneath a rather ugly black hat, which matched her coat, and despite her size she moved quickly and with decision, for no sooner did she set eyes on Dympna than she came over to her, gave a tight, perfunctory smile and snapped, 'Miss Byrne? I'm Mrs Ditchling's housekeeper, my name's Mrs Palfrey. Hurry up, the car is waiting outside in the road.'

A car! Dympna had never even sat in a car, let alone travelled in one, but somehow it no longer seemed exciting. Mrs Palfrey took almost no notice of her on the short journey and though Dympna saw that the man in a smart dark uniform, who drove the car, kept eyeing her through the little mirror that hung in the middle of the windscreen, he never once smiled or seemed friendly. She sat on the edge of the rich leather seat, clasping her new handbag with one hand and the side of the car door with the other, and prayed that she would not be sick, for she, who had withstood the perils of fierce Atlantic storms, found that travelling in a well-sprung motor car could make you feel every bit as queasy.

Fortunately the car drew to a halt before she could begin to feel really ill and the driver jumped out, opened the door for Mrs Palfrey, and then went round to the back of the car and extracted Dympna's case from wherever he had stowed it. He stood it on the ground, waited until they were both on the pavement, got back in the car and drove away.

Mrs Palfrey tutted. 'I can't think what Mr Strawn was thinking of, putting us down out here,' she said sharply and almost as if it were Dympna's fault. 'However, I dare say he thought it would be easier for us to go through the front door than to traipse all the way round by the jigger.' She turned a far from friendly eye on her companion. 'And don't think, Miss, that servants usually come and go through the front door, for that they do not. It's the back door for you, as you'll soon realise, I hope.'

Nevertheless she made her way up the short flight of steps and rang the doorbell so imperiously that Dympna marvelled at the wait. Surely anyone inside would have come running at once upon hearing the bell peeled so decidedly?

She stood and waited, however, not liking to ask Mrs Palfrey if they might not be wiser to go round the back, and presently their patience was rewarded. The big, black-painted front door with its brass knocker and long, plush-handled bell-pull started, slowly, to open. Dympna's new life, it seemed, was about to begin.

# Chapter Nine

Elsie Taylor finished polishing the last apple on the display at the back of the counter and looked hopefully across at her employer. He was a cross-grained elderly man by the name of Josiah Cannell, not an easy man to work for, but it was past eight o'clock and the April evening was already darkening. Besides, she was only paid to work until seven – surely he would let her go now? She cleared her throat. 'Ah-hem . . . Mr Cannell, sir, I done all them apples just like you said. They're like perishin' mirrors, honest to God they are, you can see your bl . . . I mean you can see your face in 'em. Can I go now?'

Mr Cannell was sitting on a tall stool behind the counter, totting up figures in a large ledger. He tutted at her and put his fingers in his ears just to prove, Elsie supposed crossly, that he was *far* too busy to listen to a chit of a thing like her. But experience had already taught her that he could make life very unpleasant for his staff if he took against one of them, so she sighed patiently and waited until he had finished adding up and had ruled a neat double line beneath the final figure. Only then did he look up and poke his spectacles further down his nose so that he could see her over the top of them. 'Yes, Miss Taylor?' he said in a mean, whining voice. 'How many times do I have to tell you not to interrupt me when I'm addin' up?'

It didn't seem worth repeating all her earlier

remarks so Elsie just said: 'Can I go now, sir? It's past eight and I'm only paid till . . .'

'Have you finished polishin' them apples?' Mr Cannell said sharply, proving either that she had not interrupted his adding up of the figures or that he was completely stone deaf. 'As for time-keepin', I clearly remember tellin' you when you took the job that I'd no hintention of employin' a clock watcher and you *assured* me . . .'

Elsie thought of the meagre wages she was reluctantly paid each Saturday night and of the over-time she was forced to work. Then she remembered his constant nagging and seriously wondered whether to throw discretion to the winds, together with this altogether horrible little job. He took it for granted that she would willingly go upstairs and clean his kitchen before making them a couple of jam sarnies and a cuppa at noon, and then had the cheek to take sixpence off her weekly wage for what he termed 'them dinners'. There were no perks here, either, not so much as a bag of fades to take home to her mum or a ha'penny knocked off the price of a cabbage. Oh, how she would love to give him a piece of her mind and let him search for some other poor kid to do his dirty work! But it was possible that Mr Cannell saw what was crossing her mind because he suddenly got down from his stool, breaking off in mid-grumble, and began to stow his ledgers away, saying over his shoulder as he did so that she might as well leave as not, only he trusted she'd be in early tomorrow, since according to his figures trade was down again this week.

Elsie longed to remind him that the entire country was groaning beneath a Depression and that if it hadn't been for the fact that money was short and jobs shorter she would not have dreamed of demeaning herself by working in his rat run of a shop, but she was sixteen now and had been in and out of three jobs in the last six months, ever since she – and a number of her friends – had been given their cards from the little biscuit factory down Great Howard Street.

'It were last in, first out,' she had told her mother tearfully, the day she had been sacked, for what else could you call it when all was said and done? 'And to think I were doin' awright wi' Jacobs . . . doin' well, in fact . . . only this here Sylvester chappie was payin' more, for shorter hours . . .'

'I did warn you, chuck,' her mother had said comfortably, pressing a fat ball of suet pastry into a white china pudding bowl and beginning to ease it up the sides. 'But the young 'ave to find out for theirselves the 'ard way. Well-known fact. Anyroad, you'll gerranother job, see if you doesn't.'

Well, she had. And lost it, as well, when her new boss went broke. So when she had seen the little card in old Cannell's window it had seemed heaven sent. Even the wages, poor though they were, were better than nothing and, with her usual optimism, Elsie had managed to convince herself that she would soon get so useful to old Cannell that he would raise her money and start treating her like a human being instead of a slave.

It had not happened, however. The old skinflint still grudged the tiny wage he paid her, and always kept her late and expected her to come in early. I've nearly had a bellyful, Elsie told herself grimly, fetching her old brown beret and flimsy raincoat out of the back room and heading for the shop door without another glance at her muttering employer.

I've bloody nearly had it with the old bugger. But me mam 'ud kill me if I quit one job afore I'd landed another.

She began to walk swiftly along Byrom Street; things could be worse, she reminded herself. It was about time she started looking for another job, though Mam would tell her that no one wanted to employ girls who had had four jobs in six months and advise her to stick it out for a bit longer. And it ain't because she wants her share of me huge wage packet, Elsie told herself, whistling a little tune under her breath as she walked. You had to hand it to Mam, she never pressed an underpaid kid to hand over their money, not when she'd got enough coming in from the others. In the good days, when Elsie had been working at Jacobs – oh, why had she ever been such a fool to leave? – she had paid her share into the family coffers happily enough. But now it was different. She needed every penny for things like stockings, a bit of powder and lipstick for when she went dancing, and tram fares.

But at least I don't have to pay for me seat at the flicks, she reminded herself as she passed a brightly coloured poster advertising the programme at the Burlington Cinema the following week. At least – I *do* bleedin' pay for it, she remembered crossly. Oh, not in money, but in . . . in takin' evasive action every time Geoff Sale stops grabbin' for me hands and starts in grabbin' elsewhere.

The thought of poor Geoff's abortive attempts, the previous Saturday night, to get a large and sweaty hand between the little pearl buttons on her accordion-pleated white blouse made her giggle. He was a nice lad, was Geoff, but . . . well, he's not the one for me and that's the truth of it, Elsie told herself, dodging three young men, arm in arm, who seemed to consider they owned the pavement and swept along at a good pace, regardless of who was in their path. Geoff's good to me, her thoughts continued. He takes me to the flicks, tries to pay for me at dances, though I'm not givin' in on that point – he'd think he bleedin' *owned* me if I let him hand over his gelt – and he's forever waitin' for me outside the shop and swearin' he'll give old Cannell a thick lip if he don't treat me wi' more respect.

'You don't appreciate Geoff,' her mother had said only the previous weekend, when she'd shot in like a kid being chased by a scuffer as soon as they reached her front door, shouting good-night to Geoff over her shoulder as she did so. 'That young feller must be a saint to keep on courtin' you when you won't give him no encouragement, norreven a kind word.'

'I do give him kind words,' Elsie had said indignantly. 'But that don't give him the right to start maulin' me as though . . . as though I were a bleedin' dockyard tart.'

'Elsie!' Mam had said, really shocked. 'Well, I won't say you were a dockyard tart – and nor shall anyone else whiles I'm around – but you're certainly norra lady.'

Her sister Suzie, drying dishes whilst listening with appreciation to this interesting talk, said: 'What's a bleedin' dockyard tart, our Mam?'

'There, now look what you done,' Mam had said reproachfully. 'You need a damned good paddlin', our Els – I shouldn't ha' been so soft on you when you was Suzie's age, that's the trouble. Anyway, if you don't mean to let Geoff give you a kiss in the porch afore you come indoors then you shouldn't let him pay for you to go dancin'.'

'I don't lerrim, I pay me own wack,' Elsie had said

triumphantly. 'And I can't *help* Geoff followin' me around like a lovesick parrot, can I? I wish he wouldn't, I tell you straight, our Mam. As for the fillums, I can't enjoy a real good cry in the cinema no more, norreven a good laugh. He's all over me, like a bl . . . I mean like a perishin' octopus and he's got the hottest hands in the whole of the Pool, what's more.'

That had more or less finished the conversation, but it had, if the truth be known, left Elsie feeling a trifle guilty. It was true that Geoff was both kind and generous, and that he never used his strength against her, which he could have done, for he was six foot tall and broad with it, whereas Elsie had never gone an inch above five foot three and was built accordingly. But Elsie knew very well that she was still holding a candle for Jimmy Ruddock and she'd not set eyes on him now for nearly three whole years, though he did write from time to time.

It had been a rotten affair, that. Jimmy's horrible old aunt and his cousins had sworn blind that Jimmy had thieved some money from the Lumleys' fish shop, and taken various articles from the flat above the shop and all. Jimmy had fled, too, which might not have gone down too well. It was hard for Elsie to piece together just what had happened, since the entire Blaney family had lied their heads off – had they been little Pinocchio, Elsie thought, their noses would have touched their knees by the time the scuffers left – and the Lumleys had steadfastly refused to discuss the matter.

But it seemed the police weren't the idiots that the Blaneys had thought them, for though right from the start pretty well they had realised Frank was trying to frame his cousin, they had not been able to prove anything until about six months later, when they had arrested Frank Blaney for possession, which meant, apparently, that they had found him spending money which they had marked and then planted in the till of a shop where Frank had become friendly with one of the young shop assistants. He had done his best to get out of it, of course, swearing that he had got the money in his change, but this time there was too much evidence against him and Frank was where he belonged, Elsie thought, in Walton gaol. Elsie was delighted and hoped this would bring Jimmy hurrying back to Kennedy Court, but the difficulty was discovering where he had gone and how she could reach him. When she went round to help peel spuds at the chip shop Mr Lumley had asked her to get in touch with Jimmy and tell him that the fuss was over; his cousin had been arrested and the police, as well as the Lumleys and all Jimmy's other friends, now acknowledged that he was innocent of anything shady.

'Tell him we want him back, lass,' Mr Lumley said earnestly. 'He were a good little worker, our Jim.'

It had taken a long time, though, to get the news that he was no longer under a cloud across to Jimmy, simply because she did not have his address or any idea where he was right now. Oh, he wrote to her, but the letters were postmarked from London usually, and Elsie, who had known Jimmy better, probably, than almost anyone else, was sure that he had not gone to London. But finally, after a year, he had written to her, actually giving her a poste restante address where she might send her letters, if, he said humbly, she would like to get in touch again.

So she had written, delighted with this breakthrough, telling him to come home and claim his old job back again. *Mr Lumley's real sorry for all the fuss, he says you need never have left though, for he'd telled the scuffers over and over that it weren't you who done the deed*, she had written. *Do come home, our Jimmy – we misses you ever so. Mam says Auntie Raddles will give you a room, cheap, and then we can all be comfortable again.*

But then he had written back, telling her all over again how he was working on a trawler and loving every minute of it. *I don't think I could settle down to an indoor job again*, he wrote. *Besides, Abel needs me. The others are all old fellers and I'm the one who can climb over the side when a net gets tangled, or jump for the quayside with the mooring rope when the weather's so bad that you have to jump or you'll be dashed to pieces between the boat's side and the quay. I'm earning good money and all, our Els; man's wages Abel says, so it 'ud be a real downer to come back to being a spud-basher, like I were before.*

He had promised to come back for a bit of a holiday, though, some time when the fishing wasn't good or the boat was in for repair, and she had had to be content with that. Not that she was. Somehow, Jimmy had become an important part of her life and the fact that he had been entirely out of it for three years did not stop her from missing him.

I suppose it were that kiss, after the Blackpool trip, she told herself now, hurrying down Gay Street in the direction of the court. Probably be now he's norra bit like I 'member him, I've sort o' *glamorised* him, as if he was a fillum star, because I've not seen him for so long. Why, when he does come back I'll be that disappointed that I'll probably tell Geoff I'll marry him after all.

But she did not believe it; not in her heart. She and Jimmy had been little more than kids when he'd done a moonlight, but sometimes kids know their own feelings a good deal better than adults. Jimmy might now be a spotty, greasy-haired lout, like Edwin Blaney, but she did not truly think it likely. Even if he was, she told herself defiantly, crossing the court and running up the steps to her front door, he'd still be kind o' special to me, would Jimmy. You don't stop likin' someone just because they've been away for a while. And right from the first moment we met, almost, I'd decided that I were goin' to marry him when I were old enough. Oh, I didn't tell *him*, o' course I didn't! How he'd ha' laughed, even though he'd probably have felt dead embarrassed, too. But I reckons if a girl feels like that when she's almost fourteen, two years won't change her feelin's that much.

She entered the house and went through to the kitchen. Her mother was ironing on the big kitchen table, the fire roaring hot despite the fact that it had been a warm and pleasant day, the flat irons ranged before it. She turned and grinned at Elsie as her daughter came through the doorway. 'Hello, chuck,' she said, resting her iron on the board for a moment and wiping the back of her hand across the sweat which had beaded her brow. 'Late again – I suppose the old skinflint thought up something to keep you busy.'

'Polishin' perishin' apples,' Elsie said wearily, dragging off her mackintosh and the faded beret, and hanging them on the hooks by the back door. 'As if they'll sell better polished than unpolished – I asks you! Oh Mam, what a great mound o' shirts. I bet you wish you'd had more gals and fewer boys when you was havin' your fambly.'

It was true that the older girls did their own ironing but Lucy, who was not yet four, seemed to create a lot of work, and though Suzie was a help in many ways, Mam did not let the eight-year-old touch the heavy flats, nor go too near the fire, for that matter.

'Oh aye, there's a good few shirts, now all your

brothers are in work,' Mrs Taylor conceded, picking up her iron again. 'Mind, we're lucky to have 'em all in jobs, an' I don't mind ironin' office shirts an' the blue workin' kind, but when it comes to these here ones for dancin' in . . . well, I told our Alan I'd as soon he married young Peg, so's she were the one who'd have the ironin'. And d'you know what he said?'

'Something saucy,' Elsie said. She walked over to the draining board and picked up the loaf. 'Mind if I cuts a slice, Mam? Only I'm fair starvin'.'

'Oh . . . your dinner's in the oven, keepin' warm,' Mrs Taylor remembered. 'Gerrit out an' sit yourself down. It's salt beef tonight, wi' carrots an' onions. You're fond o' that so I left you a good portion. Not that it seems to stick to your ribs,' she added, looking at her daughter's skinny frame. 'Anyone 'ud think I kept you short to look at you.'

Elsie went to the oven and took out a loaded plate, mouth watering at the sight of it. She put it at the end of the table furthest from the fire, sat down and began to eat. With her mouth full she said: 'It's good, Mam, real good, one o' your best meals, I reckon. Tell me what Alan said about marryin' Peg.'

Mrs Taylor laid another ironed shirt on the neat pile by her side and reached for the next. She sprinkled water on its rumpled surface, then changed the cooling iron for a hot one and began to work, raising her voice above the hiss of steam. 'He said when he got hitched he wouldn't need to go dancin' no more, so that 'ud halve the shirts what needed ironin'. I had to laugh, but isn't that just like a feller? Poor Peg, once Alan's gorrer in his clutches she won't be doin' no dancin' again.'

'Typical,' Elsie agreed. She cut a dumpling in half and wedged it into her mouth, effectively cutting short any further conversation.

Mrs Taylor glanced across at her and raised her eyebrows. 'Dear me, cat got your tongue? I were just goin' to tell you something that 'ud mek you smile an' all, but I suppose I'd best wait until you've finished your dinner.'

Elsie chewed, swallowed and smiled engagingly at her parent. 'Oh, go on, Mam, tell me whatever it is,' she said hopefully. 'All the way home I've been thinkin' . . . well, about the past, to tell you the truth. About Jimmy. I suppose it ain't a letter?'

Mrs Taylor paused in her work, the iron standing for long enough to make her give an exclamation. 'Lor' love us, if I singe his majesty's bleedin' best shirt me name'll be mud. Well, if that ain't odd, Els, I don't know what is. I were about to say there's a letter . . .'

Elsie jumped to her feet, pushing back her plate. 'Oh, Mam, I just knew it,' she said exultantly. 'Ever so often, when I've been thinkin' of Jimmy, there's been a letter when I get home. Where've you purrit?'

'On the mantel, to the right of the fire, behind the picture of Queen Mary,' her mother said. 'Now be careful, the fire's real hot – I should know, I've been sweatin' over this perishin' ironin' for hours. Now finish your dinner . . .'

But Elsie had reached up to the mantel and got hold of the letter. She scrutinised it for a moment, then sat down at the table again and pulled her plate towards her. 'Awright, Mam, I'll finish me dinner first, afore I reads it,' she said placatingly, picking up her knife and fork. 'I've had this funny feelin' all day that he might be comin' to see us . . . wouldn't that be just the grandest thing?'

'Oh aye, very nice,' Mrs Taylor said absently, her eyes on the fat white envelope propped up before her daughter's plate. 'Well, now you've gorrit, I dessay there's no harm in openin' it, seein' wharr 'e's got to say for himself.'

Elsie, still eating, spluttered. 'You're as curious as a perishin' cat, Mam,' she said accusingly. 'Go on, admit you're longin' to know what Jimmy's been up to.'

'No, I . . . oh, all right, then, I'm curious,' Mrs Taylor admitted. 'You're a little wretch, Elsie Annabel Taylor, you read me like a perishin' book. Go on, open it up.'

Elsie let her hand hover tantalisingly over the envelope for a moment, then pounced on it and tore it open. For a few moments she read in silence, then she looked up at her mother's enquiring face and smiled. 'Well, it's good an' bad,' she said. 'Which d'you want first?'

'Oh, good,' Mrs Taylor said. 'Spill the beans, chuck.'

'He's comin' home . . . back here, to Kennedy Court. Of course as you know, he didn't intend to come back for good, only for a visit. But do you remember me tellin' you that this old Abel Totteridge chap had a son . . . can't remember his name . . . what was in the merchant fleet, on a timber ship?'

'Aye, that's right,' Mrs Taylor admitted. 'Bertie, was it?'

'You're right, Mam, Bertie it was. Well, it seems he's coming home. He was injured when a pile o' plankin' fell on him as they was off-loading, and he's goin' to stay ashore until his hurts heal and then he'll join his dad in the trawler.'

'Oh,' Mrs Taylor said doubtfully. 'But surely they'll still need our Jimmy? I mean if this Bertie's hurt bad . . .'

'It ain't that bad. Jimmy says Bertie'll sail at the end o' the month, and in the meantime acourse the

312

Totteridges will want their son's room back, which is where Jimmy was sleepin' up till Bertie's arrival. So anyway Jimmy says he'll be comin' home at the weekend – oh, Lor, that's only a couple o' days away – and can we find him a bed, just till he's gorrimself settled.'

'A bed!' Mrs Taylor said, eyes rounding. 'Dear Lord, there ain't a spare inch in this house, our Els – if there was, Jimmy could have it an' welcome. I allus used to say as Aunt Raddles would be glad to oblige, but it just happens as she's full at the moment. What about the Blaneys?'

'Oh, Mam, he couldn't possibly go back there, not wi' Frank in the nick and his aunt and uncle still swearin' blind as Frank were framed and it were Jimmy all along. Besides, they's all a lot bigger now, not just Jimmy. They couldn't cram him into that horrible little room where they all used to sleep . . . he wouldn't go, I'd say.'

'No, course not. Dunno why I suggested it,' Mrs Taylor said. 'I wonder whether the Lumleys might obliged? They want him back, you said?'

'Well, they *did* a couple o' years back,' Elsie pointed out. 'But times change, Mam. They've got all their own kids workin' now and I don't know whether they'll still want Jimmy. They might find him a corner, though, just for a night or two. Until he got himself settled, like.'

'Well, if he's arrivin' this weekend you'd better go round there right now and ask,' Mrs Taylor said brightly. 'Because there won't be enough time for you to write and tell him we've nowhere for him to sleep. Wharrabout a job, though? They ain't no easier to come by than they were.'

'He's that much older and more experienced,' Elsie

said, though rather doubtfully. 'It's a pity there ain't no fishin' fleet sails from here . . . but couldn't he take a berth? The sea's the sea, Mam.'

'No it ain't. That's to say bein' a merchant seaman ain't much like bein' aboard a trawler, you can bet your life on that,' her mother said dampingly. 'Use your wits, Elsie! But I dare say Jimmy's put a bit aside for a rainy day, so he can use that just while he looks around for work. And anyway, the Lumleys might make a place for him. They were sorry for all the trouble he gorrin on account o' them.'

'On account of his thievin' cousins, you mean,' Elsie said. She finished the last of her meal and stood up. 'If you don't mind, Mam, I'll go over to Scotland Road right away. Mr Lumley's ever so nice; if they can find somewhere for Jimmy they will. I know it. See you later, then.'

Elsie grabbed her coat and hat, and fled across the court, her cheeks warm with excitement, pleasure lending wings to her feet. She was actually on Scotland Road and hurrying up the pavement towards Lumleys when a hand caught her arm and stopped her short.

'Elsie? Where's you goin'? I thought as how you an' me was seein' the flick at the Paramount on London Road tonight, if you gorroff from the shop in time.'

It was Geoff, looking hurt. Elsie heaved an exasperated sigh and patted the large hand on her upper arm, then gently disengaged his fingers. 'Geoff, I didn't gerroff until after eight, I've only just bolted me mam's dinner, so no chance of the flicks tonight, I'm afraid. What's more, I'm runnin' a message for Mam, so don't hold me up, there's a good chap.'

'Course not. Come wi' you,' Geoff said, falling into step beside her. 'Wharrabout tomorrer night, then?

Think the ole skinflint will let you off earlier, seein' as how you've worked late every night this week?'

'Dunno. Thing is, Geoff, I've just about had it up to *here*...' Elsie tapped the top of her shining brown hair '... wi' old Cannell. I'll mebbe tek a day sick tomorrer to see if I can find another job. Almost anything would do.'

'He won't believe you're sick. He'll give you your cards anyway,' Geoff pointed out in the true spirit of common-sense pessimism. He brightened as another thought occurred to him. 'Then you'll be able to come to the flicks whenever you want.'

'Don't talk daft,' Elsie said with asperity. Some people never thought of anything but theirselves, she thought crossly. 'I'm goin' to have a chat wi' Mr Lumley at the fried fish shop about a ... a friend o' mine. It's not private, exactly, but I'll do best if you ain't hangin' around wi' your lug-holes flappin'.'

'Oh. Well I'll wait for you here, then,' her swain said with all his usual persistence, waving a vague hand in the direction of the Swan Inn. 'I'll bring me bevvy to the doorway so's I can see you, but if I'm lookin' in the wrong direction you could give me a shout as you pass.'

'Right,' Elsie said wearily. It was no use telling Geoff he wasn't wanted, he didn't seem to understand the meaning of such phrases. Besides, if she were honest she did not want to hurt his feelings because he was a nice bloke, awright. And if Jimmy really did come home at the weekend – well, Geoff would see how things stood soon enough and would be forced to take the hint. And in the meantime ... She started to jog along the pavement, then shouted 'cheerio!' over her shoulder and began to run in earnest. Jimmy, Jimmy, Jimmy, her heart sang exultantly. My very own Jimmy's coming home!

Dympna hated the Ditchlings' grand house from the moment she set eyes on it. From its position in between two other big, grand houses to the traffic which shrieked and roared outside, from the shining, oft-polished black and white tiles of the entrance hall to the grim and blackbeetley scullery where the maids toiled at the cook's behest, she hated it.

As she lay in her bed that first night she had suffered from a feeling that she was being squeezed by the weight of house above her, for she had slept, because she was so nervous and ill at ease, in the little slip of a room adjoining the housekeeper's, in the basement. Lying stiff with fear and dread in the stuffy dark she imagined she could feel all those five storeys pressing down on her, with walls of hard brick instead of soft wattle and daub, and a roof of heavy tiles and slate instead of light, golden-brown rushes. She had lain on her back and told herself not to be a fool, and tried to remember her own home, with the gentle shushing of the sea always in her ears and the softness of the star-filled dark so different from the harshly lit city streets. But that other life seemed suddenly so far away, so impossibly distant. She tried to calm herself by saying under her breath that she could always go home, run away, but in her heart she knew that this would be impossible; it would be letting Mammy and Daddy down so badly that they might never recover from it.

'You're here for three years at the most, Dympna Byrne,' she told herself under her breath. 'Three years isn't that long – it's not a lifetime. You'll survive. Tomorrow you must get a big sheet of paper and a good decent pencil, and mark it up into as many squares as there are days in each of those three years. And each night, when you go to your bed, you may cross off one of the days. Your stay here will be up in no time, just you see.'

She had sat up on her elbow to talk sense to herself; now she lay down again, slowly, and took deep breaths until she felt calmer. And then she remembered her arrival in this alien place and went over in her mind all that had happened.

The housekeeper had taken her down to the servants' dining hall, with its long wooden table and flanking Welsh dressers, and introduced her, in a babble of sound and strangeness, to the other people who worked for Mr and Mrs Ditchling.

'This is Mr Frame, he's the butler, and this is Miss Partridge, parlour maid, and Miss Brown . . .' This list had gone on and on. A dozen people were introduced and Dympna, who was Miss Byrne to everyone, scarcely took in a word. 'Nanny's not here, or I'd interduce you to her first, since you'll probably be working under her once Madam has made up her mind that you'll suit,' Mrs Palfrey had said at last, pulling out a chair. 'Sit yourself down. You must be very hungry after that long journey.'

As she watched the faces around the table and pushed her food about her plate, Dympna had decided that Mrs Palfrey wasn't too bad at all, her bark was very much worse than her bite. She seemed to take in Dympna's nervous fears and although some of the other staff members eyed the girl askance and seemed inclined to whisper and giggle, clearly over her, Mrs Palfrey had kept her engaged in conversation until the meal, which Dympna scarcely touched, was over, and then had taken her through to the house-keeper's room, sat her in a stiffly upholstered little armchair and told her to have a quiet few minutes whilst she, Mrs Palfrey, went and saw their employer. Dympna had waited, wondering what was in store for her – whether she, too, would see Mrs Ditchling tonight or whether she might presently go to bed and cry herself to sleep. But when Mrs Palfrey came back her instructions had been changed.

'Mrs D's decided that there's no point in you sleepin' up in the nursery all by yourself,' she had said. 'The children have gone to visit one of their aunties, who live on an estate down in Norfolk, and they won't be back until next week, so Madam said you was to work in the kitchens, get used to the place, until then.'

'I see,' Dympna had said, dry-mouthed. She'd cleared her throat. 'So where'll I sleep, then, please, Mrs Palfrey?'

'There's a little room next to mine,' the house-keeper had said. She had come over to the chair and stood by it, and though her mouth remained firm the bright little eyes seemed softer suddenly. 'It's been a long while since I saw a girl from the old country as took aback by Liverpool as you are, alanna. But don't worry, you'll get used to it, if only you give it a chance. I doubt you realised that I'm from Dublin, meself?'

'You? Fr-from home?' Dympna had stammered. 'Well, I never would have guessed it. But you – you don't sound Irish at all . . . your name isn't Irish either, is it?'

'No, child. When I came over from the Liberties more than forty years ago I was Kat'leen Callaghan, wit' a brogue you could cut wit' a knife and hair black as a crow's wing an' so long I could sit down on it. I was nigh on terrified out of me life when I saw the

318

Liver Buildings an' the docks an' the grand big houses, but I'd come from a poor home, and I'd seventeen brudders an' sisters left behind me, so I knew this was me big chance, an' I'd got to stick to it.'

'I've got two brothers, and my mam and dad left behind,' Dympna had said, her eyes filling. 'I'm from Connemara, on the west coast. Where we live is right next to the sea, wit' wild common land and the hills at our back and a long walk to the village, which is only a few houses, a pub and a shop all in one. The school's small too – there are twenty-four pupils at the moment – and the church just holds us all. B-but I'm like you in one way; me daddy's boat got wrecked and I'm here so's he can buy another and go on fishing. I c-can't just up and leave either, no matter how much I may wish I could.'

'Well, there you are, then,' Mrs Palfrey, who had once been Kat'leen Callaghan, had said comfortably. Suddenly Dympna saw that she wasn't strict or cruel, she was simply trying to do a very demanding job and, now that they'd talked, her sympathies seemed to be very much with the new girl. 'What I can do, alanna, you can do. Now you ate nothing at supper. I'm going back to the kitchen to fetch you bread and butter and whilst I'm away, you may put the kettle over the fire and get two cups and saucers out of that cupboard.' She pointed. 'Then we'll have a bite and a sup before going to bed.'

'I suppose you got married, that's why you're Mrs Palfrey now,' Dympna had said presently, when the two of them were settled in their chairs with their bread and jam, and cups of steaming cocoa. 'My mammy was Mrs Ditchling's sister, you know, only she married my daddy, which is why I'm Dympna Byrne.'

'Yes, I do know. But it's something you're not supposed to mention to anyone,' the housekeeper had said impressively. 'I remember your mammy and all the . . . well, that's neither here nor there. But you mustn't tell other members of the household that you're related, you know. For a start they'd think you was boasting, they wouldn't believe it for one moment. And for another thing, it might cause resentment. You aren't a bit as I remember Miss Bea, so I imagine you take after your daddy?'

'That's right,' Dympna had said, trying to stem her tears as the mental picture of her father's gentle smile, his big hand on the tiller of the *Fair Aleen* as he brought her into harbour. 'I won't say anything, Mrs Palfrey. My mammy said her sister wanted a nanny for the kids, though.'

'She's got a nanny. She wants a nursery maid,' Mrs Palfrey had explained. 'The nanny, Miss Horsham, is highly qualified and has excellent references. But not unnaturally she likes a day off now and then. She'll want a proper week's holiday, maybe even two weeks, some time this summer, so a nursery maid had to be found. Miss Horsham's from Edinburgh, in Scotland, you see, and that's a long way off. And Madam would not let just anyone look after the children – I'm too busy, naturally – she wanted a nursery maid she could trust. She told me Miss Bea had written and suggested you might be suitable . . . she was concerned about the brogue, but that's one fear I was able to calm when I saw her just now. She'll see you herself in the morning, of course.'

'In the morning? I thought you said she'd taken the kids to her sister's,' Dympna had begun, to be promptly admonished.

'No, I said the children had been taken to her

sister,' Mrs Palfrey had corrected. 'People of Madam's class don't see very much of their children, not when they're young, and the oldest, Miss Harriet, is only ten and Master Dominic, the baby, is just four. Georgina is the middle child, she's seven. No, Nanny Horsham took all three children to their aunt Elinor, so you'll be able to meet Madam tomorrow.'

'I see,' Dympna had said in a low voice. 'Is . . . is she very like my mammy? Only I'd like to be prepared.'

'Well, she's fair-haired,' Mrs Palfrey had answered after a moment's thought. 'But Miss Bea was a beauty and though Miss Maude was well enough, she didn't have such striking looks or colouring as your mammy. No, I don't think you'll notice much likeness.'

'Right. Mrs Palfrey, can I ask you something else?'

'Ask away.' Mrs Palfrey eased her feet out of her smart black shoes with the silver buckles and wiggled her toes luxuriously, holding them out towards the fire's warmth. 'Eh, thank the Lord I don't often have to wear me best shoes – where's me slippers gone and hid theirselves?'

'They're under your chair,' Dympna had said. 'Mrs Palfrey, what will happen if Mrs Ditchling doesn't think I'm . . . I'm right to be a nursery maid? Will . . . will she send me home?'

There was a world of hope in her tone but Mrs Palfrey had wagged her head chidingly at her, then bent and pulled her slippers out into the firelight. She'd slipped her feet into them and had sighed again, leaning back in her chair and taking a sip from her cocoa. 'That's better! Well, my dear, she won't send you home, that's for sure. You could work in the kitchens, I dare say, though it's not the sort o' work I'd want for any niece of mine. But likelier she'd put you in as housemaid – that isn't so bad, you'd be workin' under me for a start and not under Cook. Mrs Stebbings – that's Cook – is a bit of a tartar. I won't deny she's a marvellous cook and makes sure the servants eat as well as them above stairs, but she's hot-tempered and that's a fact. Edie – she's one of the kitchen maids, there's two of 'em – gets the rough side of her tongue half a dozen times a day, and often and often I've gone down there near on midnight and the poor kid's still been at the sink, preparing veggies for the next day or washing up Cook's bowls and pans and that. So just you hope Madam takes to you. And the blessed children, of course. Did you know that Mr Ditchling had two sons by his first marriage, by the way? Mr Philip and Mr Lionel. You won't see much of them, they're both working with their father now and I can't say as I've ever seen them up in the nursery. Oh, by the way . . . would you object if Madam decided to call you Dolly, or Doris or some other such name?'

'Why?' Dympna had said baldly. 'No one here knows me, do they?'

'No, no, it's nothing like that. But we'd a maid called Carlotta once and Madam said it were too fancy. We called her Clara whilst she were with us.'

Dympna had heaved a sigh. 'I suppose if she's set on it I'll have to answer to whatever I'm called,' she'd said wearily. 'But Dympna isn't a fancy name, it's just ordinary.'

'Oh aye, in Ireland it is. But over here you don't meet many Dympnas. And remember, the children will always call the nursery maid by her first name, though they call Miss Horsham either Nanny or Horsy – she don't seem to mind that at all – and mebbe they'd find Dympna a bit of a mouthful, like.'

There was a short silence, whilst Dympna had digested this and decided that if she must work here

322

she might as well do so incognito, so to speak. She had said as much to Mrs Palfrey who nodded approval and presently, with their bread and jam eaten and their cocoa drunk, they'd both made their way to bed, Mrs Palfrey to the housekeeper's bedroom which led off from her small sitting-room and Dympna to the little dressing-room next door.

She'd undressed and got out one of the plain cotton nightgowns which her new employer had sent, slipped it on and climbed into bed. It had felt very odd to be sleeping in a room completely cut off from everyone else, instead of settling down on a truckle bed against a thin wooden partition which did not even go up to ceiling height, knowing that Egan was a hair's breadth away from her and Mammy and Daddy not much further off. She did not expect to sleep, for kind though Mrs Palfrey had been, the sensation of being buried under tons of masonry and surrounded by strangers was still very strong. But eventually she did drop off and slept, though she had bad dreams, until the first light of the new day came in around the curtained window.

'Jimmy's goin' to stay wi' Maisie Lumley as was and her Bill until he's settled,' Elsie reported when she got home that evening. 'They were ever so pleased he's comin' back, Mam, though they were pretty busy an' it seemed to me they'd got plenty o' staff. Still, Mr Lumley says they've always felt kind o' responsible for Jimmy goin' off the way he did, so they'll tek him back. Actually, Mr Lumley said Jimmy would know lots about fish – you know, when they're freshest an' what sort cooks at what heat, that kind o' thing – so he'd purrim on to the fryin' as soon as his present feller moves on.'

'Well, isn't that grand?' Mrs Taylor said placidly. She was sitting by the kitchen fire, darning a huge pile of socks. 'I've always liked young Jimmy.'

'Me too,' Elsie said warmly and received a hard stare from her brother Alan, also sitting by the fire studying his football coupon as though he was about to sit an examination on it. 'Want some help wi' them socks, Mam?'

'Oh, I'd be ever so grateful, queen,' her mother said, handing her a pile of socks, some lengths of grey wool and a large darning needle. 'Some of these – they're yours, Alan – are stiff as boards and niff like best Cheddar though I've done me best to wash 'em clean. If you find a really bad one, though, we'll chuck it out. No point workin' our fingers to the bone mendin' holes so big you can get your head through 'em.'

'What d'you mean, you like Jimmy Ruddock?' her brother said, loftily ignoring his mother's strictures. 'You're goin' steady wi' my pal Geoff.'

'I am not,' Elsie said stoutly. 'Oh, I go *out* wi' Geoff now an' then, but I'm not goin' steady wi' him. Or anyone else for that matter. And even if I was, I can like another feller, can't I?'

'No,' Alan said. 'If I heared Peg sayin' she liked another feller I'd . . . I'd give him a black eye an' I'd tell her to mind what she was at.'

'Oh, don't be so silly, Alan,' Elsie protested. 'We're not engaged or anything, nor we shan't ever be. Geoff's a nice feller but I wouldn't marry him if he was the last chap on earth and that's the truth. You and Peg are savin' up to get wed, aren't you?'

'We-ell, we're savin' up,' Alan agreed, looking hunted. 'I dunno about weddin's. Not for five or six years, anyroad.'

'But if she said she liked another feller you'd go round blackin' eyes? That sounds pretty much like weddin' talk to me,' Mrs Taylor observed, casting a mended sock into the basket by her side and picking up another one. 'Honest to God, what you boys do wi' your socks is beyond me comprehension. This 'un's more hole than foot.'

'That ain't mine,' Alan said in an injured tone. 'Mine's never all hole, like that. That 'un will be Tom's. Awful hard on socks is Tom.'

The talk then went on to other things and Elsie was relieved to have it so, for she knew that it would not be easy to rid herself of Geoff without hurting him and annoying Alan, Geoff's best friend these past five years. But she had never given him any reason to believe she was thinking of marriage, or going steady, she reminded herself later that night as she went upstairs to the girls' room, where her little sisters were already tucked up and quite probably asleep. The trouble with fellers was they found it so difficult to put their feelings into words that they assumed girls were the same. They kept on taking you about and hanging round you, and believing that this gave them certain rights.

Well, it don't, Elsie told herself crossly, climbing into bed and nudging Mabel over a bit. But it'll sort itself out once Jimmy's back – I'll get me pal Esther to make up a foursome, she's always been a bit sweet on Geoff.

Having settled in her own mind what was best to do, Elsie went to sleep, her conscience clear and her mind full of the exciting prospect of seeing Jimmy again soon.

Jimmy got off the train and stood for a moment on the

platform, gazing uncertainly around him. This was Lime Street Station all right, but it was not as he remembered it. It was so big, so noisy and so extremely crowded. He felt trapped by it, and the sight of St George's Hall when he left the station, though heart-warmingly familiar in one way, was strange in another. There were crowds of people, so many that they seemed pressed against each other, the roadway and the Plain itself was black with them, all moving one way or the other, all in good humour, calling out, dodging traffic, stopping to look at a stall set up by the roadside or shouting to a friend.

Was it always like this? Jimmy asked himself, taking his suitcase to the nearest tram stop and standing it down gratefully, for it was heavy with the combined possessions of the last two years. Fleetwood is a busy and successful town, but it has nothing like this. Not even on market days, or when the fleet comes in with a good catch to sell and the buyers come down to the quays to take their first look at the fish. He tried to look back over the past two years to the city he had left, and could only imagine that it had been, in those days, quite a lot quieter and less lively. There had been plenty of people, then as now, of course, but surely not all congregated in one spot? Or had the change been more in himself? Two years ago he had been a part of this great, crowded city and he had known nothing of the great open face of the sea, nor of the flat, rich agricultural land that surrounded Fleetwood. Now, the slower pace of the life he had lived for the past two years had suited him, become a part of him almost.

But this would never do. I'm standing here like a country bumpkin, baffled by the people and the traffic, Jimmy told himself crossly, and when a tram drew up beside him he jumped aboard without bothering to look up at the number and thus had a nerve-racking ten minutes, during which he almost managed to convince himself that he had boarded the wrong one and would probably be carried somewhere miles from his real destination.

But it was all right. The tram rattled along and when he glanced out he saw that they were already in Byrom Road and heading fast for the Scottie. He got out at the well-remembered stop and saw that Scotland Road was in its usual Saturday form – people everywhere, most of them loitering along in the spring sunshine staring in shop windows, licking ice-creams, eating wet nellies, which they had brought at the nearest canny house, and chattering like magpies. It's all right, Jimmy told himself, much relieved. The traffic here was not as dense as it had been on Lime Street, but there was the constant rattle of trams, the squeal of motors, the shouts and cajolements of the street traders and the banter of housewives, doing their marketing and demanding a bargain or a bit of something extra with every penny they spent. Yet despite all this liveliness, he no longer felt confused or out of place. In a day or so I won't know I ever left, he told himself. In a week it'll be me home again and Fleetwood and the *Maid Margery* will seem like half-forgotten dreams. So he hitched up his suitcase and turned into Gay Street. He would not go to the Blaney house, but to the Taylors, where he was expected and would be welcomed. He thought of young Elsie and grinned to himself. It would be grand, just grand, to see his little pal again.

'Jimmy? Oh, Jimmy!'

Jimmy stood inside the door of the Taylor's kitchen

and simply stared as the small person rocketed across the room, heading straight for him. At the last minute he tried to dodge, but could not evade the human rocket, which buried its head against his chest and said in muffled tones: 'Well, aren't you *big*? I've been expectin' a boy, but you're a proper man be the looks of you, our Jimmy.'

'Elsie?' Jimmy said slowly, trying, without success, to detach the small person from the front of his navy-blue blazer. 'Is it really you, Els? Well, if I've got bigger so've you, but it's more than that. You've . . . you've growed up something remarkable.'

He held her away from him so that he could get a good look, and realised that it was a mercy that he had met Elsie in her mam's kitchen and not in the street, for he never would have recognised her out of these familiar surroundings. She stood before him in a long green skirt which ended in tiny pleats at mid-calf, and her shapely legs were clad in what looked suspiciously like silk stockings. Silk stockings on little Elsie Taylor! She wore very elegant green high-heeled shoes with gold-coloured buckles across her ankles and the hair, which he remembered as shoulder-length, mousy and somewhat straggly, had been cut and shaped to her small head, and was as smooth and shining as a . . . as a buttercup. He admired the wonderful colour, supposing that it had grown lighter with the years. Her face, when his eyes reached it, was the same in some respects and very different in others. It was a small, pointy-chinned little face, but the lips had never been so red before, nor the skin so smooth and white. He distinctly remembered blemishes, and rather straight, uncompromising eyebrows over those large, light-grey eyes, whereas now her eyebrows were elegantly arched and her eyes were fringed with black and curling lashes.

He had not said anything, but he saw she was laughing and guessed, ruefully, that his thoughts had been written upon his face without his having to speak a word. He put a finger under her chin, tilting her face up to his and said: 'You've grown up, our Els. You aren't the kid I left behind me. And is . . . is that stuff on your mouth *lipstick*?'

She grinned suddenly and he saw a flash of the old Elsie; the crooked little teeth hadn't changed, nor the graceless, eager spirit behind the carefully painted face. 'Aye, that's it, Jimmy. And it ain't only lipstick, I've had me hair cut nice, and I've powdered me nose and plucked me eyebrows – it were hell, that – and I've got that massacre stuff on me lashes. D'you like it?'

She sounded partly provocative, partly shy. He was enchanted, could scarcely believe in the sudden flowering of his little pal, and impulsively took her hands in his and looked searchingly down at them. They had not changed, he saw. There was a wart on her index finger – he remembered the many times she had tried to root it out with a pair of compasses, crying with rage and vexation when she simply made the thing bleed and hurt herself – and her nails were well-bitten. 'Oh, Elsie Taylor, now I know it's you,' he said, not hearing the caressing tone in his voice, believing that he sounded practical, everyday. 'You always did nibble your bleedin' nails an' you've not broke that habit, I see.'

'Oh, damn you, Ruddock,' she said happily. 'I might ha' known you'd find the one thing I'd not managed to change about me. But the rest – it's awright, ain't it, Jimmy? You never said if you liked it.'

'What, the massacre?' He laughed. 'It's *mascara*, queen, not some sort of bleedin' battle. I'm not sure whether I like it or not, yet . . . but you're awful smart, you make me feel a right scruff-bag.'

'You're smart too,' she assured him. She eased her feet out of the high-heeled shoes and stood before him in her stockinged feet and he saw that she lost about four inches in height.

Somehow, it reassured him. He pulled her into his arms and, looking down at her, said: 'Wharrabout a kiss then, for your old bezzie? You give me one afore I left Liverpool, now how about another, to celebrate me comin' back?'

She smiled up at him, stars in her eyes, and stood on tiptoe so that he only had to bend his head and their lips met. He had meant it to be a light, welcoming sort of kiss but somehow it became something very different and she made a little pleased-cat noise beneath her breath, fairly plastering herself against him in a manner which made his heart bump very loudly and his knees begin to shake.

'What's all this, then?'

The voice, breaking into the utter stillness of the kitchen, had them springing apart, crimson-faced. At least, Jimmy saw that Elsie was crimson and his own cheeks burned hot. He turned towards it and there was Elsie's brother Alan, standing in the kitchen doorway, looking accusing.

'Hello, Alan,' Jimmy said at once. He had liked all Elsie's brothers. 'It's me – I'm back in the old place so I thought I'd come round and say hello to me pals.'

'Oh?' Alan did not sound friendly, Jimmy realised belatedly. 'Well, if that's how you say hello to your pals you can leave it out wi' me, Ruddock.'

Jimmy laughed. 'Well, your sister were quite a surprise,' he said easily. 'Ain't she just the prettiest thing, Al? But you needn't take on, it were only a friendly kiss. And now she's goin' to walk wi' me up to the Lumleys, I hope, so we can talk about old times.'

'She'd much better stay here, where I can keep me eye on her,' Alan said austerely. 'Flighty tart, throwin' herself into the arms of a feller she's not seen hide nor hair of for more'n two years. An' she's going steady wi' my pal Geoff Sale, so I've gorra right to expect her to behave decent, not like some bleedin' mary ellen.'

Elsie made a sound between a squeak and a snort, and drew herself up to her not very high height. She took Jimmy's hand and glared at her brother. 'I don't know why you say things like that, Alan, when you know very well I told you only the other day how I felt about Geoff, which is indifferent, to say the least. And . . . and Jimmy and me's goin' steady, ain't we, Jim?'

She pinched Jimmy's hand hard as she spoke and Jimmy tried to wipe what he was sure was an expression of incredulity off his face and said manfully, 'Well, you could say . . . I mean yes, we're goin' . . . we're goin' steady. Sort of.'

'I should think so, wi' the two of you kissin' like that, as if you wanted to . . . to do a whole lot more than just kissin',' Alan said, not mincing his words. 'If I'd come in two minutes later Gawd know what I'd ha' found. Well, I dunno who's goin' to tell Geoff I'm sure, 'cos he'll be just about as cut up as a feller can be.'

'I wouldn't want . . .' Jimmy began, to be fiercely silenced by his small companion.

'Of course you wouldn't,' she said soothingly. 'But when you're in love wi' someone you can't stop your-selves from . . . from kissin', can you? And now we'll be off, Alan, and I'll thank you in future to mind your own business where me an' Jimmy's concerned.'

Once outside the door and marching along the jigger, Jimmy said rather feebly, 'Well, Els, what've you let me in for this time? I'm awfully sorry, I didn't know you had a feller, I wouldn't want to split the two of you up, not for the world.'

Elsie stopped short and turned to glare at him. 'The only feller I've got is you, Jimmy Ruddock,' she announced. 'That Geoff, he's a pain in the arse. Always doggin' me footsteps, never takin' no for an answer . . . well, all that'll stop now that you're back an' we're goin' steady again.'

Jimmy took a deep breath. It was now or never, he felt. 'We are *not* goin' steady,' he said firmly. 'Since we've norreven *met* for two years, queen, how d'you make that out?'

'We went steady before,' Elsie said tranquilly, not one whit put out by his denial. 'Are you tellin' me you've been takin' another girl out, then?'

'Well, no,' Jimmy said truthfully, then thought he had been downright foolish to admit it when a little lie would have at least convinced Elsie that he was not a complete pushover. 'All I'm sayin', queen, is that you're being a bit previous, like.'

'You leave that to me,' Elsie said, taking his arm in a proprietorial fashion. Jimmy mentally sighed, shrugged and gave up. If he was to have a girlfriend thrust upon him, he could think of no one he would like more than Elsie, and she was such a pretty, fashionable little thing now, as well – he would be the envy of all his friends that was for sure.

So he and she walked into Lumley's fish and chip shop the best of friends, and an hour later Elsie had left and Jimmy was behind the counter swathed in a large striped apron dipping a fine, fresh piece of cod in the newly made batter and dropping it into the big square fish-fryer when the fat was just right to cook it a beautiful golden brown, whilst all around him the babble of the customers, the shouts of the staff as they repeated orders and the subdued hum of the traffic kept him from too much thought. Young Elsie, he told himself as he handled the long wire scoop with which Mr Lumley adroitly whisked the fish from the boiling fat as soon as they were perfectly cooked, was going to be a bit of a problem. But it was one, he felt, that he could face up to in the fullness of time. No need to worry at this stage. Better just to get on with the job, look for something better and hope that he would settle back into his old life with nothing more worrisome than a too-loving Elsie dogging *his* heels as she had complained that Geoff Sale dogged hers.

'Dora, why can't we go to the park now, right away? Nanny's writing letters, and she *said* you'd take us if we was good, and we has been good, hasn't us?'

Dympna looked up from the letter she was writing and smiled at Dominic. He was a dear little boy, round-eyed with the wonder of the world, always eager to be out and about with no enthusiasm for quiet nursery pursuits such as the two girls seemed to delight in. Right now he was sitting astride the rocking-horse, a dapple-grey, red-nostrilled monster with a real red leather saddle and bridle, and a lovely horsehair mane. The horse had been named Lucky and Dympna, who had several times ridden on the great wooden animal when its rightful owners were in bed and asleep and Nanny Horsham out with her friend Nanny Barclay, thought that it was the children who were lucky rather than the horse. How many kids, she had once demanded of her charges when Harriet had been particularly difficult, had a wooden rocking-horse the size of a real live pony to gallop away on whenever they liked? Harriet had stared at the new nursery maid resentfully and had said that everyone she knew had a horse as good or even gooder than Lucky, and that some children had real Wendy houses of their own in lovely gardens, and could play house by the hour together, with no grown-ups to interfere.

'You're right, Master Dominic. Just let me finish this sentence and then you shall go out to the park. Do you want to take your new tricycle? Or shall we all walk today?'

Dominic gave a squeak of pleasure and his sisters, Harriet colouring a drawing she had made and Georgina doing a jigsaw, looked up and began to tidy away their ploys. Both girls were at school during the week, only Dominic was still confined to the nursery, so Dympna did not see as much of them as she did of their small brother, but they were all nice children. Dympna got on very well with them, though she found Harriet's and Georgina's habit of whining when disappointed over some trifling matter rather trying. It seemed to her that the children had so much, yet apart from Dominic, who set about changing what he did not like and rarely grumbled, the two girls seemed to be constantly voicing their woes. The lack of a proper garden she agreed was difficult – as a child brought up with the whole countryside, the beach and the sea lough at her disposal, she did think that parents as rich as the Ditchlings could have contrived some such place for the children to play in – but on the other hand Princes Park was within walking distance and the nursery suite, as Mrs Ditchling called it, took up the whole top storey of the house and was well provided with wonderful playthings, including a swing and a small merry-go-round, which the children enjoyed using.

Rather to her own surprise, Dympna had not disliked Mrs Ditchling, even though she had been rather dismayed when Mrs Palfrey's prediction had come true and she had been asked to use the name Dora whilst she was with them. 'For though you have a pretty voice and only the hint of a brogue, my dear, it really isn't quite the thing to have an Irish nursery maid. Scottish ones are very popular, because the Scots, particularly from Inverness they say, speak the purest English of all, but I don't want people to wonder . . . if you've a name you'd rather use . . . Dorris? Dolly? then of course that will be just as suitable.'

Forewarned, Dympna had agreed meekly to the name Dora, but that did not mean she liked it. It was all the more distasteful to her since she thought Mrs Ditchling a sensible woman for the most part, and what did it matter whether your nursery maid was Irish, Scottish, or a heathen Chinee, so long as she did her work well? But it did not do to give voice to such thoughts, Dympna realised that, so she tried to like Mrs Ditchling for herself and forget her own renaming.

Mrs Maude Ditchling was above average height with what Nanny Horsham told Dympna was called an hour-glass figure. She had light-brown hair, chestnut-brown eyes and an infectious laugh, and though she strove to remove them with lotions and potions, a band of freckles across the bridge of her nose that made her look even younger than her years, which Dympna imagined must amount to thirty-five or so. Although she did not see a great deal of her children, their obvious affection for her would have made Dympna inclined to like her, even without her employer's anxiety for her new nursery maid's comfort.

'Your mother and I were great friends, though there was a big age difference between us,' she had told Dympna when they first met. 'I'm glad to have been able to help her financially, and I hope that by the time you leave my house you will be able to get a job as a nursery maid or even a nanny to the very best sort of family and keep yourself in relative comfort. Although you may prefer to marry and raise a family of our own,' she added with a slight uneasiness which Dympna did not at all understand. 'Because you are rather pretty, even though you're nothing like Bea – or not as I remember her.'

Dympna tried out the little half-bob which Mrs Palfrey said would be appreciated and said: 'Thank you, Mrs Ditchling. Only I've . . . I've other plans for when I go back to Ireland. All my life I've wanted to teach and if I can go into my old school as a pupil teacher . . .'

Mrs Ditchling smiled again, but perfunctorily, and began at once to talk of her children and her hopes for them. Dympna honestly wondered whether her employer had actually listened to what she had said, but only a little thought was enough to show her that pleasant though Mrs Ditchling was, she saw very little of any of the servants apart from a flat-chested spinster called Miss Florence Vaughan who was her personal maid. Their doings, therefore, were of no interest to her and since she had never been to Ireland she probably had no idea how homesick Dympna was.

And she was homesick. Even after more than two months she could not reconcile herself to the noise, the fumes, the bustle, and the fact that one was never alone. She had one day off a week, though it was less a day than part of a day, since she was expected to get the children dressed and breakfasted before she left, and to be home in time to help Nanny put them to bed. At first she had explored the city, as much of it as she could cover in the time at her disposal, but later she had saved up her pennies until she could afford a ticket on the overhead railway, which the rest of the staff called the Dockers' Umbrella. She went to Seaforth sands, where she could look wistfully out to sea and remember Connemara and her home there.

But even on the sands she was not alone. There were always kids playing there and the odd fisherman, casting his line out over the grey sea or wading thigh deep in the hope of a bite. And the trains were crowded with even more people, all coming and going on their rightful errands no doubt, but to Dympna, a means of seeing that she was never quiet and alone, as once she had been at will, more hours of the day than she had company.

'Have you finished that sentence yet, Dora dearest? Only me and Harriet . . .'

'Harriet and I,' Dympna murmured. Her employer had been eager that the children should learn to speak more like their nursery maid – and less, presumably, like Nanny Horsham – and had laid upon 'Dora' the charge of correcting their grammar.

'Yes, sorry . . . Harriet and I are ready to go out and Dom's gone downstairs to get the tricycle ready so if you've finished . . . it's a hot day, will we need coats?'

Dympna stood up. From the window she could see that it was indeed a fine day. 'No coats,' she decided. 'But the little cream-coloured linen jackets that your mother bought you and the brown and cream tam-o'-shanters would look nice, don't you think?'

'Yes, lovely,' Harriet said, appearing in the doorway between day and night nursery. 'I thought you'd say jackets, Dora, so I've got mine on already. I'll just get my tammy.'

She disappeared again and Dympna reached down from its hook her own jacket, which was navy and matched her square-pleated skirt, and her nurse's hat, which was made of navy velour and was round and basin-like. Unlike many servants she liked her uniform, apart from the hat, and thought it extremely smart, but then other girls had their wages and bought their own clothes to wear in their time off. Dympna kept her worn, threadbare garments well out of sight and always wore uniform when she could. Her pocket money went on such things as soap, toothpaste and an occasional tram ride, with nothing over for luxuries such as clothes or shoes.

Now, she checked her appearance in the long mirror by the nursery door – Nanny Horsham had told her how important appearance was to employers and their friends alike – and went through to fetch the girls.

The two of them preceded her down the long flight of stairs and into the big, shady hall with its black-and-white-tiled floor and the round Persian rugs which decorated it. Dominic was already there, uncoated and hatless, with his tricycle held in readiness and his face shining. The tricycle was a new toy and not taken out nearly often enough in his opinion, since Nanny was nervous that he might fall off or knock someone down and usually avoided trips which included it.

'Hat, Master Dominic,' Dympna said, taking a crushed brown velvet cap from her pocket like a conjuror producing a rabbit. She might sigh over his appearance – the shirt rucked up under one ear, the tie which he seemed to have chewed over breakfast, the socks already descending anklewards – but she never tried to change him. Boys, she knew, were very different from girls and Mrs Ditchling accepted her son's casualness as easily as she accepted her daughters' tidiness. 'Just pop it on until we're at the park, then we'll see.'

They would not see, of course, because Master Dominic would have the hat off his head the moment they were out of sight of the house, cramming it back into Dympna's pocket and grinning cheerfully as his brown curls were blown back by the speed of his going. The girls, who were already interested in their appearance, would walk sedately along behind the flying tricyclist with their tammies at the correct angle on their smoothly brushed hair and their jackets properly buttoned, their long brown stockings kept aloft and neat by elastic garters and their shoes, polished by Dympna, carefully avoiding both puddle and dust patch.

They reached the park and Dympna guided the children towards the lake. She had had the forethought to put a bag of crumbly dry bread into her pocket and this she now divided equally between the girls, because Dominic had shaken a lofty head at the idea of taking part in such a tame pastime. He would rather fly round the gravel paths on his tricycle, making aggressive engine noises, which changed to a screeching of brakes on corners, than feed any number of ducks.

The park was already filling up. Other nannies and nursery maids were conducting their charges along the gravelled paths and across the green, well-kept grass. Despite the wind, which had Dympna clutching her hateful hat a couple of times, it was a sunny day and young lovers strolled along, arms linked, heads close, and some of them had already taken up their stations on the grass, with their jackets and cardigans removed so that they might 'get the sun', flirting and teasing one another and eyed with considerable curiosity by passing children.

'Shall we go to the aviary now?' Dympna suggested when the ducks had eagerly gobbled up all the bread and were turning to other children who still had some scraps. 'I *know* you'd like to go on the boats, Master Dominic, but you know the rules. If you have your tricycle then you can't go boating. And besides, it's a breezy day and last time you went in a boat you were naughty, if I remember rightly.'

'He soaked us both,' Georgina said sadly. 'I was wearing my pink corduroy coat with the furry collar – Mummy laughed, but Nanny said it would never be the same again.'

'It's a winter coat, Miss Georgina,' Dympna reminded her small charge. 'By the time winter comes round again you'll have grown out of it. Now, how about the aviary?'

'Yes, yes, *yes*,' Dominic shouted, standing up on his pedals the better to emphasise his point. 'I love that parrot, I'm going to teach it to say very, very, very naughty words.'

'You don't know any,' Harriet said loftily. 'You're just showing off.'

'I am not! And I do! I know words which are so naughty to you . . . you've never heard me say them, so there.' Dominic scowled at his elder sister. 'Bloomin' girls, they all think they're the cats bloomin' whiskers but really they're dead common.'

'Dom!' his sisters shrieked in unison, much

scandalised.

Dympna had hard work to hide a smile, but she said sharply: 'Master Dominic, that's no way to talk. Just where did you get hold of . . . of those expressions?'

Dominic, his cheeks very pink, stopped his tricycle and scuffed the toes of his brown leather sandals in the gravel. His lowered eyes did not lift as he answered, which was as well, since Dympna's gravity was soon to be tested. 'Well, they said I didn't know naughty words, and I *do*, Dora. I listen to the boys when I'm in the street and sometimes when Mr Strawn is doing things to the car's engine he has a little mutter of a naughty word or two.'

'I see,' Dympna said gravely. It would not do, she decided, to let Dominic think that she was shocked by his command of street language. 'Well, Master Dominic, it may interest you to know that the words you used were not . . . not particularly naughty at all. They just aren't the sort of words that a young gentleman should use.'

'That's because he isn't a young gentleman, he's just a nasty, scruffy little *boy*,' Harriet said, giving the last word particular emphasis. 'And I know who taught him to say *dead common* like that, because we heard too, didn't we, Georgie?'

'Oh . . . d'you mean that boy Dan, who's walking out with Connie?' Georgina asked, interested. Connie was one of the housemaids. 'Oh yes, he said that Connie's pal Em was dead common. And he says bloomin' an awful lot as well. But does it matter who said it, Dora, if they aren't naughty words after all?'

She sounded disappointed. Dympna jumped in immediately. 'No, it doesn't matter at all really,' she said airily. 'Just remember, Master Dominic, that it's

341

rude to shout out in a public place. Come along now, let's go and visit the parrot.'

She walked on, with the two girls close at hand and the tricyclist just ahead. As Dominic went they could hear him muttering about the naughty words he could teach the parrot and the nastiness of girls in general and his sisters in particular, but since none of them rose to the bait the muttering gradually tailed off and presently the revving of an imaginary engine and the shrill ringing of a tricycle bell told Dympna that her youngest charge was a motor car once more and rapidly forgetting his temporary fall from grace.

When they reached the aviary peace was restored by Dympna telling the girls that they must not bait their small brother and by Dominic's apologising all round for shouting, if not for naughty words. They then bought a bag of birdseed from the vendor and began to dispense largesse, this time with Dominic in the forefront of the giving. Dympna had never seen a parrot until she came to Liverpool and was enchanted by this specimen and by all the other birds, and went from cage to cage with her charges, feeding this one, admiring that. As they walked, it occurred to her that life in the Ditchling household was, in its way, a good preparation for someone who wanted to teach in school. Because she was not their nanny but only the nursery maid, she had had to exert both charm and guile to get their friendship without losing their respect, but she really thought she had done it. And despite being the offspring of extremely rich parents, they were not uppity and selfish, as were some of the other children they met in the park. No, she could have gone a lot further and fared a lot worse than she had done, although the constant lack of more than a few pennies to spend on the various

342

items her employer did not provide was irksome, causing even the children to wonder aloud now and then why she did not spend money on herself. Now, indeed, Harriet was asking Dympna why she did not buy a pretty bird in a cage and have it in her room, where they would be able to visit it from time to time. Apparently their grandmother had a housekeeper who kept budgerigars and when they stayed with her during the long summer holidays they were allowed to chatter to the birds and to release them from their cage to fly free around the room, now and then settling on a head or a shoulder.

'Well, you see quite enough of birds, then,' Dympna pointed out, moving a little away from the circle of cages. Harriet was sharp; one of these days she would begin to put two and two together and realise that the nursery maid did not seem to have any money of her own, and Dympna did not like to contemplate the questions which would then be put to her. 'Oh look, there's a man selling ices. Who wants one?'

There was an immediate clamour from Dominic and the girls, so Dympna went over to the ice-cream seller and joined the short queue for his product. As she waited she sorted through the small amount of change Nanny had given her so that she would have the right money, and without meaning to do so, listened idly to the conversation of the couple in front of her. She could not see their faces but the man was dark-haired with broad shoulders and a narrow waist, and the girl was barely above five foot two or three inches with smooth golden hair cut short into the nape of her neck and a slim, straight-backed figure.

'I dunno, but I don't think I'll be stayin' there much longer,' the young man was saying. 'It's awful hot, Elsie, and the crowds get me down, to say nothin' of being stuck indoors, in the potato kitchen or the shop, for hours together.'

'You never minded it before,' the girl said plaintively. 'You *liked* it, Jimmy, you told me you did. The wages is ever so good, much better'n they were when you was just a kid, helpin' out, like. And you've always said the food was prime, an' the people were ever so nice to you, an' you do get out sometimes, when you go to buy more spuds, or to get supplies of vinegar an' salt and that. You used to say it were a grand life, for all the work was hard.'

'Oh aye, but I'd never known nothin' different, had I? I'd never known wharrit was to be on the deck of a trawler wi' the waves smoothin' out under a blue sky an' me hand on the tiller, holdin' her to her course. An' I'd not lived in a small seaside town, where everyone knows everyone else an' they're all your mates. An' the countryside's so . . . so fresh, an' there's quiet whenever you want it . . . I told you I was a different feller, Els, and it's God's truth. The city seems to close around me, like a hot, sweaty fist.'

The girl shrugged and slid the hand that was tucked into the young man's arm down until she was clasping her fingers with her own. 'Well, chuck, there's other jobs,' she began in a reasonable tone. 'But there's no trawler fleet in Liverpool, you know that. There's farms, though, out Crosby way. Or mebbe you could gerra job drivin' a lorry, so's you'd have time on your own as well as wi' other folk. How about that, eh?'

'I can't drive,' the young man said gloomily. 'But I could learn, I suppose. I wonder wharrit costs to learn to drive?'

'I s'pose it depends on who teaches you,' the girl said. 'But I'll ask around, if you like. Then if you really do decide you want to quit at the shop, you can . . . Hey up, we're next. Is it cones or wafers?'

The young man voted for cones and the two of them walked away clutching their purchases just as it was Dympna's turn to buy, so she only succeeded in catching a quick side view of their faces as they left, but it was enough to tell her that the feller was good-looking and the girl pretty and lively. She got one more glimpse of them as they turned away and thought they were quarrelling, then had to attend to her own purchases.

As she bought cones and handed them to the children, Dympna meditated on the conversation she had just overheard. So others beside herself were unhappy with city life. She had felt as though the young man was voicing her own feelings – but she had no willing pal to listen. She got on well with the children, but they could scarcely be termed friends, and Nanny Horsham, who was fifty-four and very settled in her ways, had nothing whatsoever in common with Dympna. She was from the city of Edinburgh, and though she frequently told anyone who would listen that Liverpool was very uncouth and rough compared with the place of her birth, she clearly took the noise, the bustle and the over-crowded conditions in her stride.

I've got to get about more, Dympna decided, licking her own ice-cream cone vigorously, for she had seen the children settled before she started hers. If I got out a bit more I'd make friends, then it wouldn't be so bad. I'm sure other nursemaids get to go out and about a bit – the housemaids do, even the kitchen maids aren't expected to work twenty-four hours out of the twenty-four. I'll have to have a talk with Mrs Palfrey; it's no use saying anything to

Nanny, she's too keen on her own time off to help me to get mine.

'Dora, Dominic's dripping all down his shirt.'

That was Georgina, licking away for dear life whilst the more motherly Harriet tried to mop her brother's front. Dympna wedged her cone into the tricycle's small basket and knelt down on the gravel to tie a white hanky round Dominic's neck, thanking Harriet for her efforts, reminding Georgina that a five-year-old on a tricycle has his hands full without adding a fast-melting ice to the mix, and took the children over to one of the benches against the orangery. There, Dominic parked his tricycle, sat down and made a good job of eating his ice and Dympna sat down too and ate hers whilst the girls, who had almost finished theirs, discussed with animation the chances of their parents allowing them a dog in the nursery.

Dympna joined in the discussion, pointing out snags, such as the distance between the top storey and the tiny back garden when a young dog needed to go outside, and the advantages, which were mainly imaginary, since she did not think that a small dog in the nursery would have much chance of driving off burglars or killing the mice that now and then appeared in the basement. But all the time she was talking she was wondering about the young man and the girl: whether he would really leave his job; the girl plainly thought he would be mad to do so. And would the life of a lorry drive be any better, really? He would still have to live in the city, she supposed, and time spent in the cab of a lorry wasn't really the outdoor life he seemed to have enjoyed so much. She wondered why, if this was so, he had given it up and returned to the city, then came back to earth again as Harriet announced that it was almost half past the hour.

'Gracious, we'll be late for lunch,' Dympna said, hastily rallying her troops. 'Come on, Dominic, you lead the way and be careful not to knock anyone down.'

They reached the house with very little time to spare and Dympna was about to ring the bell when a hand reached over her shoulder and someone pushed a key into the lock. Startled, she turned, to find a tall, golden-haired young man with aquiline features and very pale blue eyes glancing rather oddly down at her.

'Oh, I'm s-sorry,' she stammered. 'I didn't realise you were waiting to come in as well . . . you must be Mr Lionel.'

'No, it's Phil,' Dominic said. He had been standing at the bottom of the steps but now he began to try to heave his tricycle up the flight, saying as he did so: 'Come on, Phil, give me a hand, you're ever so much bigger than what I am.'

'In a moment, Dom,' his stepbrother said. 'Just let me get the girls and Miss Whatsername inside and I'll do the honours.'

'It's all right, Master Dominic, I'll carry it up,' Dympna said hastily, going down the steps again. She seized the trike and despite Dominic's spirited attempts to snatch it back from her, carried it up the steps. Mr Philip, holding the door open, looked rather impatient but said nothing and Dympna, trying to keep the tricycle clear of her black stockings, realised she had wheeled it over his shiny brown shoe, leaving a muddy tyre mark across the toecap. Cursing silently, she pushed the tricycle into the hallway and straightened. 'I'm awfully sorry, Mr Philip,' she said, trying to sound apologetic, though she was longing to say that if he'd not stood there like a cigar store Indian he would not have been run over at all. 'But it'll brush off. I was trying to keep it clear of my stockings, actually.'

She glanced up at him as she spoke and he said in a bored voice: 'That's all right, Nanny. Hurry up, Dom, or I'll shut the door on you.'

Dympna, feeling that her face was on fire, turned and began to descend the steps once more and the breeze chose that moment to snatch the pudding hat from her head, whirl it round a couple of times and send it bowling down the street. Dominic shrieked with laughter and Dympna gave him a shake, embarrassment making her wish devoutly that it could have been a good slap.

'You little wretch,' she said, through clenched teeth. 'Go indoors at once – I'll have to chase my wretched hat, much though I hate it.'

She did not wait to see if Dominic was obeying her but set off at a run, heedless now of appearances. What did it matter if she looked a fool in front of her employer's elder son, provided she caught the hat? She might hate it – well, she did – but it was part of her uniform and if she had to replace it she guessed that it would swallow up all her tiny amount of pocket money for the next three months.

But the hat, or the wind, was cunning. Almost as though it knew of her pursuit it hesitated, then leaped off the pavement and onto the road, nearly coming to grief under a taxi, which skidded and swerved, avoiding it by inches. Dympna said a bad word, which would have delighted Dominic had he chanced to hear it, and plunged off the pavement after the hat. It hesitated again, then actually took to the air for a moment – long enough, at any rate, to clear the railings of the square garden, whereupon, knowing itself now safe from pursuit, it settled meekly down in the heart of a laurel bush – visible but, alas, unreachable, until she had returned to the house and found someone to lend her the family's key to the square.

'Damn the bloody t'ing,' Dympna said crossly. She had the beginnings of a stitch and her hair had descended from its neat knot and swirled around her shoulders, and unladylike perspiration bedewed her brow. 'What'll I do now? If I go the pig of a hat will take to the air again, but if I wait here it'll sit tight, knowin' it's safe. Oh, how I hate that bleedin' hat.'

'I'll go back for the key,' an amused voice said just behind her. 'You stay here and watch it like a hawk in case it develops wings and soars off somewhere else. Or shall we leave it to its fate and go back to the house for luncheon?'

Dympna jumped quite six inches and turned round, a hand on her heart. Of course, it was Mr Philip, grinning like a Cheshire cat and clearly taking great pleasure in the incautious words he had just heard her utter. Dympna opened her mouth to apologise, to ask him not to say anything to anyone, to add that she would deal with it herself, thank you . . . and her voice went very Irish indeed and very angry, too. 'It's all your fault, so it is,' she scolded, pink-faced and furious, one hand holding back the weight of her hair from her face, because the wind would blow it about so that it half blinded her, the other stuck on her hip so that she no doubt looked like the fishwife she had sounded like moments earlier. 'I *do* hate the . . . the wretched hat, but I expect it cost a lot of money and I d-don't have money to t'row around, like some people. Just you go back for your . . . your *damned* luncheon,' she added, throwing caution to the wind, 'and I'll scramble meself over the railings and grab it before it moves on. Where are the kids, anyway? You should have stayed wit' them, that's what I t'ought you were doin'.'

'The kids have gone in and up to the nursery for their luncheon,' he said. He was looking at her in a way that made her push her hair back behind her ears and straighten her back indignantly. One moment she wasn't good enough to give a name to – *Miss Whatsername* had rankled – and the next he was looking at her with . . . well, the look that she got from the butcher's boy and the baker's man and various other tradespeople who came to the house. 'Look, wait . . . I'll go and get your hat, although I think it's a sin and a shame to cover that glorious hair – and shade that pretty, pretty little face – with the hideous thing. Stay here.'

And with that command he had swarmed up the wrought-iron railings as neatly as a kid boxing the fox for someone else's apples, and was dropping down onto the other side, a lock of that rich gold-coloured hair falling over his eyes, his long legs taking him across the garden in a couple of seconds and his long arm reaching out and rescuing her hat.

'Thanks,' Dympna said stiffly as he handed it to her through the railings and proceeded to begin to climb them again. 'I'm . . . I'm really very grateful.'

'Are you indeed?' Mr Philip said satirically, dropping down onto the pavement at her side. 'Well, allow me to tell you, Nanny, that you don't look grateful at all. You look as though you'd rather I'd impaled myself on the topmost spike, so you could have told me I was a naughty boy to do such a thing.'

Despite herself, Dympna smiled. It was a grudging smile, soon gone, but the truth was she simply could not help herself. It had been a real gas, watching the long legs of him lepping over the railings, she told herself. He had been kind, too, and had saved her at the very least a wigging from Mrs Palfrey, who usually kept the key. And Mr Philip smiled back with great charm, and suggested that he might put her hat on for her, since she had not yet attempted to do so herself. 'For I'm a great hand with women's hats,' he said earnestly, tugging at one side of the brim whilst Dympna hung grimly on to the other side. 'I can perch it on your curls so no one would ever know it had blown off.'

'It's not worth the trouble, Mr Philip,' Dympna said, retaining her hold on the hat. 'And if we pull it in two you might just as well not have rescued it from the laurels. After all, I'm going to be late for luncheon as it is. And so are you,' she added, trying not to sound pleased and sounding it nevertheless.

'Ah, but I'm privileged,' Philip said smugly, falling into step beside her as she turned back to cross the road to the house. 'I only have to say I was kept longer at the office than usual and both my papa and my stepmama will cast me glances of admiration and gratitude. Whereas you will have to admit that you nearly lost your uniform hat.'

'I can tell untruths as well as you,' Dympna flashed, then felt her cheeks grow hotter than ever. Dear God, what next would she say? This tall, golden-haired young man was in a position to get her the sack and though she had never wanted to come to Liverpool or to be a nursery maid, she could not possibly creep home to her parents and admit that her hot temper and her quick tongue had lost her the job. 'I mean . . . of course I don't tell untruths and anyway the children know what happened . . . and I'm *not* their nanny,' she added, almost tearfully. 'I'm the n-nursery maid.'

He caught her hand, pulling her to a stop, and

when she looked up at him he was neither sneering nor laughing at her, but serious and attentive. 'A nursery maid? You're far too . . . well, I'd better not say too much or you'll be angry with me again. What's your name, nursery maid?'

'Dy-Dora.' Dympna said. 'And I'm going to be dreadfully late for nursery luncheon.'

'Dy-Dora. Unusual,' he said, making Dympna bite back a laugh. 'And you're Irish, not a Scot.'

'True.' They were almost at the front steps and she stopped of her own accord this time. 'If you don't mind, Mr Philip, you'd better let me go in first . . . or I could go round the back, of course. Only I don't think I should walk in through the front door with you.'

'Very likely not, but who's to see us?' he said reasonably. 'I've got my own key, remember. Come along.'

Seeing that there was no help for it, Dympna accompanied her rescuer – or rather the rescuer of her hat – up the steps, through the front door and across the hall. But at the foot of the stairs she stopped short. 'I'll go through the kitchens and explain on the way, then go on up the back stairs,' she said. 'Thank you, Mr Philip, for getting my hat.'

He bowed, making her giggle nervously. If someone came in . . . ! But no one did. 'It was a pleasure, Miss Dora,' he said formally. 'Until next time.' And before she could do anything to stop him he had grabbed her by both shoulders and plonked a kiss on the end of her nose.

Consequently Dympna made her way through the kitchens with a heart that was beating uncomfortably fast and a face so hot that she was certain she could have fried an egg on both cheeks. Cook did look up and say that her meal had gone up a good twenty minutes ago and that she was not to be blamed if it was cold, but Dympna, too flustered to explain, merely nodded and hurried across the room and up the back stairs.

The cheek of that fellow, she was thinking as she reached the nursery door and opened it. What Mr Philip Ditchling needed was a good t'ump round the ear and the way she felt right now she was the girl to give it to him. But as she ate cold mashed potatoes, cold cod with white sauce and cold peas, she began to cool down. What did it matter if he had taken a liberty with her just now? It wasn't *much* of a liberty, after all, and she was unlikely to see him again, especially when you considered that she had lived in the house for eight whole weeks and this was the first time she had so much as set eyes on him.

Thus she comforted herself, but as she ate cold rice pudding with a spoonful of raspberry jam on top and thanked young Edie, who had been presiding in her absence, sending her back to the kitchens with one of the scarlet satin ribbons which she used to tie back her hair when she went out on her days off, she reflected that it did not *do* to bandy words, let alone anything else, with the son of one's employer.

All that afternoon and the rest of the evening she was working too hard to have much time for thought, but when she got into her bed that night, washed and plaited, with a book to read to send her to sleep, she found herself thinking a little grimly that she did not really believe she would not see Mr Philip again. There was something in his laughing, light-blue eyes which told her she was wrong. Sooner or later he would seek her out. And then, she thought, laying her book on the side table by her bed, there might well be trouble. But there was no point in meeting it half-way; for now, she had best get her rest and wait on events.

# Chapter Ten

Mr Philip, Dympna soon realised, was not actually living at home all the time, not any more. He had a bachelor flat in Quaker's Alley and found it simple enough to walk from there to his father's offices in Exchange Flags. He also found it simple enough to come home for luncheon when it suited him, and to pop in with various small tasks, which he preferred that his father's servants undertake rather than that he should have to employ someone to do them.

Dominic was quite fond of his stepbrothers, but the girls, particularly Harriet, thought that 'Philip took advantage'. Dympna realised that they had heard someone – probably their mother – using the phrase, but a little observation on her own account convinced her that it was justified. Philip did not believe in doing any work himself if he could cajole or order someone else to do it. He came round two or three times a week, either to lunch or to dine at the family home, and he brought all his used linen, causing Mrs Palfrey to ask whether there were no laundries calling along his part of the street. Other people, she told him sharply, made their own arrangements, they did not expect their parents' household to go on laundering their clothes and bed linen.

'But you don't launder them, Pally,' Philip said in a reasonable tone. 'They simply go in with my father's stuff, don't they?'

'Yes, and very well you know that they get added to your father's laundry bills, as well,' Mrs Palfrey said crossly. 'Really, Mr Philip, what you'll do when you've a proper home of your own with a wife and family I dread to think.'

'You needn't,' Philip assured her. 'Because then my wife will do the laundry.'

He sounded so triumphant that Dympna almost laughed, but since she was coming slowly down the stairs at the time, carrying Dominic's tricycle, preparatory to meeting Harriet and Georgina out of school, she kept her head down and pretended to be too absorbed in her task to notice the altercation going on below.

It was October, and a pleasant enough time of year so that Dympna had agreed without demur to taking Dominic and the tricycle with her on the school-fetching trip. She had arrived in the house in May, so she had been with the family nearly six months, and it had not been until mid-September that she had learned Mrs Ditchling was expecting a baby in early November. She had been pleased rather than otherwise, but Nanny had not been happy at all, had been downright querulous, in fact.

'I told Madam when I came that I'd no' be willing to work with small babies,' she told Dympna grimly. 'I'm no longer young, Dora, and all the night feeds and nappy changing need a younger person than I. Besides, I'm a long way from home . . . it's no' impossible tae get as good a situation in Edinburgh as the one I have here, and in Edinburgh I should be able tae get back to see my dear mother a couple of times a week instead of twice a year. And why did Madam no' tell me before about the new baby do you suppose? Because she knew full well that I'd be upset, and wouldnae be looking for the responsibility at my age.'

Nanny was tall, spare and grim-looking. Her sparse auburn hair was liberally streaked with white and pulled back from her white, aristocratic face so tightly that some mornings her eyes had an Asiatic tilt. She was firm but kind with the children, who all loved her, and in fact Dympna had speedily realised that Miss Horsham was a treasure whose ways she would do well to copy, as well as a delightful person with a sense of humour and a fund of helpful hints for any young girl who might one day raise a family of her own.

'Well, you've got me; I don't mind changing nappies and getting up in the middle of the night to give the baby its bottle,' Dympna said at once. She knew that when Nanny's voice turned suddenly Scottish she was really upset, and she had no desire to find herself working under someone who might not take to her. From her chats with other nannies and nursery maids in the park she knew that when this happened the nursery maid's life could be made miserable. 'Honestly, Nanny, I like little babies . . . well, I don't know any, but the ones in the park are lovely. I cuddled Baby Frobisher last week and he went to sleep in my arms, the little pudding.'

'Aye, very likely,' Nanny had said gloomily. Dympna could see that she was not convinced. 'But there's the dirty nappies . . . and the two-o'clock feed . . . and disturbed nights . . . Och, well, I'll have tae give it some thought, before making my mind up.'

She had given it some thought and, at the end of September, had handed her mistress her notice. Mrs Ditchling had been alarmed and upset, but Nanny Horsham had said that she would stay until the new baby was about six weeks old. 'And then, I told her, Dora, that you would be able to fill the position as Nanny admirably,' she told Dympna. 'You're a quick study and a hard worker. You'll have the new baby in your charge virtually from its birth and the other children are already fond of you. Indeed, I believe that it has been in Mrs Ditchling's mind from the start that you should replace me when I left, for she made no demur once I'd explained things.'

'Oh, Miss Horsham, are you sure I'll be able to cope?' Dympna had asked worriedly. 'And will they let me have a nursery maid? I'm sure I'd never manage without.'

'Certainly they will,' Miss Horsham assured her. 'Now don't you worry your head about a thing, Dora. Mrs Palfrey and myself are sure we're doing the right thing and we're accustomed to taking such decisions, remember.'

So now, Dympna was gradually taking over most of the nannying of the three older children and looking forward, if a trifle apprehensively, to the arrival of the new baby.

But Mr Philip, after their first meeting, seemed to have gone back into the woodwork. Dympna had seen neither hide nor hair of him until today, when there he was, standing smiling and very much at his ease whilst Mrs Palfrey, looking both hot and cross, faced him across the hallway.

All the information which Dympna had received from other members of staff about Mr Philip were obviously true, then. Mrs Palfrey had a businesslike bundle of laundry under one arm and Mr Philip was edging towards the front door. Clearly, he would not remain to argue the point, having passed on his dirty linen.

But Mrs Palfrey was not finished yet. 'I'll have to inform your mother . . .' she began, to be checkmated immediately.

'My sainted mother died when I was only three years old, Mrs P, as well you know,' Philip said soulfully. 'If you mean my *step*mother, my wicked . . .'

'I meant the present Mrs Ditchling,' Mrs Palfrey said, but Dympna saw her mouth twitch. 'It's she who will query the laundry bills and the catering bills and the sudden increase in Mr Ditchling's account with his wine merchant, and it's meself who will have to explain.'

'Oh, come on, Pally,' Mr Philip said. He put his arm round the housekeeper who stiffened with outrage. 'You know that I don't really remember my mama at all and my stepmother is the most easygoing of women. She'll quite understand that I need all of the paltry – I said paltry, not Palfrey, so don't poker up on me – all the *paltry* salary my stingy old father gives me just to keep myself in decent shirts and taxi fares.'

Mrs Palfrey snorted and Dympna, reaching the end of the stairs, stood the tricycle down and prepared to take herself and Dominic quickly out of the hall. She knew Mr Philip had seen her, but he had not so much as glanced in her direction. It would be best to get out whilst the going was good.

'That's Philip,' Dominic said conversationally. 'I wonder if he's coming to dinner? He often does, you know.'

'Is that so? Now come along, Master Dominic, or we'll be late for school coming out,' Dympna said with as much calm as she could muster. 'And that'll mean late for nursery tea, and there's strawberry jam and some shrimps with your bread and butter.'

Dominic squeaked; he loved shrimps, and the two

of them cross the hallway and reached the front door without either Mrs Palfrey or Mr Philip looking towards them. Dympna reached the front door, swung it open and was about to carry the tricycle down the steps when a familiar voice said, just behind her: 'Give me that, woman. Oh, I do so hate the modern girl who thinks she can do everything, even unto carrying tricycles, twice as well as the modern man.'

'So she can, Mr Philip,' Dympna said tartly. 'Give over tugging at it, do, or you'll have me and the tricycle down the steps a lot quicker than's comfortable.' Between them, they got the tricycle down to ground level, however, and Dominic said cheerily: 'Hello, Phil! Do you like Dora? Me an' my sisters like her ever so. She's goin' to be our Nanny when Horsy leaves.'

'I like her very much,' Mr Philip said gravely. 'So much that I'm going to walk to school with her. Won't that be nice?'

'No, it won't,' Dympna said, in chorus with Dominic, who said, 'Very nice, I fink.'

'I wonder whom I should believe?' Mr Philip mused, falling into step beside Dympna and trying to take hold of her elbow as they paused to cross the busy road. 'I think, on the whole, that I prefer Dominic's version. It's more truthful, for a start.'

Dympna had wondered whether to ask Nanny what she should do if Mr Philip approached her again, but as time went by and he did not reappear it had seemed that her fears had not only been groundless but also rather self-congratulatory. Clearly, it was out of sight out of mind so far as Mr Philip was concerned. But today, by a wretched mischance, she had hurried Dominic down the front stairs since they were a little late for the school trip, and of course, Mr Philip had immediately remembered her and decided to indulge himself in a little light flirtation. And without even consulting Nanny Horsham, Dympna realised at once that she must firmly squash this sort of behaviour in the bud. Mr Philip was handsome and knew it. He was also eligible, and as far removed from the type of 'follower' whom nannies and nursemaids attracted as the moon is from the sea. Infinitely better to tell him crisply to leave her alone . . . better to be downright rude, than for him to believe she welcomed his company and his semi-amatory advances.

'Mr Philip, I'm very sorry but it isn't at all the thing for you to be walking along beside a nursery maid, trying to hold my arm across the road. Do go away.'

He gave her a hurt look and turned on his heel. It was such an effective hurt look that Dympna felt as guilty as though she had deliberately kicked a small and fluffy puppy, but she hardened her heart and continued on her way towards the convent where, presently, the girls would come tumbling out of their classes, eager to tell her of their day and their doings, like a couple more puppies, when she came to think about it.

She half wondered whether he might turn up on their journey home, but there was neither sight nor sound of him. At nursery tea she was almost absent-minded, agreeing to Dominic sprinkling some of his delicious brown shrimps over his bread and strawberry jam and not even joining in the feminine chorus of disapproving squeaks when he joyously did so.

Bedtime came, and Dympna settled down to sleep. The trouble is, she told herself, when Mr Philip's golden head and beseeching blue gaze kept appearing in her mind's eye, I'm lonely. I don't meet many other young people and those that I do meet are either nannies or nursery maids – in other words, they're all female. I'm missing Daddy and Egan, and Kieran of course. Good heavens, I've only set eyes on old Mr Ditchling two or three times, I've never actually exchanged a word with him other than 'Good-morning, sir' or 'Good-evening, sir'. And the butler's old, and so are the gardeners, and the boys who run errands and clean shoes and so on are a lot younger than me . . . so naturally, it's nice to speak to a young man . . . it might be quite nice to flirt a bit with one, as well.

But Mr Philip was not the one, she was sure of that all right. Knowing him could be downright dangerous. So tomorrow afternoon I'll go round to the house opposite, where Amelia is nursery maid to the Thompson children, and ask her if she'd like to come dancing with me, Dympna decided recklessly. Why not? It's not a nun I'm after being, when I go back to Ireland. Daddy tells me about Egan and Maria, and how fond they are, in his letters, so why shouldn't I meet a young man and have some fun, too? I'll go round to Amelia's first thing after I've delivered the girls to school.

The dance-hall blazed with lights and everyone, both the young men and the girls, were dressed in their best. Dympna was very glad Amelia had insisted she wore her one and only black dress, though it wasn't a dance dress at all, really, and so many of the young girls here wore wonderfully exciting clothes.

'I feel a real little country bumpkin,' Dympna said as they paid for their tickets and took their places in the queue for the cloakroom. She handed over her navy-blue nanny-type coat and looked at herself in one of the long mirrors, smoothing her hands over the simple black dress, which had seemed both sophisticated and suitable when she had put it on earlier that evening. 'Oh, Amelia, thank the good God for the gardener!'

The gardener was old and gnarled, but he had come into the kitchen where she was submitting nervously to Mrs Palfrey's attentions to her hair. She had been going to wear it up, with a black velvet ribbon round her bun, but Mrs Palfrey had said disapprovingly that she looked like a mute at a funeral and had loosened the fine, night-black locks and tucked them behind Dympna's ears, and stood back, her head on one side. 'Better,' she announced. 'Have you some ear-rings? No? It needs something . . .'

The gardener had been standing by the back door, and had turned and disappeared, to reappear presently with a stem of some small, waxy flowers with cream-coloured petals and gold hearts. Silently, he handed them to Mrs Palfrey who nodded approvingly and then pinned them to the low neck of Dympna's dress. 'Very nice,' she said, standing back to view her handiwork. 'Thank Mr Evans, Dympna. That stem would ha' cost a mint o' money to buy.'

Dympna thanked the old man effusively, and he grinned and went red. 'They looks right, queen,' was all he said, however, before disappearing out of the back door once more, and now Dympna understood that he had done her a considerable service. She could see one or two other black dresses, but all were ornamented in some way – a gold link belt, worn low over the hips, or a cluster of artificial flowers or a scarf, negligently tucked into a waistband.

'You look fine, Dymp,' Amelia said now. 'Let's gerrout onto the floor, though, or we won't gerra chair.'

The chairs were small and gold-painted, with thin little legs. They stood around in small groups with girls perched upon them and if she had been by herself Dympna would have stood all evening rather than brave breaking into one of them. But Amelia was a local girl and they joined a knot of her friends, most of whom worked in domestic service of one sort or another. She presented Dympna to each and every one of them. 'This is Polly, she's a housemaid at the Cleveleys' place, more or less opposite ours. And this is Bridie, she's workin' for a family what's so stingy you wouldn't believe. Why, they won't let the servants go up the front stairs even when they goes to clean without they take their shoes off, 'cos they're scared o' the staircarpet wearin' up! And this is Sal . . . she's two streets off ours, but she's a nursery maid, like you, queen. You'll have a lot in common, the two of you. And this littl'un's Elsie, she's kitchen maid at Bellis's place, around the corner from us. She ain't been in service long so I doesn't know her very well . . . now sit down, Dymp, whiles I go and fetches the pair of us some orange squash. You can pay me later.'

Dympna had sat down on the vacant chair next to Elsie's, and began to scan the faces around her, and to glance with seeming casualness at the group of young men leaning negligently against the wall opposite. But presently her neighbour spoke. 'Did that gal say you was called "Dimmer"? I ain't never heared anyone called that afore.'

Dympna turned and smiled at the speaker. Elsie was a slim, straight-backed girl with bleached blonde hair and a lively, freckled face. Dympna, explaining that she was Irish and spelling out her name, thought that Elsie was really rather plain, for she had a small hooked nose and although her grey eyes were big and bright, her chin was jutting and her mouth too large for beauty. But she was so lively and her face so expressive that most people would believe her pretty. What was more, as Dympna talked, she realised that she had seen Elsie somewhere before. But where? Shaking a duster out of the window of a nearby house? Chatting to a tradesman on the doorstep, perhaps? Or simply going along the street on her day off, to visit her parents? Dympna could not remember exactly where she had seen the other girl, she just thought that Elsie was somehow familiar.

'Look, your pals want to join up wi' them others, so shall us sit at the next table, just the two of us?' Elsie was saying. They moved to the smaller table and several more girls joined Amelia, Bridie and Sal. 'Dympna; that's a pretty name, I wish I were called summat unusual, 'stead o' Elsie. Still, I reckon they wouldn't like a kitchen maid to have a name like that. No one thinks much o' kitchen maids, they think you're the lowest of the low, there ain't no job too 'orrible for a kitchen maid, I tells you straight.'

'I've often thought so,' Dympna admitted. 'You can't help noticing other people's jobs, can you? Our cook is a bully and a slave-driver, and once, when I was helping out, my hands got all soft and wrinkly and white, like dead fish, from having them in water most of one afternoon. I thought then it was a mercy it wasn't my permanent job because I don't think I could have stuck it, but I'm a nursery maid really; that's much nicer.'

'Oh aye, it would be,' Elsie agreed. 'Only they wouldn't have me near their brats, not wi' a scouse accent like wharr I've got. You speaks nice, Dympna.'

'Thanks – but if you hate kitchen maid, why don't you change your job?' Dympna asked. She had already realised that it was true servants were hard to get and harder to keep. Elsie was the sort of girl, she thought, who would look good in uniform, going to the front door and admitting – or denying – callers. Not many houses had butlers these days and Dympna knew that girls often took their place.

'I'm savin' up,' Elsie explained. 'I've gorra feller, he drives a lorry, an' we're both savin' up like mad. When he owns his own lorry, we'll likely get wed. Have you gorra feller, Dympna?'

'No, not really,' Dympna said. Something was stirring in her memory; a sunny day in a park, a line of people queuing for ice-creams. 'Well, there was a feller in Connemara, but I've not met anyone in Liverpool, really. This is the first time I've come dancing.'

'Aye, it's the first time I've come wi' the girls,' Elsie said. 'Well, when you've gorra feller they likes you to be wi' them. So usually we come when it's cheaper.'

'That seems sensible,' Dympna said. Was there a cheaper dance-hall near at hand, then? And if that was so, why had Elsie chosen to join the other girls tonight? Dympna glanced curiously at her companion. 'Where's your feller now, then?'

'Drivin' his bleedin' lorry,' Elsie said with gloom. 'It's always the same once you start courtin', it's all save, save, save. But if he's back in the Pool in time he'll come in here at the interval.'

'Why then? Why not as soon as he gets back?' Dympna asked. She was not particularly interested in the reply, but she had already heard another girl saying something about the place being crowded after the interval.

"Cos it's cheaper, then,' Elsie said patiently. 'Din't I just say so? Half price at the interval, an' we're savin', see? Only sometimes he don't get back in time to come dancin' at all and I were that fed up at the thought of another Sat'day night spent by me lonesome . . .'

'Oh, I see,' Dympna said. 'Oh, look, the band are striking up. What's that tune called, Elsie?'

And once the band started, so did the dancing. Amelia was eyeing up a young man so Dympna and Elsie continued their conversation and very soon Dympna realised she was enjoying herself. It was pleasant to be able to talk and laugh freely with a girl her own age, and perhaps pleasanter to realise that opposite their table a group of young men were eyeing them hungrily. It's not just the other girls, either, Dympna told herself as a tall, thick-set youth in a too-tight blue suit came over and solicited her hand for the next waltz, it's me, too. I'm all right! I'm going to have a lovely time.

Whether it was because none of the men had met Dympna before, or whether it was simply the charms of the black dress and the corsage of creamy orchids Dympna did not know, but she did not sit out one dance, and when the band went away to drink beer and relax for a bit and the compère announced that there would be a short interval, she beamed at Elsie, who had also been in great demand, very pleased with her first real night out. 'Wasn't that fun?' she asked. 'Sure and I've never danced with so many different fellers in one night, but then my local town's only small.'

'Well, sit down an' get your breath back,' Elsie advised. 'Because the fun's goin' to start again in twenty minutes or so. Which of the fellers did you like best?'

'Goodness, I only *danced* with them,' Dympna said, sinking onto a chair and fanning herself with one hand. 'They were all very polite, though. Has your feller arrived yet? What's his name, incidentally?'

'He's called Jimmy and I telled you he never comes before the interval,' Elsie reminded her. 'It's cheaper then, that's why. No, he's not . . . oh yes, here he comes.'

A young man was walking across the polished dance floor, carefully carrying two glasses of orange squash. He had dark, curly hair, dark eyes and a thin, tanned face with a deeply cleft chin. He was of medium height, broad-shouldered and narrow-waisted . . . and once again, vaguely familiar. 'There! He's brung me some orange squash, 'cos he don't realise you an' me's palled up,' Elsie said. 'I'll send him out to gerr another, if you like.' The dance-hall was not licensed, which the girls had been saying was a very good thing, but Dympna guessed that the young men would probably go out with the band to the nearest pub and that was why the room had suddenly become less congested. She said as much to Elsie, adding that she did not much care for large crowds, but would not dream of sending Jimmy in search of more orange squash.

Elsie smiled and wiggled her fingers at the hurrying Jimmy. 'Well, if you're sure . . . and as for crowds, just you wait! All the young kids an' a good many fellers come in after the interval, like I said, it bein' cheaper an' all. There'll be a real crush then, I can tell you.'

Dympna glanced around. The girls were beginning to split into smaller groups, but Amelia, Sal and

Bridie were standing in a small circle, chatting amongst themselves. She touched Elsie's arm. 'Look, I'd best go over to the others now, 'specially since your . . . I mean Jimmy's here. See you next week, perhaps.'

'Wait! Lemme interduce you to Jimmy,' Elsie said quickly. 'He's a lovely feller, he's just about me best friend as well as me feller.' Jimmy reached the table and stood the glasses down, smiling at Elsie. 'Jimmy, meet me pal. Dympna, this 'ere's me young man.'

Jimmy glanced incuriously but politely across at her, then his gaze sharpened. For several giddying seconds their eyes locked and in the pit of her stomach Dympna felt a very odd sensation indeed, as though her whole inside was turning gently and rather pleasantly over and over and over. She had the oddest feeling that she had met him before, but it was impossible, wasn't it? She went out so seldom and met so few young men. No, it was just because he had a look of . . . of Ruan, perhaps. His thick hair was dark as her own and he had very white teeth, just like her old friend's.

'H-hello, Miss . . . er . . .' Jimmy stammered as Dympna, thoroughly confused, took a step away from the table. 'Do . . . do sit down . . . I didn't mean . . .'

'She's now goin' to sit wi' the other gals,' Elsie said rather quickly. Had she intercepted that strange, long look, read something into it? But it appeared she had not, for she reached over and squeezed Dympna's hand. 'Hey, Dymp, when's your day off?'

'T-Tuesday,' Dympna muttered. She could see he was listening, taking it in, making a mental note. This was mad – terrible! 'A h-half day, from one thirty until six.'

'Right. I'll tell that bleedin' cook I'm goin' out

Tuesday afternoon. I'll call for you, back door, one thirty sharp. Awright?'

'Fine,' Dympna said. 'Bye, then.'

She left them quickly, but she could feel his glance, almost caressingly, across the nape of her neck, then dropping to the middle of her back where it burned like fire.

'Hello, queen, so you've come back,' Amelia said amiably as she joined them. 'Well, you couldn't very well stay an' play goosegog wi' Elsie an' her feller, I dare say. Enjoyin' yourself?'

Dympna admitted that she was and sat down and within a very short time the other girls were deep in conversation again. Waiting her chance, Dympna pretended to look through her handbag, whilst sliding her eyes sideways towards Elsie and Jimmy once more. Where . . . my goodness, she had it! They were the couple in the park who had joined the queue for ice-creams just before she had done so herself. The couple who were arguing about the merits of city versus country – and she had felt akin to the young man then because he found the city crowded, noisy. Well, wasn't that strange? And then, quite without meaning to do so, she realised that she could hear Elsie's voice plainly and, without even trying to listen, was doing so.

'What's so bleedin' wonderful about lorry-drivin', then?' Elsie said with more than a hint of peevishness. 'I don't see why you couldn't change your job for somethin' which left you free Sat'day nights. An' why can't you get back to the city more often, eh? This is the first weekend you've been home for . . . oh, for about a century, I should think. And then you don't come callin', like any other feller, it were only chance I come to the dance tonight, 'stead o' hangin' around in me room, wonderin' where you was this time.'

Hearing all this reminded Dympna of that other conversation. The last time she had heard Elsie and Jimmy talking Elsie had been telling him that he would soon get used to being back in Liverpool again and that if he couldn't settle at the chip shop – yes, that was it, he had been complaining that he felt stifled by the shop and Dympna, who at that time had been feeling like a prisoner in the city, had understood his feelings perfectly. But Elsie had actually suggested that he might learn to drive and then drive a lorry, Dympna remembered *that*. Jimmy must have taken her advice and become a lorry driver and now she was complaining that he didn't get back to the city often enough. Dympna had liked Elsie very much, but she thought the other girl was asking for trouble as she started on about his lorry again. But that was her affair – perhaps she wasn't that fond of him after all and was looking for an excuse to end the relationship? It had not sounded much like that earlier, but then most girls will boast about a 'steady' if a boy so much as looks at them twice, Dympna believed.

Amelia leaned over and asked for the orange squash money and Dympna picked up her handbag and pretended to examine the contents, whilst taking a quick look at Jimmy and Elsie. Jimmy was looking hunted, which was understandable. Even she, who had never really had a boyfriend, knew that nagging was not the ideal way to captivate a young man.

'Anyone would think you was *married* to that bleedin' waggon you drive,' Elsie went on vehemently. 'You an' me's been goin' steady, Jimmy, ever since we was kids, an' what have I gorrout of it?

Nothin'! Me mam keeps askin' why I don't say "yes" to Geoff, an' when I say 'cos I'm as good as engaged to you she says "Where's your ring then, chuck?" and I have to explain all over again that you're savin' up to buy your own lorry, an' then she says could I be gettin' the wrong ideas . . .'

'I've told you before, Els, that I ain't goin' steady wi' anyone,' Jimmy said obstinately. 'I like you a lot, we're bezzies, allus have been, but I dunno about marryin', or gettin' engaged. It . . . it don't seem right, somehow. Only you will keep on about it, an' . . .'

'Jimmy Ruddock, I'm in love with you!' the girl Elsie said in a hissing whisper easily audible at the next-door table. Dympna fished her money out of her purse and handed it to Amelia. She could see that Amelia's attention, too, had now been drawn to their neighbours. 'I can't help it, I wish I weren't an' that's the honest truth, but I fell for you when I were just a kid an' I can't seem to kick the habit. I spend all week dreamin' about you comin' home on Sat'day night an' when you don't . . . oh, it's as if someone had stuck a bleedin' great knife in me heart an' turned it.'

Jimmy, who had looked hunted before, now looked positively tortured. 'Look, Els,' he said in a tone which Dympna realised he was striving to make reasonable, but which only succeeded in sounding sulky. 'You can't help bein' in love, an' I can't help *not* bein' in love. Can't you understand that? Do I have to spell it out for you? I like you, queen, you're the best pal a feller ever had, you ain't never wavered or let me down. But I don't feel for you like you say you feel for me. There. *Now* do you understand?'

'Ye-es, but I don't think it matters,' Elsie said. She sounded subdued but not beaten, Dympna thought. Not beaten by a long chalk. ''Cos sometimes love, it only comes when you've been goin' steady for a good long while, some folk don't even fall in love proper-like, till after they're wed, and . . .'

'But we *ain't* goin' steady and we ain't gettin' wed,' Jimmy almost shouted. 'You're like a sister to me. There, I've said it, an' now you'll cry, an' I'll feel like a beast . . .'

'I bloody well won't cry,' Elsie said between gritted teeth. 'Right, if that's what you want . . . oh, go to hell, Jimmy Ruddock!' She put her face in her hands, then changed her mind and, picking up her own handbag, began to ferret in it. She was very pale and her eyes, tear-filled, looked enormous. Dympna, who had been unashamedly listening and rather pitying the unfortunate Jimmy, abruptly discovered that it was Elsie she should be feeling sorry for. She really did love the insensitive oaf, anyone could see that. And saying that he thought of her as a sister . . . well, surely there must have been some other way to make her see things his way?

Amelia dug her in the ribs. 'Don't look so worried, me friend Pete says they're always like that,' she said in a hissing whisper. 'They'll have made up by next Sat'day, mebbe even later this evenin', just you see.'

Dympna found this hard to believe, but sure enough, Jimmy had gone round the table and now had an arm round Elsie's shoulders. 'Elsie, love, I'm sorry, but I should of said it weeks an' weeks ago, when you started talking about gettin' engaged. Only . . . only I didn't want to hurt you, 'cos you're the best pal a feller ever had . . .'

'Don't you mean sister?' poor Elsie said coldly, getting out her handkerchief and delicately dabbing her eyes with it. 'Well, if you were me bleedin' brother I'd ha' knocked your teeth down your throat half a dozen times by now for lettin' me down, Jimmy Ruddock. Oh, I would love to punch you on the bleedin' nose!' She stopped mopping her eyes and blew her nose vigorously, then took a deep breath. 'Right. Then is . . . is this the end? 'Cos I tell you straight, if we ain't ever goin' to marry then you're no friend of mine. An' if it is the end, you can bloody well walk out, 'cos I'm not goin' to. I paid for me ticket fair and square an' I'm stayin' to the bitter end. I'm goin' to flirt wi' every feller what looks at me twice an' I'll . . . I'll probably get one of 'em to tek me home an' I'll kiss him good-night so hard he'll be seein' stars for a week. Buzz off, Ruddock!'

Only I don't believe she really said 'buzz off', Dympna thought, shocked, as the young man turned and slunk away from the table, heading for the doorway that led out into Everton Brow. Well, Mammy would say she was no lady, but from the sound of it she had quite a lot to put up with. And if that's what happens when you have a young man then perhaps I'd better just keep fellers at arm's length.

'Well!' Amelia said in a low tone, staring out across the dance floor as though she and Dympna were discussing the merits of two couples, in evening dress, doing an exhibition tango. 'Sounded awful, didn't it? But I tell you, wi' them it's all scream and scratch one minute an' the next it's kissy kissy. Wait a mo, then we'll go over an' join poor old Elsie an' she can tell us what a swine her feller is an' in no time she'll be feelin' better.'

Accordingly the two girls continued to talk and eye the dancers until Elsie had had time to compose herself, then Amelia led Dympna over to the other girl's table. 'Hey up, Els,' Amelia said cordially. 'Your feller gone awready?'

Elsie looked up at them and smiled. It was a watery smile, but better than the scowl which had hovered, Dympna thought. 'Oh . . . yes, he's gone. An' he ain't my feller, not no more. I can take so much, but bein' called his bezzie, after we've been – well, a good deal more than that – for years I won't take. So he can go to the devil as fast as he likes an' I'll find meself someone else, someone wi' a whole lot more sense.'

'Well, there's plenty of young men here,' Dympna said. 'Hello, the exhibition's over . . . what's the next dance, then?'

It proved to be a slow waltz and Dympna, Amelia and Elsie speedily found themselves being solicited as partners by three young men. Dympna's was fat, with tiny blue eyes and sweaty hands. He had almost no conversation and was a remarkably poor dancer – he had already danced with her twice so she knew the drawbacks – but it would have been rude as well as unkind to refuse when both her companions had got up. Amelia was dancing with a red-headed giant with the loudest laugh Dympna had ever heard and smiling politely up at him, and Elsie's partner appeared to be a young man she knew quite well and presently she was laughing at something he said and looking decidedly livelier.

'Now, ladies and gentlemen, this is an excuse-me,' the compère announced and Dympna's partner pulled a face. He clutched her closer – Dympna could just imagine the wet handmarks on the back of her precious dress – but almost immediately was tapped on the shoulder by a short swarthy young man in matelot's uniform.

'Excuse *me*,' the matelot said, grinning at Dympna. He drew her into his arms and beamed down at her. 'Good evenink, lovely laydee, my name ees Frenk.

Vat ees your name?'

'Good eveninck. My name ees Dora,' Dympna said wickedly. He probably thought his English perfect, so who was she to disabuse him? Was this going to be worse than sweaty hands, though? A conversation in broken English as she danced, gripped far too closely in the young man's arms, was not her idea of a pleasant evening.

'Ah, Dohra. Vat a lovely name,' the matelot said. 'Forgive: I hev no more Eenglish jus' now.'

Dympna was just congratulating herself on the end of the conversation and trying, without much success, to put some space between her own body and that of her partner, when – oh bliss – a hand touched him on the shoulder and a voice said pleasantly, and in perfectly ordinary English. 'Excuse me. My turn now, I think.'

Dympna's partner growled something which sounded very rude beneath his breath but relinquished his hold upon her and Dympna found herself clasped gently in the arms of Elsie's young man. Oh, dear God, Dympna thought, horrified. What if Elsie sees me and thinks I'm after him? Or thinks he's after me, for that matter? She'll be terribly hurt and upset, and judging from the way she behaved earlier, angry as well. I don't want trouble, I really don't.

But even as these thoughts darted through her mind, she was finding that Jimmy was just the right height for her and danced in the way she liked best. He held her firmly but did not try to sever her in twain or squash her until she could not breathe, as some of her partners had, and his hand in hers was cool and dry, the one on her waist gently guiding rather than gripping possessively. She glanced up at

375

him as they moved away, and he was looking down at her. He was smiling. He had very white teeth and there was a twinkle in his dark eyes. 'How d'you do, Miss Dympna. Don't look so scared. Despite what our Els were sayin', you'll find I don't bite. So you're in service wi' Elsie, are you?'

'No, I'm a nursery maid at another establishment,' Dympna said primly, but her heart was bumping. He really was nice, if only he hadn't been her friend's feller. Not that he was, not now, according to Elsie, but Dympna thought that Elsie had been astonished and rather horrified when he had taken her dismissal literally. And since he had come back again, she would surely assume that he had done so in order to apologise and hope to make up the quarrel.

The hand holding hers tightened for an instant. 'Another establishment, eh? An' where might that be, queen?'

Dympna was dithering between an honest answer and an evasive one, when a hand descended on Jimmy's shoulder and a voice said: 'Excuse *me*!' It was the matelot.

Jimmy twirled her round and danced her away, saying over his shoulder, 'Not twice in one evenin', pal. Don't you know the perishin' rules?' but 'Frenk' was not to be so easily dismissed.

'Excuse *me*,' he said again, holding harder this time. Then he addressed Dympna rather desperately over her partner's shoulder. 'Good evenink, lovely laydee, my name ees Frenk . . .'

Despite the embarrassment of the situation, Dympna giggled. 'It's no use your talking to him, he's like a gramophone record once he gets going,' she whispered into Jimmy's ear. 'I don't believe he understands any English at all, he's just learned enough to get by for a dance. Oh, Jimmy, do stop!' For Jimmy was whirling her away once more, ignoring the grip on his shoulder and the darkening of the matelot's complexion.

'I'll let you dance wi' the greasy little bloke if you'll tell me where you work, an' let me meet you on your day off,' Jimmy said into her ear. He said it pleasantly, and as he did so he gave Dympna's waist the discreetest of squeezes, but even so she stiffened. He had no right to try to force her to meet him by such behaviour, and anyway, Elsie was meeting her out of work on Tuesday next, what on earth would she say – and do – if she found Jimmy, her boyfriend for years, ahead of her? She'd scratch my eyes out and she'd be right, Dympna found herself thinking. No decent girl grabs another girl's feller just because they've quarrelled.

'You can't meet me,' Dympna said briskly. 'I'm going out with Elsie on Tuesday.' She turned and looked up at him and noticed, for the first time, that there was the suspicion of a dimple in one lean cheek when he smiled. Her heart did an unexpected somersault and she swallowed hard. Oh dear Lord, if only he had not been Elsie's feller.

'Yeah, I know. The following one, then?'

'Excuse *me*! You geeve me loverly laydee!' the matelot said breathlessly and this time he tugged so hard on Jimmy's arm that Jimmy lost his hold and Dympna swung away from him as he twirled, flying across the floor and colliding with another couple. Had they not fielded her neatly she would undoubtedly have fallen.

'You stupid bastard,' Jimmy roared. The matelot, looking as shocked as Jimmy, started to say something in his own language, then began to make one of those helpless shrugging gestures which are meant as an apology the world over. Unfortunately one of his outflung hands came perilously close to Jimmy's nose – and Jimmy misunderstood. At least, Dympna hoped he had, since he squared up to the matelot, called him a few choice names and punched him very hard on the nose.

For a moment there was a horrified silence. Nearby couples stopped dancing and the men got their girls behind them. Couples further away, who had not seen the first blow struck, pushed their way nearer, anxious to be in on any excitement. Then the matelot, with blood already trickling down his chin, shouted something and grabbed Jimmy by the jacket. He drew back his own fist and Jimmy ducked so that the blow whistled over his head and the matelot almost fell. Then to Dympna's horror she saw a positive tribe of small, dark-haired men in naval uniform descending on the floor and in two seconds it was bedlam. Men were punching and thumping and using dreadful language, girls were trying to get between their men and the fight, and the management were running onto the floor. Even the band had stopped playing and were apprehensively gripping their instruments as though wondering whether to flee with them whilst the going was good or whether to use them in self-defence.

Dympna, rooted to the spot, scarcely noticed as girls began to hurry past her, out of harm's way. She was staring at the mass of struggling, fighting bodies. How on earth had this happened – and so quickly? And where, in God's name, was Jimmy?

A hand grasped her arm. 'Come on out of it, gal,' Elsie's voice said in her ear. 'What happened, eh? I were t'other side of the room, I din't see nothin'.'

'Two fellers started punching,' Dympna said. Innate caution advised her not to spill the beans completely, not now. 'Oh, Els, the chap I was dancing with is under that lot somewhere . . . what'll I do?'

'Skedaddle,' Elsie said briefly. 'No feller's worth gettin' a split lip for, let alone bein' carted off by the scuffers. Come on!'

She set off in the direction of the cloakroom, but Dympna, poised on the very edge of the dance floor and gazing helplessly into the heaving mound of fighting men, had just seen Jimmy emerging from the fracas, with what looked like a black eye and his shirt collar torn clean off. And in the moment that she saw him, she also saw a matelot grab a tall glass from a nearby table, smash it against a chair, and advance purposefully upon Jimmy, with the jagged remains of the glass held at shoulder level.

'Jimmy, look out!' Dympna shrieked – and cast herself at the matelot. She hit him squarely amidships with her shoulder and the two of them went down in a tangled heap. The matelot started shouting something in a foreign language just as someone grabbed Dympna, lifted her up in his arms and began to run. 'Let me down,' Dympna squeaked. 'I'm all right, I can run . . . let me down.'

'Right,' Jimmy's voice said breathlessly in her ear. 'I say, wharra ding-dong! We'd best gerrout o' this before the scuffers arrive.'

They reached the pavement just in time. In the distance, they could hear the sound of vehicles, ringing bells, shouts. The police, Dympna saw, were coming at the double, truncheons already held at the ready. She gasped and would have run, but Jimmy caught her arm and stopped her, slowing to a saunter himself as he did so. 'Never run, it tells 'em you're the feller they're after,' he said. 'Quietly now. I'll tek you home.'

Dympna looked at him. He had a black eye and a long scratch down one side of his face but he was grinning and looking, if anything, rather pleased with himself than otherwise. 'You started that,' she said, gesturing back towards the dance-hall. 'That poor sailor had no idea of hitting you, sure and you just whacked out at him for no real reason.'

'I thought he were goin' to hit me, didn't I?' Jimmy said in an injured tone. 'I didn't want no fight, queen. Why, I could ha' been killed.'

'Then why start it? Oh, gracious, see who's at the corner? It's the girls – they're waiting for me.' She turned to her companion. 'You'd better make yourself scarce.'

'I don't see why . . .' Jimmy began, then groaned. 'Elsie's there. If she sees us together it's all up wi' you, queen.' He chuckled. 'She'll have your guts for garters, I'm tellin' you. Look, where d'you work? Can I come round, call for you? I'd tek good care o' you, I promise you that on . . . on me honour.'

'Oh, yes? Like you did in the dance-hall, when that matelot only wanted to dance with me?' Dympna said rather bitterly. 'I'll thank you to clear off, Jimmy. Elsie's my friend and I won't have her thinking me . . . well, all sorts of bad things. But I'm working at the Ditchlings', so I suppose you could come round one evening, just for a word, you know.'

'Right. I'll come round Sunday evenin', perhaps. We could go for a stroll – just for ten minutes – an' have a bit of a jangle.' He put the back of his hand against her cheek, drawing it gently round to her chin, in a tender movement which brought the blood rushing to Dympna's cheeks. 'Good-night, sweetheart – I've never felt like this before, I swear it.'

Dympna gasped, then gave him a tentative smile before turning away. He had a cheek, saying things like that – why didn't she mind? Why did she feel . . . oh, all excited and yet apprehensive? But she began to run along the pavement towards the small group of girls and as she approached one of them detached herself from the group and came towards her. It was Elsie. 'Who was that you were with, Dymp?' she asked. 'It looked awful like . . .'

'I dunno. Some feller. We left the dance-hall at the same time and he walked along with me until I saw you,' Dympna said untruthfully. She knew it was wrong to tell lies, even white ones, but she just did not have the strength, right now, to face up to telling the truth. And anyway, Elsie might not believe that she was innocent of trying to get Jimmy for herself. In fact, if she were being honest, Dympna's own motives seemed somewhat muddled right now.

'Oh aye?' Elsie said, apparently losing interest. 'Well, don't forget we're meetin' on Tuesday. What'll we do? Tek in a flick? Or go to a tea dance? Or we could just talk, an' gerron a tram an' go off somewhere.'

'I usually go to Seaforth on the overhead railway,' Dympna admitted. 'But I don't mind where we go. Shall we talk about it on Tuesday?'

'Yeah, awright. An' in the meantime, I'm goin' to see if I can't gerra job what ain't kitchen maid. Why not?' she sniffed dolefully. 'No point in savin' up to get married when you're feller's walked out on you.'

'Are you comin', Dympna?' Amelia's voice cut in. 'The Thompsons are good, but Nanny Bridgeman says in before midnight or there'd be trouble. Likely your Miss Horsham's the same, so we'd best gerra move on. If we trot . . .'

So trot they did and parted at Amelia's gate, promising to go dancing again the following Saturday.

Having seen Amelia safely in, Dympna headed for her own back door. She let herself in, wondering as she crept quietly up the little passage that led to the back stairs whether she would be able to sleep after so much excitement. That Jimmy . . . she still wasn't sure whether she liked or disliked him, but she did know that her feelings regarding him were strong ones. And when he had stroked her face like that . . . her stomach did another of its abrupt somersaults and she gasped with the strength of it. If simply thinking about a touch could do that to her, what would happen when – if – he kissed her? She went quickly up the back stairs, seeing his face, that lean and dangerous face, in her mind's eye, bending above her own, getting nearer . . . nearer . . . the eyes half closing, the mouth slowly opening . . .

She put out her hand to open her bedroom door and arms closed round her, then eased her carefully inside the room. And for that moment, Dympna let herself be cradled in those arms, for the gesture seemed natural after what she had been thinking. The arms were gentle and for that first fatal moment Dympna believed that Jimmy had followed her indoors and up the stairs, which was extremely wicked and would have to be severely punished, but after the sort of evening she had had, was comforting and wonderful. And then, even as she turned her face up to that of her captor, a mouth descended on hers and immediately she knew, without a shadow of a doubt, that this was not Jimmy.

She tried to scream and began to pull away but her captor was strong and as determined as she. He bundled her across the room and kicked the door shut behind them, then flung her onto the bed and followed her so swiftly that all the breath was knocked out of her and screaming became an impossible exercise.

'Dimples, my own little Dimples,' a voice breathed close to her ear and she smelled alcohol on his breath. 'Oh, I've waited for hours an' hours an' hours an' hours . . .'

Dympna took in a long breath for a good shriek and a hand clamped over her mouth. She bit the hand and grabbed wildly at a garment, felt it rip beneath her fingers, then found her head ringing from a vicious slap.

'All right, if that's the way you want it,' her attacker said between his teeth. 'That's the way you'll get it. Shut up and keep still, you little fool.'

Too frightened to take heed of such warnings, Dympna continued to struggle until a sound on the landing outside must have reached her attacker's ears, for he suddenly stopped short, and Dympna knew he was listening. His hand was still clamped over her mouth and her head was ringing with the pain of his blows, but nevertheless she took in breath to attempt another scream . . . even as she heard, outside the door, the gentle, scuffling sounds of Blenheim, the ancient labrador, who was sometimes allowed the run of the house at night and occasionally ventured up to the attics to see if he could find someone awake to keep him company. But even as she registered what it was, her captor leaped off the bed, turned and delivered one last, vicious blow to her head, which robbed her of her senses.

When she came round, she had no idea how much later, she was alone.

Nanny Horsham, getting up to start her day, did not miss her nursery maid until she went through into the night nursery to find Dominic, the only child now sleeping there until the arrival of the new baby, still soundly slumbering. This was very unusual. Dora was an early riser and as soon as she padded quietly down the attic stairs to go about the business of getting the nursery ready for breakfast, Dominic, usually clad in only half his pyjamas, sometimes in nothing at all, joined her. Of course, the girl then left off what she was doing to get him washed and dressed, meanwhile sparing a moment to go and wake the girls. But this morning . . . Nanny Horsham looked at the neat little watch which hung from her lapel and frowned. Was Dora not well? She was certainly not up.

Dominic, meanwhile, had sat up and knuckled his eyes. 'Nanny!' he said, sounding almost shocked. 'Where's Dora?'

'She's overslept, my lamb,' Nanny said, trying not to sound annoyed, because Dora was a good time-keeper as a rule. 'You can get yourself out of your pyjamas, can't you? That's right, then you have a nice wash whilst I rouse the girls.'

She popped her head round the door of the girls' room, to find Harriet and Georgina already up and preparing for the day ahead. Then she went up the long flight of stairs and into the attics, where Dora still slept though she would come downstairs and take Nanny's room once the new baby was born. Nanny Horsham reached Dora's door and tapped lightly. No one answered, so she opened it and went in. She looked across to the bed, then went to the head of the stairs and, in a voice which shook with fright, called for help.

The other servants were already downstairs but a door opened and Miss Florence Vaughan, Mrs Ditchling's superior lady's maid, looked out. 'What is it, what's happened?' she called back in a decidedly cross voice. 'Mrs Ditchling's still only half awake, you should not . . .'

'My nursery maid's been attacked, the room's covered in blood,' Nanny Horsham said, not mincing words. 'Get help at once, Vaughan.'

And Miss Florence Vaughan, unused though she was to being ordered about by anyone, particularly a mere nanny, was so shocked by her words and impressed by her tone that she actually ran down the stairs, crying out as she went, 'Help, help . . . someone's been attacked! Help, bring help!'

The doctor came, said that Dora was suffering from shock, severe bruising and lacerations, but would mend, given time and quiet. He then sent a nurse round to take care of her for a couple of days, for Mrs Ditchling, horrified by what had happened, had gone into labour and was about to produce her fourth little Ditchling. The nurse was a kindly, round-faced woman with a strong practical streak and she said that the nursery maid would be all the better once she was able to talk freely about her experience. Looks were exchanged at that; no one knew what had happened yet, because 'poor Dora' was still too shocked to say much, not to mention that she had been hit in the mouth, splitting her upper lip and causing her mouth to become so swollen that she could scarcely utter. But everyone, particularly the male servants, felt extremely uncomfortable. They all knew that Blenheim had been wandering around that night and had no so much as whimpered. The back door had been locked by Mr Frame at midnight; did this mean that it was an inside job?

The only male servant who slept in the house, however, was Mr Frame himself and not the most censorious of servants would have accused the dried-up old butler of such an attack. As for the only other males on the premises, one was Mr Ditchling, who scarcely knew the nursery maid, and the other was Dominic, who was far too young to be a suspect.

So 'Dora' lay undisturbed in her bed all that day, sick and sore and afraid from the very bottom of her soul, and waited until she could think logically about what had happened and decide what she should do.

'I want to see Mrs Ditchling,' Dympna kept repeating with the stubbornness of despair. She was fond of Nanny Horsham, she liked and respected Mrs Palfrey, but she had thought and thought, and had finally decided that Mrs Ditchling must be told.

'But she's just had a new baby, a brother for Dominic,' Nanny Horsham said in hushed accents. 'Won't I do, dear?'

'I thought it might be best . . . but if you say she's not well enough to see me . . .' Dympna said slowly and painfully through her swollen lips. 'I'll tell you what happened, though I'd rather you didn't say anything to anyone else.'

Nanny Horsham said she was not one to gossip and after a moment's thought, Dympna began her story. 'Well, we came back from the dance . . .'

'Are you sure it was Mr Philip?' Nanny Horsham said, when at last the pitiful little tale was told. 'It was dark, dearie, and you were frightened . . .'

It occurred to Dympna then that this was a

rehearsal for the real thing, that the time would undoubtedly come when she would have to tell someone in authority, the police, or Mr Ditchling himself, so she did not answer impatiently, but calmly. 'I know, Miss Horsham, but I did see him, quite clearly. And . . . and he left something behind . . . something I know was his. A cuff-link.'

'I see.' Miss Horsham, who had been sitting on the bed facing Dympna, suddenly turned her head away to look towards the window. She said in a stiff, embarrassed voice: 'Did he . . . did the young man . . . Mr Philip – interfere with you in any way?'

'Interfere?' Dympna said, her voice rising. 'He *hit* me, Miss Horsham, he – he . . .' Her voice was suspended by tears. Was this what she would have to face – misunderstanding? But it appeared it was she who had not understood.

'Might . . . might there be a . . . consequence of the attack?' Miss Horsham said. Colour had darkened her cheeks, Dympna saw. 'Is it . . . did he . . . will you . . .?'

'Oh!' Dympna said, suddenly realising what the other woman meant. 'No, didn't I say? Dear old Blenheim came snuffling and scuffling up the attic stairs and Mr Phil . . . he thought it was one of the servants, I suppose, and ran out. He hit me across the head just before he left, though, and I was too sick and giddy to do anything but lie there.'

'Ah, I see,' Miss Horsham said. 'Do you understand now, dearie, what I meant when I asked if he had . . . er . . .'

'Yes,' Dympna said as quickly as her swollen mouth would allow. 'It's all right, Miss Horsham, I do understand. And now do you understand that I really should see Mrs Ditchling? Or . . . or Mr Ditchling,

perhaps,' she added sadly. It would be difficult, but
she would have, she supposed, to face him
eventually.

After a frowning moment, Miss Horsham agreed
that this would have to be done and offered, to
Dympna's relief, to come and sit quietly in the room
whilst she spoke to the master.

So later that morning, whilst she was still lying in
bed with her head throbbing and all her hurts aching,
the door opened slowly and Mr Ditchling's rather
long, handsome head looked in. He also looked
acutely embarrassed and came very slowly into the
room, leaving the door open behind him. He nodded
to Miss Horsham, then came and stood beside the
bed, and after a quick, horrified glance at her bruised
and battered face, kept his eyes carefully fixed just
above Dympna's head.

'Miss – er – Miss Byrne? Mrs Palfrey says you wish
to speak to me, which is unusual, to say the least.
Surely, after what has happened, you would prefer to
speak to . . . to my wife? Or possibly you might wish
to return home? I really fail to see what I can do . . .'

'I want to keep my job – I have to keep it, sir,'
Dympna said exhaustedly. 'But I want to tell you
something about my . . . my attacker.'

Mr Ditchling's eyebrows rose and he began to
speak, but Dympna cut across him. 'It was . . . was
someone we both know, sir.' She lowered her voice
until it scarcely above a whisper. 'It was Mr Philip,
sir.'

Mr Ditchling tried to speak over her, saying
agitatedly: 'I don't think I quite . . . Miss Horsham,
perhaps it would be best . . .'

'Stay where you are, please,' Dympna said, casting
Miss Horsham a mandatory glance. She turned back

to her employer. 'Miss Horsham knows, sir. But it's only she and myself who do – and you now, of course. And neither of us intends to tell anyone else, if only you'll take some action on my behalf, please.'

Mr Ditchling drew his neck into the tall, stiff collar of his shirt. It made him look like a tortoise, and for the first time since the attack, Dympna wanted to smile. But though he was trying to look shocked, she thought she could read, in his eyes, a sad acceptance. 'That is a very serious accusation you've made against my son,' he said stiffly. 'Do you have proof?'

'Yes,' Dympna said baldly. 'When he was taking . . . when he was in this room, he wrenched off his . . . his shirt. When he was leaving he must have grabbed for his things, I suppose, and left, believing he had removed all the evidence. But he has some rather nice cuff-links, I've seen them once before when he was giving Dominic a piggy-back, and one of them was lying beside my bed when I . . . I came to myself. I shan't tell anyone,' she added hastily, seeing her employer's face grow white and bleak. 'I just wanted Mrs Ditchling to know, though. Someone else could have been blamed, or I could have been sacked,' she finished.

'How do you know that it was Mr Philip's cuff-link?' Mr Ditchling said, his brows drawing together. 'Someone else might have a similar pair.'

Dympna shook her head. 'They've got his initials on,' she said. 'P.M.D. See?' She reached under her pillow and held up the small enamelled cuff-link but when Mr Ditchling put his hand out for it, she shook her head and slid it under her pillow once more. 'I think I'll keep it if you don't mind,' she said. 'It's the only proof I've got – except that Mr Philip has been hanging around me for some time now.'

Mr Ditchling's eyebrows rose once more. 'Hanging around you? But my dear young lady, my son is – well, he's in reasonably affluent circumstances . . .'

Dympna cut in, flushing angrily. 'You mean he doesn't have to hang around after a nursery maid when he could afford to take some young lady wining and dining? Maybe so, Mr Ditchling, but there's no accounting for taste, is there? And now, if you don't mind, I'd like to know what you're going to do about it. The doctor said I could have my attacker up for grievous bodily harm and though I'd hate the whole business, I'll do it if you make things impossible for me.'

'Just what do you want?' Mr Ditchling said. He was looking ill, Dympna thought, but she had a shrewd suspicion that he had known what she was going to say long before she said it. Probably he knew that Philip could be violent – perhaps they had had trouble with other servants.

'I want to keep my job and Mrs Ditchling's respect,' Dympna said bluntly. She would much rather have gone home, but knew that a promise was a promise. She was to work here for three years so that the loan for Micheál's pucan would be paid back, and she did not intend to renege on her part of the bargain – or let the Ditchlings renege on theirs. She had realised, of course, that a person without conscience might well try to hold the Ditchlings to ransom over this matter – let me go home without repaying the loan and I'll keep my mouth shut – but she could never have done such a thing. 'And I want you to tell Mr Philip that you know, and that he's to keep well away from me. Could you tell him not to come to the house whilst I'm working here, for instance?'

'Certainly I could. Certainly I shall,' Mr Ditchling

said. 'I shall also send him away from the city – away from the country, in fact. He's an idle young scamp and needs a firm hand – he shall be given his fare and an introduction to his uncle, who has a large farm in South Africa – a fruit farm. He can work there for a few years, see how he likes that.'

'That would be a great relief,' Dympna said. She felt as though a heavy weight had rolled off her shoulders. 'Mrs Ditchling has been good to me, and I enjoy being with the children and the other members of staff. Thank you, sir.'

Mr Ditchling nodded, moved towards the door, turned back. 'Can I take it, Miss Byrne, that this will be the end of the matter? You'll not tell anyone else, or talk to the police? Only it may look a little as though I'm aiding and abetting a criminal to escape if you do so.'

'I shan't breathe a word,' Dympna said rather reproachfully. 'It . . . it isn't the sort of thing anyone would want to talk about. Once he's gone, I shall just want to forget it and take up my ordinary life again.'

'Good, good,' Mr Ditchling said, almost absently. 'And I do thank you most sincerely, Miss Byrne. You are a young woman of character, and when you take over from Nanny Horsham I feel sure you will do our children nothing but good. As for what has happened, please accept my sincere apologies. I wish I could do more, make the perpetrator apologise, but . . . he's best away as soon as possible. There will be no talk, then.'

Dympna leaned back on her pillows and closed her eyes for a moment, then opened them again. 'I'll get up tomorrow and take up my normal duties, sir,' she said. 'I know Nanny Horsham will be glad when I can move my things into the nursery bedroom so that she can have uninterrupted nights. But I'm afraid I don't want to go out for a few days – not until my face is less . . . less . . .'

'Quite. I'll see to it,' Mr Ditchling said. 'And now I'll go and explain things to my wife, and I'll send Mrs Palfrey up to make you comfortable.'

'Thank you,' Dympna whispered.

On Sunday night Jimmy went round to the back door of the Ditchlings', knocked and asked for Miss Byrne, the nursery maid. The cook, hearing the name, peremptorily called the kitchen maid away and came over to the door herself.

'Miss Byrne's ill abed,' she said, eyeing Jimmy curiously. 'She'll not be goin' out for a day or so, I reckon.'

'Oh, I'm sorry,' Jimmy said, blushing bright red. 'Will you tell her I come round, please? I'm Jimmy Ruddock.'

He tried again on the Tuesday, which was supposed to be her day off, only to be told once again that Miss Byrne had been very poorly and wasn't going out. Thursday brought him no nearer a meeting.

'She'll be goin' to the dance, come Sat'day,' Jimmy told his friend Scratcher when they met for a glass of beer at their local. 'You comin' to the Acacia, Scratch? You'll meet her if you come – she's a great looker, honest to God she is.'

But she wasn't at the dance – and Elsie was. Having thought the matter over, Jimmy decided to ask Elsie to dance in order to find out what had happened to her friend. He did not want to rouse Elsie's suspicions, but he simply had to get in touch with Dympna somehow and it was clear that the staff at the house where she worked had been told to give him the brush-off. Enquiries as to what was the matter with her, and when she would be out and about once more had been met with a discouraging show of indifference. They said they didn't know and made it clear they did not intend to discuss the matter further.

So Jimmy and Scratch went to the dance, and Jimmy, armed with his most winning smile, went and asked Elsie if she would do him the honour of waltzing with him.

'May as well,' Elsie said ungraciously, getting to her feet. 'Though I don't know why you want to dance wi' your *sister*, Jimmy bleedin' Ruddock. Where's you been all week, anyhow? Me mam saw you on the Great Homer on Thursday so you wasn't workin' out o' town *then*.'

'Oh, I did one or two long-distance trips so the boss lemme leave early a couple o' days,' Jimmy said airily – and untruthfully. His boss was getting fed up with his employee's sudden urge to spend time in Liverpool and had threatened to find someone more reliable more than once.

'Oh aye? Well, it don't matter no more. I've gorra berra job what started last week. It's live-in an' I don't have to find lodgin's nor nothin'. It pays awright, too, 'cos I'm under-nursemaid to five kids an' a new babby, so in a year or two, I could be the proper nursemaid. I like it, an' all.'

'Well, congratulations,' Jimmy said heartily. 'But you'll miss your pals, our Els. Wharrabout that little Irish gal – you'll miss her, won't you?'

'Nah! She weren't workin' in the same house as me, for a start,' Elsie said morosely. 'Never turned up that Tuesday, she din't, an' when I axed for her at the house they said she'd been took bad an' wouldn't be comin' out for a while.'

'Oh?' Jimmy said, rather heartened to hear that Elsie, too, had been given the same cold-shoulder treatment. 'Well, I hopes you'll be really happy, Els. Want me to write to you?'

'Oh yes, I . . .' Elsie stopped abruptly, the smile dying out of her eyes. 'No thanks,' she said, staring over his shoulder into the distance. 'Best when you're startin' a new life to make it really new, don't you think?'

'Oh aye, but what about that Geoff feller?' Jimmy said. He felt unaccountably guilty. Elsie had never thought about any sort of new life unless it was the new life of being married to him. He didn't love her, didn't want her to love him, but he didn't want to believe he had broken her heart, either. 'He's real keen, you've said it often.'

'Well, I'm not,' Elsie snapped. She pulled away from him. 'I'm goin' to sit down . . . you go back to Scratch. No point in diggin' up something what's dead an' buried.'

'All I said,' Jimmy began, but he was speaking to empty air. Elsie, her spine held straight as a poker, was heading back to her table.

All evening, Jimmy tried to dance with girls that he had seen with Dympna, but he had no more luck with them than he had had with Elsie. One of them, Amelia, told him that she believed, from something one of the Ditchling housemaids had said, that Dympna had fallen down the stairs and cut her face up 'something horrible', but apart from that, Dympna had not been amongst them long enough to make close friends, so no one was particularly worried over her non-appearance at the dance. I suppose she'll come out again when she's better, Jimmy told himself. But surely, even if she's made a real mess of her face, it'll soon begin to heal, and she'll be coming to dances and that? It's just a matter of waiting. And for a girl like young Dympna Byrne, he was prepared to wait and wait and wait.

'Dora, there's a young feller axin' for you. He's been comin' every bleedin' week for ages an' ages . . . won't you come to the door an' tell him you don't want to go out, if that's how you feel? Only he looks so sad, an' he – he ain't done nothin', has he? I know you say you won't go out, but your face looks just as it should, now, an' the fact is you can't hide yourself away for ever. Just come down an' have a word, there's a good gal.' The cook, coming ponderously up the stairs, had met Dympna coming down, and now she looked hopefully at the younger woman. 'Fair's fair, chuck. I don't want the feller to think I've got some reason for tellin' lies about you – you're takin' the kids in the park now, ain't you?'

Dympna stopped short on the second stair, filled with an unreasoning urge to turn and fly back up to the nursery as fast as her feet would carry her. She knew, of course, that the 'young feller' wouldn't – couldn't – be Philip. Her employer had been very straight with her and had told her the very sailing that his son would be catching.

'And if he ever comes back to England, it won't be for some considerable while,' he had added stiffly. 'Besides which, I've told him, and so has Mrs Ditchling, that he will never be welcome in our house. So you continue with your excellent work, Miss Byrne, and don't give the matter a thought.'

He was kind, but he could not know how hugely,

in her mind, the 'matter' loomed still. She could not bring herself to walk in the street without the protection of her uniform and the big, modern perambulator, and she could not exchange so much as a smile or a look with a man without a terrible sinking sensation in the pit of her stomach.

She felt terribly vulnerable and friendless, too. She could not tell Amelia, or Sal, or Bridie what had happened to change her so, and now that her face had healed there was no real reason why she should not go dancing, or out to a concert, or simply round to someone else's house for an afternoon of chatter and a cup of tea. Miss Horsham had left and she was now firmly ensconced as the Ditchlings' trusted Nanny, but she found that she was clinging to her job in a desperate attempt to distance herself from any sort of ordinary life. Even Cook, it now seemed, had realised that she was still hiding away.

And . . . and she had liked Jimmy very much. Only everything had changed, even her memories of the first part of that terrible evening. She remembered Jimmy touching her cheek – but now she recollected it with horror, thinking how easily his hand might have slid down onto her neck, gripping it, choking her . . .

Her dreams were all nightmares, now. She knew very well she was safe as houses in the pretty, handsomely furnished bedroom adjoining the night nursery, where her two young charges now slept, but if she woke in the night it was to lie in a sweat of terror, waiting for the outer door to open and a man to appear round it. The fact that she always shot the bolt across so that no one could reach her save through the night nursery did not put these ridiculous fears in their proper place, which was out of her head. There was nothing logical or sensible in the way she felt, but she could not help it. I'll never marry, she told herself despairingly over and over. I'll never let anyone, not the nicest man in the world, get close to me again. Besides, I thought Mr Philip was quite nice until that night. All men may be like that, underneath. But even if they aren't, I don't want to find out. I want to be safe, that's what I want. Safe and single.

'Miss Byrne? Nanny? Come down, queen, he's at the kitchen door this very minute an' I told him I'd fetch you down if I could. Please, Miss Byrne, do tell him to his face if you don't want to see him no more.'

Dympna took a deep breath and smiled at Cook, then marched down the remainder of the stairs, across the hall and into the kitchen. Jimmy was standing on the doorstep, leaning against the door jamb, and at the sight of her his eyes lit up and a big smile spread across his face.

'Dympna! Oh, I've been that worried, queen. Come over here, so's I can look at you. I've been callin' an' callin' at this here perishin' house . . .'

Dympna looked at him. At the dark, curly hair falling across his tanned brow, and the dark, bright eyes, and the smile, the white teeth . . . and suddenly it was as though a mist had fallen between them and as it cleared it was no longer Jimmy Ruddock who stood there but Philip Ditchling, his hands coming out to grab her, his face changing into that terrible look, which she would never be able completely to forget. The look of a ravening wolf, she thought, beginning to tremble. She remembered how Philip's fair hair had flopped across his brow and how his eyes had glittered; the cruel twist of his lips and how his hands had . . . had . . .

'I'm not coming any nearer,' she heard her voice say, rather high but quite flat and emotionless. 'I'm not coming out with you, either. Not today, not ever. I . . . I really don't like you at all. Now go away, please.'

He stared at her as though he couldn't believe his ears. Then a slow, painful flush crept up his neck, his face, right up to the tips of his ears. He stood up straighter, staring at her as though – as though she had hurt him, struck him. For a moment she was sorry; she wanted to run to him, to say that it was all right, that she had been ill . . . But she remembered what Philip had done to her and hardened her heart. Better to finish it right now, before it had really begun, then she could go back to being Nanny Byrne again and need never remember the soft and silly Dympna who had so enjoyed – enjoyed! – the touch of this young man's hand.

'Look, love, I don't know what's been happenin' to you, but it weren't none o' my doin', so why send me away? We . . . we got on right well, that night, an' I been comin' round here every week . . . I've damn' near lost me job over it . . . if only you'll come out wi' me for a walk in the park, say, so's we can talk, explain . . .'

'No,' Dympna said. She began to tremble. She could not stand much more of this. 'I don't ever want to see your face again, Jimmy Ruddock, so will you just listen to me? Go away. Chase after that Elsie – heaven knows she was keen enough to . . . keen enough . . .' Her voice faltered, then strengthened. 'I've got a feller back in Ireland, we're goin' to get married when I'm old enough. Does *that* satisfy you?'

He stood there as if turned to stone for a moment. He had been red but now he was white, still. Then he took a step backwards. 'I'm sorry,' he said. His voice cracked when he spoke; if he had been a girl she would have thought he was fighting back tears. 'I'm real sorry, I didn't mean to upset you, I didn't realise . . . about the feller in Ireland, I mean. Of course . . . of *course* if that's how it is, there's nowt more to say.'

Even at this late stage there was a part of her which was agonising with him over her words – her untruthful, hateful words. But the frightened part of her was uppermost and all it wanted was to see him leave so that she could be Nanny Byrne once more, safe with her little charges and her work and her comfortable letters home.

He turned away, was actually walking down the short path, she was moving across the kitchen to close the door behind him when he suddenly turned. She was as terrified as if he had pounced on her; she gasped with fear and a hand flew to her mouth. He was going to attack her for what she had said, he knew it was all lies, he would be angry . . .

'Goodbye, Dympna,' he said. 'If you ever change your mind, let me know, eh?'

He was smiling, raising a hand. She said nothing, watching him stonily as he heaved a sigh and left. She closed the door after him then and went upstairs again, to the nursery. It was empty of children for the older ones were all at school now and the baby was fast asleep in his cot. Dympna checked that he was all right, then flung herself down across her own bed and began to weep.

Jimmy went back to his yard and when the boss started shouting he shouted right back. The boss said he might have his cards and welcome, and just let him find himself another job with the Depression tightening its stranglehold on the country and lorry drivers ten a penny. 'If you want this bleedin' job then stop arsin' around an' git back in your cab, an' don't think of leavin' it no more,' his boss growled at him. 'Else you'll find yourself on the bleedin' street wi' your bum hangin' out o' your kecks an' norra penny piece to bless yourself with.'

Much I care, Jimmy thought, picking up his bits and pieces and making his way back to his cold and unsatisfactory bed-sitting-room. I'll not stay here in this dump when I could be somewhere else, somewhere better. I'll find meself a berth, I'll go to the States and jump ship and never come back here no more.

And to an extent, he did just that. He gave his landlord notice and got a berth on a transatlantic passenger ship as a deckhand. Within a week he was far away from Liverpool, nursing the pain of Dympna's rejection and determined to make a new life for himself, as Elsie had. There were other pretty girls in the world, a great many of them, and once you'd made up your mind to wed, it should be easy enough to find a girl who was both pretty and intelligent, and willing.

When his ship had sailed Jimmy had stared up at the Liver Birds and thought bitter thoughts of Dympna, who had not bothered to let him know that she was returning to Ireland – though how she could have done so, lacking his name and address, he never thought – and planned how he would grow rich, buy his own boat and sail to Ireland to search for her there. He knew he was being foolish, that it was an impossible dream, yet when he told one of his messmates why he had come to sea the older man was comforting.

400

'If you're meant for each other, pal, you'll find each other,' he said. 'My ole woman an' me, we found each other, din't we? She's Spanish, couldn't speak hardly a word of English, but we met, an' we knew, like. We didn't know each other's names nor nothin', mind you, 'cos she were wi' what they called a chaperon, an' us fellers weren't allowed nowhere near the females, not the young 'uns, anyroad. So when me ship sailed I thought that were that. An' six months later, I were took bad on board ship wi' a belly-ache like you ain't never dreamed of, an' they put me in a little boat an' rowed me ashore at a place called Corunna an' carried me miles an' miles, an' put me in 'ospital where only two o' the nurses spoke any English. An' one o' them were my ole woman . . . Anna, I calls her, though she's gorra fine Spanish name about six times the length o' that. Now your gal's only in Ireland – she might come back to Liverpool any minute – so you'll find each other, never fret. I b'lieve there's someone up there . . .' he pointed to the smoky ceiling of the crew's mess room '. . . what looks out for lovers.'

When the ship reached New York he thought about leaving her, but decided that to do so without a penny to bless himself with wasn't a wise act, so he stayed on. And once he began to make friends in the crew the obvious solution occurred to him. He could not face going ashore in Liverpool, so why not travel down south and get a job on a liner that berthed in Southampton? Several of his mates did just that from time to time. Why should not he – and his broken heart – join them?

With Jimmy, to think had always been to act. In no time at all he was sailing with a ship out of Southampton and only thinking of Dympna half a dozen times a day, and for the first hour or so of every night. He would, he told himself, come to his senses. And if she ever came to hers – a rush of delight filled him at the very thought – then he had told her to get in touch with him immediately.

It did not occur to him for several weeks that she simply could not do so. He had neither given her an address nor told her of his intention to take a berth aboard ship.

But dreams do not take note of such inconvenient facts and for many, many weeks his favourite dreams included Dympna coming to him and confessing that it had all been a dreadful mistake, that they must be together. In his dreams he took her in his arms and kissed her, and all their troubles, disagreements, misunderstandings were over. But in reality he tried very hard to live his life without her. He met other girls, took them out, told them they were beautiful and sometimes reaped his reward. But he did not fall in love again.

Dympna started night school when the baby was six months old. By then she had a nursery maid of her own, because Mrs Ditchling understood that she needed to have time off just as much as Nanny Horsham had and employed a sweet-tempered, sensible young girl of sixteen called Polly. But Dympna did not go to dances, or to the cinema, and at last Mrs Palfrey told her that she must begin to forget the past. 'I know I'm not supposed to discuss what happened to you on that dreadful night and I've never asked you any questions, but I'm fairly sure that you were attacked in some way by a young man. It's a dreadful thing, my dear, but it's over and you must forget it. You must start living a normal life again, otherwise you're going to end up a sour old spinster, always looking after other people's children, until at last you're too old for nannying and they turn you out to fend for yourself.'

'What should I do, then, Mrs P?' Dympna asked. The two of them were in the housekeeper's room, shelling peas for staff dinner. 'I used to want to go in for teaching, but that all went by the board when . . . when I came here.' Even now, she did not intend to let Mrs Palfrey know that she was working so that her father could own his own pucan.

'Go to evening classes at the technical college,' Mrs Palfrey said briskly. She had plainly thought it all out before tackling Dympna. 'You can actually get your school certificate there – your higher, as well, if you want that. You'll be mixing with young men as well as young women, of course, but they won't be . . . well, they won't be the rough sort of fellers you might meet at dances or the cinema. They'll be wanting to better theirselves, like you do. Will you go along, my dear? You'll probably find you know some of the young people once you get there.'

She had, too. A girl from Dublin, with whom she was already on speaking terms, was also putting her name down for classes.

'Hello, Miss Byrne,' Annunciata had said shyly. 'I never knew you were comin' here to sign up. What're you doin'?'

'I'm going to have a try at getting a school certificate,' Dympna admitted. 'What about you?'

Annunciata smiled. 'I'm the same,' she said. 'I love nannying, so I do, but you can't be a nanny once you're gettin' on in years. I'd like to teach.'

The two girls stared at one another. 'We're twin souls,' Dympna said joyfully. 'You're nannying for

403

the Sidmouths, on Croxteth Road, aren't you? I've seen you in the park and someone said you were there.'

'That's right,' Annunciata agreed. 'So we'll sign on together, shall we? And when the classes start, in September, I'll call for you so we can go in together. It won't be nearly as frightening wit' the two of us.'

And so the two girls became friends and began to study, to 'hear' each other's work and to compete for a good place in the class. And gradually Annunciata, who knew nothing of Dympna's horrible experience with Mr Philip, wore down her friend's attitude to dancing, cinema and other attractions. When the two of them went to a cinema or a concert they stayed together, neither being keen on getting involved with a young man whilst their exams were not yet behind them and their certificates not yet won.

'But it'll be different when we've got our school certs,' Annunciata said as they watched the young girls in their bright dresses going into the Acacia dance-hall one evening. 'Once we're part-way to being qualified, we can relax, wouldn't you say?'

But Dympna just laughed. She would wait until she was qualified to attend a teacher training college, she said airily, knowing that this would put off the evil day for several years at least. Then and only then would she start going out properly again.

# Chapter Eleven

It was July and a fine, hot day, the sun pouring its molten gold down from a deep-blue cloudless sky. Beatrice had seen Micheál and Egan off for a couple of days' fishing on the Porcupine Bank and had settled down herself to a grand house-cleaning, for Nicholas, his course finished and his degree won, was coming home for a short stay – would be home, in fact, by tea-time.

As she rubbed and scrubbed, however, Beatrice found her thoughts wandering from Nicholas's imminent arrival to her still-absent daughter. Dympna had obediently gone off to England to be a servant in her aunt's house so that her parents might accept the Ditchlings' loan and continue to make a living from a new boat, and also, of course, so that Nicholas might complete his training at the university. She had done just as she had promised, had never even attempted to come home for a holiday, and although the three years were up and her debt to the Ditchlings paid, she had not so much as mentioned returning and now actually sent what must be the lion's share of her earnings home.

In the beginning Beatrice had secretly expected Dympna to land on Irish soil before the end of her time and had been surprised when this had failed to happen. After all, she could quite fairly have taken some holiday after three years during which, it seemed, she had been happy to take her breaks from her work in days off rather than all in a lump together, so that she might have come home.

When Beatrice, at Micheál's insistence, had written to her asking her why she did not return to them for a week or so at least, Dympna had replied that she had suffered so dreadfully from homesickness when she had first crossed the water that she had decided not to come home until she could do so for good. Yet now that the debt was repaid and she was free to do so, she had not come. Micheál had sighed sadly and said he had lost his little girl, that the big city had claimed her, but Beatrice did not think that this was true. She believed, however, that Dympna would do a good deal better for herself in Liverpool than she could in Ireland and continued to write to her weekly, and to tell anyone who asked that her daughter was doing well, and was happy both in her work and in her social life.

But in her heart, Beatrice had never believed her own propaganda. Dympna wrote home often, rather brief letters to Beatrice, longer, chattier ones to her brother and replies to Micheál's lengthy, ill-spelled epistles, which Beatrice had never been permitted to read, though he occasionally left one carelessly about, where Beatrice could scan it guiltily whilst he was out of the way. But in all these letters Beatrice could sense the girl's constraint behind her seemingly innocent chatter about the house, her employers, her fellow servants. It might not have been obvious to Micheál or Egan, but Beatrice was sure that something had happened to Dympna, which had changed her in some deep and painful way, and equally certain that this was the real reason why her daughter had not yet returned.

Yet why should Dympna not be as happy and content as she pretended? Indeed, why should she pretend? There was nothing wrong in admitting to homesickness – she had done so – nor in saying that she would rather be at home. Only of course had she said that, Micheál would have been clamouring to have her back, which would not have been possible until the three years were up.

Nevertheless, now that she was about to welcome home her son, Beatrice became aware of a little niggle of sadness that Dympna, too, would not be returning to Connemara. She had proved herself to be a good girl, a daughter to be proud of, and gradually, over the years of her absence, all Beatrice's foolish fears and vague jealousies had been laid to rest. Dympna, she had realised, was no threat to her happiness with Micheál. She knew she had been downright foolish and unkind to resent the girl and intended to make it up to her when next they met. Only . . . well, it seemed that they were not going to meet, not in the immediate future, at any rate. And Beatrice, who passionately desired Micheál's happiness, had come to realise, of late, that her husband was fretting for Dympna. Seeing Nicholas might be enough for Beatrice, but it would not satisfy Micheál's longing for his daughter, who had been so long away.

However, it was useless to wonder about Dympna; she had best count her blessings and revel in the thought of Nicholas's impending arrival. It would be grand to have him home, Beatrice told herself as she cleaned the cottage window-panes with rolled-up newspaper dipped in vinegar until they shone like diamonds, especially now that he was *Doctor* Byrne and not just a student. Oh, she had been proud of him as a student, there was no question of it, but to be able to say *My son's a fully qualified doctor* would give her enormous satisfaction.

Finishing the last window, she remembered something else. Micheál had reminded her once again that morning that there was no financial reason, now, why Dympna should not come home too. He had never fully understood the terms on which Dympna had been taken on by the Ditchling family and her heart had given an uncomfortable series of little jerks at the mere sound of the words, because she was still a little afraid of Micheál finding out about her bargain with Maude and could not bear the thought that he would despise her if he knew that she had virtually sold his daughter into a sort of slavery. Instead, she had said that no doubt Dympna would come as soon as she felt able to leave the children and that in the meantime they must enjoy Nicholas's arrival instead.

Beatrice fetched the round tin of beeswax and began to polish the Welsh dresser, rubbing round and round, on and on, until she could see her face in the dark wood. Of course, had Dympna not admitted that she was studying to better herself so that she might one day return to Ireland, even Micheál might have been suspicious, because the girl had loved the country so, but her letters to the family were always cheerful and never included so much as one word of complaint. She did say she was longing to see them all again, that she dreamed of the cottage and the lough every night as she lay in her bed in the nice little room she had taken over when Nanny Horsham had left, but that was just the way she talked, dreaming of home as somewhere special. Beatrice told herself that Dympna would not really want to come back to this godforsaken corner of Connemara, not now that she'd tasted the sweets of city life. And Maude, good Catholic that she was, had given her lord and master another baby in the years since

Dympna had arrived in Liverpool. In her letters she spoke of the child almost as though he had been her own, for had she not had full control over him since his birth? Someone else's baby, Beatrice told herself, would be much more acceptable than one's own because Dympna had a nursery maid to see to the little ones' wants, as she had the weekly washer-woman to wash dirty nappies, bibs and other clothing.

What was more, in her letters Dympna spoke of cinemas, theatres, concerts and, occasionally, of young men, though never of one in particular. She had been a pretty girl, so of course there must have been young men. But she was twenty now, too sensible to be cajoled into an unsuitable alliance. She would choose someone who could support her in the manner to which she had become accustomed, and then she would come back to Connemara for long enough to see them all and to convince both Beatrice and Micheál that she really was happier in England and go away once more.

So Beatrice told herself that she was a lucky woman, with a daughter in a good job, earning good money, and a son – what a son! – who had got his degree in medicine and was now about to start his career as a doctor.

And Beatrice, cleaning with vigour and enjoyment, had another reason for happiness today. Egan, who was sixteen, had found himself a very nice girlfriend in Maria, the daughter of the Sullivans up at the farm. Mr Sullivan doted on his youngest daughter and so did his wife; Maria would bring a very nice dowry with her when she eventually made her choice and as things stood at the moment, it would be Egan because the child never looked at anyone else. Of course she was a child still – though a mature fifteen – but Beatrice could read the look in a young girl's eyes, and that look boded well for Egan.

Presently, her work done, Beatrice decided she would like a cup of tea. She had lit the fire long since, despite the heat of the day, for she meant to bake this afternoon so that when Nicholas came into the kitchen the good smell of his mother's cooking was sweet on the air. She went over to the bucket, tipped the contents into the big black kettle, pulled it over the fire and went out into the summer sunshine to refill the bucket at the spring.

It really was a lovely day, she mused, going briskly down the garden path and out into the lane. The apple trees overhung the fuchsia hedge, the apples already well-formed, and the patch of Queen Anne's lace – meadowsweet – which grew close to the spring made the air heady with its sweetness. She bent over the spring and the water gushed into the tin pail; when it was full she stood it down, then picked a sprig of meadowsweet and pushed it into the bosom of her cotton dress. She felt like a girl again, she almost plucked more of the rich, creamy spikes to decorate her hair, then, laughing at her own foolishness, bent to pick up the full pail and return to the house.

She did not know what caused her to look round as she straightened; movement probably. But look round she did, shielding her eyes against the noonday sun, and saw, coming heavily up the path from the quay, her husband and younger son. They were walking slowly, as though with difficulty, and Micheál's arm was looped around Egan's shoulders almost as though he was having to encourage the boy to keep walking.

Beatrice stood down her bucket and walked towards the two men. 'Micheál!' she said as he looked up and saw her coming towards him. 'What's happened? Why are you back so early? I thought you said you'd be gone for a couple of days, are the fish not biting?'

'It's not . . . not the . . . fish,' Egan said, panting. Beatrice now saw that he was clutching his side, his fingers pressing deep into the flesh beneath the grey flannel shirt. 'It's . . . it's me innards, Mammy. I've a pain in me innards like as if someone – a fox or a wolf – was tearin' me guts out. Oh Mammy, the pain's awful bad, so it is.'

'I t'ought we'd best come back ashore straight away,' Micheál said, taking the bucket from his wife's hand and standing it down. 'Will you gi' me a hand to get the young feller into bed, Bea? Then I'll come back for your bucket. 'Twas only be the grace o' God,' he continued as they helped Egan to climb the stony little lane, 'that we weren't far out when the pain struck. I'm no medical man, Bea, but I t'ink we'll be needin' a doctor before the day's out.'

'A doctor!' Beatrice said, her eyes widening. 'You don't think it's something he ate, or . . . or a twisted muscle?'

'I don't know what it is, but Egan's not a feller to fuss,' Micheál said almost sharply. 'We'll put him to bed wit' a hot brick at his feet, and if he's no better in half an hour I'll go in to Clifden for the doctor.'

'Doctors cost, so they do.' The thin words came from Egan's deathly white lips. 'It'll go off, won't it, Daddy? Janey mac, I can't stand much more o' this!'

'Don't fret yourself, Egan,' Micheál said quickly. 'We've had a good week, so we have, wit' the cod an' the halibut bitin' well. We can afford a few shillin's for the doctor. And as for the pain goin' off, it'll go the quicker if you're give the right medicine.'

'Don't try to talk, Egan,' Beatrice said gently. They eased the boy – who was a man's height now, with a man's broad shoulders, and weighed accordingly – up the narrow path to the front door and then, very gently, inside it. But Egan groaned twice before they got him sitting before the fire, and the sweat ran in great drops down his face and darkened the collar of his grey flannel shirt.

'I wonder, should we give him a hot drink?' Beatrice asked timidly as she came back from the outhouse with a brick to wrap in flannel and warm by the fire. 'I seem to recall . . .'

'Bed first; then if he wants a drink he can have one,' Micheál said firmly. 'Dear God, Bea, he's passed out.'

But he came round again as they lifted him and gave a great shout when they put him down as gently as they could on their own double bed. 'He'll be easier to nurse here,' Micheál said as they stood looking down on their son's pale, pain-racked face. 'Poor lad, and at daybreak he was merry as a lark, so he was, and lookin' forward to the sail out to the Porcupine, and now look at him.'

'I'm . . . easier now,' Egan muttered. 'It's good to be warm, Daddy.'

His parents exchanged worried glances over his head; the day was a hot one and the heat in the cottage kitchen had been quite oppressive. 'I'm goin' to go for the doctor, Bea,' Micheál whispered after a moment when Egan had closed his eyes and turned his head sideways into the pillow. 'I'll be as quick as I can, but I'll be after gettin' the man himself an' not his deputy. The pain's too bad for messin' wit' anyone else.'

'Thanks, Micheál,' Beatrice murmured. 'Can you bring my knitting through from the kitchen? I'll need something to keep my hands occupied whilst I sit by him.'

'I'll do that,' Micheál said. And presently returned to the room with Beatrice's knitting in one hand and a cup of tea, steaming gently, in the other. 'The boy won't want to drink, I doubt,' he whispered. 'But no need for you to go thirsty; drink it down, lass. And I'm bringin' through a cup o' cool water an' a piece o' cloth so you can wet his lips from time to time.'

'Oh Micheál, you always think of just the right thing,' Beatrice murmured, acknowledging her husband's deeper sensitivity, though she did not realise it. 'Don't be any longer than you need, my love. Couldn't you harness Rosa and drive in – in the trap?'

'Well, if she'll let herself be caught,' Micheál said. He touched his wife's soft blonde hair. 'Don't worry, I'll be back as soon as may be.'

Nicholas came whistling up the lane with his suitcase pulling one arm down almost to his knees so that he was lopsided with it and a great thirst rising in him. He reached the spring and paused; the sound alone was enough to make a man thirsty, he thought, and stood down the case to lean over, his hands cupped, to catch enough water for a quick wetting of his mouth and throat.

That done, he paused for a moment, letting the feelings rush over him. He had been home perhaps half a dozen times since he had started at university, but this time, in particular, with his career waiting for him, he had expected to feel impatience with his parents for their insistence that he come home and a certain weariness with the place where he had been brought up. Why should he feel anything else? They knew nothing, his parents and his brother. They were proud of his achievements but had no idea what those achievements could bring him. He could do anything – be anything. He had done well in his last exams, in his practicals, in all his work. He could go into hospital as a houseman and rise through the ranks until he was a surgeon – he enjoyed surgery, was quick and neat. 'He cuts without scruple,' one of his tutors had remarked and had then qualified the remark, hastily, by adding that Byrne knew that the incision must be made in order that the diseased organ could be extracted. Some of his students, he went on to complain, hesitated, fumbled a bit. But Byrne simply cut.

Or I could go into general practice, he continued in his thoughts, standing before the spring and watching the surge of bright water as it spurted from the rich grass and undergrowth at the top of the bank and tumbled down into the round tin basin which had stood there as long as he, Nicholas, could remember. He fancied a practice in a rich neighbourhood so that he would be paid promptly and without having to go from door to door, reminding people. But he knew, really, that you needed money to start a private practice – unless you were lucky enough to be taken on as an assistant to a rich doctor with a busy existing practice. And there were snags to that; he would probably end up doing all the work at all hours and getting precious little remuneration for it.

Perhaps it would be best to apply for a houseman's post. But he would think it over whilst he remained at home, talk it over with his mother, perhaps. When he had been a needy student she had given him money, but he did not think she could give him any more. He vaguely remembered the panic-stricken letters when his father and Dympna between them had lost the boat. That was why Dymp no longer lived at home. She had gone to Liverpool to work with children in some capacity – he was not sure what: a teacher? a nanny? – and had not returned to Ireland so far as he knew. It was a pity in a way; Dympna was sufficiently bright; he could have talked his situation over with her. She would be old enough, now, to understand his dilemma and it would have been interesting to hear her views. But she was not here, so he would use the next couple of weeks to go over and over his choices, thus making sure that his decision was the right one. He did not consider consulting Egan for one moment; thick, Egan had been, both at school and in every other way so far as he could remember. He shook his head slowly, thoughtfully. No use talking to Egan – or the daddy, for that matter. Mammy was a different kettle of fish, though. She came of a good family – he wondered whether one of them might be willing to help him? It was a curse, poverty, especially when it meant that a feller with a brain like his could not simply choose his path and follow it. But he would find a way; he always had.

Having slaked his thirst and gone over his problem in his mind he continued up the lane, reached the crooked gate, opened it and walked up the path. The cottage was freshly whitewashed and even to Nicholas's unappreciative eye it looked nice, the white contrasting with the golden-brown of the thatch, which was held down against the Atlantic storms by lengths of rope which, in their turn, were attached to large boulders that his father, as a very much younger man, had brought up from the shore.

Because it was summer the apples which leaned

over the fuchsia hedge into the increasingly steep and stony lane were reddening and in the scrap of garden the main-crop potatoes were in full flower. When the flowers fall the roots are ready for digging, Nicholas thought, and was surprised that he, who had spent most of his childhood evading such tasks, could still remember the old country lore.

He did not knock of course. Sure of his welcome he simply pushed open the wooden door, the tar which helped to preserve it from the weather sticky to the touch, he noticed fastidiously, and walked inside.

The room seemed smaller than he remembered it, but since this happened every time he came home he took little notice of the phenomenon. He stood down his suitcase by the worn sofa and went to hang his mackintosh and his brown velour hat on the stand to one side of the back door. Then he strolled over to the fire and gave it a kick; the turves smouldered redly into life and Nicholas pulled the blackened kettle over them, then checked that there was water in it. By God, he could do with a decent hot drink – the spring water was all very well but nothing quenched the thirst like tea. Or beer, of course, but Mammy wouldn't be after having beer in the house except on a special occasion.

The kettle was half full, which was plenty of water for a good pot of tea. Nicholas had left the back door open, and a good thing too, on such a hot day. He had better pull the lower half closed, though, he decided. He understood enough of country ways to know that, if he did not do so, he would be joined, presently, by a number of the hens which croodled and scratched around the cottage, to say nothing of the odd dog from the farm, or even the pig, if his mammy had let it out of its sty so that it could have a wander and graze on the long, summer-bleached grass.

Having performed that task, he heard a sound from the direction of the bedroom. He walked across the kitchen, smiling. Mammy had obviously been cleaning the house all day – everything shone – and now she was finishing up in the bedrooms. He went towards the door.

It opened abruptly. Three people came into the kitchen. His mammy, his daddy and a stranger in a Harris tweed jacket – Nicholas knew quality when he saw it – dark-grey flannels and a flowing tie patterned in red and blue. The stranger was talking and for a miracle neither his mammy nor his daddy noticed that Nicholas had arrived home, they were concentrating so entirely on the man.

'. . . Nasty case of appendicitis,' he was saying, and immediately all Nicholas's finely tuned instincts came into play. A doctor, and a well-to-do one by the look of him, with clothes that cost . . . what was he doing here, in this humble fisherman's cottage?

'. . . Take him to the hospital?' That was Mammy, white-faced.

Nicholas stepped forward. 'Mammy, what's going on? I arrived home and thought the house was empty – I was wondering where you and Daddy were when I heard someone talking from the direction of the bedrooms and I was about to come through . . . Oh, good afternoon, sir, I'm so sorry . . . I'm all at sea. What's happening?'

The doctor glanced quickly at him and then back to his parents. But he spoke to all three of them, turning his head to include Nicholas as he did so. 'I'd like to get hold of a trained nurse, to assist me . . . the boy's very sick . . . I suppose there's no telephone around here? It would be best if I could get him to hospital as soon as possible, which means Galway, of course, but it's a long ride to Galway in the back of my car, and even if one of you came along to hold the patient still . . . in short, his best chance is an immediate operation, but I'll need someone to administer the anaesthetic and I don't . . .'

Nicholas cut in without even thinking. 'I'm a doctor, sir. Oh, a very new one, I got me degree only a couple o' weeks ago, but I . . . I think I could assist. Of course, I've only worked in the big hospitals in Dublin, but if it's best . . .'

'The quicker the better, really,' the doctor said. He looked keenly at Nicholas, taking in with one glance the respectable grey flannel suit, the sombre tie, the neatly cut hair and clean and well-trimmed nails. 'You're another son, I take it? My car's right down at the end of the lane, but it can come up as far as the spring. If you'll give me a hand wit' my instruments and such we can get your good parents to clean down here and make all as sterile as possible . . . but he's your own brother, me boy. Are you sure you aren't too involved to do your part?'

'He's barely been home these past five years,' Micheál said gruffly before Nicholas could answer. 'They're almost strangers. An' young Nick's done well, both in his work at the college an' at the hospital. Sor, if it'll help me son . . . me younger son . . . I'd be grateful . . .' He did not complete the sentence but looked hopefully from Nicholas to the doctor and back again.

'Right,' the doctor said. He seemed to have made an instant decision. 'As you know, I'm not your regular physician, Dr Doyle. I'm his cousin from Dublin, come down to Clifden for a holiday, but since Dr Doyle wasn't available, I've come meself. Me name's Farrell.'

'We only ever called Dr Doyle out when I was half drownded, sor,' Micheál said with a trace of pride in his voice. 'Us Byrnes are a healt'y lot, by and large.'

Mr Farrell was about to answer when Nicholas cut in, stammering in his eagerness, 'N-Not the Mr Farrell who works at P-Paddy's Dun – St Patrick Dun's, I mean, sir?' Nicholas said, a note of awe in his voice. Mr Farrell, the surgeon, was well known to all the medical students in St Cecilia's Street. 'I did wonder . . . I've never met you, but I saw a wonderful car at the end of our lane . . . I've seen your car in Dublin, sir,' Nicholas finished in a rush. He had wondered what such a nice car was doing in a neck of the woods like this. He should have guessed that it meant emergency, trouble.

'That's me. So you'll trust me to operate on your young brother,' the surgeon said with a twinkle, then turned to Micheál. 'I'll go down to me car and bring it as close as I can, in case I need to reach a telephone. Then you and meself and your good lady here will get to work on this room.' He smiled reassuringly round at them all and Nicholas realised that Mr Farrell was not only a brilliant surgeon but a charming man, too. 'Shall we get to work?'

Very much later that night, Nicholas let himself quietly out of the cottage and stole down the path. At the gate he paused. He could go up the lane and up into the hills and stroll amongst the gorse and the big grey noses of the eternal rocks, which pushed through their thin earth counterpane, and be quite alone with his turbulent thoughts. Or he could go down to the harbour and watch the sea – the old enemy – either breaking against the stones of the quay or creeping slowly across the flat golden sands of the lough. Either way, he realised, he would be alone because it must be well past ten o'clock and everyone in Connemara, he believed, unless they were night-fishing, went to bed well before ten.

God, but he was tired! He had assisted the surgeon, more on his mettle than he had ever been before, determined to prove himself, knowing this to be a man of influence who could easily make – or break – his future career. And yet even whilst he was straining every nerve to show what he could do he was aware, in a part of his mind that he had scarcely known existed, that anxiety for his brother was making his hand shake when it should be steady, making the sweat runnel down the sides of his face in a way it never did when he was assisting – even operating – on an unknown or little-known patient.

But he had got through it somehow and so had Egan. He had administered the anaesthetic, making sure that the boy had got enough but not too much, monitoring his pulse and handing the surgeon the sterilised instruments sticking out of the old milk saucepan, which had been the most suitable object for boiling them in. He had watched eagerly as the incision was made and then, uncharacteristically, had found himself forced to turn away as he saw the dreadful mess which was his brother's appendix. He found he could not watch those strong, dextrous fingers doing their work with the scalpel because he was full of the dreadful fear that the appendix might rupture under the surgeon's instrument. He had thought himself immune from such feelings and was astonished to realise how much his younger brother still meant to him. If it had been the mammy, he found himself thinking, or Daddy, or even Dympna, I don't know how I'd have coped. Of course, he and

Egan had shared first a bed and then a room for years, but he had honestly believed himself to have sloughed off his family as a snake sloughs its old skin; apparently it was not that simple.

However, Egan had come through it so far because he was strong. It might be the only thing the sea does for you, but it shouldn't be altogether forgotten, Nicholas found himself thinking as he felt Egan's pulse beating with only the slightest falter beneath his fingers. If I'd had to endure hours of pain and then a protracted kitchen-table operation, would I have come through it as well as Egan has? I doubt it, I doubt it very much.

He had been standing by the gate whilst his mind wandered, now he turned towards the sea; he would go down to the quay and make sure the new boat was safely tied up and that the nets were folded and put away. He had had almost nothing to do with the boat for years, but knew that he would never forget how everything should have been left. He also remembered how differently he had once felt about the boat, how intrigued he had been with everything to do with the fishing. As a child of three or four he had dogged his father's heels, wanting to know how this worked and that, picking up the big, curved netting needle in his small hand and trying to imitate Micheál's quick, confident moves with it.

Then Dympna had been born and he had gone to school and things had no longer been the same. The baby had been fretful and his father, who had spent so much time with his small son, now seemed to assume that Nicholas could manage very well without him. Many and many a night Micheál had come in from fishing and gone straight to the cradle, picking the grizzling little creature out of it as though she were the most precious thing in the world and walking up and down with her, singing songs, old lullabies, until she quieted. He had fed her patiently with the double-ended bottle, or spooned mashed potato into her, and Nicholas had felt himself pushed out by this horrible, red-faced baby who had become such a favourite with the father he had idolised.

I should thank Dympna, then, for my sudden revulsion against the fishing, he told himself now, as he neared the quay. He could smell the curious odour of seaweed, wet stone, tar and fish, which was as familiar to him as the aroma of a peat fire smouldering on the hearth and found that he knew already that the tide was out, the sea a distant line against the dark night sky and the trembling stars. What a blessing, then, that Dympna had arrived and forced him to look beyond fishing and the *Fair Aleen* to the life of the mind, which was captured in books and learning. But he knew that this was not so; he had taken to book-learning as soon as he had realised that such a thing existed, for there had been no books in his parents' crowded little cottage nor in the homes of their neighbours.

He reached the quay and dropped from its five-foot height onto the hard wet sand. The boat – his father was not a man of imagination and had named this one *Fair Aleen* as well, as though he could not think of sailing a pucan with any other name – was pulled up close to the grey stones and a rope led from her bows up to a bollard around which it was securely tied. Micheál must have taken the opportunity some time or other to pop back here, because the nets were folded and in their right places and the ropes – save for the one which fastened the *Aleen* to the bollard – were neatly coiled. A couple of lobster pots were arranged by her side on the sand and as Nicholas bent over them something moved.

'Who's there?'

The voice, coming softly out of the blue darkness, made him jump and catch his breath so that he turned wrathfully upon the speaker. 'Who the hell . . .? What on earth . . .? Where . . .?'

There was a soft laugh and a figure detached itself from the shadow of the quay and came towards him. It was a slender girl, probably in her mid to late teens, with long, dark hair caught back from her face with a ribbon and sparkling dark eyes. He could see very little more than that in the faint starlight, save that she was clearly not at all afraid of him, stranger though he must be to her.

'I'm Maria Sullivan, from the farm, an' you'll be Nicholas Byrne, the feller Mrs Byrne's so proud of. I ought to remember you, but I don't t'ink I do. You've not been home over much so's I recall. But I'm wonderin' can ye tell me the latest news of Egan? I came down to the harbour earlier, to try if I could meet him, an' his daddy had come out whilst the doctor saw to Egan, so's he could bring the boat up and tidy the nets. He told me Egan's appendix was bein' took out, but he was in a quare old state, so he was, tanglin' nets more than he was tidyin' 'em, so I give him a hand. I like Egan's daddy – your daddy, that's to say. So how's Egan now?' She came closer, so that he could see her pale oval face and the anxiety in the big, shadowed eyes. He saw that she was a little nervous; she kept playing with a slender silver bangle, which she wore around her wrist, pushing it up and then pulling it down again until it almost reached her knuckles. 'You'll tell me the trut', won't you? Sure an' I'd rather be knowin' what's happenin' to him, it's worse bein' kept in iggerance, so it is.'

'He's had his appendix removed and he's asleep now, in our mammy's big bed,' Nicholas said, wondering how much he should tell her. He was longing to confide his worries to someone, but dared say nothing to either of his parents. It was not fair to let them know what Mr Farrell had been so careful to keep from them. The surgeon had managed to get the appendix out without it rupturing, but it had been a tricky and awkward operation. There was – there must be – a strong possibility of infection and, fit though Egan undoubtedly was, an infected wound was no joke, particularly when you were trying to nurse the patient at home. He looked consideringly at the girl in the faint starlight. Was she close to his brother? He had no idea whether Egan was particularly friendly with one of the Sullivan girls, but then he scarcely knew his brother as an adult at all. The Egan he knew had scarcely noticed girls, far less made a special friend of one. Would it be safe to confide in her or would she burst into wailing sobs and fly up to the cottage to get reassurance from Egan's mammy and daddy? But he could say enough to make her see that things were not too rosy without frightening the life out of her and she had said she would rather know the score than not.

He took a deep breath. 'You know that I'm a doctor, I suppose?' he said and, at her nod, 'Well, the surgeon who did the operation is a famous man, no one else could have managed it the way he did, it was a grand job, but what worries me is the chance of infection. An appendectomy is a tricky operation, particularly when there's a fear of rupture, and though Mr Farrell managed to get the organ out complete, or so I believe, it was . . . it was messy. And Egan's being

424

nursed at home, not in sterile surroundings. Mr Farrell says Galway's too far off to take him in safety and I'm certain he's right, because of maybe bursting the stitches and other complications, but it adds to my worries. Egan's strong, though, so I'm telling meself right now that he'll come through it if anyone can and that makes me feel better.'

'I see,' Maria Sullivan said seriously. 'Thank you, Mr Byrne, for tellin' me the trut' straight out, even if it worries me. Will I be seein' Egan in the mornin', do you t'ink?'

'No reason why not, only probably the surgeon will want him kept quiet,' Nicholas said, adding in a rallying tone, 'And a pretty girl like yourself, Miss Maria, is inclined to excite a feller.'

Maria smiled, but perfunctorily. Nicholas could see that she was thinking about Egan and had little time for his gallantries. 'I'll come round tomorrer, so, when I've done milkin' the cows an' a few other messages,' she said. 'Good-night to you, Mr Byrne.'

'I'll walk you home,' Nicholas said quickly. To his own surprise he found this odd little country girl attractive and would have liked to see more of her. 'It's a dark old night for a girl to be out in the countryside by herself.'

She turned and flashed him a quick smile; he saw her teeth gleam white for a moment, then she was whisking round and away from him. 'No need, Mr Byrne. I know every stick an' stone of the way betwixt your cottage an' the farm like the palm of me hand. But I'll see you tomorrer, if you're still wit' the family when I come round.'

'Oh, I will be,' Nicholas said to her back. 'Sweet dreams, Miss Maria.'

She made no reply and he watched until he lost her

figure in the shadows of the little lane which led, he remembered, up to the Sullivans' farm. Then he made his own way slowly back to the cottage, suddenly aware that he felt a good deal better. Mr Farrell had promised to come round first thing the following morning to see how his patient did. If Egan was showing signs of feverishness or if the wound had a bad appearance, Nicholas had promised that he would have his brother all ready for a journey in the back of the doctor's car to Galway if necessary. But he hoped it would not come to that. With luck, Egan would be better by morning, wanting a drink and a mouthful, perhaps, his forehead cool and the wound pale and mending. And in the meantime, his mother was sitting with Egan, so he had best go in and try to persuade her to go to bed. No sense in wearing herself out and he would rather do the night-watch himself, since this was the likeliest to be a difficult one.

He went up the garden path and in through the black-tarred door. He wanted to get some sleep himself before the morning, but he would persuade Beatrice to rest first. It made sense that Egan would have someone qualified by his bedside during the long hours of the night, but tomorrow, if Mr Farrell came and was pleased with his patient, he would have plenty of time to rest.

'It's my brother, Mrs Ditchling. He's had an emergency operation to remove his appendix and he's not so well. Me mam – I mean, my mother – wrote, and her letter seemed quite cheerful and optimistic but then on the bottom of the sheet she's just scrawled *Egan's not as well as I thought when I began this letter, maybe you'd best come home. To tell you*

426

*the truth, dear, I'm rushed off my feet and would be grateful for your presence.* Apparently he was taken ill at the beginning of July and now we're into August and he's still not right. And I've not taken more than a week's holiday since I've been working for you, so I thought, if you don't mind, I'd take a couple of weeks and leave tomorrow morning, early. There's a boat that will get me to Dublin in time to catch the train for Galway – I can be home by tomorrow evening if I'm lucky with my connections.'

Dympna was in Mrs Ditchling's little sitting-room, standing by the door, whilst Mrs Ditchling, who had been sitting in the little blue velvet armchair embroidering delicate sweet peas on a fine damask table-cloth, put her work down on her knee and stared interrogatively up at her. When Dympna had finished speaking Mrs Ditchling nodded slowly. 'Yes, they'll need you at home, I can understand that. But – a whole fortnight, Nanny? Surely your brother will be fit enough to leave after a few days? Only it's not as if we've had any notice, this is all rather sudden and I don't quite know . . . the children are such a handful when you're on your day off, let alone . . .'

'I couldn't give you any notice since I've only just heard myself,' Dympna said patiently. 'And Nanny Horsham always took a fortnight's holiday in the summer and a fortnight at Christmas, Madam, if you remember. I wish it hadn't happened just as much as you do, but . . . but my brother Egan is very dear to me, and I feel I must go to him. My mother, too, needs me at home – she's said so and she isn't the sort of person to ask anyone for help unless she's really desperate.'

'Well, of course you must go,' Mrs Ditchling said. She picked up her needle again. 'What a blessing it's the school holidays, though. I shall send the children off to their aunt in Norfolk; they love going there. And the babies, the little ones . . . is Gill capable of taking care of them do you think, Nanny? My sister-in-law has children the same age as mine and the cousins get on very well, but the little ones . . .'

'Gill will manage the little ones, I'm sure,' Dympna said firmly. She did not intend to let Mrs Ditchling, who had talked herself into letting her nanny go, talk herself out of it again. 'So will that suit, Madam? I'd like to go to my room and start my packing but I'll tell the children now so that they don't wake up in the morning and think I've deserted them.'

'Oh, they wouldn't think that,' Mrs Ditchling said quickly. 'They're so fond of you, Nanny, and you're so good with them. Very well then . . . ah, can you manage the fare, Nanny? Or would you like me to advance you some money?'

'I'd be grateful if you could pay me up to the end of the month,' Dympna said stiffly. It was half-way through the month and she had just about enough money to see her through the coming fortnight; after all, she should have had holiday money these past three years, so it was not unfair that Mrs Ditchling should pay her for the next fortnight right now. When she had become the children's nanny her wages had risen and after talking it over with her employer, who assured her the loan would be repaid without taking her rise into consideration, she had decided to keep the extra money for herself. And now that they were fair and square, she sent a good deal of her salary straight to Beatrice in one of her weekly letters home. Besides, Micheál, in one of his painfully penned letters, had assured her that they were doing well and he was able to pay Egan a small wage.

So Dympna had saved some of her money and spent the rest sensibly. She had bought herself some clothes and shoes, and had taken to going to the cinema and to concerts and other entertainments with Nanny Hazell, who was Irish, like herself. But later she and Annunciata had decided to better themselves by starting evening classes, and she had used her funds to buy books. She and Annunciata had passed their school certificate examination at the first attempt and once the initial hurdle was satisfactorily behind them they had decided to try for the higher school certificate so that they might both enter a teacher training college, thus enabling them to go back to Ireland with qualifications, which would ensure that they got decently paid work.

So now, having cleared things with her employer, Dympna went to her room and began to pack. She was still carefully folding clothing into her case when there was a small knock at her door and Harriet's neatly braided head came into view. 'Nanny, I'm so sorry about your brother,' she said in her cool, precise little voice. 'Mummy says you've got to go home and I do understand, but we'll miss you most dreadfully.'

'That's kind of you, dear,' Dympna said, swiftly folding her best white blouse with the ruffles around a piece of pale-blue tissue paper, to stop it creasing. 'But didn't your mother tell you that she's sending you to your auntie, at Uplands? You like it there, don't you?'

'Oh yes, it's lovely,' Harriet said enthusiastically. 'I wish you could see Uplands, Nanny – you'd love it, too. But each time we've gone Mother's kept you here, hasn't she?'

'Your mother doesn't like the little ones to go, so I stay and look after them as a rule,' Dympna said diplomatically. 'But it's nice for me to be going home to my own parents, even though my brother's probably too ill to spend much time with me. Poor Egan, he's never had a day's illness in his life I don't think. He must be very bored, lying in bed whilst his appendix wound heals.'

'Egan. That's a funny sort of name,' Harriet said. She came fully into the room and sat down on the little chair before the dressing-table. 'Can I help you, Nanny? Your poor brother, I do hope he's better by the time you get back. Mummy said your brother was very poorly, that was why you'd been called home.'

'You could take these flowers and the vase as well into the nursery, and put them on the window-sill there,' Dympna said tactfully. Harriet, at thirteen, had grown out of her whining fits and her sulks, and was beginning to be both pleasant company and useful, though she was still, unfortunately, the plainest of the family. 'I won't be able to enjoy them since I shan't be here, but you and Gill and the other children will probably not get to Norfolk for two or three days. Especially since I shan't be around to do your packing,' she added and felt her heart lift at the prospect of someone else – probably Gill, the nursery maid – having to face that dread task. The girls weren't so bad, but Dominic always wanted to take his toy of the moment – a very large clockwork train set, rails and all, or the rocking-horse, or his brand-new two-wheeler bicycle. Explaining that such objects were impossible to pack led to either tears or tantrums – Dominic, at seven, was still susceptible to both when thwarted – and even when he realised that he would have to do without his best things, he was apt to try to smuggle his wooden revolver and cartridge belt into the case, to say nothing of his cowboy outfit complete with tall leather boots and a swaggering stetson hat.

'Well, I shan't do it,' Harriet said, going over to the window-sill and picking up the vase of roses, which sweetened the air. 'Who gave you these, Nanny?'

'Oh . . . just a friend,' Dympna said, aware that her cheeks felt warm. A member of her evening class, Bobby O'Hare, had given her the roses when the college broke up for the holidays and she had been touched by his thoughtfulness, but did not intend to take him up on his invitation to 'Come out for a drink an' a bit of a dance when the results come through, 'cos we'll either be celebratin', or drownin' us sorrows'. That kind of thing, she had long ago decided, led to the sort of friendship she simply had no wish for. 'And when you've done that, dear, perhaps you might run down to the kitchen for me and ask the housemaids if any of my clothing has come in off the line, needing ironing. I think there's a white petticoat and some underwear. I don't suppose you'd like to ask Gill to run the nursery iron over my things, would you?' she added without much hope.

But Harriet, it seemed, was really determined to be useful. 'I'll do it,' she said eagerly. 'Only not with the nursery iron, Nanny. Mother bought a lovely new one a few weeks ago, an *electric* iron. You don't have to heat it by the fire or anything, you just plug it into the wall,' she added.

'Well, isn't that grand?' Dympna said. She went over to her wardrobe and checked that she had put enough clothing into her case. No point in packing her uniforms. Just a couple of summer cottons, sufficient underwear and her navy-blue wool cardigan, the one Annunciata had given her last Christmas. Annunciata was a marvellous knitter and had made it herself. Running an eye over her clothes, Dympna decided she would travel in her brown pleated skirt and the pale-yellow jacket. Annunciata liked that outfit; she said it was coffee and cream, so it was, and Dympna trusted her friend's judgement. If Annunciata thought the outfit smart she was probably right.

Harriet came over to the case as Dympna added her black strap shoes and said: 'You do pack nicely, Nanny. I wish you'd teach me to pack like that.'

'Nanny Horsham taught me and if you like I'll show you how, some day. Not that you'll ever need to pack for yourself I don't imagine,' Dympna said, without really thinking, and then remembered some of the things Bobby said about the revolution which was overdue in England – and probably in Ireland too. The people who had the money were the *wrong* people, Bobby stated. He was strong Labour and told Dympna that the rich hugged all the money to their greedy bosoms and underpaid their dependents, and then grumbled that they no longer got good service. Well, the world was changing, Bobby often said so, and you only had to hear Mrs Ditchling complaining about staff to know that it was true. Girls did not like domestic service. It did not pay well enough and the house were not conducive to leading a good social life. And young men did not want to spend all their time digging other men's gardens and driving other men's cars. Ordinary people did not expect riches, holidays abroad, meat at every meal, but they wanted a better life and Bobby thought they ought to get it, even if a few heads had to roll first. Dympna liked him as much as she liked any young man – which was not much – but did not want to get involved in the politics which were meat and drink to him.

'I like your blue Sunday dress with the flounced skirt,' Harriet said enviously. Her clothing was good but plain – a bit like Harriet herself, Dympna supposed. 'I'm going to ask Mother to buy me a silk dress when she brings me out. Oh, I know the coming-out dress is special, you have to have the same as all the other girls, but once I am out then I'll have a blue silk dress just like yours, Nanny. Did you buy it at Blacklers?'

'It isn't silk, goose, it's just imitation,' Dympna said. 'Could you go and ask about my washing, please, dear? And then could you see if there's some stout cord which I could use to tie round my small suitcase? It's only some sort of cardboard and I don't want it collapsing half-way home.'

'Oh, I'm sorry, of course I will,' Harriet said, making for the door. 'Shan't be long, Nanny.'

And Dympna, hastily taking down the rest of her clothes from the wardrobe and dragging out from under the bed the very old suitcase she had meant to leave behind, realised that she had decided it was best to take all her possessions with her. It was all very well to say that she was coming back, but would she? What if she decided to stay? Feeling guilty but determined, she began to put the rest of her clothes, except for the black dress, into the old suitcase.

Dympna found a seat near the bows of the ferry and settled down in it, preparing for a long and probably boring journey. But as soon as she was comfortable and turned around so that she could look out at the waves and the birds that skimmed over them, her mind took a dive back in time and she began to remember.

Once, she had so loved the sea. She had worked on

it, played in it and beside it, regarded it both as an enemy and as the means of making her livelihood. And now that she was at last on her way home she began to wonder just why she had not gone back ages ago, just to see her family and friends, to know for herself that all was well with them. She had told herself that it was because she was afraid of the terrible homesickness, which had almost drowned her when she first came to Liverpool, but now, with the advantage of being older and wiser, she knew that it had been no such thing. Ever since Mr Philip's horrible attack on her she had been living in a sort of dream. She had worked, ate, slept, talked, but the real Dympna, the one who had come over from Ireland to help to buy her daddy a boat, had simply gone missing, into some sort of hibernation. That way, no one could hurt her. Young men were dangerous, therefore she kept away from them, studied, worked hard, discouraged any but safe feminine friendships.

Ever since that dreadful night I've been little better than a shell, Dympna told herself, snuggling into her corner seat. Nothing has really touched me. I've loved the children, of course, but in a fairly cold-blooded sort of way. Even the new baby had not managed to get inside her shell – it was too dangerous. If she had not rather liked Mr Philip, perhaps encouraged him to believe her not indifferent, then his attack might never have happened. Dympna knew that a good many people, Mr Ditchling amongst them, probably believed that she had led Mr Philip to think she would welcome his advances and, though she had assured Mr Ditchling that it was quite otherwise and he had seemed to believe her, she was not sure, in her heart, that she had believed herself. After all Philip was young, handsome, rather fun to be with. Why should she not have smiled at him, laughed at his little jokes, let him put her hat on her tumbled curls? But if letting a young man straighten one's hat had led to such a terrible misunderstanding . . . well, she was better keeping everyone back from her, refusing all human closeness.

And that was what she had done, until the moment when she had decided to take all her things away with her save for the black dress. It had been as though she had cast off the life she had lived in Liverpool and pulled down over her head, like a comfortable old jersey, the Irish life she had known before. And now she acknowledged that no matter how she had behaved, there were many people who would know very well that it had been all Mr Philip's fault and none of her own – Daddy, Mammy and Egan, just for a start, probably Nicholas, who had been a kind big brother to her when she had been small, and her friends at school, the Sullivans, other neighbours, and . . . and that other feller, the one she had sent away. For the first time since Philip's attack, she remembered the earlier part of that dreadful evening, which had not been dreadful at all. It had been the evening the nice young man had danced with her, whispered sweetly in her ear, stroked her cheek. What was his name, now? But it had gone, she could no longer remember. Yet his face . . . when she really thought about him she could see it in her mind's eye, the thin cheeks, the jutting chin, the dark, amused eyes.

I shouldn't have sent him off like that, without so much as telling him what had happened, Dympna thought, and for the first time felt shame for an action which did not concern Mr Philip Ditchling. I do wish

I could tell him how sorry I am – but that's not possible, so I'll simply pray that one day we'll meet again and I can explain. Oh, not all the dreadful details, not what Mr Philip did . . . but enough so's he can understand. And Daddy and the boys, they'll know it was no fault of mine . . . so will the mammy, though I'll have to explain what happened to her first.

She peered over the rail at the troubled sea beneath her and realised that in order to put Mr Philip's attack behind her, she was going to have to come out of her shell and start to feel things again. Liking and love, warm and comfortable, were good things to feel, but she knew, now, that they would be accompanied by pain, by anxiety, by worry, even by loss, for the young man whose name had disappeared into limbo had been lost to her, through her own actions and that hurt. And of course there was Egan; he and she had always been close. She had been worried and upset to hear of his illness when she had first received Beatrice's letter, but now she knew the painful, gnawing anxiety caused by the suffering of one you love.

If this is coming back to being the real Dympna Byrne, I'm not sure that I want it to happen, she told herself rebelliously as worries began to rush back into her mind. But even as she thought it, she knew it wasn't true. She had stood outside real life long enough; now she wanted to play her part in it once more.

The journey was a long and tiring one, but as it passed and the day lengthened, Dympna found herself feeling both more worried and also more excited. When she came down the gangway and onto the quays she felt a big, beaming smile spread across her face and sniffed the smell of Liffey, weed, damp stone, as though she had been born here, though in fact she had only seen Dublin once, and that was on her previous journey when she had been travelling to England and her despised job. Now she looked around as she lugged her suitcase across the city to Broadstone Station and wondered where Nicholas was in this great place. He would be able to give her news of Egan, probably he knew a great deal more than her parents did since Beatrice had written proudly that Nicholas, now a doctor, had assisted at the operation and had looked after Egan until he had to return to Dublin. But as her mother had not said whereabouts in Dublin Dympna's brother was to be found, and he did not meet the ferry, she had to board the train for home without having her curiosity satisfied or her fears eased.

She was met at Clifden, though. To her immense surprise and delight, the first thing she saw as she stepped down on to the platform was her daddy, Micheál. He, too, looked just the same, and came over to pick her up and give her a great bear hug as though she were still his little girl and not a grown woman of past twenty. She felt as safe in his arms as if she had never left home, never suffered from homesickness in a far country. She knew, then, that she was home.

'Daddy! Oh, Daddy, isn't it great to see you? Isn't it grand?' she gasped, clinging to his arm as he stood her down again and took her suitcase from her. 'How's Egan?'

'He's doin' pretty well, considerin',' Micheál said, after some thought. 'But he'll not be workin' for many a long day. He got an infection . . . but he's a deal better now, t'ank the good Lord. I've brung Rosa an' the cart to meet you, so's you can have a ride home.'

'Oh yes, and you'll walk, I know you,' Dympna said. 'I'm happy to have Rosa carry my case, but I'll walk with you, Daddy. There's so much to talk about – have I changed? I don't feel any different, now I'm home, but I expect I am.'

Dympna smiled, as Micheál looked at her consideringly, and glanced around her. The single platform which was Clifden Station was just as it had always been, clean and tidy, with the white-walled, red-tiled station master's house shining in the sun. 'Sure you're different in some way,' he said at last. 'You look a real young lady, so you do. But if we put you into your ould raggedy skirt an' blouse now, I dare say your pals 'ud know you. You've not done anythin' to your hair, have you, alanna? I like a woman's hair left natural, so I do.' They had reached Rosa and the donkey cart, and Micheál dumped his daughter's suitcase in the well of the cart and then put his hand to Rosa's bridle. 'Come on, me old gorl,' he said, shaking the reins, which were looped over the front of the little cart. 'You've not cut your hair, have you?' he repeated rather anxiously. 'Your mammy would be disappointed, so she would.'

Dympna pulled off her hat and shook out her hair, laughing up at Micheál as she did so. 'It's not the sort of hair to take kindly to a bob or a shingle,' she said. 'And they're not in fashion so much now anyway. But nannies aren't fashionable, you know, we aren't allowed to be. Our mistresses wouldn't like it.'

'Ach, mistresses,' Micheál said dismissively, as though such things were behind her now, for ever. 'Well, you won't have to worry about t'ings like that while you're at home. It'll be your work, alanna, to keep Egan happy. He's not a feller for books, you know, nor letter writin'. So he cheers up somethin'

438

wonderful when someone comes a-callin'.'

'And how are you managing with the new pucan?' Dympna asked as Rosa led them from the station past the Catholic church and along Main Street. 'I take it Egan won't be fishing for a while yet?' They crossed the square and she glanced up at Church Hill to their right waving to one of the Brannegan boys who helped carry her daddy home that fateful night. It won't be long now before everyone knows I'm home, she thought. Young Brannegan could never keep his mouth shut and his mammy's worse.

'You're right,' Micheál said heavily. 'But our Nicholas has a job now in a big hospital in Dublin – he calls it the Mater – and he's sendin' money home for the first time in his life. Of course I'm grateful, though as you know, Dympna, a grosh o' money went the other way before. So even though I'm havin' to pay a feller to come out wit' me, we manage.'

'I hope the money I've been sending helps a bit?' Dympna enquired, highly daring. She knew that it was one thing to question Micheál now and quite another to have the courage to do so when her mother was present. Beatrice would see that he did not answer anything which she thought it better Dympna should not know. But I earn every penny of it by hard work, she reminded herself now. I should be told, willingly, where it goes. She turned and looked up at Micheál, who frowned, puzzled.

'Your money, alanna? Come to t'ink, your mammy's never said a word on that subject, so I suppose she t'ought I knew what went on. But for why should you send money home?'

'I thought it might help a bit,' Dympna said sturdily. 'I'm earning a good salary now, Daddy, so I felt I could spare some for the extra expenses you have that I don't – the house, your keep and so on. I have all my food, uniforms and such paid for by the family.'

Micheál shrugged. He looked uncomfortable and Dympna began to wish she had never started to ask questions. It was not fair; after all, Mammy probably had her own reasons for not telling Daddy that their daughter still contributed.

All this time the three of them, Dympna, Micheál and Rosa, had been heading out of town and into the hills. And Dympna had been stealing glances around her, seeing the gold of the gorse and the purple of heather, the rough, summer-dry grasses and the blunt noses of rock, lichen-embroidered, as they went deeper into the countryside. And presently they turned sharply left and began to go downhill to where they could see, at last, the sea lough, shimmering gold in the evening sun, and the cottages and farmhouses scattered over the great hills and snugged into the shadow valleys.

'Stop a moment, Daddy,' Dympna said. 'Dear God, isn't that the most beautiful thing you ever did see? Streamstown, crouched beside the lough and the water all gold with the setting sun. Oh, how I've managed to live without this land I'll never know. And how I'll make meself go back . . . eh, it'll be hard.'

'And why should you go back, alanna?' Micheál demanded, giving a tug on Rosa's bridle so that they started down the steep and rocky path once more. 'I told you, we're managin' just fine, wit' the money Nicholas sends and . . .'

He stopped and the frown on his forehead deepened. Dympna waited for the penny to drop. Her father was a slow thinker, but he was not a stupid man. And presently, he turned to her, his expression grave. 'Is *that* what it's all about, then? There's nothing comin' from Nicholas, is there? Isn't that what you're after thinkin', alanna? 'Tis the money you yourself send each month . . . but your mammy didn't like to tell me, in case I t'ought it wasn't fair, now the debt is paid, that we should take your earnings. But it's not right, that's one t'ing I'm sure of. I'll have to speak to her about it.'

'Better not,' Dympna said. 'It . . . it won't make the mammy love me more, Daddy. And I would like to have a . . . a peaceful couple of weeks.'

In the silence that followed she looked around her. The sun was just a tiny sliver of red on the western horizon and as they neared the bottom of the long slope she could see, through the grove of trees which hung their lazy, heavily leafed branches across their path, the dazzling blue of the water, the golden sand and the dancing red and gold path of the last glimmers of sunset. The beauty, which she had taken for granted before, caught at her throat and brought tears to her eyes – tears which slid, unbidden, down her cheeks. She was on her way home. What did it matter if her money had been belittled, if her mother had allowed Daddy to believe that it came from Nicholas? Perhaps he was contributing something, now that he had a proper job as a doctor. But it really did not matter. What mattered was that she was nearly home and the past, which had seemed so important, had suddenly shrunk to an insignificant dot on some far horizon. Dympna smiled at her father and tucked her hand into his arm. 'C'mon, Daddy,' she said gaily. 'Best foot forward, as Madam is so fond of saying. Oh, aren't I longin' to see me home again?'

*

441

Dympna felt almost shy as she and Micheál approached the cottage. She took in, without really paying much attention, the heavy apple crop in the trees overhanging the lane, the pink and purple of the fuchsia hedge, the well-grown haulms of the potatoes, their mauve and yellow flowers beginning to fade and drop. She passed through the bit of garden feeling as though she trod on hallowed ground and went into the cottage whilst Micheál unharnessed Rosa and turned her out into the hill field, and there was Egan, sitting by the fire, though the warmth of the August day still lingered.

He looked up as she came through the doorway and a pale grin spread across his face. 'Dymp! Sure an' aren't you the best t'ing I've seen since I took ill? Janey, you've growed into a beauty, so you have! Come nearer, so's I can look at you.'

Dympna crossed the room and kissed him heartily, though secretly she was shocked by his appearance. 'Oh Egan, it's so good to see you! Good to be home, as well. But you're not yourself yet, lad, anyone can see that. Why, your skin's white as milk and I doubt you weigh as much as me. Is . . . is it just the appendix operation? Or are they trying to hide something from me?'

Egan laughed, but Dympna noticed that he took the first opportunity to sit down again and did so with a tiny sigh of relief, as though getting to his feet to welcome his sister had taken all his strength. 'And whyfor should we try to hide anythin' from our darlin' Dymp?' he enquired indulgently. 'No, don't fret, 'tis only the appendix that's taken the strengt' from me an' the flesh from me bones. Give me a few weeks an' I'll be joinin' Daddy in the *Aleen* again. She's a grand little pucan, the new *Aleen*, Dymp. You must get the daddy to let you have a sail in her, you must indeed. She answers to your hand like a well-trained horse – a good deal better and quicker than our Rosa, I'm tellin' you.'

'Only the operation? But that was weeks ago, back at the beginning of July, Daddy told me whilst we were coming home from the station.' Dympna protested. 'What went wrong, Egan?'

'I got an infected wound,' Egan said, not without pride. 'I was real ill, so I was. Sick, an' hot, an' achin' all over. One day I didn't know me own mammy, would you believe that, Dymp? And when Maria came to see me I told her to go away, I t'ought she was a witch come to tip me out o' me boat . . . I kept haulin' on the ropes an' swingin' the tiller and I told her I'd chuck her in the sea if she didn't get off me pucan.' He laughed, pulling a rueful face. 'Can you imagine? Me, t'inkin' little Maria was a witch.'

'What, little Maria Sullivan? What was she doing, visiting you? She's only a kid,' Dympna said, then put a hand to her mouth and laughed at Egan over the top of it. 'Of course, she was a kid when I left but now she must be . . . what, fifteen?'

'Older,' Egan said. 'Getting on for seventeen.' He looked quickly at Dympna, then down again, to the turfs on the hearth. 'She . . . she's me sweetheart, so she is. We're goin' to get married one of dese days, an' we'll buy our own farm . . . Not yet, though. We're too young yet.'

'You've got to get fit, as well,' Dympna reminded him. 'Where's Mammy? I thought she'd be here when Daddy and I got home.'

'She's pickin' mussels,' Egan said. 'You like mussels, don't you, Dymp? I told Mammy you did because I wanted to go pickin' 'em, but she's that scared I'll take bad again that she went instead. Said she knew where the best mussels growed just as well as I did, an' that she needed some relaxation so I shouldn't try to keep all the fun for meself. An' just in case you t'ink you're in favour,' he added cheerfully, 'Nicholas is comin' home this weekend an' he loves mussels best of all.'

'Ye-es, but mussels are nicest the day they're picked and cooked,' Dympna said, reluctant to lose the little glow which the thought of her mother going down to the shore for her sake had brought. 'If he's coming at the weekend she'll be picking mussels for him then. Anyway, if you'd like it, perhaps you and me could go then,' she finished.

Egan looked doubtful. 'We-ell, I'd like it, awright, but I don't know whether I could get back from the shore, even if I could get down,' he said. 'I . . . I don't seem to be gettin' well as quick as I'd ha' thought. But Mr Farrell said it 'ud take a while. Do you want to put your t'ings away? I'll pull the kettle over the flames an' have tea ready for you by the time you get back.'

Dympna agreed, and went to the little partitioned-off slip of a room which she had had when she lived at home. She began to hang her clothes on the nails behind the piece of curtain, thinking about Egan as she did so. He was so weak, and pale. Fancy him actually admitting that he could not get back from the shore – that he might not even be able to get down there. She had taken a good look at him whilst he was talking and had seen how paper thin his skin seemed, how fragile his bones. He looked like an invalid of long standing, not a healthy young man who had had an operation a month ago and was recovering from it. But then I know very little about illness, she reminded herself, stowing her suitcase under her little truckle bed. And Egan says Nick's coming home at the weekend; I'll have a word with him then. After all, he's a doctor, he should know whether Egan's getting well as fast as he should. I won't worry Mammy or Daddy with questions they can't answer, or perhaps don't want to.

So she went back into the kitchen presently, talking as she entered the room, and found Micheál there, standing before the fire, a finger to his lips. She glanced across at Egan and her brother was asleep. Sitting in the easy chair before the fire and sound asleep, and it not yet eight o'clock in the evening.

So as not to disturb him she tiptoed across to the door and let herself out, Micheál following on her heels. As soon as it was softly shut and they were a sufficient distance from the cottage he said: 'It must have been after shockin' you terrible, alanna, to see Egan so changed. Bea and meself was worried stiff, but Nick says the feller's had a 'trocious bad time, an' 'tis only to be expected that he'll be wore out for a while. What's more, Egan's havin' the best treatment, so he is. The doctor comes once a week – don't worry, we can bear the cost of it, especially as he's a fine man an' takes his fee in fish – and we buy him all the tonics an' the good food he needs. Dr Doyle's a good physician; Mr Farrell, the surgeon who done the operation, says we couldn't have a better, an' Nick likes him, so he does.'

'Oh. Right,' Dympna said. Her father's words were reassuring until she remembered Egan's thinness and his having to sit down after he had greeted her so cheerfully. 'Well, I'll have a word with Nick too, when he comes. And Egan says Mammy's down on the shore, pickin' mussels for my tea because I like

445

them, so I thought I'd maybe walk down and give her a hand bringing them back.'

'Want me to come?' Micheál said, and almost immediately shook his head and answered his own question, making it unnecessary for Dympna to do so. 'No, you'll be after havin' a bit of a crack wit' her – women's talk, I dare say. I'll go back in, get the kettle off the fire before it begins to boil over an' damps the turves.' They had reached the path which led down to the shore and Micheál gestured to his left. 'She'll ha' gone that way. See you later, alanna.'

Dympna began to walk down the little path, then across the top of the quay. From there she jumped on to the hard sand and looked ahead of her. If Beatrice had walked right to the edge of the bay there were fine mussels there, but the ones on the rocks no more than a hundred yards from the quay itself were pretty good. She was wearing sandals and a cotton dress and walked fast, turning her head now and then to see her footsteps dimpling into tiny pools. That meant the tide had only just gone out, so she would not have to come back along the cliff top but would be able to retrace her steps.

It was fine on the beach, with the wind lifting her hair gently off her forehead and the smell of the sea in her nostrils. Dympna stopped for a moment to slip off her sandals, feeling the firm wet sand beneath her toes with all the pleasure that a city girl might have felt to tread pavements once more. I'm home, Dympna thought exultantly. This is my place, where I was born and raised, and I never want to leave it, never. But that was foolish thinking, so she concentrated, instead, on the pleasure of the moment, walking perhaps a little more slowly and letting her gaze wander over the beach, the sea, the outline of the opposite coast – even to the little white bay where their pucan had been lost. It was beautiful and dear to her, and wherever she went she would always come home to it but for now, that must suffice.

Despite the slackening of her pace, it did not take her long to catch up with Beatrice. Her mother was walking along the long ridge of black rock which led down to the sea, picking mussels and dropping them into her bucket as she sang an old Irish ballad Micheál had taught the children when they were small. To Dympna's astonishment she was singing it in gaelic, a language which she professed both to be ignorant of and to despise. Yet I suppose some of it must have rubbed off, Dympna thought, rather amused. Daddy's always talked gaelic at home, translating for Mammy if she were in the room, and there was a lot talked in school, though the teachers pretended to look down on it as a barbaric language. She had a vague memory of being told to speak only English when she had first gone to school, but that was before we kicked the damned English out, she reminded herself, feeling comfortably wicked at daring to have such a revolutionary thought. And once Ireland had her independence it was no longer thought imperative to prevent schoolchildren speaking the gaelic in order to acquire what someone had once called 'The International Language of English', whilst in their own homes the children – and their parents – would have thought it a strange form of showing off to speak anything but the gaelic.

But not us, of course, because of Mammy, Dympna reminded herself as she walked along the top of the beautiful beach with all its happy childhood memories. Beatrice was an Englishwoman and though her opinion of her countrymen had been

447

considerably shaken during the troubles, and had reached an all-time low when the Black and Tans had attacked Clifden, Micheál had instilled in his children that criticism of the English was unfair on their mother. Even after the Tans had entered Clifden, killing and burning as an act of retaliation for the death of two Royal Irish Constabulary men, Beatrice's being English was respected by everyone who knew her and the matter was never discussed in her hearing.

And now here was Mammy, the epitome of Englishness, singing an Irish ballad, in gaelic, when she thought herself alone. I wonder, did Mammy listen all those years ago when Daddy was teaching us the song and feel . . . well, kind of left out? Dympna asked herself. Would Daddy – and the rest of us – have done better to remind her that she was an Irishwoman by marriage, that her children were Irish and proud of it, rather than shielding her from unpleasantness to the extent that she felt herself separated from her family?

But those questions would probably never be answered. Instead, Dympna hurried up behind her mother and called out 'Mammy! I'm home!' half hoping Beatrice would cast down her bucket and open her arms to her only daughter.

And indeed, Beatrice did stand down her bucket and smile brightly, taking Dympna by both shoulders and looking with what seemed like affection into her face once she was close enough. 'Darling,' she said. 'How you startled me! And how very smart you look – quite the young lady. Daddy met you all right? You've seen Egan? We've been dreadfully worried about him.'

'He's very thin. And very weak, too,' Dympna said,

choosing her words with care, for long habit had made her careful never to say anything which might antagonise Mammy if she could help it. What was more, she found she was fighting a mixture of emotions; pleasure in her mother's apparently spontaneous greeting, wariness, because her mother had never used a love word to her before, and a sort of shyness which was the result, she supposed, of the long separation. 'But Daddy says Nick will be here at the weekend; he'll be able to tell us a bit more. Here, let me take the bucket.'

'It's all right. I've been carrying buckets of mussels for myself for some time now,' Beatrice said, and immediately Dympna felt that her mother was blaming her for her long absence and the prickly feeling of being unjustly criticised stiffened her back.

'I'd have come home before . . .' she began, but Beatrice shook her head, smiling at her. Dympna saw incredulously that there was a warmth in her mother's eyes when they rested on her, which she had never seen before. How nice it was to feel wanted, welcomed.

'No, no, I didn't mean . . . how could you come back when Maude had sent us most of your wages home to buy the pucan? I've never said it, my dear – I'm bad at giving thanks – but if it hadn't been for you we wouldn't be as comfortably situated as we are now. And Nicholas, of course,' she added. 'He's been most good, most generous. He sends me money every month . . .'

'Really? As I do?' Dympna said innocently. 'Is this just since Egan's illness, or was he doing it before?'

'Oh . . . well, that doesn't really matter, does it?' Beatrice said evasively. 'I can't remember exactly when he began to send money home, but I suppose it was after he had got his degree and was in a proper hospital job.'

'I see. He's not been doing it all that long, then,' Dympna said. 'I'm going to take Rosa and the cart down to the station to meet him on Saturday. I'll ask him then how he's managing financially, because as I remember, money went from us to Nicholas, not the other way around, when he was at college. But there, no doubt he's much better paid than myself – I'm a mere nanny, he's a properly trained doctor.'

There was a strained silence, then Dympna stopped in her tracks and faced her mother squarely. 'Mammy, why didn't you tell Daddy that I was still sending a good deal of my salary home? It's not that I mind the money coming home – quite the opposite – but it does seem strange that when the three years were up and I could have stopped paying Nick suddenly begins to fork out.'

For several moments Beatrice said nothing but continued to look steadily and with definite hostility into Dympna's eyes. But if it was a battle of wills it was easily won, for her gaze dropped first to her own hands and then to the hard, wet sand on which she stood. 'It's a long story,' she said quietly. 'I know you've a right to understand just why I feel Nicholas is so . . . so special to me, so very precious, and why I've . . . I've always thought you more able to take care of yourself. But it's a hard admission for me to make.'

Dympna said nothing but waited. She did not intend to help Beatrice out by pretending that she had never been hurt by her mother's attitude towards her and presently it seemed as though Beatrice realised it, for she took a deep breath and began to speak.

'Nicholas was born after Micheál and myself had been married six months. No, he wasn't a premature

450

baby, I went full term. So in a way, the baby was a constant reproach to me – do you see that? If I'd not behaved in . . . in the way I did behave, I wouldn't have had to marry Micheál or live in a fisherman's cottage and scrape a living as best I might. I could have stayed in Liverpool and married a man who could keep me in the style to which I had always been accustomed. And I wished very much that I'd not been so foolish, because at that time I didn't love Micheál, you see. I came to love him very deeply, but that was later, when I was a woman and not a silly, romantic girl.'

She stopped speaking and Dympna said cautiously: 'I didn't know that, Mammy, and I do see that it might have made you bitter. But why not against Nicholas? It was he who tied you to Daddy, not myself.'

'Ah, but I didn't resent Nicholas. He was the last reminder of my old life, the way I had once been. I ignored your daddy as much as was possible and simply poured all my affection and hopes over Nicholas. And he repaid me by being bright, intelligent beyond his years, very loving . . . I was determined that my little son should not suffer because I'd ended up married to a poor man. Everything I had should be his, I was adamant that he should have a good career and a good life. My own, I thought then, was finished, over. I was condemned to the life I'd had to choose, but my son could better himself.'

'Mammy!' Dympna gasped. 'Isn't . . . isn't Nicky Daddy's son?'

There was an appalled silence. Dympna saw the colour creeping up her mother's long, white neck, across her face, right up to her hairline. She could even see, through her mother's fine, pale-golden hair, the pink advancing across her scalp.

But then, just as she was about to apologise, to admit she had no idea what had made her say such a thing, her mother gave a deep sigh and a small, shamefaced nod. 'I don't know how you guessed, but you're right, of course. Nicholas was the result of one mad, foolish moment with a young man who proved later to be thoroughly unworthy. I don't need to tell you that your father is one of the best and finest men you're ever likely to meet because I believe you know already, but he's never, by word or deed, let me feel that I behaved . . . badly . . .'

'No, Daddy wouldn't,' Dympna agreed in a small voice. 'He loves Nicholas and he's proud of him, though when you think back, Nick's let him down more than once. No, Mammy, it's no use you ruffling up and beginning to hate me again because I've said what's true, but I don't think Nicky will ever be as good a man as Daddy.'

'He'll be good, but in a very different way,' Beatrice said. 'He'll be a brilliant doctor, the sort of man who saves lives and helps people. But he'll never have the understanding and sensitivity that Micheál has.'

'No. Because Daddy's not his father,' Dympna said quietly. 'Well, Mammy, this explains an awful lot, but it doesn't explain why you wanted me away.'

'Wanted you away? But my dear child, it was the only way we could possibly . . .'

'. . . get the new pucan,' Dympna finished for her, her voice as cynical as her expression. 'No, no, Mammy, now that there's some truth between us, let's not slip back into our old ways. You didn't feel bitter towards Nick, but you certainly felt bitter towards me and I never have known why.'

'There was no good reason,' Beatrice admitted with a sigh. 'Let's sit down on these rocks, dear, and pick over the mussels. That's better. My goodness, there are a lot. They'll make a decent meal, with bread and butter.'

'Sure they will,' Dympna agreed, beginning to turn over the shellfish in her mother's basket. She waited, but the silence stretched between them until she was forced to say, 'Mammy? You were saying?'

Beatrice sighed again and pulled a piece of seaweed from a shell. 'Oh, yes. Where was I?'

'You said there was no good reason,' Dympna prompted. 'But there must have been a reason, Mammy. I couldn't have been *that* repulsive as a kid!'

Beatrice laughed. 'No, you were very sweet, really. But your arrival killed stone dead the secret hope that I'd had of returning to Liverpool and my own family with my little boy. Oh, I'd probably never have done it, it was just a foolish dream, but when you came along I knew that it was just that – a foolish dream. So I think I resented you for making me face reality. And I know I resented you because your father simply doted on you,' she added with a rush of honesty. 'He'd always been good with Nicholas and very patient, but he couldn't do enough for his little girl. Afterwards, as you grew, I . . . I was jealous, I suppose. I thought Micheál cared for you more deeply than he cared for me.' She smiled across at Dympna, her fingers busily and needlessly rearranging the shellfish in the bucket. 'More foolishness, you see. The way a man loves his wife and the way he loves his daughter are so different – but all I saw was the love flowing to you and not to me. Nor to Nicholas. And somehow, I got it into my head that when you grew up you'd go away, go into service somewhere, and I'd have Micheál all to myself once more. I . . . I wanted that. I wanted it quite badly. So when the tragedy took away the pucan, and your Daddy and I talked about getting help from my family, it was natural to think of you. Well, I thought that my sister was having a job to find servants and I knew she'd be good to you – she promised and I'm sure she is good, isn't she? – so you could go away and earn money and we could buy the boat and . . . and everything would be all right again,' she finished with a rush.

'And now?' Dympna said levelly after a moment. So much foolishness! But it had made her childhood harder than it need have been, made her relationship with her mother something not to be envied. 'Now that I've been gone almost three and a half years, and you've had Daddy to yourself all that time? Did it work for you? And why did you send for me? Why not just go on getting the money and saying it came from Nick and being happy, if that's what you wanted to make you happy. And you are happy – you were singing, in *Irish*, when I came up to you on the shore.'

'Yes, I am happy,' Beatrice said. She sounded surprised, as though she had not realised her happiness herself until this moment. 'Oh, not because you were gone, I promise you that. Just because I'm older and wiser and know, now, that your daddy's a fine man and I'm lucky indeed to be his wife. But I sent for you because you mean a lot to Egan and he needed to see you. He said so and Micheál backed him up, so I wrote the letter. I didn't want to worry you . . . but you can see for yourself Egan's not the man he was.'

'I can,' Dympna said. She repressed an urge to say that this was the first time she had seen the grown-up

454

Egan, so it was hard for her to tell. She put her hand on her mother's arm. 'Then . . . then we can be friends? You won't resent me, or try to send me away?'

'Not again. Not if you want to stay,' Beatrice said. She sounded calmer than ever, more self-assured, but the affection was still in her voice. 'But you've been pretty happy yourself, haven't you? You've friends, a well-paid job . . .'

'Only a good deal of the money comes home to Ireland,' Dympna said. 'I'm not saying that because I mind any more – I don't. I just want to remind you that I'm scarcely a young woman of independent means.' She was laughing, but Beatrice looked solemn.

'Yes, I know, I'm sorry. I'll tell Micheál about the money when . . . when I've a chance to explain. Are you saying that you don't want to go back to Liverpool, then?'

'I may go back, because it wouldn't be fair on Mrs Ditchling to let her down by not returning,' Dympna said. 'And I'll need to explain to my friends, of course. But in a little while I'll be coming across the water for good. I've not said much about the examinations I've been taking, but I've done all right at them so far and if I pass the tests I took earlier in the summer then that means I can go to a teaching college. I'd rather go to one in Dublin because I want to live – and teach – in Ireland. But I may never live at home again, except in the holidays,' she finished rather sadly.

'I'm glad for you, dear. And now tell me about my sister, and her house, husband, children . . . and about my parents. You must have met them – of course you have, you've been to Uplands – I expect they've changed a lot since I saw them last but I'm still interested.'

Dympna laughed. 'Sure an' your sister is fashionable, popular, a pretty good employer. Her husband is quite nice, but I don't see him often, he doesn't interest himself in the children very much. As for your parents and your older sisters, I've never met them, Mrs Ditchling has seen to that. Don't forget, Mammy, they're my relatives too.'

'Oh,' Beatrice said rather blankly. 'But you've talked of the children visiting Uplands, in Norfolk ... naturally I thought you meant you went as well.'

'I didn't feel I could explain in a letter that I was considered a risk,' Dympna said quite gently. 'It seemed so foolish, really. After all, I'm not a bit like you and your parents never knew Daddy well, did they? I've always had the impression that they didn't even attend the wedding.'

'That's right. They never met Daddy,' Beatrice admitted. 'That *is* odd, isn't it? It isn't as if you've a very broad brogue or anything, or anything to make them suspect. Your accent is very slight. I wonder, could it be your name. Dympna is a very Irish name.'

'They called me Dora when I was the nursery maid,' Dympna said, giggling. 'But now I'm Nanny Byrne, so I suppose that might have given me away. Only it's not an unusual name in Liverpool – the city is absolutely bursting with Irish, and Irish names. No, I think Mrs Ditchling was just playing safe – and I was more useful to her at the Liverpool house with the baby than I would have been up in Uplands.'

'True,' nodded Beatrice. She got to her feet. 'Time we were getting back, dear. I'm going to cook these mussels in a new way and I don't want supper to be too late so I really should be in the kitchen right now.'

She smiled at her daughter. 'Do you understand things a little better now, Dymp? And am I forgiven for the way I've behaved in the past? Jealousy is a dreadful thing and I'm so relieved to be rid of it at last.'

'Of course you're forgiven,' Dympna said stoutly. The relief of hearing her mother speak to her without reservation or some sort of implied criticism was wonderfully warming. 'It must have been nearly as bad for you as it was for me. And you can show me how to cook mussels when we get home, because nannies only deal with nursery meals, which means lots of mince stew and rice puddings.' The two women began to walk back up the beach and Dympna glanced across at her mother, took a deep breath, squared her shoulders and began to speak. 'Have you a little more time to spare, though, before you rush home to cook the evening meal? Because there's something I . . . I really would like to tell you. Something I'd rather talk about quietly, whilst we're alone.'

'We'll walk the long way home, by the cliffs,' Beatrice said. 'Go on then, my dear, tell me what's been bothering you.'

Dympna took a deep breath. 'Well, one evening some of my friends and I decided to go to a dance . . .'

With many pauses whilst she considered her words, Dympna continued to tell out loud the story that had so often reverberated inside her head. And as she spoke, as her mother gasped and frowned, and turned to touch her hand, she realised that a good deal of the discomfort and guilt she had felt over the whole horrible affair was becoming a thing of the past with the telling of it. And when she had finished, when she had explained that Mr Ditchling had, in the end, believed her and sent Mr Philip away, her mother drew her to a halt, put down her bucket of mussels and took her tenderly in her arms.

'My dearest chid,' she said, her voice breaking. 'That you should have had to suffer like that and without telling anyone. Oh why didn't you come home?'

'I . . . I don't know,' Dympna admitted. 'Perhaps I really was afraid that if I did I'd never go back again and Daddy would never get his pucan.'

'Well, you know, now, that we've both had . . . had sad sort of experiences,' Beatrice said after a moment. She turned to face Dympna, taking both her daughter's hands in hers and gripping them fiercely. 'But Dympna, my dear child, you mustn't let it ruin your life. You've clearly not been out with . . . with young men since the . . . the terrible occurrence. And we did get the impression, your father and I, that you had met someone you cared about.'

'I didn't really have a young man, but there was someone I . . . I liked,' Dympna admitted. 'I . . . I sent him away, though, and I've never seen him since, so perhaps the feeling was all on my side. And I'm not sure I felt so very much, really,' she added with more spirit. 'We only met the . . . the evening before I was attacked, so we did.'

'And you sent him away because you felt smirched, dirty,' Beatrice said quietly. 'That was how I felt, when I realised that Rupert had not loved me at all, that he was going to see me sacrificed. I suffered agonies of guilt, remorse, self-blame . . . yet I truly think that it was your poor father who suffered most. I blamed him, most unfairly, because he was a man and had married me against my wishes, though of course he had no inkling of that. And your young man, my dear, probably thinks it was something he had done or said which suddenly turned you against him. I made my peace with Micheál long ago, however. If you ever see that young man again I think you should make your peace with him, as well.'

'You're right,' Dympna said humbly. 'When I go back to Liverpool I'll try to trace him and explain – without telling him what happened, of course.'

'That's wonderful. And you'll put it behind you now? And along with that, you'll forget all the things that have kept you away from us for so long? Because that's all over now. Can you trust me? I'll never treat you like that again, my dear.'

'I do trust you,' Dympna said quietly. 'And I do believe you're right. We're starting again, Mammy. We'll do better this time.'

# Chapter Twelve

Dympna walked up the track which led over the mountain, enjoying the fresh breeze and the scent of gorse and sea mingling. It was her last day and she was torn between sorrow at leaving her home and her family, and a strange sort of elation at the thought of returning to the life of friendships, work and the studies she had left in Liverpool, though she was already determined to give Mrs Ditchling her notice once she had all the qualifications necessary to become a teacher.

What was more, there would be some point, now, in her return to Liverpool, quite apart from her work and friends. Quietly but strongly, the desire to find once more the boy she had danced with on that fateful night nearly three years ago and, if possible, to take up their friendship where it had left off had been growing steadily in her mind, and with it, a flowering of pleasant anticipation she had not felt for a long time. She could still remember his face as though she had seen it only yesterday – the dark eyes, the thick, tumbled dark curls, the way his mouth went when he smiled, the feel of his hands on her . . . but what was his name?

Normal, Dympna told herself, astonished. I feel absolutely normal again. I want to see him and explain to him, and then I want to go dancing, to the cinema, to concerts and entertainments – but with him, not with my girlfriends. She could scarcely wait to start the search and would do it by contacting Elsie once more. Although she knew very well that Elsie had not met him – Elsie was all but engaged to another feller – she was pretty sure that the other girl would still have contacts.

Of course, she knew that he might have gone his own way. Why, he could be married, with a couple of kids by now. But calm and serene, inside her head, she did not believe this. Well, they had seemed right for each other. He had felt it just as she had, she was sure of it. So she would not allow herself to think she had lost him until she had some definite proof.

She was more anxious about leaving Egan. She had talked to Nicholas two days earlier and he had admitted he was worried. 'But he'll be his old self, given time,' he had told her. 'By Christmas, Dr Doyle says, Egan will be doing light work about the place. By spring he might give Daddy a helping hand on board the *Aleen*. By next summer he should be able to hold his own on the boat and dig the fields if he's a mind.'

'But they never knew Egan before,' Dympna had reminded her elder brother. 'I've not seen him for a long while, but even before I left he was very strong . . . very big, too. Will he be like that again?'

'It doesn't matter, Dymp,' Nicholas had said impatiently. 'Size isn't important, it's health and strength that count, and Dr Doyle says he's sure Egan will regain both. Doesn't that satisfy you?'

'It's got to,' Dympna had said rather gloomily. 'Only – I don't think he's any better now than he was when I arrived, and that's two whole weeks ago.'

'Two whole weeks,' Nicholas had echoed sarcastically. 'A lifetime, no less. You expect miracles, Dymp, that's the trouble. Come home again at Christmas, then you'll see.'

'Oh well, all right. And . . . and you'll write to me, Nick? Let me know how they all go on? Mammy doesn't want me to worry and Daddy isn't a great hand with the pen. Egan says he can't concentrate for long or he gets bad headaches – Egan, admitting to having a headache. So if you can't write I'll be cut off again, like I have been these past three and a half years.'

'I'll write,' Nicholas had promised. 'I'm never going to allow myself to get so out of touch with my family again, either. I'm going to come home as regularly as I can to check up on Egan and the parents. And every time I come home I'll write you a nice long letter. Will that satisfy you?'

Dympna had heaved a great sigh of relief. She and Nicky had got on better this time, it seemed as though they understood and liked one another for the first time for many years. 'Thanks, Nick. I'll write back if you send me your address. Have you never thought of coming over to England, incidentally? There are huge hospitals over there, all longing to employ a handsome young Irishman like yourself.'

'Huh!' Nicholas had said. 'Ireland trained me, Ireland shall have the advantage of employing me as well. And now let's turn for home or Egan will guess we've been talking about him and that might worry him.'

So now, climbing steadily upwards, Dympna told herself that she had no reason to worry. She would be home again at Christmas; Mrs Ditchling valued her too much to object to her going home from time to time, and by then Egan would have begun to regain his old strength. She understood Beatrice better than she had ever done before and Micheál was his old, loving self. She hated leaving, but oddly, she was

462

quite looking forward to getting back to Liverpool again. Soon it would be term time so the children would come home from Norfolk and life would take up its old even tenor. She would go back to her beloved evening classes at night school, with Annunciata and Bobby, and she would study like anything so that she would pass the higher next summer. She still remembered the way Micheál's eyes had shone when she had produced the piece of paper proving that she had matriculated. She had written at once, of course, but they had not seen the lovely framed certificate with her name on it. Egan had given her three cheers in his thin, reedy voice and Mammy had looked pleased as well.

She had gone out with Micheál on board the new *Aleen*, too, and had recaptured some of her old ability. She might not be as strong as she once had been, but she still had the knacks which had enabled her to hold her own when out with the fleet. She had enjoyed it immensely, but she knew that it would no longer be enough for her. She had grown accustomed to using her brain as well as her body. Now she needed work for her brain even more than the rest of her. Teaching, she was almost sure, would satisfy some deep need in her, and to do a job one enjoys and which stretches one is imperative for a happy life. That was what Bobby said and he knew a lot.

She reached the top of the hill and began to run down the other side for the sheer joy of it. A mile or so further along she would come out on the flat headland that overlooked the islands and would see once more the cliffs down which she had once scrambled in order to collect gulls' eggs. She doubted very much that she could do it now, but that didn't matter. What mattered was revisiting the place where she had been so very happy, where she and Egan had often come, to clamber about the cliffs and play on the shore, beyond the reach of parents who might prefer that one worked.

On the headland, she sat down in the grass and contemplated the islands spread out before her a bit like the relief map that the geography teacher had used at school. It was too late in the year for the cliffs to be white with sea-birds, but come the spring the birds would come back and nest, and kids like her and Egan would climb down with their collecting bags and take some of the eggs. Some, not all; Micheál had been firm on that point.

Having sat down, Dympna thought about Egan. She did love her brother and wanted him to be better. He was a fighter, Dr Doyle had told her only that morning. When they first realised that the wound was infected they had almost despaired, but Egan had rested and done all the things they told him to, and his appetite for life had pulled him back from the edge. 'Now he should begin to recover faster,' Dr Doyle had said. 'Come Christmas you'll not believe the change in him.'

Well, that suits me, Dympna told herself, lying back and contemplating the blue of the sky overhead. And it'll suit Maria too, because it's plain as the nose on your face that those two adore each other. Of course, Maria's only young, but she's very mature for her age. She seems to be quite content to sit by the bed and read to Egan, or talk to him. As he gets better she'll go walks with him – gentle ones at first, then gradually longer. She's a nice girl; I'll be glad to have her for a sister-in-law.

And presently, with the sun on her face and the

breeze so gentle that it scarcely stirred her hair, Dympna fell asleep.

A day later, Dympna arrived in Liverpool, took a taxi – vast extravagance – to the Ditchlings' house and went at once to see her mistress.

Mrs Ditchling was lying on a day-bed in her small parlour, knitting. As soon as she set eyes on Dympna, however, she threw down her work and sat up. She smiled. 'My dear Nanny – so you've come back. I've been having the most frightful nightmares, imagining that you would get to Ireland and decide not to return. I should have known you better. Now tell me, how is your brother? And the rest of the family, of course?'

'My parents and elder brother are well, but my younger brother isn't strong,' Dympna admitted. She and her employer had never mentioned any relationship between the Ditchling and the Byrne family, and Dympna thought now that it had been for the best. After all, when she came to leave there would be no feeling of letting anyone down on either side, she hoped. 'How are the children, Madam? And how is Gill coping? Because if I'm sent for again in a hurry it's useful to know that she can manage.'

'She's managed very well in Norfolk,' Mrs Ditchling assured her. 'And she and the children return home tomorrow, so you'll be able to judge for yourself. But right now, Nanny, it's just lovely to have you back and to know that life will begin to take its normal course once more. I've really missed you.'

'I'm glad to be back,' Dympna admitted. 'Though I expect I'll miss my own people badly, at first. And since the children aren't yet back, I'll just pop out again, Madam, if you don't mind, and contact one or two of my friends. I've been too busy to write to them, so no one will know that I'm back.'

Mrs Ditchling advised her to get Cook to make her a cup of tea and a sandwich first, and Dympna accordingly went straight down to the kitchen, but she found herself alight with excitement and had to force herself to sit down and eat and drink quietly, before getting to her feet and making her way out into the road once more.

I'm starting my search, she told herself exultantly as she set off towards Belvidere Street to find Elsie. Any time now I'll be seeing him, speaking to him. Oh, how ever shall I wait?

Egan missed his sister badly when she first left. They had been so close as kids, he supposed, that she had a place in his heart that his older brother and even his parents could not enter. Even Maria, who was his dear love, did not know him quite as well as Dympna did. But he told himself that she had a life of her own to lead now and a career to prepare for, and did his best to ignore the pains that plagued him and the weakness, which frequently made him dizzy and sick if he walked more than a few steps, and tried to get himself well.

Maria was wonderful, but she must have been sick and tired of his being sick and tired, he told himself with wry humour. She came and sat with him almost every evening, she talked to him about what was happening on the farm, she told him funny stories about the boys and girls they had both been at school with, she helped Beatrice about the house and encouraged Micheál to tell them what had been happening to the fishing fleet.

Oh, but he did love her! Their love-making had

been of the gentlest, most innocent kind, for they had agreed long ago, when they were scarcely more than children themselves, that they would marry one day. But they knew it would be a good way off before they could afford any such thing, so they had been careful and respectful of one another. But still, there had been wonderful kisses and cuddles, snuggled up underneath an upturned boat in summer and in her father's barns in the soft, sweet-smelling hay in winter. He ached to hold her now, and when his parents were out of the kitchen, where he usually lay now that he was supposed to be getting better, he would take her gently in his arms and kiss her soft and willing mouth.

But it exhausted him and brought on the grinding, stabbing pain worse than ever. Sometimes his own weakness frightened him and he determined to tell Nicholas, to see if something could not be done. Dr Doyle looked at him sometimes with the worry clear to see in his brown eyes, but Egan told himself that naturally Dr Doyle would worry. He had had this awful infection and was ill still, but Dr Doyle had not known Egan's strength and endurance from before. So he said nothing to the doctor, nor to his brother. What was the use of going over and over it? How could he say to another man that he no longer felt he could cuddle his girlfriend, because when he tried to do so the pain in his groin and lower belly was like bein' stuck wit' a knife, and after that he felt as if his heart had fled from his breast? No, he must listen to what they said, try his best to take their advice and await results.

Rather to his surprise, furthermore, Nicholas was as good as his word. He came back to the cottage not just once a month but twice or sometimes three times.

467

He was something called a houseman in one of the big hospitals in Dublin, working extremely hard and from his own account, being very much appreciated both by his patients and by his fellow medics.

'But it's good to spend me spare time wit' me little brother,' he had said jokingly, last time he had come over for a forty-eight-hour break in the middle of the week. 'And I like to breathe the fresh air and walk along the beach a piece. And then there's Mammy's cooking – I'd come a long way for that.'

He did not come by train, either; on a houseman's salary he could not have afforded the long journeys. But he was friendly with a rich man's son who was courting a girl from Connemara and gave him a ride in his motor, and would not even take a share of the petrol money.

'It's the company he likes,' Nicholas explained as he sat beside Egan's couch, pulled up close to the fire, for now that he was so thin Egan felt the cold terribly and scarcely ever went outside the door. 'We go over our more interesting cases and talk about the surgeons and the other medics – oh, we have a grand jangle, so we do, and the time passes in a flash. It would be a long and borin' drive but that we've so much in common, so many interests the same.'

'I'm glad of your company,' Egan said. 'Sure an' 'tis a borin' ould way to spend me time, layin' on this bleedin' couch like a fish gutted an' ready for the table.'

So when Dympna's letter arrived, addressed to himself, Egan was glad on two counts. He would enjoy the letter, every last syllable, and he would have something to give Nicholas when he came the following day, for it was fun to be able to tell his brother something for a change. Nick appreciated, perhaps better than anyone else could, how damnably lost he felt without anything to occupy his big, once-capable hands, for Nick had told him that he, too, had once felt like that. It was whilst he was at the village school and in the top class, with all the lessons learned and Mr O'Neill too busy with the other kids to give him the work he needed and craved for to stretch himself. 'Me brain was just lyin' in me head, bored out of its mind wit' nothin' to occupy it,' he had told Egan. 'So I understand how you must be feelin', old feller. But it'll pass, believe me.'

'Would ye like to give a hand wit' the net mendin'?' Micheál had asked in the early days, but now he knew better. Egan would have dearly loved to help with the net mending, but he could not hold the needle for long enough to do more than a stitch or two and it pained him to have to give over after such a seemingly small attempt.

He began to read Dympna's letter, but Beatrice, pottering about the room, came over and told him that the light was poor in this corner, and had he not better wait until she could read it to him – or until Maria came?

'It's a turble t'ing, Mammy, not bein' able to read me own letter,' he said, ashamed. 'But you're right, the light's awful poor, so it is. I'd be glad if you'd read it for me.'

So his mammy came and sat down beside him and read the letter. It was a grand letter, Egan thought contentedly, watching his mammy's face in the firelight as she heard the city in which she had been born and brought up described in detail, for Dympna said frankly that she had come back to Liverpool largely to find a friend, and told her brother all about her search, which had included, it seemed, some

469

areas known as the courts, which had quite shocked his country-bred sister.

In between these descriptions, however, there were others. She had taken the children to the home of a friend of the Ditchlings who had a number of glasshouses in his grounds, and he had made the children, and their nanny, free of them. Egan had seen such a glasshouse once and had longed to go inside. Dympna, who wrote very well, told how she had stolen in with the older children – her cousins, did they but know it – to examine the peach and apricot trees growing against the glass walls. She talked of the dry warmth within when the wind blew cold without and the grapes hanging overhead with the bloom on them still, the fruits coddled and kept at this warm, even temperature whilst the roots were outside, braving the cold. Egan lived the experience with her, as he did her ride in the big motor car, which had carried the family out of the city.

Shortly after this, she and the nursery maid had taken the children to Southport by bus, with the wonders of that town described in minute detail, from the smart shops to the big hotels along the promenade, from the miles of golden sand to the sea, which went out so far that she had not, for the first few hours of their stay, managed to glimpse it.

*It was great fun and I enjoyed it as much as the kids did,* Dympna had written. *But now we're back in the city, the children are getting ready for school, and I shall go on hunting for my friend. I do hope you're feeling very much better, poor old Egan, and I have to keep reminding myself that I'll be seeing you again at Christmas or I don't know how I'd stand being away from you all, but until then, Eggy, it's just letters. So don't you forget that a line or two is the next-best thing to seeing you myself. Lots of love, Dympna.*

When the letter was finished he sighed with pleasure and took it from his mother, folding it up into its original folds and slipping it under his pillow. When he was alone he would get it out and read and reread it, but now Mammy was in a talkative mood, wanting to ask him what he thought of the fine time his sister had been having in the city of her birth.

'Well, it all sounds very grand,' Egan said judiciously, having thought it over. 'But me sister loves Connemara, Mammy, and I reckon she'll come back here like a bird to its nest just as soon as she's able to earn good money this side of the water as well as t'other.'

His mammy agreed that this seemed likely and admitted that she would be happier with her daughter back in Ireland, and then she went back to preparing the supper. And very soon after that Maria arrived, and then his brother came breezing in, talking as he came, and Maria sat on the couch by Egan and held his thin hand in her small, warm one, and when Daddy came in Mammy asked Maria to stay for supper, and they all sat up round the table except for himself and the mammy. There was good food and talk and laughter, and Mammy helped him to eat so that none of the others noticed, and then whilst Maria and Mammy cleared and washed the pots Nicholas came and sat on the couch and talked to him and asked him about his walking, and just what he did with himself when it was just him and the mammy.

Nicholas was a grand feller, Egan thought contentedly, asking his brother just what he himself had been doing over the past two or three weeks so he would not have to tell his brother how very little he had managed. As he lay there, half listening to his brother's voice, he decided that later, when Nick walked Maria home to the farm and stopped off and had a few words with her brothers and parents, he would get up off his couch and try to walk round the room once or twice. If he did it more often, perhaps it would not be so terribly painful, like a knife turning in his guts, and perhaps the more he practised the better he would feel, which was what Dr Doyle had been telling him for weeks.

So Nicholas gave him a bit of a talk about doctoring in a big hospital, and about one of the nurses who was so pretty that all the fellers wanted to grab her and give her a kiss, only it wasn't allowed, and how Nick had followed her into the sluice (that sounded pretty odd to Egan, but he said nothing, only nodding wisely, as if he understood every word) and was just about to suggest that she should come out wit' him one evening, after work, when Matron came in and didn't she just glare at the poor girl, who had done nothing wrong, only blushed like the prettiest little rose and her as innocent as that flower herself?

And then, whilst Egan was still laughing at the thought of the poor girl blushing over nothing, he repeated his question. 'And what have you done wit' yourself lately, Egan? How far have you walked today, or is this a bad day to choose, what wit' meself coming home and Maria here to wait on you hand and foot?'

Egan began to mumble a reply, trying to make it sound as though he was getting on better because he was damned if he wanted Nick to know what a useless brother he had, Maria called across to him to look at this now, one of the sheepdog's puppies had followed her down from the farm and was sitting, bold as brass, on the slab of rock that he and Dympna used to pretend was a mounting block when they were kids. The puppy was watching them through the window, Maria said, and wagging its tail whenever anyone glanced out at it.

'Hurry, Egan, or it'll be after jumpin' down an' runnin' over to the back door again,' she urged him. And Egan got quickly to his feet and went to go over to the window, and a terrible pain, like a sword being struck through his stomach, made him totter, and he saw the floor rushing up at him through a veil of blackness and the pain got worse and worse . . .

He tried to say something, to tell them he was all right, that he would be all right in a moment, and a great groan of pain was forced out of him. Then consciousness left him before he struck the hard earth floor.

'Egan!' Nicholas had shouted, as his mother and Maria screamed and his father leaped across the room, trying to catch his youngest before he hit the floor, only Egan was there already. Nicholas took his brother's legs as Micheál already had him by the shoulders and together they lifted him onto the bed. Nicholas looked down at his brother's face for a moment; it was white as a sheet. And he saw the weakness, and the hollow eyes and the thinness, and he thought, I've been coming back here for weeks and I've never really looked at him before, because I had other things on me mind, but this is serious. By now he should be a great deal better, he shouldn't be passing out when he stands on his two feet – and he's terrible brave is Egan, I've never known him shout with pain, but that great groan came from agony . . . we've got to get him into hospital fast, or it'll be a wake we're holding over him.

'What is it? What is it?' Mammy was on her knees by the sofa, with Maria, tears wet on her cheeks, bending over and smoothing the hair off Egan's brow. 'Is he dead? Is my boy dead? Oh, dear God, don't let Egan be dead!'

'Of course he isn't dead, he just passed out,' Nicholas said briskly. 'Look, I've got to make some phone calls. I won't be long. Just keep him very quiet and if he comes round, Mammy, wet his lips wit' some water but don't let him drink if you can help it. I'm going to ring Mr Farrell; Egan's got to get to hospital, so he has, and quickly, too. I shan't be long.'

He did not wait for argument or questions but rushed out of the cottage, down the path and along the lane. He ran. I should have noticed, should have realised, he kept saying to himself, then scolded himself in the same breath for crying over spilled milk. He had not noticed and nor had Dr Doyle, a man with far more experience than he, but all that mattered now was to put things right.

He reached the telephone box and rang Mr Farrell in Dublin. He got through before his change ran out and was told to get Egan to the hospital in Galway with all possible speed. 'I'll instruct a surgeon at the hospital and come meself just as soon as I can,' he said. 'I'll tell them to have a theatre prepared – and a bed, of course.' And before Nicholas could more than stammer his thanks the surgeon had put down the receiver.

Nicholas got out the rest of his change and rang the friend with the car, who said he would be with Nicholas in ten minutes and was as good as his word. Within twenty minutes Egan, wrapped in blankets and still barely conscious, was laid along the back seat and the car was speeding as fast as it could for the bad surfaces, along the road to Galway.

'It was touch and go whether they would manage to save him,' Beatrice told Mrs Sullivan a couple of days later, when Egan was still thought to be seriously ill but was at least out of the worst danger. 'He'd never told anyone how frightful the pain was whenever he tried to move more than a little, but from what Nicholas told us, the wound had healed in a way it shouldn't have done, so that he couldn't move for the tugging ... if he had tugged too hard, he would have died. Or that's what I think Nicholas meant,' she added conscientiously. 'Only he does use such long words and such professional language. Still, he says Egan will be in hospital for a good many weeks, but should come out at the end of it pretty well his old self.'

'It's glad I am that he's better, poor feller,' Mrs Sullivan said. 'Our Maria was that worried about him. She's goin' to catch the train to Galway just as soon as he's able to have visitors, so she is. They've been close since they were children ... I dare say Egan will be glad to see her?'

'I'm sure he'll be delighted,' Beatrice said truthfully. 'We've been twice, me and Micheál, but he was still very ill, then. You tell Maria just as soon as she can spare the time, give Nicholas a ring on the telephone. I'll give you a note of the number and when he'll be there. He'll tell her when his brother's well enough to see her.'

'Good, good,' Mrs Sullivan said. 'Nicholas is in Dublin, isn't he?'

'Yes, he's gone back now, though he stayed in Galway until he felt his brother was out of danger. I can't tell you how marvellous Nick has been – why, if it hadn't been for him I don't think Egan would be alive today. But anyway, he telephones the Galway hospital each day to get a progress report, so there's no one better qualified to say when Maria may go over to see Egan.'

Egan sat out in the chair beside his hospital bed and read the latest letter from Dympna without any assistance from anyone. He felt so much better. The terrible weakness had actually seemed less within days of coming round after the operation to put right whatever had been wrong inside him, and although he was still careful how he moved, the terrible tearing pain had not returned.

Mr Farrell had explained what had happened. It was not that the first operation had gone wrong, it was because the healing process had failed to go according to plan so far as he could make out. Nick had explained it best. 'When a wound heals, the two halves of the wound heal together again, right? Just leaving a line as a scar. Understand?' Egan had understood perfectly. 'Well, what happened with you was that your good strong healing body decided that it would join two pieces inside you that should not have joined up – in other words you've had lesions as we call them: pieces of your inside which were never meant to be together joined up after the operation, so you got the terrible tugging pains whenever you tried to move quickly or turn or twist. Get it?'

Egan said he got it and he did, pretty well. So anyway, the surgeon had opened him up again and done a bit more slicing and embroidery – Mr Farrell's own words – and now the correct healing was going on and they would keep a sharp eye on him to make sure that it continued and did not again go awry.

Apparently, if he had told someone about the terrible tearing pain, the agony of feeling that his guts were being sliced up with a large sword, then they might have realised earlier what had gone wrong. But he had not. He had kept going, hoping each day that the next would be better, not even admitting to Nick that there was still terrible pain, especially as it would have meant admitting that hugging Maria hurt worst of all.

Still. He was better now, very much better. He was eating so well that the nurses had to beg extras for him from the kitchen staff, and whenever he had a visitor, he or she would be eyed hopefully, for most people arrived with grapes, chocolates, biscuits . . . something, at any rate. His parents came often and brought proper food, thick slices of home-made bread with home-cured ham sandwiched between them and apples and pears from the garden. Maria came when she could, with eggs for the nurses to boil for him and pats of golden butter and meat pies with a whole egg buried in the pink of the meat. The last three times she had visited, Nicholas had too. He was continuing to visit his parents frequently and made a point of coming in to the hospital either on his way to the cottage or on his way back. He was very pleased with himself for getting Egan to the hospital in time and for explaining what he thought had happened so that the surgeon had been briefed at once and had been able to operate immediately to put things right. He was also pleased because his mammy and daddy were so proud of what he had done, and told all the neighbours what a good son they had in him. Micheál had actually said he would take Beatrice to Dublin to visit his son just as soon as

Nicholas had got a place of his own.

'They would have done that anyway, so they would,' Egan had insisted. 'Mammy's been longin' to see Dublin again and it'll t'rill her to see where you're livin'. They're both so proud of you, Nick.'

'Oh, well, I did me best, so I did,' Nicholas said easily. It occurred to Egan for the first time that his brother was developing a proper brogue and no longer tried to speak like his mother. He supposed that it was the result of living and working with Dubliners; well, there was no harm in it. In fact, Egan felt better now that the two of them had a brogue.

'Well, my boy? And how are you feeling now? Sitting out of bed, I see – very soon you'll be walking around the hospital, then it'll be strolls around the street . . . in a month you'll be walking in at your own front door, I'm telling you.'

The young doctor smiled approvingly at Egan, who grinned back. 'I've walked up an' down the ward till me legs told me to stop,' he assured the doctor. 'And tomorrer I'm goin' to get me some clothes. Soon an' I'll be after havin' a try at a walk round the town. Janey, I'm so much better you've no idea, Doc. I'm gettin' me strength back at a turble quick rate o' knots, so I am.'

'There speaks a true fisherman,' the young medic said. 'Let's check your chart . . .' He picked up the chart that hung on the end of the bed and scrutinised it. 'Yup . . . everyt'ing's normal . . . you'll be home before you know it.'

Egan agreed and presently got up to help the nurses with the tea trolley. He was well enough now to be itching to get home, and he had written as much to Dympna, though he had sworn her to secrecy.

*I'm going to walk in and supprise them* [he had told
her in his last letter]. *They'll all be pleased, becos it's a
long way to come a-visiting, so it is. And it's spensive.
Still, not long now. I've been into the town although they
made a nurse go with me and I pop in and out of the
shops like a native of the place, so I do, and I been to the
cinema! The doctors are pleesed with me. The nurses say
it's been like a miracule. I'll write agin when I get home
and tell you what they all say. Maybe you could have
some time of, and come home and see me? I'm as different
from what I was as can be. I can even think about
working with Daddy again. So get some time of – I don't
want to have to wate until Christmas to see your ugly
face, nor for you to see mine!*

And here was Dympna's reply. It was lovely, as were
all her letters, and she told him about her search for
her friend and how close she was getting to finding
him again, now that she knew where his pal lived.
She was meeting Elsie, she wrote, and maybe they
would go to dances and the pictures again as they
had done long ago, when she had first come to the
city. She even made the search for this feller sound
fun, telling him about the courts and the children
with bare bottoms and rags who were still full of
energy and played very similar games in their city
courts to the games she and Egan had played as kids.

But though she wrote lightly, Egan knew his sister
well enough to realise that she was whistling into the
wind. She would be pretty upset if this friend she
talked about never turned up, or almost worse,
turned up with a wife and a packet of kids as well.
She might pretend – she did pretend – that she only
wanted to find him so she could explain why she had
been so horrible to him the last time they had met, but

479

Egan was not fooled for one moment. A fellow you searched for like that must mean more to you than a chance acquaintance, turned off years before.

Egan gave a sigh and folded the letter, stuffing it into his locker drawer. Dympna would be all right. She was pretty, clever and quick-witted. If she wanted this chap she would have him, but if she preferred to come home to Ireland and start in on this teaching, which she seemed to regard so highly, then she would do that instead. Satisfied that Dympna would manage her life very well he turned his thoughts to his own future.

Maria. His illness had made him realise that time was not, after all, a commodity of which anyone had an infinite supply. Something could happen to Maria, or indeed to himself – quite a lot already had – and their dream of being together could just vanish into thin air. They should tell people, he should buy her a ring. They might have a long engagement, though he hoped now that this would not be so, but in any event, they would be promised and everyone would know it. Then they could both start saving towards a home of their own and a wedding. As soon as he was back at work he would tell Daddy that he needed actual money and not just his keep and some pocket money for specific things, such as a new shirt. Daddy would understand and he could begin to save.

Satisfied on that score, he wondered whether to tell Maria next time she visited him that he meant to buy her a ring as soon as he was out of here, but decided against it. Besides, he had no idea when she would be visiting next, but he had a good idea when he would be going home. The doctor had said that when he could walk a mile he might go, and Egan knew that he was near his goal already. In two days, or perhaps three, he would be walking that distance with ease. What was more, he had considerably increased his knowledge of what young men and young women did together by his trip to the cinema. He had seen very little of the film, but had watched, entranced, as couples all around him began to kiss and cuddle in a way he had at first thought very wicked. But then he had realised that there was nothing wrong in showing your love for someone and, when he went home, he was resolved to try his newly acquired ideas on Maria. That she would like it he was certain, for she had always been the most demonstrative and loving little creature. So he had bought a stamp and this very evening he would write to Dympna and ask her to lend him the train fare home. He hugged himself at the thought of walking into the kitchen whilst Mammy and Daddy were eating their supper, talking about him, planning his homecoming in two or three weeks' time. And as for the welcome Maria would give him – he closed his eyes with the sheer ecstasy of it. Oh, wouldn't it be just grand now to hold his little sweetheart again?

But he had been out of bed ever since his breakfast. No point in running himself down when he had so much to work for. He climbed back between the sheets, and was soon asleep and dreaming of Maria.

Dympna walked blithely along the pavement in the late sunshine of the autumn afternoon. She had just despatched a letter home, or rather not home but to the Galway hospital where Egan was incarcerated. She had been told about Egan's sudden second operation only after it was over and her brother was making a good recovery because her mammy had not seen the sense of worrying her when she was so far away. And last week he was so much better that he had sent her a desperate note, asking for money for the train fare home.

*I'm going to suprise them by gettin home before they think I will,* he had written in his cramped, ill-spelled handwriting. *They know I'm better, but not that I'm real well agin, so it will be a good suprise for them, won't it? I'll be back at the fishing before you know it, so send the fare money, me dear sister, and I'll pay you back out of me fishing money when I'm earning it again.*

Dympna had posted a note with the money in it as she left the house and then had allowed herself to dream, a little, of that far-away home, and of the excitement which everyone would feel when Egan walked in, right as rain, to surprise his parents and, according to him, to take up his job once again.

She had gone round to see Elsie, thankful that after her first recoiling from all her old friends, she had taken to seeing Elsie again, though they only went to the cinema occasionally, or met, each with their charges, in the park for a chat. She had never told Elsie what had happened to turn her against such things as dances, but now, she realised, she would have to do so. Accordingly, she took a deep breath, squared her shoulders and decided on the truth – or as much of the truth as she was free to tell. So as soon as she and Elsie were ensconced in her friend's small room, she had started.

'Look, Els, I've never told you this before, but I'm going to have to do so because I want to ask you a favour. After that dance we all went to, the one where you . . . you and your feller fell out, I was attacked,' Dympna said, keeping her voice low and knowing that her face was turning lobster red. 'That was why I never met up wit' you on the Tuesday, after work, and why I haven't gone to dances or mixed with fellers since then. I can't tell you how awful it was, Elsie. He beat me until I went unconscious, he hurt me badly, my face was a mess for weeks. And it put me off dances an' that, I promise you.'

'No bleedin' wonder,' Elsie had breathed, her eyes like saucers. 'It 'ud put me off dances an' all. Was he after your handbag, chuck? Did they catch the feller?'

'No, he wasn't after money, he . . . well, they knew who it was, 'cos I told them. He'd been . . . been attached to the house, like, so the Ditchlings got rid of him, he went right away. No one wanted the police brought into it, but he was punished, believe me. I was so ill that I was in bed for days and after that I stayed in the house except when I took the kids out. Then, when I began to feel a bit better, I started evening classes and began to work for me school certificate. And . . . and somehow, I just didn't want to go around eyeing up the fellers any more, though I was happy to meet you and Amelia and a few others from time to time. And of course you started going steady with Harry, which meant you didn't want to go dancing with me . . . anyway, I told myself all that sort of thing was behind me, that I would work hard and become a teacher and never look at another feller. Only I went home recently, and me mammy talked some sense into me, and told me to find the last young man I'd been out with and explain. So I'm searchin' for him – he was that young man you had the row with at the dance, only I can't remember his name.'

'You mean Jimmy Ruddock – oh Gawd, you aren't tryin' to tell me as Jimmy attacked you, is you?' Elsie had squeaked, wide-eyed. ' 'Cos I've knowed Jimmy since we was kids together and he ain't never struck me as that kind. Why, I were bleedin' furious wi' him that night, but . . .'

'No, no,' Dympna had said quickly. 'Jimmy Ruddock – yes, I remember now. No, it wasn't him who attacked me, that was . . . was someone else altogether. But I had danced with Jimmy, you see, and he'd been really kind and we seemed to get on well, so I'd agreed to go out with him some time when we were both free. And then one evening after the attack he turned up on the doorstep and I . . . I just froze him off, told him to go and not to come back, said I never wanted to see him again. That kind of thing.'

'But *why*?' Elsie had asked, mouth rounding now as well as eyes. 'Why din't you explain, Dymp? It were the least you could do. Unless the feller . . . he din't . . . you weren't . . .'

'He didn't get the chance, he was frightened off before he could do what he'd come to do, and as for explaining to Jimmy, I couldn't say much, because he came to the kitchen door when Cook and all the other servants were there,' Dympna had said miserably, seeing herself becoming positively bogged down in lies. 'You see, Mr Ditchling made me promise not to say anything . . . I can't even tell you the whole story, Els, or I would, honest to God.'

'I see,' Elsie had said, speaking knowingly but somehow almost absently, as though her mind was elsewhere. 'So you know our Jimmy?'

'Not really,' Dympna had said in a hurry. She had seen the little green light in her friend's eyes and sensed danger, still, in too much truthfulness. 'But I was so rude and unkind, Els, and I would like to see him again and . . . and explain a little bit. Like I've done to you,' she finished.

'Hmm,' Elsie had said thoughtfully. 'Well, there ain't much I can tell you, queen. Last I heard, he'd gone on the transatlantic liners, which ain't much help to you. But that must ha' been three years gone. He may be ashore again by now. Come to think, his home port was Southampton, but he must turn up here from time to time, whilst his ship goes into dock an' that. I'll put the word around, if it 'ud help, see whether we can find him.'

'I'd be ever so grateful, Elsie,' Dympna had assured her friend. 'If there's ever anything I can do for you, you've only got to ask. So what would you do next, if you were me? Ask down at the docks? You don't know the name of his ship, do you?'

'Strikes me you want our Jimmy for more than just apologisin',' Elsie had remarked shrewdly. 'Still an' all, I were fond of him once, and anyroad, it's your business, queen. I'd start wi' his pals . . . know Scratch, do you?'

'Scratch?'

'Tall, skinny feller. Ginger hair an' about a million freckles. They was mates from school, so if anyone knows where our Jimmy's gone it'll be Scratch. Wait on, I'll give you his address.'

And that was why Dympna was walking along in the autumn sunshine, smiling to herself and thinking of Jimmy. Because she had searched out the court in which Scratch lived and had speedily discovered, to her initial dismay, that Scratch, too, had gone to sea.

'He don't come home here much no more,' his mother had told Dympna, chewing what appeared to be a small cigar – Dympna hoped it was a small cigar; if it was not, imagination boggled. Mrs Scratch – whose real name turned out to be Mrs Smith – was a fat, ginger-haired woman in a filthy black dress over

485

which she wore a surprisingly clean calico apron.
'But he an' Jimmy signed on together, so they're still
mates, like. My Scratch, he goes round to Jenny
Anyone's. She's in the next court, four doors down.'

What an odd name, Dympna had thought as she
made her way there, but she soon realised that it was
probably extremely apt, having knocked on the door
in question and had her knock answered by Jenny
Anyone's.

'Scratch ain't here yet, but he'll be dockin' in
around a week,' her informant, a slovenly young
woman with hair that would be golden fair if it were
ever washed and a pair of bold blue eyes which
stared out from a brightly made-up face, had told her.
The two of them had been standing at the top of a
flight of four filthy, greasy steps which led up to a
broken front door and the woman had gestured to a
group of small children playing on the paving
outside her home. 'That 'un's his'n, the one wi' red
'air, an' he's fond of the little bugger so I mek sure to
treat 'im right. I got several others, but Scratch ain't
interested in 'em, only in his own get. Still, he allus
comes to the court when he's in dock to see the little
feller an' give me some money for his keep. An' he
likes to tek me out an' about too, acourse,' she added.

'Naturally,' Dympna had said, wondering why it
had not previously occurred to her that this woman
was quite possibly Scratch's wife. Jenny Anyone's
must be a nickname. 'Umm . . . does he live here,
then? With you? I mean are you his wife?'

The other woman's full, red-painted mouth had
stretched into a broad grin, revealing a number of
broken but very white teeth. 'Me, married? That'll be
the day, gal! I'm a free agent, that's wharr I am, an'
glad of it. Nah, Scratch just comes here when his ship

docks, so's he can treat me an' the nipper to a good time. Why d'you want him? Money?'

'No,' Dympna had said briefly. 'I'm looking for Jimmy Ruddock and someone told me he and Scratch are pals. So I thought . . .'

'Oh aye, been pals since school. Scratch'll know where Jimmy's hangin' out, that's for sure. You come back in a week, chuck . . .'

And now the week was up and Dympna was going back. She turned into the court where Jenny and her children lived and began to cross the filthy paving stones, edging round some of the most disreputable children she had ever seen. There were little girls in ragged dresses playing hopscotch, bare bottoms showing every time they bent to pick up the piece of broken tile they were playing with. There were babies, snotty-nosed and scabby, held in the impatient arms of six-year-olds. There were filthy little boys in men's cut-down trousers playing football with a bundle of rags. Thank God I didn't bring the Ditchling children with me, Dympna thought with an inward chuckle. Madam wouldn't be at all pleased if she found me introducing her brood to these scruffy little souls.

She lingered for a moment to watch a shot at goal, then went rather diffidently towards the greasy steps, but before she could mount them the door shot open and a man appeared on the doorstep. He was – her heart quickened – at least six foot tall with bright ginger hair, a great many freckles and a beaming grin. He wore the navy trousers and jersey of a seaman and he was carrying a small boy so like him that no one could have doubted his parentage.

Dympna went towards the steps. She felt like saying: 'Dr Livingstone, I presume?' but decided on the safer 'Are you Scratch Smith?'

'Aye, that's right,' the young man admitted. 'An' you'll be lookin' for me pal Jimmy, from what our Jenny's been tellin' me. He's got lodgin's in Upper Milk Street – right 'andy for the brewery.'

'Where's that?' Dympna asked baldly. She had got herself lost several times in the maze of tiny streets leading off the Scotland Road and had no desire to do so again. 'I don't know this part of the city very well.'

'Well, you cross over the Scotty into Cavendish and then turn down Marybone. When you reach Pickop Street . . . here, I've a better idea, since it's gerrin' on for dusk,' Scratch observed. 'If you'll hold on a minute whiles I dumps this little feller on his mam, I'll walk wi' you. I need to see our Jimmy afore mornin', anyhow,' he added.

'That's kind of you,' Dympna said gratefully. 'It is getting rather dark and I know I'd only get lost by myself. Would you like me to hold the baby while you go indoors?'

'Never you bother yourself,' Scratch said. 'Shan't be a mo.' And he disappeared inside Jenny Anyone's battered front door.

Jimmy Ruddock had been back in Liverpool for two whole days and he was getting fidgety. It wasn't that he didn't love this great, sprawling city and its people, because he did. He had friends here in plenty, there was a good social life available for the asking and the smell of the sea was everywhere, but he had realised some time back that the life of a deckhand on a big transatlantic liner was not for him. The trouble was, an atlantic liner wasn't like a Fleetwood fishing trawler and what Jimmy yearned for, he had realised a good twelve months previously, was the free life of a fisherman, untroubled and untrammelled by passengers or officers or crew members who got their kicks from making their fellow workers' lives difficult.

But if he went back to Fleetwood he might never see the girl Dympna, who had seemed to like him very nearly as much as he liked her, but had then so suddenly and inexplicably decided that she hated him. He racked his brains over what he had done to be sent packing, but nothing seemed to fit. He had not known her long enough to have got fresh with her and the same applied to having offended her in some way. He simply could not understand it. One moment all had been set fair, the next, stormy weather had not just set in, it had blown him clear out of the sea.

So he had soldiered on, or rather he had sailored on, he thought with grim humour, and had formed the habit of spending a good deal of time when his ship docked in the area of Devonshire Road and the park, trying to see her. He had succeeded several times, but at first she had looked so pale and harassed, so ill, in fact, that he had decided it would be kinder not to approach her. And later, when she began to get her looks back, something still told him not to interfere. There was an air about her of always being on her guard, which said as plainly as any words that this girl was suffering from some kind of shock or dreadful experience and he would be wiser not to meddle.

But he could not go on any longer like this. Coming home in the hope of seeing a girl who was clearly not interested in him, then going off again, earning good money, it is true, but not enjoying the work he was doing one bit. And nice though Mrs Hulme, his landlady, was, Upper Milk Street was not by any

489

stretch of the imagination a home. It was a lodging house, clean and respectable, used by single seamen mainly, most of whom spent their evenings either at the Great Eastern Public House on Cockspur Street or, less reputably, in skulking around Lime Street searching for young women willing to satisfy a sailor's needs.

Being only human, Jimmy had spent a good deal of his time in pubs, and had also managed to find himself a dancing partner now and then who was not averse to a spot of slap and tickle when being escorted home, but further than that he did not intend to go. That girl Dympna had got under his skin, and unless he met up with someone else who attracted him even more, he could not see himself going steady with anyone.

So this evening he was sauntering along Marybone Street, trying to talk some sense into himself. He had almost made up his mind not to sign on again when the liner sailed in a couple of days' time, so he thought he ought to chance his arm with young Dympna. He had decided to go to the house again, ask to see her and try to persuade her at least to explain what he had done to offend her so badly when last they had met. And if she was still offhand and cold with him, then he would take it she didn't intend to change and would get the next train up to Fleetwood and get back onto trawlers. If he did not immediately succeed he had savings now, quite a handsome sum, and could, he supposed, find some way of making money in Fleetwood until such time as a berth was offered.

Yet here he was, on Marybone Street, knowing that he was only a tram ride away from Devonshire Road, and could he make up his mind to go to the house of the people who employed the girl? He kept putting it off, nipping into the Marlborough Hotel for a half of bitter and a chat with the barmaid, a pretty blonde who had a soft spot for him, and then going along to Mrs Annie Marshall's fried fish emporium and treating himself to two penn'orth of chips and as nice a piece of cod as he'd seen for some time.

He had just come out of the fish shop and was dipping into the chips when he saw, above the heads of the crowd, for it was a fine evening, though the street lamps were already lighting up the blue dusk, a crop of ginger hair. He knew at once that it would be Scratch, out looking for him so that the two of them could go to a pub, or a dance, or simply spend some time together. For although Scratch had fathered a baby boy on Jenny Anyone's, he had made it plain that he did not intend to tie himself to a girl like her and was still searching, on and off, for a decent girl who would marry him and take care of his child.

'Shall I scoot before he sees me, or shall I give a shout?' Jimmy asked himself. Now that it had come to the point, it occurred to him that it might be more sensible to catch a tram up to Seffy tomorrow and waylay Dympna when she was taking her charges for their daily walk in the park. So he might as well give Scratch a yell and they could go along to the Lighthouse for a bevvy or two. Tomorrow can wait, Jimmy told himself, and shouted, 'Hey, Scratch! Over here!'

He saw Scratch turn towards him and was beginning to grin when all of a sudden his knees turned to water and he felt his heart give a great, unsteady bound. Scratch had a solicitous hand on the arm of a girl – a girl he recognised, would have known anywhere.

She spotted him only a second or so after he had spotted her and he saw the colour flood her face and a smile begin, broadening until he could see, even across the space that separated them, the dimples in both cheeks.

He never did know quite how he got across to her – or whether, in fact, it was she who had got across to him. He only knew that they were holding tightly to each other's hands and that all of a sudden her smile had disappeared as she said in a small, choked voice: 'I'm sorry, Jimmy, I'm so dreadfully sorry! Will you ever forgive me for the way I behaved that evening? Sending you away as though the whole thing was your fault, when . . . but I've been trying to find you . . . then I met Elsie and she told me you'd gone to sea . . . oh Jimmy, I really am so sorry!'

Her hands in his were small and they trembled a bit, and now that he looked at her properly he could see that there were tears on the tips of her long, curling lashes. She was looking up at him, her lower lip trembling. He swallowed. God, but she was the loveliest thing, quite the loveliest thing he had ever set eyes on – what on earth was she trying to say? She was sorry? What did it matter, now? The past was the past, and right now her hands were in his and her eyes were on his face and . . . and he would never let her go again, never, never.

'S'awright,' Jimmy Ruddock said, and let go one of her hands in order to stroke down along the softness of her cheek and into the smooth ivory of her neck. 'I've . . . I've missed you, though.'

'I've missed you, too,' Dympna said. 'Jimmy, can we go somewhere, have a bit of a talk? Only I went home and my mammy said you deserved to know why . . . where can we go?'

'Go back to Upper Milky,' a cynical voice behind them said. 'Ax your landlady to let you entertain in her front room, our Jim. She can only refuse, after all – an' worse things happen at sea.'

'Oh . . . Scratch,' Jimmy said. He turned to his friend for an instant, then back to Dympna. 'Sorry, I forgot you were there.'

'Don't I know it,' Scratch said. 'Oh, gerroff, the pair of youse! I'll see y'around, Jimmy.'

When he had melted into the crowd Jimmy pulled Dympna back against the window of the fish shop and said tentatively: 'Wharrabout goin' back to me lodgin's, then? All respectable, an' that. Mrs Hulme wouldn't let nothin' go on . . . we'll go to the front room, I wouldn't dream o' takin' you . . . not that I'd do anythin' . . .'

He lost himself in a morass of half-sentences and Dympna laughed and tucked her hand into the crook of his elbow. 'Let's try Upper Milk Street, then,' she said gaily. 'Because quite apart from the explaining I've got to do, we'll need to catch up on each other's news, won't we? It's been a long time, Jimmy.'

'Oh aye,' Jimmy said dazedly. He still felt as though this might be some sort of wonderful dream from which he might presently wake. 'Off we goes, then, to Upper Milky!'

When Jimmy escorted Dympna home that night it was very late and quite chilly enough to justify the arm which he kept protectively around her shoulders. They did not talk much, having talked themselves hoarse earlier in the evening, but they walked in step and Dympna felt that their minds, too, were in perfect tune. Jimmy's teeth had ground with rage when she had told him about Philip's attack, she

493

remembered with deep contentment, and he had been extremely interested in her brother Egan's health, and her father's pucan and even in Nicholas's career as a doctor.

'Wish I had fam'ly,' he had said at some point, and Dympna, quite without meaning to, said 'You'll share mine, I hope', and had then been so embarrassed that she had not known where to look until he had gently taken her hands once more – they were sitting in Mrs Hulme's respectable front room, on her hard little horsehair sofa – and drawn her close so that he might, very gently, kiss her mouth.

'That's the nicest thing anyone's ever said to me,' he had told her. 'Oh, Dymp, I wish I had more to offer you. But everything I've got, all me savin's, and me future, it's all yours. If you want it, that is.'

'We're running before we've learned to walk,' Dympna had warned him, then reached up and kissed him back. 'Only we've wasted so much time being apart that we've got to run a bit, wouldn't you say?'

But now they were fast approaching the big house in Devonshire Street and Dympna was wondering how she could possible let Jimmy go. In the few short hours that they had been together they had both, she thought, realised that this was the real thing. It was the magic love at first sight, which she had read about and never really believed in. And now that they'd met and talked they would never let themselves be parted again.

Jimmy was saying as much as he took her round to the side door which Gill, the nursery maid, had left unlocked for her. 'I'm not signin' on again this voyage,' he told her earnestly, folding her small, cold hands in his big, warm ones. 'So I can see you every day for – well, until I gerranother job, I reckon.'

'Tomorrow? I'm not off until seven thirty, but if you'll come round then . . . don't come to the door, it's . . . it's a bit difficult. Wait for me under the lamp outside; is that all right? I'll be there as soon after seven thirty as I can manage it. Oh, Jimmy!'

'Oh, Dympna!' Jimmy said, taking her in his arms at last and holding her so close that she felt almost a part of him. 'Oh, oh, my . . . my dear girl!'

They kissed, tentatively at first and then with passion so that when Jimmy finally held her away from him her mouth was pink and her eyes shone like stars.

'Until tomorrer,' Jimmy whispered. He kissed the top of her head, where the dark hair parted, then turned away. 'It's nearly tomorrer awready. Under the lamp, an' don't you be late!'

Dympna laughed softly and let herself into the house, then turned in the doorway. 'You've got a good walk home,' she whispered. 'Take care of yourself, dear Jimmy.'

Going slowly up the stairs to the nursery floor, she was sure that no one in the whole world had ever been happier or luckier than she. Jimmy had understood everything, he had not blamed her for her dreadful behaviour, and he had treated her with such sensitivity and gentleness . . . oh, he was the best, the nicest man she had ever met and nothing, *nothing*, would make her let him down tomorrow evening.

# Chapter Thirteen

Everyone conspired with Egan to make his leaving the hospital both secret and special. The nurses kissed him and wished him luck, and said he was the best patient ever, so he was, and his girl the luckiest creature alive, for by now Egan had confided in most of them that he was in love with Maria, the girl who came visiting, and she with him.

'We'll get engaged just as soon as I can buy the ring, so we will,' he assured his new friends. 'And isn't she a dote, now? We've knowed each other since we were kids in school and I've always t'ought she was the prettiest little t'ing. Of course, when I was ill all the time I couldn't even t'ink of marriage, but now I'm better . . . well, it's all I do t'ink of, to tell you the truth.'

'Give her a great big hug and a kiss,' one of the younger nurses said. 'Like this, Egan.' And she hugged him so hard, and kissed him so sweetly, that he felt his cheeks burn, even though all the other nurses laughed and did likewise, making it clear that they were joking, so they were.

Dympna, who knew how to do things, sent extra money for presents for the nurses, a nice thought which, left to himself, Egan confessed, might just have slipped his mind. So he went round the big shops with one of the housemen who was off duty and they bought a great many small boxes of chocolates and a few larger ones, which the houseman said would do nicely for the sisters, so they would.

Egan duly delivered himself of his gifts and got kissed again, only this time he did not blush. Why should he? He had told them all that he was getting engaged and that meant that they could kiss him without fear of anyone compromising anyone else. And at last he said his goodbyes to the other patients, though few had been on the ward anywhere near so long as he, and slung his bags with his few possessions in it over one shoulder and his coat over the other, for though it was November it was mild and pleasant, and set off.

Everything went smooth as clockwork. He caught the right train and sat in a corner seat eating his sandwiches – the nurses' parting gift had been a packed lunch of superior proportions – and drinking his bottle of cold tea and feeling like a king. Freedom, he told himself as the train slid smoothly across the countryside, was all the more precious when you've had it taken away from you for weeks and weeks. Now he was free to do – more or less – as he liked. His brother Nicholas had told him he would be a fool to do too much and spoil all the hard work the doctors and nursing staff had put in on him, so he would be careful. But oh, how he would walk! Up into the hills behind the cottage and down the other side, across the cliffs to where the sea-birds would nest when spring came and along the coast until he could see the broad Atlantic, its mighty waves pounding on Connemara's strangely convoluted shore. He would go in to Clifden and greet all his old school friends now working there, he would go out with Daddy in the pucan and catch up with the doings of the fishermen. He would take the bus and go and see his uncles and aunts and cousins who lived in the area, and tell them all about Maria and how he and she had plighted their troth and would get married one day.

He would work again, too. Not too hard at first, because Nicholas said that could do more harm than good, but as hard as he was allowed. He would dig the garden, because Micheál had been too busy with the fishing to do much digging, his mammy had told him so. And he would take a plough to the fields if Mr Sullivan would lend him the plough and a team. He did not think that Rosa would be much good with a plough coming on behind and besides, Mammy said they were doing well with the fish, so they were, so Rosa would be needed whenever Daddy brought home a good catch, to carry it to Clifden where it would be sold either to local folk or to the people who came from Dublin and Limerick and Cork, wanting the good fresh fish and shellfish which the men brought in daily from their fishing trips.

The train stopped at several stations but at last it was Clifden and Egan packed his empty sandwich papers neatly into the tin box which the nurses had given him and shoved it into his carpet bag along with his other possessions. He threw the apple cores out of the window and popped the plum stones into his pocket. He fancied growing a plum stone until it was a proper plum tree, then it would remind him of his friends in Galway for ever and a day, he told himself, patting his pockets and bringing out his ticket for the porter on the station, and checking that he had left nothing behind.

There was no one waiting on the station, but how could there be? This was to be the best surprise any of his family had ever had and it could scarcely be a surprise if he had got someone to call for him. He thought about a taxi, but it was an extravagance, so it was, and the walk home from Clifden no more than four or five miles at the outside, and hadn't he been walking that far and further for exercise every day now at the hospital?

So he set off, his bag now weighing quite a lot less than it had on his departure from Galway. His eyes were everywhere, appreciating things he had always taken for granted: the lush green of the grass on the verges by the dusty road, the way the thorn trees bent to the push of the prevailing wind and the sweet clearness of the air, which he drew into his lungs eagerly, as though he were a thirsty man and it was crystal-clear water.

He walked with his old stride now, too. A long, swinging stride, which ate up the miles. He turned on to Sky Road and presently passed the little church where the whole family worshipped every Sunday and quite often on other days too. He passed the little lane which led to the farm next to the Sullivans – a long little lane, which climbed two hills before it reached its destination – and a couple of cottages where the men scraped a living from their tiny, odd-shaped fields and went out in their curraghs to fish inshore or to pick mussels and oysters from their beds.

At last, he reached their lane. It was smaller, stonier and dustier than the Sky Road, but he loved it because it led home. He turned into it. Not long now, not long now! His heart was hammering and his palms were suddenly damp. He stopped and stood still for a moment, looking ahead of him up to the curve in the lane that hid the cottages from him. No point in getting himself all over-excited, there was plenty of time. It was still only mid-afternoon and Daddy would not be back from the fishing yet nor would Mammy have returned from the Sullivans', if she was working there.

Presently he reached the place where the little track led down to the stone quay and the harbour. He hesitated, wondering whether to go down and just take a look around, see how things were shaping. But he would have to climb up again, and that might not be such a good idea; he wanted to arrive home looking fit as a fiddle and feeling it, too. So he stopped for a moment, breathing deeply and slowly. When his heart could no longer be felt thumping in his chest he moved on up the lane, round the corner, to the spring and the tin bath, and a thousand thousand memories.

It was just the same, but he had never appreciated, before, quite how beautiful it was. True, the hazel trees which overhung the spring were leafless now, but the water tinkled down as musically as ever, into the tin bath and out again the other side, to pour across the lane on its stony bed and over the edge of the small cliff on its way to the sea. And there – his heart gave a jump, but it was a happiness jump – was the cottage. Just the same as when he had left, except that now it was almost winter and the apple trees were bare, save for a few scarlet fruit grimly hanging on, and the dark green of winter cabbage in the long narrow beds that lined each side of the path.

He approached the gate, unlatched it, slipped through. He was careful not to make a noise – he wanted this to be a surprise – and reached the front door on tiptoe. It was closed top and bottom, which almost certainly meant that Mammy was not in, for had she been there she would have opened the top of the door to let in the mild air and to let out the smells of cooking, of the smouldering turf fire and of the fish that Micheál cleaned on the long wooden draining board.

He unlatched the top door and pushed it ajar. The kitchen, as he had guessed, was empty, though the turves smouldered, well banked up. Mammy had known she was going to be out for several hours and did not want the job of re-laying and relighting the fire, so had damped it down with plenty of turves. All it needed to get it going again would be a lift with the poker so that the air might go in underneath and start a-roaring.

Egan opened the bottom half of the door and let himself in. The journey, and the excitement of being home, had tired him, so he would stir up the fire and sit down by it for a while. He would put the kettle on as well, as it was a long time since the last of his cold tea had been drunk and anyway, what he wanted now was hot tea and plenty of it. And griddle cakes would be nice – or a slice of Mammy's special fruit cake, which she always kept in the big round tin with the picture of Queen Victoria looking very regal on the lid.

He was half-way across the room when it occurred to him that he ought to take off his good shoes and find up some old ones. And he could put away the stuff he had in the carpet bag at the same time.

Egan removed his cap and hung his coat on the peg. There were no coats there already, so Mammy and Daddy were both out. It was the weekend, so he rather hoped that Nicholas might be coming home either this evening or tomorrow, but clearly he had not yet arrived. Egan stretched, yawned and made for the bedrooms. Already beginning to relax, he went into his room.

*

Nicholas was there, lying full-length on the bed. With ... Egan's eyes widened and widened. Sick shock and horror rose up in his throat, choking him, so that he could not have spoken even if he had wished to do so.

For a moment he just stared, stretch-eyed. Nicholas and ... and a *woman* lay on the bed in which he had lain ever since he grew to man's stature. Their bodies were moving with an urgency which seemed horrible to him and the woman had long, dark hair with a strong curl to it, and her bare arms were beautiful, made more beautiful by the narrow silver band with the strange marks carved into it which had got pushed up her arm half-way to the elbow ...

Egan went down to the quay, but there was no one there. The sea was coming in and a curragh was pulled up on the narrow strip of sand, which the tide rarely invaded. It was being tarred and the tin of tar and the stubby stick with a piece of rag wrapped round it, which the owner had been employing to spread the tar, lay beside the upturned craft. Egan was sweating and the old, sickening pain was throbbing away somewhere in the region of his stomach, but his mind it was that ached worse. His girl! Little Maria, whom he had loved ever since he was old enough to love anyone, lying on his own bed with no clothes on, bold as any Jezebel. And his own brother! He felt as if he were drowning in anger and pain and, strangely, guilt. What had he done for Maria, he asked himself, sitting down on one of the stone bollards on the end of the quay. He had kissed her with devotion, to be sure – but so dully, with so much respect. Once he had seen the young men and women in the cinema he had realised that he was slow, slow, slow! No girl could bear to be engaged to such a one as he had been, a feller without the gumption to rouse the feelings in her, which he had only been dimly aware of in himself. Ah, but I was going to be very different as soon as I was better, he reminded himself miserably, and felt the tears begin to form in his eyes and slide down his cheeks. But she couldn't wait for me – didn't wait – wouldn't wait. Why should she wait for a thick, slow, stupid eejit of a feller like Egan Byrne when she could be havin' a fine ould time wit' a grand feller like Nicholas Byrne, who knew how to pleasure a girl, how to persuade her out of her clothes and into bed?

And now what? Go back, pretend he knew nothing, wait for them to tell him that they were to be married? Dear God, perhaps they all knew, Mammy, Daddy, Dympna. Perhaps it was only thick old Egan who had not realised a girl like Maria would not want to be tied to a dolt like himself, wit' no ambitions and no skills, either, save that of catchin' fish and diggin' the land.

But . . . what sort of life would it be for him now? With no Maria? She had been the star by which he steered, his reason for existence. Why, when he had been at his worst it had been the thought of Maria which had got him through. He honestly did not think he wanted to face a future which not only would not contain Maria for him, but which would damn him to being her brother-in-law. To seeing her marry, bright-faced, his elder brother, who had a great future as a doctor of medicine, or a surgeon even, before him. To watch her swell with Nick's child, dandle that child on her knee and put it to the breast . . . he would rather die.

To die. He nearly had died, lying there in the hospital. But he had fought back, struggled for life.

Was he going to throw that all away just because . . .? But every time he faced what his life would be like without Maria, death seemed . . . oh, like a comfortable sleep. At least if he was dead there would be no questions asked as to why Maria had suddenly changed her mind. They would think well of Nicholas for comforting the girl who grieved for Egan Byrne. His death would free Nick and Maria to marry as nothing else could, for the Sullivans had teased him often about his fondness for Maria, and his own parents, his sister Dympna, all knew that the childhood sweethearts planned to wed just as soon as they could afford to do so.

But dying isn't so easy for a man on the way back to health. Egan got to his feet. He walked over to the curragh and looked down at it. No, he could not steal another man's livelihood and besides, what was the point? He could swim and he had a horrible feeling that no matter how far out he rowed, he would somehow manage to swim ashore if he sank the curragh out there in the deep sea.

But you can't fly, a little voice said in his head as he turned and trudged back up the beach and onto the lane which led to the cliffs. You've watched Dympna many and many a time climbing down those cliffs after sea-birds' eggs and never could you find the courage to take her place. When she left Streamstown that was the end of a glut of gulls' eggs, he told himself now. Go on, Egan, walk faster, run. You aren't supposed to run, it's not good for your mending guts, so run.

But he soon slowed to a walk. There was no need to drag his belly apart, the rocks below the cliffs would do that for him.

*

Beatrice saw the coat hanging on the hook of the kitchen door and the carpet bag under the wooden table as soon as she entered the room and guessed their meaning at once. Egan, the little devil, was home. He had been hinting, last time she and Micheál had visited him, that he would not be tied to his bed for much longer. Maria had said she expected him to come home within a couple of weeks, and he had done it. All by himself . . . oh, if only they had known she and Micheál would have arranged something, had a celebration . . . but no, that would be to come, when he was truly strong enough to enjoy such a gathering. Her eyes roamed the room; he had got the fire going, had pulled the kettle over the flame – and then? She smiled. Of course, he was worn out after the long journey and the thrill of coming home. He would have gone through to his room for a lie-down on the bed and probably had fallen asleep. It would do him good and Nicholas was coming home later today, so the lad should get all the rest he could. But she would just peep in, make sure he was all right . . .

Beatrice went quietly across the kitchen and through into the tiny passageway from which the bedrooms led. Very quietly, so as not to disturb him, she pushed open the door of the boys' room . . .

Beatrice ran out of the cottage. She was wearing the print dress which she used for dairy work and her old shoes, which were good for running in, but she had no idea which way to run and all of her own accord her mouth had opened and she was screaming, 'Egan! Eeeegan! Come back, my dearest, my best of sons! Where've you gone, what're you doing? Eeeegan! It's your mammy, wantin' you. Egan, what you saw don't mean a thing, it was . . . I'll kill

Nicholas wit' me own hands for what he's done to me son, I'll bloody kill 'um!'

She heard herself and wondered why, after more than twenty years of clinging to her English, she was talking as Micheál talked, as her dear son Egan talked. In a muddled sort of way she supposed that she was admitting something, giving in to something. She was one of them, she was Micheál's wife, Egan's mother. She wasn't Beatrice Campion, the beautiful Campion girl who would, one day, make a good marriage. She was what she had become and what she was now proud of being – Micheál's wife, Egan's mother.

The harbour was empty, but a black boat with its red sails half down was gliding in across the water. She screamed again. 'Micheál! Egan's home but he's gone! He saw . . . something terrible. Where would he go? Ah, dear God, where's me son?'

Micheál pointed. He pointed away from the cottage, to the cliffs two or three miles away. He must have been able to see his son's figure there, for without demanding any other explanation he suddenly began to bring the sail up again and to turn the boat. He could get there quicker than she and he would find some way of stopping Egan doing . . . whatever he had it in mind to do. Beatrice remembered when she was young, how she had felt. Everything so distorted by youth, so important. Ah, God, she had thought about killing herself when she and Micheál had first wed, but the baby had been within her and it had seemed the final wickedness to destroy, along with her own worthless life, the life of one of God's innocents. And now, looking back . . . I've had a grand life, so I have, Beatrice told herself breathlessly, running as fast as she could along the dusty lane. Why, my whole life has been full of riches, which I never even thought twice about until this moment. What a blind eejit I've been not to realise.

She picked up her skirt so that it would not encumber her and ran faster, until a sharp stitch in her side advised her to slow down if she wanted to reach the cliffs at all. And when her shoe fell off she swerved off the track onto the wiry cliff grass and kicked off the other one and ran like a girl, and felt like one, save for the gnawing anxiety which told her that she might yet be too late.

Micheál had wondered about Nicholas's constantly returning home and once or twice lately had also noticed, without really thinking about it, that he was being very sweet to Maria. He took her out, bought her little gifts that she could take for Egan, talked to her without trying to show off his superior knowledge all the time. Now, Micheál's mind was putting two and two together and making four. It was working slowly, because that was Micheál's mind for you, but it was getting there.

Maria's a very pretty girl, his mind said. Nick's not a bad-looking young feller, if you don't mind the weedy look of 'm. Maria's innocent, unawakened. That might well appeal to Nicholas, who had been meeting girls who had a good deal of experience one way and another. And Egan, God love him, is as innocent as she and that isn't always a good t'ing.

So what had happened to send Bea, in her print dress and apron, shrieking down to the quay? What could have happened? She had said Egan was home and that he had seen 'something terrible'. Oh, janey, he must have seen that self-satisfied young doctor, Nicholas Byrne, kissin' little Maria – worse, he must have seen Maria kissin' him back. And it had turned his head from t'oughts of his own marriage to . . . to blacker t'oughts. And he'd gone off at a run, like Bea, for hadn't Micheál seen some young feller just now, sloggin' away across the cliffs, black against the greying sky of evening?

Whilst he thought these things, Micheál had not been idle. He had set the sails once more and Liam, the little lad who was working with him, had cottoned on at once to the idea that they were not making for harbour after all. He had sprung to the sheets and as the wind puffed out the red sail the *Aleen* got the bone in her teeth and they swung her round towards the distant line of the cliffs. Micheál took the tiller with his left hand and the mainsheet with his right, and grinned at Liam. 'Me son's come home,' he said cheerfully. Not for worlds would he have admitted that there might be trouble. 'He's gone along the cliffs a piece. We'll go round and meet 'um.'

'Awright, Mr Byrne,' Liam said. He grinned. He was a cheerful urchin who said he was fourteen though Micheál had his doubts. 'Sure an' the wind's right for it.'

'Aye,' Micheál said. He got out his pipe and began to puff at it, though it had long been cold. 'We'll get there before me woman's half-way, so we shall.'

But what to do when he got there he did not know. How could he stop the boy doin' somethin' mad if Egan had a mind to it? And as if God was listenin' and waitin' for to give advice, a little voice in his head said: Be there. That'll do it. Just be there, so that if he jumps – he felt the cold sweat form and run down his back at the thought – if he jumps it'll be with the knowledge that he's doin' it in front of his daddy. Egan's never after hurtin' anyone, so he'll not want to do his daddy such a turble hurt. And the *Aleen* swept confidently on with her master at the tiller, bringing her close up to the rocks at the foot of the cliffs where once his daughter had scrambled after sea-birds' eggs and his son had danced on the cliff top in an agony of apprehension lest she should fall, yet too afraid of heights to go down further.

Egan saw the pucan coming round the coast just before he reached the cliffs but he did not immediately connect it with his father. His thoughts were turned inward, too confused and complex to be able to take in what was happening in the real world when the world of his mind and imagination were in such turmoil.

As he hurried, he was fighting off imaginings of such disturbing clarity that he could scarcely bear it. He kept seeing his room, the couple on the bed, their bare limbs entwined and entangled, their thoughts so totally involved with one another that the opening of the door – and the quiet closing of it – had not caused either of them to lift a head.

He reached the cliffs and walked slower and slower as he neared the edge. He had always hated heights, had never been able to understand Dympna's complete indifference to them. 'What does it matter how far you fall, if you're going to fall?' she had once asked him in genuine puzzlement. 'And when there's water under you, and you swim well, as you do, why should you fear a dive into it?'

He had not been able to explain the inexplicable – why one person is afraid of heights but can fearlessly handle a live spider or a dead, feathered hen. Dympna was terrified of spiders and loathed the feeling of the feathers still warm on the hen. 'Each to his own,' his mammy had been wont to say. 'We're all different, thank the good Lord.'

So now he approached the edge of the cliff with all the flutterings of the heart that had always accompanied a close approach to a long drop. And before he got anywhere near the edge he looked out, and there was the *Fair Aleen*, with her mains'l coming down and his father bringing her gently head to wind – right below. If I were to jump now, Egan thought, wouldn't I go bang t'rough the bottom of me daddy's boat? Wouldn't I likely kill all t'ree of us, meself, me daddy and young Liam? And wouldn't that make me a murderer of the worst kind, to kill an innocent man an' a child?

But he took a step nearer the edge and swayed, and forced himself to stand firm. He could jump well to the left . . . that would mean he could clear the boat all right. Or he could jump very shallow, more or less walk over the edge, and . . .

Terror gripped him now. He no longer wanted to jump, but knew, in his bones and heart, that he would do so. He would do so because now that he was so near the edge, the rocks below and the green, translucent sea were calling him, calling him. He could not resist, he was so frozen with fear that to end it he was even willing to tip over the cliff, to tumble down, down, down, turning over and over as he went . . .

He gulped down a desperate desire to vomit and tried to turn away – and could not. His feet seemed to be stuck to the ground, but he was fascinated by the drop. He could feel his body swaying forward, as though it wanted to feel that awful void sucking at him, dragging him down . . . down . . .

'Dymp,' he said, and his voice came out dry and hollow. 'Dymp – will ye be after helpin' me now? Will ye tell me what I'm to do?'

And he heard Dympna's voice quite distinctly in his head, sounding half amused, half angry. 'Are you just going to give your Maria up to that . . . that Nicholas?' her voice said. 'Aren't you even going to fight for her? You can't think she's worth much, Egan Byrne.'

He was so astonished – and indignant – that he stepped back from the cliff, turning as though he expected to find Dympna herself standing just behind him. He said angrily: 'She's worth the world to me, so she is. But . . . but Nicholas is the better man. He's a doctor, he can give her a good home, plenty of money, all that she's ever wanted . . . how can I stand in their way?'

'You eejit,' Dympna's voice said. 'You think Nick is a better man than you? Well, boy, you're twice the feller he is, he's just a weed of a feller with lots of learnin' but no common sense. What sort of wife would Maria make for a feller like that? What sort of husband would he make for her, come to that? Just you go back to the cottage, Egan, and tell the pair of 'em to stop making fools of themselves, because you're set to marry Maria just as soon as you can afford it and you won't take damaged goods.'

'But they've . . . I saw them, they were . . . they were *bare*,' Egan said. His voice sounded apologetic, even to him. 'And they were lyin' on me bed, so they were.'

'Bare? You didn't see them that clearly, I'll be bound. You were much too shocked,' Dympna's sensible, practical voice pointed out. 'Egan Byrne, if you don't go right back to the cottage now, this minute, and take what's yours, you're no brother of mine.'

Egan, wretchedly undecided, turned back to look

down over the edge of the cliff and there was his father, the boat right underneath him now, smiling, actually smiling up at him. Feeling trapped, Egan spun round again . . . and there was his mammy, panting hard and with a hand to her side, coming in her bare feet and her cooking apron across the grass towards him.

'Egan! Oh, my darling . . . my dearest son,' Beatrice said and almost jumped into his arms. 'Now just you come on back to the cottage – you've been very ill, you shouldn't be out here . . . Whatever's gone wrong we can put it right. Come alone, now.'

'It's . . . I don't . . . I came here to . . . to . . .' Egan said and let his voice fade into silence. His mammy took his arm and gripped it tightly.

'I'll kill that bloody Nicholas wit' my bare hands,' she said. She looked up into his face with anxious, motherly eyes. It was nice to be looked at as though you were the favourite son and very precious, nice to hear Nicholas called names. 'He's been playing fast and loose wit' Maria, my dear boy, and maybe her head was turned a little . . . you've been ill a long time and Nicholas – I realise it now – must have been very attentive. But it's a game to him, Egan, it isn't real. Oh, how I'll make him smart.' She turned away from the cliff, back towards the path, and because she was holding his arm and because he felt warmer now, and better altogether, he turned with her, naturally, and went with her across the grass.

'How did you know what had happened, Mammy?' Egan said as they rejoined the lane. 'Did you go in, like I did? Did they see you?'

'See me? They would have had to be blind not to have seen me, and deaf not to have heard some of the things I called them,' Beatrice said. 'But I swear to you, my son, that it looked far worse than it was. Now we'll go in together and face them out, how's that?'

'I . . . I don't know,' Egan said slowly. His body was still shaking from his recent experience. I nearly went over, he thought, awed. I near as dammit kilt meself, an' me just recovered from the operation an' happy as Larry, and just because me girl hadn't been true. And now here was his mammy saying it wasn't as bad as he t'ought and to face them out wit' what they'd done, and all of a sudden he wasn't at all sure that he wanted Maria. Not now. Not having seen her in Nick's arms, rolling on his – Egan Byrne's – bed. He voiced the thought aloud. 'Mammy, it's . . . it's changed t'ings. Mebbe 'twould be better if Nicholas married her and took her away from here, because he'd not stay in Connemara, not our Nick. He's headin' for the top, everyone says so, even the nurses at the hospital.'

'If that's how you feel you must tell them and give them your blessing,' Beatrice said. 'But you've loved Maria a powerful long time, Egan.'

'Ye-es, but it was me own little Maria I loved. She was just a kid really, Mammy, a kid who didn't know what it was all about, any more than I did. Mammy, she an' me, we never did anything at all at all, an' she said she loved me, yet there she was, wit' her body pressed against his as though . . . as though . . .'

'Yes, well, every woman on God's good earth does foolish things sometimes,' Beatrice said hurriedly. 'I've done bad, foolish things myself, Egan, but yet good came out of it. Maybe – who can say? – good will come of this day's work.'

Egan shook his head dubiously. He was walking more and more slowly, not only as the stress of the

513

day caught up with him but as a sort of horror of walking into the cottage awoke in his mind. To face Nick and Maria, joined against him, how would that feel? To see on Maria's pixie face a look of . . . of what? Contempt? Chill? Indifference? Oh, God, not indifference, he prayed fiercely and dropped further back. But his mammy was having none of it. She slowed down too and caught his elbow. 'No turning back now, my son. You're in the right, remember, and they're deeply in the wrong. This thing must be faced and sorted right here and now, because I'll not have my family torn in two by a selfish son and a boy too weak to say his mind.'

'I'm not too weak at all,' Egan said, stung. 'I'll say me mind, Mammy, even if it means Nick an' Maria walk out of Streamstown an' never come back again. And don't you be blamin' me if that happens, Mammy, for it's the sort o' t'ing Nick would do, rather than face the music.'

'Right,' Beatrice said. She sounded as determined as Egan suddenly felt. 'Here we go, then.' And together they approached the cottage.

'*Marry* her?' Nick said. His voice rose almost to a squeak. 'Marry Maria Sullivan? But dear God, Egan, 'twas only a bit of fun, I don't know why you're making such a fuss about it, indeed I don't. Look, we didn't know you were on your way home, I teased her into lying down on the bed with me, we had a bit of a kiss and a few cuddles . . .'

'You had the clothes off her back,' Egan said, coldly but almost mildly. 'I *saw* you, Nick; you were so . . . so busy wit' one another that you never even noticed the door openin', nor closin', neither. When a feller treats a girl like that then he marries her – or he does round here. I don't know what they do in Dublin, t'ank God, but round here he marries her.'

'Oh, janey mac, I've said it enough times, *I didn't do anythin' wrong to the little innocent*,' Nicholas shouted. His face was red as a lobster and the fair curls he was so proud of stood up all over his head as though a strong wind blew. 'Has she told you different, then? Has she said I seduced her, or raped her, or whatever I'm supposed to have done?'

Maria had been gone by the time Egan arrived back at the cottage and since he, his mother and Micheál had arrived there just about simultaneously, they had gone in together, to 'face it out', as Beatrice had put it.

Nicholas had been standing before the fire, drinking tea. His face had been pink then, not lobster red, but there was something about his eyes, the way they darted round the room, never fixing themselves on anyone – or anything – for longer than a few seconds, which would have told most observers that he felt extremely guilty about something. But at first he had been calm enough, saying that he believed his mammy had got a 'totally wrong impression' when she had walked into the boys' room and found him there with Maria.

Indeed, it was only when Egan said, as generously as he knew how, that it was all right, so it was, he would not dream of trying to stake a claim to a girl who obviously no longer loved him, particularly when it was his own brother who had taken her fancy. 'It won't be bad for me, because after you're married you'll be livin' in Dublin, or London, or wherever your doctorin' takes you,' he had said, and raised the present storm.

But now Nicholas was glaring at them all, waiting for a reply, though he knew very well that there had been no time for anyone to have spoken to Maria. They had come straight in, all of them, expecting to find her there.

Finally, it was Beatrice who spoke. 'If her father knew that you'd taken the girl into your bedroom and taken the clothes off her back, he'd take a stock whip to you first and then a shotgun and the priest would be marrying the pair of you before you'd had time to turn round. What was left of you, that is. So don't trifle with us, Nicholas. If Egan withdraws his claim then you'll marry the girl and that's flat. The Sullivans will be pleased enough. You're quite a catch, in your way.'

'But Maria doesn't want to marry *me*,' Nicholas wailed. Tears stood in his eyes. 'It was just a bit of fun, I'm tellin' you . . . ask Maria. Ask anyone!'

'She can't want to marry Egan,' Micheál said quietly. It was the first time he had spoken. 'Or she'd never have gone wit' you into the bedroom. She's a dacint young girl, she'd not be playin' fast an' loose wit' you if she still intended to marry Egan.'

Nicholas turned on Egan, his voice suddenly hopeful, his eyes bright. 'Egan, you're me little brother, you must know I'd not take your girl. And . . . and didn't I save your life now, when you lay ill, mebbe dyin', and I rang for Mr Farrell an' fetched you into hospital? Honest to God, Egan, I was just . . . just so bloody *bored*, and Maria missed you, she kept tellin' me how much she missed you, and I'd no idea of marriage, certainly I never mentioned marriage to Maria. It 'ud ruin me career, wreck me chances utterly. She's . . . she's a nice girl, but she's a country girl, she's not up to all the tricks . . . she'd be bloody miserable in Dublin, she wouldn't be after knowin' a soul, or what to do wit' herself . . . and I'm set for better t'ings than a country practice, you know I am. Give me a chance, Egan. A life for a life, eh?'

The silence in the small room stretched and stretched. Beatrice was gazing at her eldest child as though she had never seen him before in her life, as though she had just turned over a stone and found him wriggling beneath it. Micheál was staring at his eldest son too, with compressed lips and a dark frown, the distaste clear on his face for all to see.

Egan was the only one who looked at Nicholas calmly, thoughtfully, without either judging or condemning. Finally, he spoke. 'Fair enough. I'll talk to Maria. I'll go up there later, when I've had a bit of a sit-down. It's . . . it's been a quare ould day so far.'

'And . . . and you'll not try to force either of us into a marriage that neither of us wants?' Nicholas said eagerly, taking a step towards his brother. 'She's no manner o' use to me as a doctor's wife. Well, a woman, any woman, would only hold me back, spoil my chances . . .'

Egan stared at his brother as though he, too, had just seen clearly, for the first time, the monstrous egotism and vanity that were Nicholas Byrne. Then he punched him on the nose so hard that Nicholas staggered back against the mantel, and sat down on the sofa and smiled at his parents. 'I'd not be sayin' no to a cup of tay, Mammy,' he said sweetly. 'And a piece of sody bread would go down well before I go down to the quay to take a look at the *Fair Aleen*.'

A month had passed since Egan's return and Beatrice and Micheál were close to despair. All that time they had been trying to come to terms with what had happened, whilst Egan refused to discuss it. Needless to say, Nicholas had disappeared back to Dublin and had not answered one of Beatrice's increasingly frantic letters.

'Nicholas won't have nothin' to do wit' marryin' Maria,' Micheál said sadly, as they climbed into bed one night. 'And I'm not about to come the heavy father and try to mek him change his mind – some marriage that would be to be sure. Besides which he'd not attend to me, not Nicholas. But it's plain to me, me darlin' Bea, that Nicholas had his way wit' the gorl and because they've been so close in the past, it's Egan who'll get the blame if Maria's in the fam'ly way.'

'Yes, I know,' Beatrice said heavily. 'I've never been so ashamed of Nicholas as I was that evening. Such total selfishness . . . I wondered where I'd gone wrong in bringing him up, indeed I did. But I had hoped, and believed, that Egan might still marry Maria, because they've been closer than twins, the pair of them, and loving as two turtle doves. Yet when I mentioned it . . .'

'He cut you down wit' a remark about damaged goods, I dare say,' Micheál said gently. 'He said much the same to me, so he did, but you must remember he's hurt, me darlin', to the depths of his soul an' he can't see straight right now. I was hopin' that he'd remember how he loved his wee gorl and begin to understand that what happened was certainly not her fault, the poor crittur. Why, when they meet . . .'

'If they meet,' Beatrice said gloomily. 'Egan's always been the easiest of sons, Micheál, but now he's turned in on himself and won't listen to a word I say. Come to that, I doubt he'll listen to you either, my love. He's mortal fond of you, but he's terribly hurt and confused, too, and in this mood I'm afraid he'll make a terrible mistake, a mistake which he'll regret for the rest of his life. Only he won't listen to me. What should we do, dearest?'

There was a silence whilst Micheál thought. It was such a long one that Beatrice found her lids drooping over her eyes, for the last couple of days had been exhausting for them all.

But then at last Micheál stirred, cleared his throat and spoke. 'Get Dympna home,' he said.

'Get her home? Oh, but she's scarcely been back from her last visit a couple of months back . . . how can we ask her to come home again so soon?'

'Just ask her,' Micheál advised. 'Write her a letter, Bea. She's closer to Egan than any of us and I don't believe that he will shut her out, the way he's done wit' us. Just drop her a line, explain and she'll come.'

'I could try,' Beatrice said doubtfully. 'But God alone knows what I could say . . . after all, I never asked her to come back when Egan was rushed into hospital, did I? We both agreed that because he was out of danger so quickly there was no point in disturbing her again.'

'Well, he's not out of danger now,' Micheál said. 'He's in greater danger than ever he was wit' his health I'm thinkin'. Write, me love.'

'I will, then,' Beatrice said. She snuggled down and rested her head against his broad chest so that she could hear the steady beat of his heart. 'Oh, Micheál, you're so . . . so *sensible*.'

Micheál's deep chuckle rumbled through his chest. 'Well, I do me best,' he said modestly. 'Now let's sleep on it, alanna.'

They did so and next morning, as soon as she had cooked breakfast, Beatrice walked in to Clifden and posted a letter to her daughter. It did not go into much detail, but she thought that it would do the trick and bring Dympna back to her.

So Beatrice, making her way back along Sky Road, thought that she had done all she could, now. The daughter she had always undervalued was, she now knew, a young woman of good sense and intelligence, with a far deeper understanding of her younger brother than she herself had ever possessed. Dympna, she was sure, would sort it out.

The letter arrived whilst Dympna was taking the children to school, but Mr Frome had taken it in for her and handed it over, with a little half-bow, as soon as she came in through the front door. 'Letter, Nanny,' he said gravely. 'I hope all is well.'

Dympna took the small envelope with a sinking heart and tore it open, her hands shaking. Oddly enough, so much had her feelings changed in the past forty-eight hours, she thought immediately that it must be from Jimmy. Something had gone wrong, he was cancelling their date, telling her he had changed his mind, paying her back for what she had done to him more than two years before.

But the first words showed her that it was not from Jimmy, that it was a very serious business indeed. For Mammy, who was so cool, calm and collected to say that something bad had happened to Egan, to beg her to come home . . . She shoved the letter back into its envelope and turned to the butler, standing courteously by, his eyes fixed on the front door but all his attention, she was sure, on her. 'Mr Frome, it is bad news. Is Madam up yet?'

'To be sure she is, Miss. She's in the breakfast parlour, though I believe she's finished her meal. Will you go to her?'

'Yes,' Dympna said baldly. 'Oh . . . could you get one of the servants to go up to the nursery and tell Gill that I'll be up presently? She can start getting the children ready for the park.'

'But if you've had bad news, Miss,' the butler began, to be crisply interrupted.

'I shan't be taking them to the park, Mr Frome, but Gill is quite capable of doing so.'

And Dympna turned on her heel and went swiftly across the hall to the breakfast parlour, knocked on the door and let herself in, closing the door gently behind her.


An hour later, she had made all the necessary arrangements, packed a bag and given Gill instructions for how she was to carry on during Dympna's absence. 'I may be away for a few days or possibly for a week or so,' she had said. 'You coped before, Gill, so I'm trusting that you can cope now, but remind Mrs Ditchling that you need a temporary nursemaid whilst you're acting as temporary nanny. Now there's an errand I want to run before I leave, so if you would just carry my bag down to the hall and get Cook to make me up a few sandwiches, I'll be on my way. Can I rely on you to see to these things?'

'Of course, Nanny Byrne,' Gill said at once. 'I'll get her to make you up some of her lemonade as well, shall I? Is it a long journey, back to your home?'

'Pretty long. And my brother's been very ill, so I shall make what speed I can,' Dympna said. She sat down at the nursery table and pulled a writing block towards her. 'I'll just write a letter . . . I must let people know what's happening . . .'

She wrote, of course, to Jimmy.

*Dear Jimmy,*

*The most dreadful thing – I've been called home to Connemara, in Ireland, to the little village where I live. My brother is ill or in trouble, my mother does not say which, but I hope you know, dear Jimmy, that it had to be an emergency for me to disappear out of your life again, even for a few days.*

*I suppose it isn't fair to ask you to come? We live just outside a tiny village called Streamstown, which is five miles or so outside Clifden, Connemara. You could sleep in the boys' room, with Egan, or on the couch in the living-room, if you would rather. You can get there by train from Dublin . . . to Clifden, I mean. You can only reach Streamstown by boat or by the old horse and cart which brings visitors from the station at Clifden. However, if you can't come, is there any chance that you might write to me? I'll write to you, or I would, if I knew which number Upper Milk Street you were lodging in. I'm afraid I didn't notice when you took me back there the other evening, so if you possibly can write first I'd be grateful.*

*Dear Jimmy, I'm so sorry about all this, but it could be a wonderful chance for you to meet my family – don't worry, they will love you. As I do.*
*Your Dympna.*

She put the letter into an envelope, sealed it, wrote Jimmy's name on it and ran across the nursery, down the stairs, over the hall and out into the road. She was going to Elsie's house, because she could not bear the thought of Jimmy standing and waiting under that lamp – waiting in vain. If only Elsie was agreeable, she could take the letter to Jimmy, give Dympna's apologies in person and actually see the precious epistle into his hands. That way, she, Dympna, would not feel quite so bad about the whole business.

It was chilly outside, with the gusty November wind picking up the last of the fallen leaves and whirling them across the park, to land in the front gardens of the big houses opposite, and Dympna had to hold on her hat as she scurried round the corner, but she wasn't thinking about the weather. She was thinking that these houses mostly contained a number of small children, yet not one was visible on this wild and windy day, to jump up and try to catch a falling leaf or to play a game on the broad pavement. Those other children, the children of the courts for whom she had felt so sorry, had one thing that their richer neighbours lacked. They had the freedom of the streets, to come and go as they pleased, and a good few of them, Dympna thought shrewdly, probably had a deal more love than those little inhabitants of the smart nurseries which surrounded her, who seldom saw their parents for more than a few minutes each day. What a pity, she thought as she turned the corner into Belvidere Road, that there could not be some sort of division of worldly and unworldly goods, so that the children of the rich might have some of the companionship and ease of their poorer cousins, and the poorer cousins might have some of the good food and wonderful toys, which rich parents lavished on their kids in such abundance.

However, such lofty thoughts soon turned to more practical matters. Egan, Dympna reflected, must be in desperate straits for her mammy to have sent that letter. A relapse, perhaps? But if so, surely Mammy would have said so, and would, furthermore, have directed her daughter to go to Galway rather than to come all the way home and then, presumably, retrace her steps by forty miles or so.

Still. Whatever it was, she would soon know. And she would go off on her long journey a good deal happier if she had left her letter with Elsie for delivery that evening.

She knew better than to go to the front door, of course, when enquiring for a nursery maid. But the cook, who opened the back door to her, was a merry, obliging woman, who sent for Elsie at once and then despatched the two of them out into the backyard to have their conversation in peace, whilst they drank a nice cup of tea together.

'Isn't she nice?' Dympna said wonderingly. 'Mrs Stebbings is all right, but she wouldn't hand out cups of tea to a total stranger.'

'She's me mam's first cousin,' Elsie said. 'Blood's thicker'n water, gal! Now what is it that's so urgent you hauled me away from me ironin'?'

Quickly, Dympna explained about the letter, then added the rider that she had found Jimmy Ruddock and that he and she had meant to meet that evening, under the lamp which was directly opposite the Ditchling house.

'Only I've got to leave right away, 'cos the letter was urgent,' she continued. 'But I hate to think of him standing out there, believing that I've stood him up. Even if I posted the letter I've written, it couldn't possibly get to him in time to stop him coming round, and anyway, I don't know what number he lives at in Upper Milk Street. So Elsie, could you be a real friend and meet him this evening, under the lamp-post, and tell him what's happened and give him my letter? I'll be eternally grateful if you would,' she concluded hopefully.

'Course I will,' Elsie said with commendable

promptness. 'Give it over. Half seven this evenin',
you say, under the lamp directly outside your place?
Can't go wrong, can I? Tell you what, though, I'll
drop you a line, immediate like, if you give me your
mam's address, telling you that the deed was done.'

'Oh, thanks, Els,' Dympna said gratefully. 'You're a
brick, so you are.' She fished the letter out of her
pocket and handed it over. 'Look, I'll give you the
money for a stamp . . . oh, damn, I've not got me purse
on me. Never mind, I'll pay you when I get back. And
now I must fly or I'll miss the perishing ship. Cheerio
for now, Els!'

'Bye, Dymp. Have a good journey. And I hope as
how you'll find your brother awright when you gets
home,' Elsie said. 'Be good now, and I'll do as you
say. Seven thirty this evenin' under the lamp.'

Frankly, Elsie thought as she got ready to go out that
evening, I'm as curious as any cat to see old Jimmy
again. I reckon Dympna's done me a good turn,
lettin' me have a peek at him and a word or two,
without it lookin' as though I was interested, like.

It was not that she cared a button for Jimmy now,
of course, not with Harry MacBride willing and eager
to marry her. They would need to save up for a few
years, probably, but her man always said that those
were the relationships which lasted. It was the fall-in-
love-overnight, wed-after-a-week marriages that
went to the wall.

She chose her earth-brown jacket and skirt with a
cream blouse and earth-brown gloves, and put on a
pair of large gold ear-rings, then combed her hair into
kiss-curls across her forehead and checked her
stocking seams in the nursery mirror. She then
donned her most tottery – and elegant – shoes and a

small brown hat with a curly feather, and returned to the mirror to examine her face closely. Damn, there was an incipient pimple just coming to fruition on her chin but a dab more powder – she applied it with Nanny's swansdown puff – would hide it well enough and apart from that she looked pretty damn' good, though she said it as shouldn't.

She was oddly nervous, though. You've known the feller since you was both kids, she scolded herself as she made her way down the back stairs, so why should you feel that it's something special to be meeting him now? But there was no accounting for it. She might not be daft about him any more (that was how she had been putting her feelings for Jimmy ever since she began to realise the solid worth of Harry MacBride) but the truth was, she supposed, that Jimmy had been her first love and because of that, he meant something to her still, no matter how little she might relish the fact.

So what I'm doing, she told herself as she pirouetted before her aunt, the cook, and got her usual good-natured approval, is proving to meself that there's nothing special about Jimmy Ruddock. That I can meet him, chat, tell him about Dympna and go away again and feel absolutely nothing for him except for old friendship.

Accordingly, she set out for the rendezvous, trying to ignore the fact that the palms of her hands were damp and her heart – unreliable organ – was beating a tattoo under the cream blouse, which was enough to make her breathless.

Elsie got to the street lamp at twenty minutes past seven, but even as she turned into its glow she saw that Jimmy was there first and her heart, which had been beating so fast, suddenly did a series of small, hopping somersaults. Blast him, he looked so . . . so . . .

'Hey, Jimmy!' Her voice, to her considerable pleasure, came out calm and quiet, with just the slightest of lifts to show that this meeting was a happy one. 'Over here, mate – it's your old pal, don't you reckernise me?'

He turned towards her, his face lighting up, his eyes blazing . . . and she realised, all in a split second, that he had not recognised her, that he had been expecting Dympna and that her own appearance was of no account to him. His face fell, the light went from his eyes and she could see that he was acting when he came towards her, trying to summon up a smile.

'Els, me old darlin'! Well, I never expected to see you tonight. I . . . I'm waitin' for a pal only I'm a bit early . . . how are you keepin'?'

'I'm fine, thanks,' Elsie said. She spoke tartly. 'You're waitin' for Dympna, aren't you? Dympna Byrne?'

'Umm . . . yes, that's right. Is she . . . she told you, did she, that we was goin' out tonight?'

Elsie smiled. Tightly. The pain in her heart when he had recognised her and looked so deeply disappointed! Damn his eyes, couldn't he know, guess, how she still felt about him? Oh, she might not want him for her feller, she might know she was a sight better off wi' her dear Harry, but . . . well, they'd meant something to each other once, he was the first feller ever to kiss her . . . it left a mark, did that. 'Yes, she told me,' she said quietly, however. 'And when she got the letter from home she asked me to come along, so's you didn't feel as how you'd been stood up.'

'Stood up? A letter? My Gawd, what . . .?'

Elsie sighed. She said, with assumed patience: 'She had a letter from her mam telling her there was summat up wi' that younger brother she's so fond of. Her mam asked her to go home at once, today. So she's gone. She said to say she was sorry and she'd be in touch.'

He stood very still. He looked shocked, as though he could hardly take in her words. 'She's gone? Where?'

'Home to Ireland,' Elsie answered. 'But she'll be back. It might be a few days or a week, or two weeks, she said. But she'll be back.' As she spoke she put her hand into the pocket of her jacket to get out the letter – and it was not there. How stupid she was! She had been so desperate to get her appearance right, so that he saw what he was missing, that she had clean forgotten to pick up the white envelope with Jimmy's name scrawled across the front. She could see it as clearly as if she was still back in the nursery, sitting propped up on the nursery mantel, so she could not possibly forget it.

She should tell him there had been – was – a letter. There might be something important in it, like Dympna's address. Elsie took a breath and licked her suddenly dry lips. The look on his face when he had realised it was she and not the little Irish girl. Even remembering it hurt like a stab in the ribs. But Dympna had given her the letter and she ought to hand it over . . . only she would make a kind of test of it, like. She moistened her lips again. 'I'm awful sorry, chuck, I can see you're upset,' she said. 'But how about if you walk back wi' me, now, to Belvidere Road? It ain't far and we . . . we can talk about old times and you can tell me how you come to know Dympna.'

If he accepted, she would tell him to hang on a mo, and go indoors and fetch the letter down. That was only fair. If he was still her pal, like he'd swear he was if she asked, he'd do a simple little thing like that for her, especially at this time of night, when you never knew who was walking the streets. She lifted her face to his and smiled. 'Well, our Jimmy?'

'Oh . . . no, I'd best not,' he said almost absently, as though she meant nothing to him – less than nothing. 'I'd best be gettin' back. It's a long walk to Upper Milky.'

And before she could utter another word – for she told herself, afterwards, that it was on the tip of her tongue to tell him about the letter – he had raised a hand, given her a pale grin and was striding off down the road.

Elsie stood and watched him until he disappeared round the corner, then she straightened her shoulders and began to walk along the pavement after him. Damn his eyes, she thought wrathfully, why couldn't he have *pretended*, for Gawd's sake? After all, they were old pals when all was said and done, he could just have walked home with her for old times' sake. But the high and mighty Jimmy Ruddock couldn't pretend some affection just to save his old pal's face, could he? Oh no, he had to make it painfully clear that he were head over heels in love wi' damn' Dympna Byrne and din't give a toss for little Elsie Taylor.

Elsie stamped along the pavement, wrath burning within her and revenge, just at that moment, tasting mighty sweet. Whatever Dympna had said in that letter, and she suspected it might have been a request to Jimmy to write, he would not know about it now until Dympna came back to Liverpool – and serve him bleedin' well right, the bastard! Which made it all the odder that, by the time Elsie reached Belvidere Road once more, she was crying bitterly.

# Chapter Fourteen

Dympna was met at the station again, but this time by her mother – and a very worried mother, at that. When she jumped down off the train Beatrice ran across the platform and gave her a hug, then held her daughter away from her, a tremulous smile on her mouth.

'Oh, my dear, I knew you'd come, I told Daddy you would and he said of course, only . . . well, it was such short notice and it's all been so upsetting and . . . but I've got Rosa and the cart, so I'll tell you what's been happening as we make our way home. And don't forget, my dear, that there was no letter, no one got in touch with you, you simply decided to come home for a few days because . . . oh, I can't think of a reason, but I'm hoping you'll be able to. Only I don't want Egan to suspect that we're desperately worried about him.'

'Tell me what's been happening since I left, Mammy,' Dympna said gently, heaving her bag into the donkey cart and taking her mother's arm. 'I know Egan had to go back into hospital and I know he wrote to me for his fare home, so's he could surprise you all. What's happened since then?'

The sordid little story was soon told and at the end of it Dympna whistled under her breath. 'Dear God, what a terrible thing, Mammy. For Egan to see . . . to know . . . and you say Nick isn't interested in marrying Maria?'

'He holds to it that he did nothing which Maria didn't play her part in eagerly,' Beatrice said soberly. 'Dymp, Maria Sullivan is sixteen and Nick more than half a dozen years older. What's more, he's experienced, a man of the world, and she's just a sweet, easily impressed child. I'm sure she knows that what she did was wrong, but she was seduced. And I'm sure she still loves Egan, but . . . well, since he won't see her or have anything to do with her, that's neither here nor there.'

'Oh, Mammy, what a tangle! Is Maria going to have a baby?' Dympna asked bluntly.

Beatrice, though she stared wonderingly at her daughter, could only sigh. 'It's too soon to say, but I'm afraid . . . The Sullivans know there's trouble between their girl and Egan but they don't have the slightest idea just what that trouble is, nor what part Nicholas played in it. I shudder to think what they'll do when they find out – if they find out. And Egan won't talk to me or your daddy, which is why I've asked you to come home.'

'Mammy, what do you want?' Dympna said. 'Do you want Egan to marry Maria? They're both awful young . . . do you truly think that it's the best thing?'

'The Sullivans are a respectable family, well liked and much admired for the way they've changed a poor little farm into one of the best holdings in the area. If Maria is expecting a baby everyone is going to blame Egan, because they know nothing of her . . . her liaison with Nicholas. If she tells them about Nicholas they'll do something awful . . . I'm sure they'll expect him to marry her and he's adamant that he'll do no such thing. So you can see, dearest, that we don't know which way to turn.'

'But how can Egan marry her?' Dympna said after

a moment's thought. 'He has no home to give her, no savings, nothing. And as you say she's the daughter of a well-to-do farmer. And Egan's so *young*, Mammy! As you say, she's sixteen, but he's only one year older than she. What if it's all a mistake? What if they've mistaken puppy love for the real thing and they marry and then discover they're not in love at all?'

Beatrice sighed. 'Will you talk to Egan for us, Dymp? If he says he doesn't love Maria, never did, never will, then there's nothing more to be said. Your daddy will make Nicholas do the decent thing by the girl – he says he will and I dare say he means it. But just talk to your brother, dearest, because I believe that if Nicholas and Maria do marry, then Egan's heart will break in two, whether he's willing to admit it or not.'

'All right, Mammy, I'll have a talk to him,' Dympna agreed. 'Is he fit again? Can we go for a walk along the shore after supper?'

'He's very well, though understandably moody,' Beatrice said. 'Yes, you go off by yourselves, dear. It will be easier for everyone.'

'Well, Egan, what's been happening since I was home last?' Dympna said as the two of them skirted the quay and began to walk along the firm, dark-gold sand. 'When I told Mrs Ditchling that I would be leaving come the spring it seemed a good idea, to her, to see how Gill, the nursery maid, coped without me, so I said I'd come home for a week or so. But that's my news, such as it is. What's yours?'

'They've told you,' Egan said flatly. 'You'd not have come home, else.'

'They've told me there's been some trouble, but I'd

like to hear your version of it,' Dympna said cautiously. She had never been in favour of telling Egan a tissue of lies, but so far no one had lied at all. Egan had simply accepted that she had come home for a while and had not mentioned his own homecoming, a week or so earlier.

'It's not a nice story you'll be after hearin',' Egan said rather cautiously. 'I've not telled anyone the whole . . . Oh, Dymp, I'm in such a muddle! I don't know what to do for the best, and Mammy and Daddy are worryin' at me like dogs at a bone. It's like this . . .'

He told the story well, with a depth of detail that Dympna doubted if Beatrice and Micheál knew. And when he got to the part where he had decided to kill himself, and had been sternly admonished on his stupidity by a voice that sounded just like Dympna's, she stared at him in real consternation. Her baby brother, the little boy who had dogged her footsteps, who had dithered on the edge of cliffs when she went down for birds' eggs because he was so afraid of heights – and he had meant to kill himself by jumping over the cliff! Her heart went cold at the thought of his agony of mind – he must care very deeply for Maria no matter what he might tell himself.

She said as much. Egan, after a pause, nodded slowly. 'Aye, I did care for her. I loved her, Dymp, we meant to marry. But . . . how could she do it? Go wit' Nicholas, of all people? And now he turns round and says it was as much her fault as his and he'll have nothing further to do wit' her.' He looked at Dympna and shrugged helplessly. 'What am I to do, Dymp? Because I still love her, of course I do, but she . . . she can't love me. If she did, she'd never have gone wit' Nicholas whiles I was ill in me hospital bed, wit' no chance to put me own point of view.'

'Egan, she's only a kid,' Dympna said rather helplessly. 'She must have been very flattered that Nick took any notice of her at all – he'd never done so before, I'll swear. And when he'd teased her into letting him kiss her . . . I don't know very much about it, but I can't believe she loves him.'

'I dunno,' Egan said drearily. 'I can't bring meself to go up there and Maria's not come down to the cottage. And I won't have Daddy an' Mammy interferin', because they might make things worse. But you, Dymp, you're a girl as well, could you understand how Maria feels? If you talked to her . . .'

'I'll go up tomorrow morning and take her for a walk and find out how she really feels,' Dympna promised him, considerably heartened. 'Has it not occurred to you, though, Egan, that she's afraid and ashamed to face you? That she still loves you very much indeed, but knows what a dreadful thing she's done and dare not come down to the cottage?'

'I dunno,' Egan repeated. 'You talk to her, Dymp, find out what she's really feelin', thinkin'.'

So Dympna promised, and the two of them turned and began to retrace their steps along the beach.

Maria, when Dympna went up to the farm next day, was pathetically eager to go out for a while with the older girl, particularly when Dympna suggested that they might go and look at Mrs O'Connor's kittens. She thought Maria looked positively haggard, with dark circles under her eyes and hollow cheeks, and her body looked all angles instead of curves. She also realised how worried the Sullivans were when Mrs Sullivan took her to one side for a moment, having sent Maria to fetch her coat.

'Dympna! 'Tis glad I am to see you, alanna, and I'll be more than glad if you can find out what ails our Maria. I don't doubt she and Egan have quarrelled, for she won't go near nor by the shore, but over what, we ask ourselves? But when we question her she bursts into tears . . . I asked if he'd done something he shouldn't, though to think such a t'ing of a boy who's been so ill seems . . . but she cried louder than ever and swore he wasn't after doin' wrong t'ings.' Mrs Sullivan's round, innocent face was red with puzzlement and anxiety. 'Dympna, she's our only gorl, so she is, and me and me husband are half out of our minds wit' worryin'. If you can persuade her to talk to you, tell you what's gone wrong . . .'

So now Dympna and Maria set off to walk up the hill to a cottage a mile or so distant, where they might choose a kitten from the litter the woman's cat had recently produced, for Beatrice had decided to get a cat to help keep down the mice, which had taken to coming indoors during the heat of the summer.

They chatted idly at first, of Dympna's job, of the children in her care, of a dress which Maria was having made by the local dressmaker so that she might attend her cousin's wedding in the spring. Only when the younger girl seemed relaxed did Dympna raise the question which was foremost in her mind. 'Maria, why don't you come down to our cottage any more? Mammy and Daddy would like to see you, and Egan . . .'

'You know why.' Maria's voice broke. 'I can never go into your cottage again, Dympna, never, never!'

'Why, Maria?' Dympna asked gently. 'Because of . . . of what happened between you and my brother Nicholas?'

'Yes,' Maria muttered. 'I'm goin' to have to tell Mammy . . . I t'ink I'll kill meself, that's what I'll do – or else Daddy'll do it for me, when he finds out.'

'If you would go and talk to Egan, you might find that there was a solution other than killing yourself,' Dympna said gently. 'What a pair you are – he was going to kill himself because he said you loved Nicholas and not him and you're going to . . .'

'Egan t'inks I love Nicholas?' Maria interrupted, the colour flooding her small face. 'Oh Dymp, I know he's your brother, but I *hate* him! He made me do t'ings I knew were wicked and wrong, only he's a doctor and I thought he could make it all right. Then when poor Egan walked in . . . oh, I could have *killed* Nicholas, I swear to God I could. To hurt Egan so! Only of course it were my fault, too . . .'

'Nicholas should know better; he's the wicked one, to treat you so,' Dympna said between her teeth. 'And if anyone kills Nicholas it'll be me – if Egan doesn't get to him first, that is. Or Daddy – now Daddy said he'd tear Nicholas limb from limb when he saw him next, so mebbe there won't be much of my older brother left for you to kill.'

She had meant to make Maria laugh and succeeded, then Maria clapped a small hand guiltily over her mouth and looked up at Dympna with big, tear-filled eyes. 'Only how can I expect Egan to marry me, after this? And anyway, it'll be *years* before we've saved enough to get married.'

'What about Nicholas?' Dympna asked, greatly daring. 'After what happened, dear, you could demand that Nicholas marry you, you know.'

Maria looked absolutely horrified. 'Oh, *no*, I couldn't possibly marry him. He doesn't like me at all, not really, he just wanted to . . . to do *that* with me.'

She shuddered. 'And I couldn't bear it,' she ended positively.

Dympna sighed, but not aloud. If her experience with Nicholas had given Maria a dislike of . . . of *that*, it didn't look as though any marriage would be successful. But she had felt just the same after Philip's attack and now she found that she could contemplate being married to Jimmy with positive pleasure. Surely the same would happen to Maria, when the man who held her in his arms was the right one?

She said as much and Maria, having thought it over, nodded violently. 'Oh, Egan's different,' she agreed. 'He's so kind and we know each other so well . . . oh look, Mrs O'Connor's in her garden. What sort of kitten does your mammy want, d'you t'ink?'

'You choose it,' Dympna said presently as the two of them bent over the box of hay in which the kittens were disporting themselves. 'But only if you'll come back to the cottage with me for a nice cup of tea and a slice of soda bread.'

'Oh! Well, if it were to be mine I'd have the ginger and white one,' Maria said longingly. She picked the kitten out of the hay and held it under her chin, so that it rubbed against her, purring like distant thunder. She heaved a sigh. 'I suppose I've got to start facin' your mammy and daddy soon. But I'll not be lookin' them in the eye at first, Dymp. I . . . I'm so 'shamed.'

'Don't worry,' Dympna advised her gently. 'Take things as they come. So we'll take the ginger and white kitten for Mammy, and then we'll go down to our place.'

It was not an easy meeting; Dympna had never thought that it would be. She and Maria, with the younger girl hugging the kitten, went doubtfully into the cottage kitchen. Beatrice, gutting fish, looked round and said calmly: 'Hello, Maria. Wait on and I'll pull the kettle over the fire,' but Egan, who had been sitting on the sofa staring into the fire, jumped to his feet, a smile spreading across his face, then sat down abruptly once more and turned away from them.

'Egan? We've chosen the kitten for Mammy,' Dympna said. 'Want to see it?'

Egan turned and Maria bent and put the tiny kitten into his hand. It looked up at him with huge amber eyes and miaowed, and Egan, despite himself it seemed, smiled.

'D'you like it?' Maria asked in a voice almost as small as the kitten's. 'I chose it, Egan.'

'It's very nice,' Egan said politely. He put the kitten down on the floor and stood up. 'Mammy, shall I be after puttin' the kettle over the fire?'

'Certainly,' Beatrice said cordially. 'I'm sure Maria will stay and have a bite to eat with us. I'll lay an extra place.'

'T'anks, Mammy,' Egan said when Maria seemed unable to speak. 'Then whiles the tea's brewin' Maria an' me will walk down to the quay, see if we can see the *Aleen*.' He turned to the white-faced girl who was standing very close to him, looking up into his face with anxious eyes. 'Is that all right, Maria?'

'That's fine, so it is,' Maria answered almost inaudibly. Egan took her hand and led her across the kitchen and out of the door.

Dympna collapsed onto the sofa with a sigh of relief. 'Oh, Mammy, pray it'll be all right,' she said urgently. 'I know they're far too young to marry – but I think it's the best solution. She really doesn't like Nicholas at all and I believe she still feels as she always has about Egan.'

Beatrice came over to her, sat down on the sofa beside her and kissed her cheek. She was smiling but there were tears in her eyes. 'The relief! I knew she'd talk to you, Dympna. Somehow, you're easy to talk to, and you and Maria are the same generation. Her poor mother! She met me in Clifden a week gone and said she was worried sick – she'll be so pleased everything's all right.'

'Ye-es, but Maria and I didn't talk about the possibility of a baby,' Dympna pointed out. 'Egan and Maria will have to tell her parents what happened, you know, otherwise they might not want them to marry.'

'If she isn't in the family way, perhaps they could wait for a while,' Beatrice said hopefully, but Dympna shook her head.

'I don't think so, Mammy. I think we ought to get them married as soon as may be and then there'll be no more trouble. Maria's a very appealing little thing and Nicholas is bound to come home again some time.'

'Your father won't have him in the house.' Beatrice's voice was sad. 'And I'm not sure I blame him, Dympna. What a wicked way to behave . . . but it's no use dwelling on what's past and done. We'll ask them how they feel about marrying when they come indoors again.'

It took a lot of understanding from everyone concerned, but eventually it was decided that with the help of their parents Egan and Maria would marry and move inland, to a little place owned by an uncle of Mr Sullivan's. The old man needed help on the tiny smallholding and was willing, in return for such help whilst he lived, to leave the land and the little cottage to Maria and her husband when he died.

'For I won't have people adding up on their fingers and nodding their heads and believing that we've done bad t'ings,' Egan said austerely. 'If there is a babby, to the folk in our new village it will be *my* babby, an' there will be no nasty talk and that's all that matters, so it is.'

'I've telegraphed Mrs Ditchling that I won't be going back and asked her to send my trunk on,' Dympna told her mother. 'I had hoped to return there for a short while . . . but you'll be needing me here, I can see that.'

'It's good of you, dear.' Beatrice sounded as though she meant it. 'I can see these next few weeks are going to be difficult ones for us all.'

So Dympna settled down to help her family as far as in her lay, but her heart was sore because Jimmy had neither written nor come whistling up from Clifden Station to tell her – show her – that she mattered to him. She knew that Elsie had met him, as arranged, because her friend had sent her a postcard telling her reassuringly that she had kept her assignation with Jimmy Ruddock. So he knew how she was situated, must realise that she could not get back to Liverpool just yet. Yet he had not written, not a line. But surely he would write? Any day now there would be a letter, she told herself so repeatedly when she went to bed at night and first thing when she woke in the morning. And quite often in between, as well. So Dympna worked in the house, went out on the *Fair Aleen* and saw her hands gradually toughening, the soft, blistered patches hardening, and watched and waited.

\*

Jimmy waited too. At first, with what patience he could muster, then, increasingly, without any patience whatsoever but with despair beginning to creep into his heart. She had sent Elsie along with a message to let him know that she could not come, in case he feared that she would not – did not wish – to come. Surely, having done so, she had meant to get in touch with him, write him a letter, do something?

For the first week he was patient, only going round to Devonshire Road two or three times, to stand outside the house that once contained Dympna, looking searchingly up at where he guessed the nursery windows to be. He had gone to the park, too, and watched the nursery maid, Gill, pushing the pram with the latest Ditchling baby in it, whilst two or three other children ran ahead, threw bread to the ducks, played chase on the smooth park grass.

But the second week taxed him further. He could not imagine what had happened and began to fear the worst; that she had gone home, met an old flame, decided that this was the real thing . . . he ground his teeth at the mere thought, but was helpless to do anything more. He went repeatedly to the park now, and actually knocked at the back door of the Ditchling house, only to be told what he already knew – that Miss Byrne had been called home and had not yet returned.

At the start of the third week, he did what he should have done right from the beginning. Immediately after he'd had his breakfast he went round to Belvidere Road. He had no idea in which house Elsie worked, but again he hung around until he saw her, surrounded by children with straw-coloured hair and posh tweed coats with velvet collars, trying to keep them in some sort of order whilst a nanny in navy-blue uniform with the most hideous bonnet he had ever seen pushed a pram and occasionally commanded Elsie to keep her charges quiet.

He did not accost her there and then, but waited until he had followed them back to their house – it was number eight – and then, after a discreet interval, went to the back door and asked for Miss Elsie Taylor.

Elsie was sent for and came. The moment she set eyes on him she went very red and looked fixedly down at her feet. She tried to say she was too busy to talk to him but Jimmy took her by the wrist and said, in an undertone: 'Come for a little walk in the garden wi' me, young Elsie; we've gorra have a chat. Where's Dympna, eh? She telled you more than you telled me, that much I *have* guessed. Come on, spill the beans. What didn't you tell me, Els?'

'Oh, leggo me wrist, our Jimmy,' Elsie said in a tone that was perilously close to a whine. She tried to turn back to the house but Jimmy prevented her, leading her towards a small arbour set back from the main lawn. 'I dunno what you's talkin' about, honest to God I don't.'

'You do,' Jimmy said grimly. He gave her wrist a quick half-turn and heard her gasp with pain, feeling a mixture of guilt and pleasure at the sound. Fancy wanting to hurt little Elsie – but he felt in his bones that she was holding out on him. He pulled her into the shelter of the arbour, then faced her. 'Come on, Els, let's be havin' the truth.'

'Well . . . there was a letter,' Elsie said sulkily after a moment. 'I forgot to bring it wi' me, honest to God I forgot, Jimmy. I would of give it to you, only you wouldn't come back here wi' me, an' I thought if you couldn't be bothered to walk a few hundred yards . . . well, then you could whistle for the bleedin' letter. Anyway, it probably din't say much.'

'It said . . . but never mind that, I'll have it now,' Jimmy said through gritted teeth. 'Just you go and fetch it, Elsie Taylor. It's . . . it's a crim'nal offence to withhold a letter, that I *do* know.'

'I can't fetch it,' Elsie muttered. 'I chucked the bleedin' thing away, I felt that guilty. No, Jimmy, don't look like that, it's the truth I'm tellin' you.'

'But you read it first,' Jimmy said implacably. 'I know you, Els – curiosity's always been your besettin' sin as they said in school. Tell me what it said right away now, or I'll . . . I'll . . .'

'What'll you do, Mr Clever Dick?' Elsie said, apparently deciding that she had been meek long enough. 'If my feller could see you now . . .'

'Interferin' wi' someone else's mail is a matter for the scuffers,' Jimmy interrupted remorselessly. 'Now come on, Elsie, tell me what me letter said or . . .'

'Awright, awright,' Elsie grumbled. She rubbed her wrist. 'It weren't important, I can tell you *that*. I dunno why she bothered to write. She just said as how she'd gorra go home an' . . . an' she hoped you'd either write or go to see her in Conny-wotsit, 'acos she didn't know the number of your lodgings in Upper Milky,' she finished. 'So I don't see as I kept any important information from you, do you?'

'Her bleedin' address, that's all,' Jimmy groaned, glaring at her. 'What was her bleedin' address, Els? I can't write or go there without an address, can I?'

'Oh, lor',' Elsie said. Jimmy could see that she was genuinely dismayed. 'I never thought o' that! But I dunno as she had much of an address, not so's I 'member, at any rate.' She faced Jimmy squarely, her mouth trembling a little. 'Jimmy, I am sorry, really I am, but I do 'member it was that Connywotsit place, if that's any help.'

'Connywotsit,' Jimmy said with scorn. 'What made you do it, Els? What made you destroy the bleedin' letter?' Elsie sat down with a thump on the bench at the back of the arbour. Jimmy sat beside her. 'Can't you tell me, our Els?' he said at last, as the silence stretched. 'You and me's been pals for a long time, don't that count for nothin'?'

Elsie looked down at her hands, gripped tightly in her lap, and gave a little sob. Then she looked up at him. There were tears on her lashes. 'It were the l-look on your face when you saw it were me an' not that perishin' Dympna,' she said. 'You looked so . . . so mis'rable, Jimmy, as though she were the only person in the world you wanted to see. You an' me, we'd not set eyes on each other for ages, but you never even smiled at me, you was so disappointed that I weren't Dympna. An' . . . an' you'd been me feller once, an' . . . an' I'm fond o' you still, in a friendly kind o' way.'

Jimmy put his arm round her shoulders and gave her a hard hug. 'I'm sorry Els,' he said humbly. 'You are me pal still, only . . . well, we've growed apart, wouldn't you say? But it were wrong of me to behave as though it were only Dymp what mattered, even if . . .'

'Even if that's how you feel, now,' Elsie finished for him. She heaved a sigh and took a handkerchief out of her sleeve, applying it first to her eyes and then blowing her nose on it with a blast like a trumpet. 'Tell you what, I can't remember much more, only I thought wharran odd place to live – it were somethin' about a stream, I think.'

'Well, thanks, Els,' Jimmy began. He got to his feet.

Connywotsit would be Connemara, but that was a huge area of Ireland, he didn't see . . .

And then, into his head there flashed a scene. A quay, with black-tarred fishing boats pulled up beside it and the sea beginning to retreat as the tide turned. And against the background of nets and wet stone, and the broad sweep of the Connemara hills he saw a small, heart-shaped face framed in night-black hair. A fishergirl, whose mammy was English, who had got furious with him when he had said something about her mammy being English . . . who had flown off in a fury, all blazing navy-blue eyes and scarlet cheeks, because he had made some stupid comment . . .

Dympna! He had never made the connection before, despite the name, her appearance . . . but of course it had been she on that Irish quayside all those years ago, and that meant he knew very well where she lived. Well, he could not remember the name of her village, but he could find it again, if he could only persuade Abel, of the trawler *Maid Margery*, to take him fishing off the Porcupine Bank and then to drop him off at that little harbour near where his old friends, the Sullivans, had lived.

'What's up?' Elsie said. She had risen from the bench too and stood beside him, looking up into his face with some anxiety. 'You look . . . kind o' *weird*, Jimmy Ruddock. Are you goin' to chuck up your brekfuss?'

Trust Elsie to bring you back to reality with a bump, Jimmy thought wryly, grinning down into the eyes which were fixed on his. 'No, I'm not ill, though I've been every kind o' fool,' he told her. 'But I guess I know where Dympna's gone . . . thanks, Els.'

*

'Well I'll be . . . damned,' Elsie said, as her one-time boyfriend disappeared out of the garden as though shot from a cannon. 'Wharrever d'you mek o' that?' But since she was speaking to herself she did not get an answer and presently she got up from the bench, brushed the back of her skirt, which was covered in dew and fragments of wood from the seat, and made her way slowly back to the house.

'That were Jimmy Ruddock, weren't it?' her mam's first cousin, the cook, said curiously. 'You two was sweet on each other once, wasn't you?'

'Yeah, but that were a long time ago; he's goin' to marry one of me best pals; I wouldn't want to marry the feller,' Elsie said airily and realised that she was speaking no more than the truth. 'Thanks, Cook. I'll get on wi' me ironin' now.'

They were pleased to see him in Fleetwood; old Abel was still the master of the *Maid Margery* and when Jimmy explained his errand he said that he could always do with an unpaid hand aboard and agreed to take him when they next sailed, at the end of the week. As for putting him ashore in Connemara, why not?

'But I'll not wait longer than an hour or two,' he warned. 'Three, mebbe, if you need more time.'

But Jimmy assured him that all he wanted was to be dropped off. Once there, he would make his own arrangements for his journey home.

'We've still got your room, Jimmy,' old Mrs Totteridge told him. 'Since your time, our Bertie's got hisself a wife, so he don't live wi' us no more. So you just move back in there until the *Maid* sails and no talk o' rent or such. You're welcome as a second son to me, our Jimmy.'

So Jimmy, boiling with such impatience that he felt inclined to chuck himself into the sea and swim to Ireland, had to settle down into the tall old house, help Mrs Totteridge with her domestic chores, talk to Abel of fish prices, the ruinous cost of good nets and the vagaries of the sea.

But the week passed, and the day came when he dressed himself up in his thick jersey and borrowed oilskins and set sail, once more, with the crew of the *Maid Margery*. And his impatience, which had bubbled and boiled and all but exploded during that week, was suddenly rewarded. There he was, helping with the chores on board the trawler, ready to cast the trawl or help to pull it in again should they strike a likely shoal, and all the time he had only one thought in his mind: I'm gettin' there at last! Soon, soon, soon I'll be steppin' ashore in Ireland and takin' the only girl who ever mattered to me into me arms.

Dympna and Micheál had been out on the boat and had brought home a good catch of herring, having found a shoal almost as soon as they had cast their nets. Now, returning in the pale gold of a winter's afternoon, she felt a deep satisfaction, despite her worry over Jimmy. Why had he not got in touch? She had begun to wonder whether Elsie had told her the truth or whether her friend had seen Jimmy, felt the tug of old affection, and – well, simply told him nothing.

She would have confided in Egan, but he and Maria had gone; up to the little holding somewhere at the foot of the Twelve Bens, the great mountains that reared out of the flat Connemara bogs. Dympna had been up to visit them the previous day and had found Egan just coming home from a day's work at the peat digging whilst Maria, with her skirts kilted up round her knees and her face running with sweat, toiled over enlarging their potato plot. Maria had looked happier than Dympna had ever seen her and the welcome they had given her had convinced her all over again that they had done the right thing. Nicholas was forgotten, it was as though he had never been, and Egan treated Maria with a warmth of teasing affection which Dympna thought she had never seen equalled. What was more they spoke of the expected baby as though they already knew him, calling him, 'our Mick', and planning his future as though they owned a palace and not a turf digger's hut and a few acres of bog.

Uncle Patrick had clearly never been happier. He was fussed over as though he were the baby they so eagerly awaited. He could have kept to his bed all day, he told Dympna, had he wished to do so. As it was, he had his warm chimney corner by the fire, or a bench in the sun, and little Maria to wait on him hand and foot, to read to him and tell him stories, whilst when Egan got home they had a rare old time, going over family history and planning for the wee boy who would arrive.

'But suppose it's a girl?' Dympna had said, and Uncle Patrick said that would be grand, indeed so it would, but he just had a feelin', like, that it would be a young feller for him to dandle on his knee and take a-walking down by the lake.

Going back home, Dympna had known a real stab of envy. They were so poor, their main diet was potatoes, with freshwater fish when Egan caught any – he used Uncle Patrick's little curragh and fished on the lake when it was too wet for peat digging – and Maria kept hens and a pig, and planned to sell eggs and to kill the pig before the baby came so she would have some money to make baby clothes.

I wouldn't mind living like that, if I were living with someone I cared for, Dympna found herself thinking as she sat in the bus that would take her back to Clifden. They're like a couple of kids, playing at being married – but what fun it all is, and how bravely they face up to the hard toil and the small rewards.

Today, however, she meant to go up to the Sullivan farm and tell Mrs Sullivan all about her visit to the young couple. She knew that the older woman worried, particularly since Mr Sullivan had said he would not visit them until the baby was born and he felt less confused about the suddenness of their marriage and the rapidness of their departure. Beatrice and Mrs Sullivan, talking it over, had decided that Mr Sullivan, who was quite a bit older than she and very set in his ways, should not be told that the child was Nicholas's, nor that Maria had already been pregnant when she and Egan had wed. This had seemed better at the time, but now Dympna realised that it left Mrs Sullivan in a similar position to her own – they neither of them had anyone with whom to discuss the main trouble on their minds.

In the farmhouse kitchen, she and Mrs Sullivan settled down over a pot of tea and a slice of potato cake to discuss the little family on the croft. Mrs Sullivan told Dympna that she was knitting as fast as she could, and wondered whether to tell Maria that a fine quantity of little woollen jackets, shawls and bootees would presently be winging their way to her.

'Mammy and me are making little nightgowns,' Dympna admitted. 'Only I'm no good with me needle, so Mammy does the sewing and I do the cutting out and a bit of the fancy stuff across the front. Just a few lazy daisies and some simple chain stitch, but it makes the gowns look prettier.'

'Me man gives me strange looks sometimes,' Mrs Sullivan said. 'I'm wonderin' whether he'll do the countin' on his fingers when the babby's born.'

'If he does he'll just tut a little and then forget it when the baby catches hold of his finger and smiles up into his face,' Dympna said wisely, as though she were the mother of ten and not merely an ex-nanny. 'He'll be your first grandchild, won't he?'

'He will. Unless he's after bein' a girl, of course,' Mrs Sullivan said somewhat confusedly. 'Eh, wouldn't a little girl be a wonderful t'ing, Dympna? There's me wit' three sons and only the one daughter . . . aye, a girl would be grand, so she would.'

'Well, boy or girl, it'll be your first grandchild and the first one is always special,' Dympna observed. 'It's the same for Mammy, of course, and for . . .'

She stopped short. Suddenly, without rhyme or reason, she felt she wanted to be out of the house and in the open air. Mrs Sullivan, however, was getting ponderously to her feet, unaware of any anxiety which Dympna might be feeling.

'I'll just wet the tay again so's we can sup another cup,' she was saying comfortably. 'And there's a gingerbread I made last week, which'll be good and sticky to eat now. I'll cut us both . . .'

'Mrs Sullivan, I have to go,' Dympna said urgently, jumping to her feet. 'I . . . I forgot I promised my daddy to clean down the docks of the *Aleen* before dark, and to fold up the nets and put them away, too. And . . . and there's supper to get, and the table to lay . . .'

'I t'ought you cleaned down afore you came up

here, alanna,' Mrs Sullivan began, but she was speaking to Dympna's back as her erstwhile guest grabbed her coat off the hooks on the back of the kitchen door and swung that same door wide. 'Why are you hurryin' away before you've so much as tasted my gingerbread?'

'Oh . . . I have to go,' Dympna called distractedly over her shoulder as she ran through the farmyard. The tall gander, sensing a possible victim, came towards her, neck extended, beak gaping in a threatening hiss. He tried to jab at her legs as she passed him but she never even paused and he straightened, looking affronted. 'Goodbye, Mrs Sullivan, and thanks very much for the tea.'

She ran down the little bit of a lane with the hazels and their browning nuts overhanging it, and out onto the smooth, sloping pasture which, not so very long ago, had been a mass of thistles. It was easy running here and she did not even pause at the gate but flung herself over it with as much abandon as though she were ten again, instead of twice that. She still had no idea why she was hurrying, where she was going, but something kept her moving as fast as she could . . . downhill, downhill, heading for the cottage and home.

She burst into the lane just above the cottage and immediately knew that she was not wanted here. She ran past the gate and did not pause until she reached the sandy path that led down to the quay. From here she could see it, the sturdy shape of Micheál's pucan, the stretch of hard, dark-gold sand, for the tide was on the ebb and would be so for several hours.

She stared, with excited anticipation building up within her as she saw that there was another boat pulled up on the sand for the sea no longer stretched up as far as the jetty. There was a man, too, about to relaunch the boat and climb back into it. She could see his sturdy figure, his seaboots, even his head silhouetted against the strong, golden light of the setting sun. She knew at once that he was a stranger to her but felt no lessening of her excitement because of that. Something had brought her down here at such a pace, and it had to do with the boats, she was sure of it.

She dropped down onto the pathway, then paused again. A figure was walking across the sand, heading for the shore – heading for her. Immediately the anticipation focused and she was like a magnet which feels, for the first time, the tug of the steel. She must go down onto the sands, the man . . . she could only see his silhouette too, black against the light of the setting sun . . . the man was important to her, she must hurry, hurry, hurry! Her fate, her life, her whole future was down there, sturdily seabooted and jerseyed, making his way up the beach.

She ran down the path and dropped onto the sand. She stumbled a little, then began to run. The man stopped short, stared, then started to run too. He held out his arms and Dympna flung herself straight into them, tears of joy pouring down her face, her body aching with love for him.

'Jimmy! Oh Jimmy, you're here, you're here!'

'Oh, me darlin' Dymp,' Jimmy said against her hair. 'Did you think I was never comin', then? Did you think I could ever leave you, ever forget you?'

For a moment longer they clung, kissed. Then Jimmy turned her back to the shore and put his arm around her shoulders, gently propelling her towards the pathway she had just run down with such abandon.

'There's a feller up there, in a cottage garden, watchin' us as if he thinks we've both run mad,' he said a little breathlessly. 'All I can say, queen, is that if this is madness I'm happy to stay that way.'

'And me,' Dympna murmured, clutching him as though she never meant to let him go. 'That's me daddy up there, Jimmy. You'll like him so much. Oh, and I've such a lot to tell you. Things have been happening here . . . you'll be astonished.'

'It's not been all that quiet back in Liverpool,' Jimmy said ruefully. 'Come on, then, Dympna luv, let's go an' meet your daddy.'

Together, still entwined, they went towards the cottage.

## Buy *FLYNN*
### Order further *Katie Flynn* titles from your local bookshop, or have them delivered direct to your door by Bookpost

| | | | |
|---|---|---|---|
| ☐ | A Liverpool Lass | 0099429993 | £5.99 |
| ☐ | Liverpool Taffy | 0099416093 | £6.99 |
| ☐ | The Mersey Girls | 0099443279 | £5.99 |
| ☐ | Strawberry Fields | 0099416034 | £5.99 |
| ☐ | Rose of Tralee | 0099416336 | £6.99 |

### FREE POST AND PACKING
Overseas customers allow £2 per paperback

PHONE: 01624 677237

POST: Random House Books
c/o Bookpost, PO Box 29, Douglas,
Isle of Man IM99 1BQ

FAX: 01624 670923

EMAIL: bookshop@enterprise.net

Cheques (payable to Bookpost) and
credit cards accepted

Prices and availability subject to change without notice
Allow 28 days for delivery
When placing your order, please state if you do not wish to receive
any additional information

www.randomhouse.co.uk